READ ME

LAUREN CONNOLLY

CITY OWL
PRESS

READ ME
Forget the Past, Book 2

CITY OWL PRESS
www.cityowlpress.com

Cover Design by Mibl Art. All stock photos licensed appropriately.

Edited by Yelena Casale.

For information on subsidiary rights, please contact the publisher at info@cityowlpress.com.

Print Edition ISBN: 978-1-64898-085-5

Digital Edition ISBN: 978-1-64898-086-2

Printed in the United States of America

For my Durango friends. Your plan worked; I am now a cat person.

Author's Note

As I wrote *Read Me*, I explored some important issues, including LGBTQ youth homelessness and animal rescue. If you would like to learn more about these topics and find out how to get involved, here are a few organizations looking for your help:

True Colors United : truecolorsunited.org

The Trevor Project : www.thetrevorproject.org

Louisiana SPCA : www.louisianaspca.org

Animal Rescue New Orleans : animalrescueneworleans.org

Content warning: Some scenes describe stalking and assault.

Chapter One

SUMMER

The massive stack of books hides the face of a god. A god like Hades. Beautiful, hard, and shrouded in the shadows of his hardcover stronghold. A being who knows only how to walk the world alone, scorning the help of others.

Especially librarians.

Will today finally be the day he gives in?

I can always tell I'm getting near the end of my shift when I start comparing patrons to mythical characters. Nothing like a little storytelling to keep me going after the caffeine wears off.

Before leaving the circulation desk, I press a button that rings a bell throughout the entire building. This is the third and final ring. In five minutes, the security guard will give people their last notice that the library is closing. Today it's Johnny, a newer guy. He's friendly, but I hope not so friendly that he lets stragglers guilt him into allowing them to linger a few minutes longer.

I love working in a public library, but that doesn't mean I want to stay an hour later than my scheduled shift. Which is why I leave Karen to handle the final checkouts as I approach the makeshift book fort.

When I reach the fortress walls, I have a strong urge to topple the lot of them with a growl and declare that Hades' castle has been conquered by a fire-breathing dragon.

But I'm mixing myths, and dragon attacks are not recommended for proper book upkeep.

I clear my throat, twining my fingers together behind my back to keep from reaching for an armful of the reading material.

A window appears as the man hidden behind the parchment ramparts slides a few off the top. A set of Icelandic blue eyes trace over my eager form. I'm not sure if Icelandic is technically a shade of blue, but the country name brings to mind sharp icebergs floating in blood-freezing oceans.

And that's his blue. Sharp and cold.

The color mixes beautifully with his Nordic blonde hair and the silver piercings that decorate the rims of his ears and accent the edge of his eyebrow and lower lip. Briefly, I wonder if any of his tattoos have the same color blue of his eyes. There's a good many on display, twining down his arms and creeping up his neck. There are bits of color inside the black outlines, but I've never gotten the chance to leisurely study the images to answer my question.

Everything about this patron conveys a simple message: *I'm not friendly. Don't talk to me.*

But I talk to everyone, even sexy, intimidating men who surround themselves with fortresses of books.

"Yes?"

Yes, he asks. As if he doesn't know why I'm here. Why I always approach him at the end of my Sunday shift. The way he says the one word does things to my chest. Good things. Bad things. Burning things.

"You've amassed quite a collection today." One of my hands sneaks free, reaching to fiddle with the cover of a worn volume at the top of a stack.

"Yes."

Yes, he says.

One of the first things I learned working in customer service is how to smile. No matter what.

I smile at him now.

"Well, I would be happy to put away whatever you don't plan on checking out. Seeing as how we're closing. In five minutes."

Say yes. Say it now.

Let me help.

"No. Thanks."

Damn you.

Still I smile, even though I want to glare until he accepts my aid.

Let the librarian help you. I try to telepathically implant the notion in his brain, but I think all the metal in his face messes with my signal. My smile begins to ache.

"You sure? I don't mind. It's my job." My fingers itch with the need to make sure the titles end up in their proper shelf locations.

"I've got it." And, as if to prove his point, he rises from his chair and palms a handful of the materials before sauntering away toward the shelves. I'm left staring at the rest of his hoard, practically sweating from the need to help replace them. But I don't know which titles he plans on checking out.

I linger, eyeing him as he stretches one long arm up to a higher shelf. Admittedly, that would've been a stepstool task for me. But still.

He never lets me help.

I try not to huff in frustration or stomp too hard as I return to the circulation desk. Less than five minutes later, he's standing in front of me, placing a much more reasonable number of titles on the counter.

Triumph has me grinning. "You left the rest on the table?"

"No." His lips twitch into a smirk. "I put them away."

"That's..." I stumble over what to say. "You can't have. Did you? Even I'm not that fast. And I work here!" Disbelief has me abandoning him to jog back into the reading room.

His table is empty.

Frosty eyes watch me as I return.

"You didn't shove them someplace random, did you? Because that's way worse than letting me shelve them."

Without answering, he tucks his hands deep in his pockets before strolling past me, back toward the shelves. And I follow.

He pauses, reaching out to tap a call number on one of the book spines.

"Military science. Housed under Dewey decimal 355."

Before I can think of an answer, he moves on.

"European folklore. Housed under Dewey decimal 398"

He leads me to another shelf.

"Medicinal plants. Dewey 581."

Every number he lists off is correct, and I decide that no man as hot as an inferno should be allowed to talk about library organizational methods. It's too much. I need a fan. Or a respirator.

"Are you a secret librarian?"

The corner of his mouth curls. "No."

"But you have the Dewey decimal system memorized?"

"The important parts."

"Well. It's all important. Because it's information."

He shrugs, and his dismissiveness allows me to regain a minuscule amount of control over my hormones.

"Okay. You've made your point. You know how to properly shelve books. I promise not to bother you anymore. You can construct and dismantle your book fortresses in peace."

When I glance up, I expect to catch a satisfied smirk on his sharp handsome face. Instead, the man frowns at me.

And I realize that this is the first time he ever has.

COLE

I don't want her to leave me alone.

I fight off a frustrated sigh. The cute librarian's continuous attempts to help me are one of the highlights of my week.

This is what happens when I try to impress her. I just fuck it all up.

Ask her out. A voice taunts in the back of my mind.

The urge has never been stronger as I follow her back to the checkout desk, my eyes briefly hypnotized by the sway of her skirt against her knees. She's always wearing skirts and dresses.

Like she knows how they torment me.

For months I've been coming to this library. At first, I showed up for the writers' group on Thursday nights. Then I came in on a Sunday and realized I'd never written more in one sitting than that day.

So it became a habit. Sunday afternoons are writing and research days at the public library.

They're also the days I plan how I'll eventually ask out Summer.

Learning her name wasn't hard. She wears a name tag, always pinned to the neckline of her outfit. The place my eyes seek out after they're done tracing over the long dark lashes and the sinful curve of her mouth.

Today, she has on an orange lipstick. What I wouldn't give to look in the mirror and see smears of that color on my mouth. Down my neck. Across my chest.

Wait till you get home, I tell myself.

When I'm at my place, late at night, imaging all the things I want to do to the sassy librarian is my favorite pastime. But playing out the fantasies when she's scanning my library card seems disrespectful, bordering on creepy.

"Everyone is out. This is the final straggler." A guy in a uniform leans against the counter, smiling at Summer like they're good friends.

Maybe they are friends. That's fine. I like the idea of Summer having friends. People she can rely on.

As long as friendship is all it is.

Ask her out now, the greedy part of my brain murmurs. But I hold myself back. Not yet. Not until I have my ace card. Not until I know she'll say yes.

I'm not the type of guy to badger a woman. When I ask Summer out, if she tells me no, then I'll accept it. It'll be hard to give up on the idea of us together. The future where every one of her smiles is for me.

But I take a woman's *no* seriously.

So my goal is to make the word yes so much more appealing.

Doesn't help that I suck at flirting. Pissing people off comes more naturally.

This sensation, the craving I have for her to like me, is new. Normally, I find the world easier to deal with if people just leave me alone. But I don't want Summer to leave me alone. I want her to walk up to my stack of books and give me her sweet smile and angry eyes as she practically begs to help.

Only now that I've shown my understanding of the library's cataloging system, she might not bother me anymore.

I want her to bother me.

"This is quite a stack of books." The scanner in her hand beeps as she points it at the final barcode. "You shouldn't carry them all at once."

Maybe I should point out how I was able to carry them all up to the checkout desk on my own. Maybe then she'll look at my arms and consider how strong I am.

That's how flirting works, right?

But she's talking again before I can make up my mind.

"It's unsafe for you and for the books. What if you drop a few on your way out and trip on them?"

"He seems capable enough," the security guard offers while backing away from the desk. The guy is probably worried I'll ask him for help.

Yeah, no thanks. Me and any type of law enforcement do *not* get along.

"You should let me grab a few. I'm on my way out anyway. Karen and Johnny are in charge of closing tonight." Summer isn't even looking at me as she continues to offer her aid. She clicks away on the computer, working her librarian magic.

Keeping to my plan requires me to say no. It would be even better if I could turn down the offer in a flirtatious way. Maybe lean on the desk and stare deep into her eyes and tell her...

...

Damn. My mind is blank. This never happens when I'm writing. Only when I'm talking.

Mainly when I'm talking to Summer.

Because I can never come up with the right words, I tend to opt for a stoic, silent demeanor, knowing that with how I look, people tend to think I'm brooding.

Often, I am.

But in this case, I want to give her an answer, and I'm only able to formulate one.

"Yes."

Summer continues talking as if she didn't hear me. "I mean, seriously. Just let me help you. For once." Her fingers fiddle with my giant stack of books, straightening them until all the corners align.

"Yes."

"I don't understand why you're so stubborn. Yes, I admit, you know the Dewey decimal system, but that doesn't mean you have to turn me down. Everyone needs a little bit of help sometimes."

I can't keep the grin from creeping over my face. "Summer." Damn her name tastes good on my lips.

She jerks her head up to stare at me, surprise coloring her face.

"I said yes."

"No, you...you did! You said yes!" She shimmies a little happy dance, clapping her hands as if I just told her she won a basket of kittens.

"I did." I smooth my fingers over my mouth, trying to push away the foreign expression that curls my lips.

"You *never* say yes to me helping you." As Summer hurries around the desk, reaching to gather a few of the volumes in her arms, the full meaning behind her words hits me.

She's asked to help me so many times, and I constantly turn her down. I always thought she'd be impressed by my ability to navigate her domain on my own. One more way that I'm bad at this slow-burn wooing I've been attempting. Clearly being able to help someone makes her happy, which I can't pretend like I didn't notice. Summer is always wandering around the library, checking in with patrons, offering her assistance when it comes to locating items or answering questions. And she's always smiling one of those happy-mouth, happy-eyes smiles when she does.

I'm the only one that gets angry eyes.

When Summer has an armful of books, she waves a finger at me. "Wait here. I just need to grab my purse from my office."

I nod. She has half of my books held hostage, so it's not like I can leave without her. Should I tell her I'm completely willing to have her hold my body hostage too if she gets the urge?

No. That's weird. And might scare her off. I never want to scare Summer.

She disappears behind a Staff Only door, and I lounge against the front desk, eyes fixed on her exit, waiting until the moment she reappears.

"You come here a lot, huh?"

The security guard is just across the way, his eyes tracing over me. He's judging me, I'm sure. Looking at the ink and metal in my skin, and giving me a label.

Bad news, his frown shouts.

"Yes," is the only word I give him. Authority figures have never been on my good list.

"Got nowhere else to be?" He grimaces with both his eyebrows raised. There's another question hovering just below the one he spoke.

Are you homeless?

It's not an outlandish conclusion. Public libraries are often a haven for those without a home. But the tone he uses, the one that makes it sound like I *should* have somewhere else to be, and if I don't then I'm lacking, makes annoyance prick over my skin.

Gathering all my disdain for his perceived authority over me, I infuse the disgust into one word.

"No."

His face creases into a glare which smooths out immediately at the sound of a door opening.

"He didn't leave did he?" At Summer's question, I realize the guy shifted to block her, so all she sees is his back.

"Still here. Wouldn't leave without you." I say this with my gaze on the security guard's, who seems to be fighting another frown.

"Good. I've been on my feet all day, and I didn't want to chase you down." She comes into view, bright red purse over her shoulder, wide smile on her orange-painted lips. The colors should clash, but Summer could wear a technicolor outfit and still look adorable.

"No need." I lift the still-considerable stack of materials left on the counter as she reaches my side.

"I would have though. If I needed to."

As we turn toward the exit, side by side, the greedy part of my brain shouts at me again, demanding I stop waiting. Begging me to make some kind of play. Any type at all.

But I don't. Because a yes is not guaranteed.
Instead, I speak low enough so only she can hear.
"Chase me whenever you want to."

Chapter Two

SUMMER

He said *yes*, and not in the usual way that makes me want to claw his eyes out. A very kind clawing. I only maul people with my help.

As we head toward the parking lot, I barely notice the sore soles of my feet. Joy makes me light.

I am helping my most elusive patron.

And yes, I think of him as mine. But I think of a lot of the patrons as mine. My regulars. The ones who I know by name because I've scanned their library cards so often.

That's how I know his name.

Cole Allemand.

I love all the Ls it contains and how my tongue gets to play with those letters. Well, it would if I ever had a chance to say his name. When I see him, I'll often find myself mouthing it, wanting to speak the moniker aloud. But I haven't had a reason to yet. He's never officially introduced himself.

He knows my name.

How can I get him to say it again?

Maybe if I talk about the change of seasons we'll eventually get around to the one I share my name with, and then I can pretend he's talking about me. These are not the thoughts a librarian should be having about one of her many patrons. I should be friendly but not...affectionate.

Out of the corner of my eye, I observe the lithe way he walks, all casual and smooth. Cat-like. He's a giant cat, and I want to reach up and scratch behind his ears.

Stop it! Not appropriate.

But I can't seem to force my mind to appropriate topics around Cole Allemand.

Maybe if I talk, that'll shut down the strange, sexual thoughts this tattooed man inspires in me.

"You go to the writers' group on Thursday, right?"

His iceberg eyes cut to me. "Yes."

Score. Another good yes.

"How are you liking it?"

Cole stops next to a beat-up blue truck that's a few decades old. It's blocky, and the paint has chipped away in places. The vehicle is not what I would have put him in. I might have thought a guy with his style and give-no-fucks demeanor would opt for something dark and sleek and fast. Maybe a car with a tricked-out stereo system that he could blast metal music on while cruising through the streets and flipping off the police.

But no. His truck, despite its clear age, seems downright reliable.

And it's not even that old. The thing looks like a teenager compared to my ancient Volkswagen. I like to refer to my transportation as a classic, but it loses some of the prestige of the word because of the duct tape keeping the bumper on.

"You could come to a meeting." His smoky voice has my mind off cars and back to my original question.

"Me? At a meeting? Oh no. No no, that wouldn't work."

"Why not?"

"Well, for one, and the most main one, I don't write. Composing a tweet is almost too much for me to handle."

"You could listen." Cole watches me, and his intense stare has my hands wanting to twist around in flustered flapping. Luckily, the stack of books I'm holding keeps them weighed down.

"I couldn't though. I mean, I wouldn't talk while someone was reading. Of course not. That would be horribly rude."

"So then what?"

"It's once they stop reading that's the problem."

Cole leans a shoulder against the driver's door. "You don't have to comment."

"But I would! Only, no one would call it commenting. I...well...I gush."

"You gush?"

"Yes. I gush. I gush more than a massive crack in a levy. If I went to a writers' group and heard someone read a piece of their own writing, something they created with only their imagination and gift for words, I would gush all my adoration all over them until everyone within a twenty-foot radius would be ill and pity me. It's a problem. I went to a romance writers' convention a few years ago, and I practically fainted. I think a few of the authors put out restraining orders on me." The whole thing is a blur in my memory. I got drunk on their glorious talent, and I blacked out.

"Hmm." Cole keeps his response short, not even a real word. But the way he looks at me seems like a different form of communication. His face holds an entire dialog. Only, I haven't learned the language yet.

"It's bad," I promise. "Better if I keep my distance."

Then Cole does something unbearably unfair. He tongues the stud in his lower lip. Not suggestively, exactly. I shouldn't even be able to pick up on the movement because his mouth stays closed the entire time. But I can see the tease under his lip. The shift of the metal.

And now my mind can only imagine getting the chance to fiddle with his piercing with *my* tongue.

"I think I'd like to see you gush."

Silence descends between us after his statement. I can't tell if he meant for those words to sound as dirty as they did. The problem is Cole has a dark, almost sultry voice that can make anything sexy. I bet listening to him read a cellphone contract could get me wet.

I worry, though. That maybe his voice doesn't naturally come with that raspiness. That maybe a chemical cloud has been eating away at his bad-boy lungs to give him the panty-melting tone.

"Do you smoke?"

His eyebrow, the one with the cute little barbell spiked through it, jerks up.

"No."

"Good," I sigh with a smile. "You shouldn't. Bad for the lungs."

So he's deliciously smoky all on his own. Like those fancy smoked drinks bartenders with suspenders make at speakeasys. I went to one of those places once in college. My roommate offered to treat me to one of the pricy drinks that would've cost the same amount I spend on food for an entire day. Accepting her charity with only a slight bit of guilt, I ordered the special.

Honestly, I could've done without drinking the actual thing. The alcohol burned my unaccustomed throat and had me making weird flinching faces. Luckily, my roommate thought it was hilarious and didn't mind that her money didn't result in my enjoyment but instead an amusing show for her.

So the taste wasn't for me, but the creation process was mesmerizing. The skilled man poured amber liquid into a glass that was both elegant and sturdy, then tucked the drink under a glass dome where he piped a copious amount of smoke, enough to infuse the drink with its flavor.

I sat at the bar, hypnotized.

Cole is that drink, standing in front of me, all gorgeous and tempting like tendrils of smoke that promise you can drink them down.

If I got the chance to taste him, I'd probably act just as foolish as I did with my glass of bourbon.

"Anything else you want to know?" Cole's question brings me back to the present.

"Everything. I want to know everything."

Oh no. I just said that out loud. And I'm staring at him. *Stop staring at him.*

Cole watches me, cold eyes examining my overeager face.

Why can't I ever be cool? Aloof? Mysterious?

But no. I'm eager. I'm helpful. My coworkers often call me peppy. They ask if I was a cheerleader in high school.

They wouldn't ask that if they saw a picture of me in high school.

"What are you thinking about?" he asks.

Damn. I want to lie, but it's not like I was thinking of what he looks like naked. Which I have thought about. Too many times.

So I answer with the truth. "How I had to wear braces for all four years of high school."

Cole blinks at me. "You're thinking about braces?"

I nod. "What are *you* thinking about?" My voice is all excitement, ready to get a small peek into his brain.

I bet it's a fascinating brain.

My heart gives in to the sudden urge to beat harder in my chest. Not necessarily faster, just with more conviction than normal. I can feel each valve's contraction.

We're standing close, gazing at each other in a deserted parking lot. A strange thought pops into my head.

He's going to ask me out.

"I need to get home," Cole says, all cool detachment.

My heart valves shudder and give up their confident stride. They settle back into their unnoticed rhythm of beating.

Cole does not want to date me.

I try my best to ignore the melancholy this realization brings.

Stop being ridiculous. He is a bad boy. Just look at him.

Cole is all smoldering temptation and heartbreaking hotness. He is exactly the type of man made to destroy a woman.

And I will not be destroyed.

This is good. He doesn't want to date me, and that is good.

I repeat the mantra to myself as I step back so he can open the door. I chant it to a marching tune as I lay my share of his book burden on the front seat of his truck. I mouth it as I move so he can close the door again.

Cole Allemand doesn't want to date me, and that is good.

But could we be friendly at least? Maybe enough to use each other's names?

Screw it. I'm introducing him to myself because I want to say those goddamn Ls.

"Cole Allemand!" Why did I shout? Oh yeah. Because I have no chill.

If we were in a regency ballroom, I would be the subject of ridicule, forever a wallflower because I yell people's names as a means of introduction. They may even go so far as to commit me to an asylum. They were pretty quick to use asylums in the olden days.

"You know my name?" Cole asks, seeming more surprised by the content of my outburst rather than the volume of it.

A deep breath helps me regain some sense of normalcy. "It's on your library card."

"But you know it."

"I do. And now I've used it. And I plan on saying hi to you in the future and using your name. And you should say hi to me. And say my name." Oh no. I think I just purred that last part.

It's official. Tonight I need to take some me-time. I will use my vibrator until I've fulfilled my orgasm quota for the week. Or the month. Basically, I need to wear my clit out so I stop wondering if Cole would be willing to take on the task.

"Summer."

"That's the one!" Without books to hold, my hands decide to do a jazzy shake for emphasis. This is why I need pockets. I'm wearing one of those nonsensical skirts without them, as if pretty and practical cannot exist in the same universe.

This is a good time to retreat. I said his name out loud, so this has been a successful day. Better take my winnings before I gamble too much. But when I step back, Cole follows the movement. Only, his legs are longer than mine, so his step covers more ground. We're suddenly much closer. His long fingers, perfect for typing and writing, reach up. For the briefest moment, I'm sure his hand is going to cup my boob. And I wonder if I'd have any inclination to stop him.

But he only uses the tip of his forefinger to trace over the surface of my name tag where it's magnetically attached to my neckline.

Cole's eyes drop to my mouth. As if he wants to do something. With my mouth.

"You have great teeth," he says, then closes his eyes and frowns.

Oh. Okay. "I'll let my orthodontist know those four years weren't in vain," I declare valiantly, as my cheeks stain with mortification.

Cole blinks, then steps back, moving to his truck. "See you, Summer."

Three times. He's used his ear-orgasm of a voice to say my name three times. Unfortunately, this last one I'm still too twisted up in thoughts of my teeth to fully appreciate the sound.

"You too." I make my retreat, hoping he'll leave the parking lot before he has to see the hot mess of a car I drive.

"Summer."

Four. My body shivers and jerks around, a puppet to the strings of his voice. "Yes?"

Cole stands on the driver's side of his truck, hand on the open door, elbow on the roof of the cab as he peers at me across the darkening parking lot.

"You said you were going to use it."

"Use what?"

"My name."

Oh.

"Cole Allemand!" I shout again, embarrassment fading, erased by my laughter and his willingness to look past my overeager introduction. "I'll see you around, Cole Allemand."

Chapter Three

SUMMER

The slight chill in the air has me grateful I'm clutching two hot coffees. Of course, I shouldn't complain. New Orleans' winter is mild by comparison. But when you're used to the warmth, low fifties seems downright frigid.

I'm also proud of not having spilled either of the coffees, seeing as how my car has no cupholders. None. It's like a skirt without pockets. Still, I try not to insult it too much. Out loud. I'm afraid it will take offense and give up on working, and then I'll have to rely solely on the public transport system.

As I approach the front doors, a familiar figure sits on an outside bench.

"Jamie!" I call out, smiling wide even as I drag worried eyes over his form. The teenager sits with an ankle propped on his knee, a composition book in his lap, messy black hair falling in disarray over his forehead. None of that worries me. What does is his T-shirt and jeans that appear worn, and lack of a coat. "Why are you sitting out here instead of inside? It's chilly."

"Fresh air helps me write." The young man grins at me through his floppy dark hair. The strands tangle in odd ways, begging for a comb and a pair of clippers.

"You need a jacket." I know I'm scolding him, but it's only because I worry. Sometimes I worry all night about Jamie.

"Here. They doubled my order again." I offer him the extra cup of coffee, eager to hand him something warm to clutch.

"Funny how they always do that." Jamie smirks as he eyes the cup. One of these days, I'm worried he'll turn it down.

But today, like all the Thursdays before, he reaches out to accept the beverage. I know there's research about caffeine affecting the growth of teens, but as Jamie rises to his six-foot-three height, I reason that he might prefer some stunting.

"You're romance-hero tall, you know?" I hold open the library door for him, and he gives me a confused grin.

"I'm what?"

"Romance-hero tall. Survey the height of heroes in the genre, and I'd bet over ninety percent surpass six foot. It's like only tall men are allowed to fall in love."

Jamie snorts and continues to smile down at me. "I don't think I'm mainstream romance novel material."

He knows I know what he's referring to. There's been a time or two I teased him about the way he likes to ogle Daniel, one of our more handsome security guards.

"Your version of romance is becoming more mainstream. Still," I lean in closer and he bends down to hear me, "find yourself a tall man. Under six-foot, and I'm sorry to tell you, the relationship will be doomed."

Jamie chuckles, eyes sparkling, and I glow with happiness. He's a sweet kid, just turned sixteen, and spends most of his afternoons at the library, working on homework or writing in one of his beat-up composition notebooks. At my urging, he started to attend the weekly writer meetings. On Thursdays, his smiles seem to come easier.

Only now I watch with despair as the upward curl of his lips retreats.

"My dad always said I'm basketball tall." His comment lacks the amusement we were sharing moments before, a lost, dark look behind his eyes.

Damn it. I want to hug him so bad.

My dad always said... Past tense.

I have suspicions about Jamie's home situation. Or more like, his lack of a home situation. But the teenager is as elusive as he is sweet, and I've never been able to get him to fess up. I guess I can understand. If social services knew there was an underaged kid in an unstable situation, they might decide to put him into a foster home.

That's not always a good thing. The foster care system is...in need of improvement. But when the other option is sleeping under some random bridge?

Still, I don't know anything for sure. It could just be that his dad left.

Or passed away. Like mine.

My mind does a Cirque du Soleil worthy leap over that thought, avoiding the pain of good memories gone.

Both Jamie and I need to focus on something else.

"Do you have a new story to share today?" I tilt my head at his notebook as I unlock my office.

"Maybe. Not sure yet. I have a few hours to decide."

It's only three p.m., and the writers' group doesn't meet until six. Jamie usually gets here right after school lets out, then stays till closing.

Which is at nine p.m.

One more reason I'm almost certain he doesn't have a home to go to. Or if he does, it's not one he wants to spend much time at.

My office is tiny, but I've done what I can to make it a cozy space. A couple of flea market lamps to avoid using the overhead fluorescent lighting. An armchair my mom found left behind at a house she sold. Framed poster-sized covers of some of my favorite novels.

And pillows. I love throw pillows. There are at least six in my office, which is quite restrained when compared to the number in my apartment. As long as I don't count the number at home, I can pretend the amount hasn't reached unhealthy proportions.

Opening the door of my mini-fridge, I reach in and come out with a granny smith apple in hand.

"Here."

Jamie avoids my eyes. Men and their pride.

"You don't want coffee breath. You'll drive all the group members to the other side of the room. Apples are like fruity toothbrushes."

"I think I need to see the research on that," Jamie says. But he accepts the apple.

Good. He has food and caffeine.

Next, a jacket. I can't solve that right now, but I have my whole shift to come up with a solution. Just like with food, I need to trick the kid into accepting help. He's adamantly against handouts.

"You don't trust me?" I fake offense. "I'm a librarian. We know everything."

He wrinkles his nose at me before taking a large crunchy bite out of the apple, his disbelief clear in the way he chews slow and cow-like.

"Stop sassing me and go do your homework. I'm on the reference desk at four if you need help."

"Yes, Ms. Pierce."

Jamie strolls away on his way to claim his favorite desk in the far corner of the library. His backpack slaps against his back as he moves, and I notice the dull silver shine of duct tape around one strap.

My heart breaks just a little bit. But I force myself to concentrate on the massive amount of emails cluttering my inbox. If I worry too much, I won't be able to work. If I don't work, I'll lose my job, and then I'll have no money to sneakily buy Jamie things.

Work it is.

Chapter Four

SUMMER

"Thank you, Mrs. Faun. Your disregard for due dates keeps the library event account well-funded."

The eighty-year-old woman smiles at me as she pushes her handful of dimes across the counter.

"I'm a rebel. Always have been."

"I can believe it." I'm careful to place the stack of mystery novels evenly in her cloth tote and only allow half my attention to track the writers' group filing out of the front meeting room. From their animated talking, it sounds like an hour wasn't enough.

"Happy reading. See you on"—I glance at her check out receipt—"January third." I try to make my voice stern even as I smile.

"We'll see!" She cackles and strolls out, maneuvering through the dispersing writers with ease.

I only realize I'm searching for a certain tattooed person when my attention gets pulled away by the sound of my name.

"Summer. I've been thinking about you all day." A handsome man steps up to the desk, smiling down at me with beautifully white, perfectly shaped teeth. I bet he was born with them that way, too.

Joshua Perry.

Joshua goes by Joshua, not Josh. Calling him Josh will earn you a small tight smile and a polite correction. I know because I received the gentle rebuke the first time he asked me out.

"I hope they were happy thoughts," I chime, not sure how else to answer.

"Everything about you is happy."

Hmm. Not the strongest flirting game I've dealt with, but I give Joshua the benefit of the doubt. Just because someone isn't a smooth talker doesn't mean they don't have an engaging mind or a kind heart.

"I aim to please!" Again, my answer feels off. Like it doesn't quite connect with his statement. A puzzle piece that is just a tad too large to fit into place, even though it appears as though it should.

But Joshua doesn't comment, maybe giving me the benefit of the doubt, too.

"I had a good time yesterday, and I was hoping you might want to get dinner with me on Saturday?"

See? Joshua is a good guy. Plenty of men would have forgotten that I said I work Friday evenings and asked me out then. Then we'd have to play the *eh that doesn't work for me, what about this day* game, which drains the romance from the spontaneity of asking.

"Saturday works for me."

A deep throat-clearing snags my attention. Across the way, I catch the eye of Daniel, one of our regular security guards. He tilts his head. At his hint, I glance around Joshua's stocky frame and find a line has formed during our brief conversation.

Realizing our poor attempt at flirting has resulted in me appearing negligent on the job, I can't help as a flush creeps up my neck. This situation calls for my *I'm a super nice librarian, please don't yell at me* smile. I up the wattage and aim it at the first patron in line.

My sunshine smile collides with ice.

Cole hovers—no, that's not right. Hovering denotes a sense of nervous energy. Cole never looks nervous. If anything, he looks pissed.

His iceberg eyes bore into the back of Joshua's neck.

Damn, he must hate waiting for his books.

"Sorry, Josh...ua." Whew, almost tripped myself there. "I need to get back to work. You have my number. You can text me about Saturday."

"Sure thing, Happy Summer." Joshua winks and flashes his beautiful smile before stepping to the side.

Oh hell. Was that supposed to be a nickname?

I love my name and all the warmth associated with it, but there is no way I want any type of romantic interest referring to me as "Happy Summer."

Weirdest pet name ever.

I guess if he does it again I can correct him the same way he corrected me.

All thoughts of Joshua stroll away with him, and my mind has a new —for some reason more interesting—subject to focus on.

"Hi Cole!" I thought about saying his whole name, but that almost seems like revealing too much to the general public. Like I'd be betraying his confidence and privacy. So first name it is.

"Summer."

Wow. Chills.

But not the good kind. His voice is even more frosty than usual.

Without another word, Cole slides a stack of books toward me he must have grabbed before the meeting. I pull out my little scanner gun and start knocking them out. And sure, my hands might fumble a couple of times, drawing out the interaction.

"Was it a good meeting? Get some insight and ideas?"

"Yes."

No.

Don't say yes *to me like that.*

It's like he's using the word as a guillotine to end any further conversation.

I'm cut off.

Cole stares toward the exit, his long-fingered hand resting on the counter, a tease of ink peeking out on his wrist. He has on a long-sleeved black sweater, which means I once again don't have the opportunity to make out what the designs are.

How expansive are the tattoos? Has he only covered his lower arms, or do they claim more of his body? Maybe to his shoulders? Even on his chest? Down his back...

"Due date?" Cole asks, his gaze on me.

Maybe I imagining things, but I think the ice has melted. Slightly.

"Oh. Yes. You have to come back"—that was an odd way of putting it —"by January third."

The tiniest corner of Cole's mouth twitches, and I release a tension I hadn't realized gathered in my chest.

"I'll be back sooner."

"Of course. On Sunday. To build your book fortress."

A grin! Or, okay, a smile wide enough for me to catch a slight glimpse of his teeth. But it feels like a jackpot on the first quarter dropped into a slot machine.

"Are you stalking me?" he asks.

Any warm happiness I'd been experiencing rips out of me in an instant, leaving my nerves raw and my heart beating way too fast for anything as simple as a conversation in a library.

"No." The word comes out low and harsh. A plea.

Cole's mouth thins into a tight line, eyes raking over me.

I should calm down, but instead I lean forward and cover his hand with mine.

"I would never do that, Cole. Never."

His eyes widen as he takes in whatever expression is on my face. "Summer—"

Another throat-clearing has me snatching my hand back and throwing Daniel an apologetic half wave.

What is with me this evening?

"Sorry! I'm holding up the line again. Bad chatty librarian." I give the back of my hand a playful slap and bring my sunshine smile back to the surface. "Here you go, Cole. Have a good night!" I slide the pile of books across the counter to him, receipt on top.

Cole hesitates, still watching me. I click away on the computer as if I'm doing something other than closing and opening the same windows.

"Goodnight, Summer."

Three times. He said my name three times, and each one felt different. I open a little lockbox in my memory, shove them inside, and close the door, knowing I'll want to take them out later tonight when I have time to fully admire them.

"He's romance-novel tall."

Jamie. Of course he had to be the next patron in line, observing all the awkwardness that is me interacting with a handsome man.

Handsome *men*. I almost forgot Joshua was here, too.

"Who?" My attempt at nonchalance fails. There was a reason I only ever worked on the stage crew for my high school theater productions.

Jamie glances at Cole's retreating form. Then back to me. I fidget with a cup of pens, looking to see if any caps are loose.

"And you're romance-heroine short."

I gasp in indignation. "I am not. You are looking at five foot four inches of average woman height right here. Add in these wedges and I could be hanging out at the top of a beanstalk, thank you very much."

I don't mention that wedges were a horrible choice of footwear for an eight-hour work day. I've been finding places to lean every chance I get. Not even sure why I opted for them, choosing to ignore how they happen to put my eyeline closer to a certain library patron.

"Sure. I take it back. You're a giant."

"Do you have any books to check out?"

"Touchy." The teenager grins at me and hands over the first volume of the graphic novel *Saga*.

"I love this one."

"Because there's romance in it?"

"Oh shut it," I grumble.

"He's hot."

I gasp again, which Jamie seems to enjoy making me do. "I'm not discussing this with you. Cole is one of my patrons, nothing more." And he can't be anything more. Not with the words "bad boy" and "naughty" as clear on him as his tattoos.

I learned early on in life that if I'm going to fall for someone, they need to be nice.

"Who said I was talking about Cole? Maybe I was referring to Josh. Your Saturday night date."

A blush comes back, full force and aggravated by Jamie's trickster smirk.

"His name is Joshua," I grumble, feeling exposed.

"Of course. *Joshua*. The guy you're dating. I'll write that down so I don't get confused." The kid saunters away, back toward his corner table, and I try not to glare at his retreating form.

After helping the last two patrons in line, I'm suddenly patron-less. A few glorious seconds of leaning occur, just before Security Guard Daniel returns from his rounds.

"You're popular tonight." He gives me his kind smile, and I return it, guilty for the many throat-clearings my distracted mind required.

"Guess I make a lot of friends."

"Not surprised. Everyone's favorite librarian." He leans on the circulation desk, eyes scanning the space.

"I try."

His knuckles rap loud on the counter before he steps away. "Careful. You'll make them all fall in love with you."

The words remind me of a box I keep tucked in the cabinet under my bathroom sink. The darkest area of my apartment.

And I can't help wondering if my friendliness is the root of my trouble.

Chapter Five

SUMMER

Joshua is a nice guy. He says nice things. We're in a nice restaurant. He smells...nice?

Maybe. There is a decent cologne drifting past my nose as we settle at our tiny table. But it might be from the man who's sitting behind me with his date.

I hope it's Joshua's cologne. I'd rather not lean in at the end of this date for a kiss and realize he smells like his own musk. Why would anyone want to be around someone that smells like musk? You know who has musk? Forest creatures. They're cute to look at, but you wouldn't want to breathe too deeply around them.

Because musk.

Maybe musk was good in medieval times when bathing was rare. Need to make sure your guy has quality musk, or else you're going to be stuck with a shitty-smelling partner.

Literally.

They did not have good plumbing situations in medieval times.

One of the reasons I would turn down the option to time travel if it were ever offered to me. Sure, the dresses are pretty. But they all probably smelled like poop and musk.

I'll stick with my thrift store clothes and running water, thank you very much.

"And that's the third loan request I had to turn down this week. I'm not sure why people go through the trouble of filling out the paperwork if they can't fulfill all the requirements. They're just wasting everyone's time." Joshua lets out a chuckle and shakes his head, reaching for his beer.

Shoot, he's been talking, and I haven't been listening. My mind does that sometimes, drifting off down twisty tangent roads. I'm glad Joshua didn't notice and ask me what I was thinking about. Then I'd feel obligated to tell him I was pondering ornate dresses that smell like musk and shit. Not a good second-date discussion.

"Yeah. That's too bad they went through all that effort." I hope my answer is sufficient, having only picked up the last few sentences.

"Hmm. I guess some people don't have anything to do." He chuckles. Again.

For some reason, the noise gives me a headache. Which has never happened. Normally, I love it when people are amused. If I hear laughter as I'm walking down the street, I can't keep from smiling myself.

Maybe it's because I'm not sure *why* he laughed. It's not a joke. Or funny. It sounds like some people needed money, and he turned them down.

More than anything, that makes me sad.

Objectively, I realize it's part of his job. Banks can't give loans to everyone. There are rules in the world.

But too often I see those rules only benefiting a certain wealthy group of people. I've gotten too close to the lowest end of the economic spectrum to find someone being denied money amusing.

"Let's talk about something other than work," I say.

We covered hobbies and family on our first date in the few minutes before the movie theater went dark. Joshua is a runner, baseball player, and has weekly poker nights with his buddies. Nice, normal pastimes. Not necessarily great fodder for conversations, but still. "Read any good books lately?"

"Hey, isn't reading books your job?" Joshua smiles at me, pointing his finger with a little teasing wave.

"Ha. True." Not true. Not true at all.

But I've heard the joke before. Everyone imagines a librarian's day involves finding a cozy chair and flipping open the latest bestseller.

Would I love to be paid to do that? Of course.

Does that job exist in the world? If it does, the job title certainly isn't *librarian*.

An awkward silence descends as I wait to see if Joshua will answer the question. To look busy I reach for my wine glass and suck down a hearty gulp, congratulating myself when I don't scowl at the taste.

But it's so fucking fruity I want to gag. When we'd first sat down, I'd mused aloud how I wasn't sure if I wanted a glass of white or red wine.

"Oh, my sister's favorite wine is on this list. Let me get you a glass." Joshua had grinned his perfect smile at me, and I'd given in.

If it's someone's favorite, that's got to be a good endorsement.

Unfortunately, I'm too trusting.

The waiter brought out a moscato. I despise moscato. It's like drinking a watered down pear mixed with cough syrup. My wine should be drier than centuries-old paint on a sun-exposed sign in the middle of the desert.

But no. Joshua saw the flowers on my dress and the petal-pink lipstick I'd carefully applied, and he categorized me as sweet.

Fucking sweet. Just like this goddamned wine.

I can't believe I let him order for me. My mom would have flipped a table if she found out.

You are a strong, independent woman! No man should have a say in your life! Why are you even on a date?

And that is the moment where we would diverge.

I *am* a strong independent woman. I *do* want to have the final say on every aspect of my life.

But I think I can have those two things and also find a partner. Someone to love and make plans with.

I know I don't need a man. But I want one. A nice one.

Like Joshua.

But...maybe not Joshua exactly.

He still hasn't answered my question, and I think I might finish my disgusting wine before he gets around to it.

"So, books." Maybe I should just go first to get the conversation flowing. "I read a good one last week. It was an autobiography about a chef." I figure Joshua doesn't want to hear about the fantasy series I've been devouring, so I stick to my non-fiction reads. "He kept running into roadblocks because of the neighborhood he grew up in and the way society viewed him, but he relentlessly pursued his dream, which was inspiring. And every chapter ended with a recipe, which I thought was a great publishing idea. If I was a better cook and had an oven that worked, I might try to make some of them."

"Your oven doesn't work? Have you called a repair man?"

Bleh, that's what he's interested in?

"I'm renting. I let the owner of the building know. I'm sure they'll get around to it. Honestly, I shouldn't even complain. This chef had to cook on an oil tanker—"

"How do you make dinner without a working oven?"

Joshua is still on my oven? It's just an appliance.

"I get by. Using a toaster oven and the microwave."

"You can't cook very much in those." He frowns at me across the table as if the portion size of my food legitimately concerns him.

I fight the urge to groan and lay my head on the table. Despite how very mature that would make me look, I restrain myself and paste an overly bright smile on my face, hoping that if I look happy, maybe I'll start to feel happy.

"I'm just cooking for me, so I don't need a lot." Seems he's not interested in Kwame Onwuachi's life story, so I give up on that track of one-sided conversation. "Are there any meals you like to cook?"

"Oh." He chuckles as if my question is amusing, which again, I don't get. After sipping what I'm sure is a delicious dry whiskey, Joshua gives me a small smile.

The expression comes off as patronizing.

"My mother never let me in the kitchen. She and my sister always handled the meals."

"And you and your dad took care of clean-up duty?"

He laughs. A full, belly-rumbling laugh.

I take another swallow from my glass, polishing it off.

"You liked it?" He grins across the table at me, still riding the high of finding my not-funny question hilarious.

"I'm going to try something else." I wave the waiter down, keeping their eyes locked with mine so they know who is in charge here.

It's me. I'm in charge. And I need a dry red.

Because this is going to be a long evening.

Chapter Six

COLE

Sansa encircles my neck, claiming me as her own. She's draped across me, with no care for how her placement might make it difficult for me to perform my job duties.

And the second she thinks I'm ignoring her, I hear about it.

"Mrrrrooww."

The grumbled complaint sounds directly in my ear. I smirk, turning my head slightly to meet her beautiful green eyes.

"Yes, Queen of the North?"

The eight-year-old tabby is such a deep orange she almost appears red. Hence the name I chose for her when she was abandoned at the shelter. I'd been the first to arrive at work that day and found a cardboard box waiting outside. People abandoning animals on our front steps isn't out of the ordinary.

When I pulled open the top flaps of the box, I prayed that the animal inside would be alive and in not too bad shape. Luckily, the russet tabby only appeared slightly underfed and didn't even try to swipe at me when I reached a hand out for her to sniff.

Just over a month has passed since that morning, and Sansa was recently cleared for adoption. I doubt it will take long, so I enjoy her clingy-ness while it's still me she clings to. If it weren't for my doesn't-play-well-with-others cat at home, I might have considered claiming her for myself.

She rubs her head on my cheek before letting out another grumpy meow.

Cats. Never clear about what they want, but will make sure to punish you if you don't figure it out.

"Let me finish here," I murmur, reaching for the disposable litter box with my gloved hand and shoving it into the trash bag with all the others. The amount of litter we go through in a single day is staggering when I think about it. But I try not to get too concerned about the cost of materials this place requires. Money is not my responsibility. Keeping the cats clean and comfortable, and from going insane in their confined spaces, is.

I know how they feel, locked up all day. There was no one around who cared about my mental health during that dark time in my life, and these innocent animals don't even understand why they're kept in such tight living quarters.

Just as I'm tying up the bag and considering if I have time to play with Sansa before moving on to my next task, there's a knock on the door.

"Come in!" Sansa isn't one for bolting, so an open door to the rest of the shelter isn't a flight risk like it might be with another of the animals.

My boss, Cheryl, walks in, her sharp eyes resting on the cat lounging across my shoulders. Her serious mouth twitches.

"You have something on your shirt," she deadpans.

"Really?" I pretend to glance down at myself. "Where?"

Cheryl sighs then, and there's a defeated note in the exhale. I try not to tense, wanting to keep the feline on my shoulders relaxed.

"Do you have a minute to talk?"

"Yes." I pride myself on my ability to keep my emotions from showing, so the word comes out flat. Probably too flat because Cheryl's gaze narrows as she examines my face.

Normally, when people narrow their eyes at me, they're judging me. Worrying about what I might do. People think I'm dangerous.

I guess I am. Or, at least, I used to be.

But when Cheryl looks at me this way, I know she's more concerned than anything. She's the one who brought a collection of rescued dogs to the prison where I was incarcerated, looking for nonviolent prisoners to work with the animals. To learn how to be responsible for the health and happiness of another living creature.

She gave me a chance, a path out of the darkness, and I've been grateful ever since.

So now I don't put up a wall between us. But I also don't spill my soul.

"How are things going?" she asks.

One of my eyebrows creeps up, and I decide to answer her question in the only way that makes me feel comfortable. "Everything is on schedule for the day. Just finished cleaning the adoptable cat enclosures. I'll move on to the strays' cages next."

She's shaking her head before I'm even done.

"No, I mean in your life. Outside of here."

"Fine. Good." Other than the woman I'm obsessed with going on dates with a button-up douche bag.

"You're spending time with friends? With Dash?"

"Yes."

"You're still writing?"

"Yes."

"Visiting your family?"

"Yes."

"Looking at other jobs?"

"Y—what?" I'd almost stopped listening to the questions, confident I'm living my life within the parameters she'd find acceptable. But that last bit threw me.

"Other jobs. I wouldn't be offended if you want to work somewhere offering a higher salary and better benefits."

"Do you want me to go?"

"No, Cole. You're one of my best employees. It's only..." Cheryl hesitates. She never hesitates, and I reach up to scratch Sansa's fluffy chin to ease my worries, waiting for Cheryl to figure out whatever she's trying to say.

"We're running out of money."

My muscles clench, threatening to lock up. Sucking in a deep breath through my nose, I convince myself that there's no reason to panic. It's a hard lie to make myself swallow.

"Is the shelter closing?"

Cheryl glares at the ceiling. "I'm going to do everything in my power to keep that from happening."

"But it would be easier if you didn't have to pay me." I don't frame it as a question because of course, the answer is yes.

"You're not doing busy work Cole. You serve an important role here. But I just wanted to let you know that if something else comes up, you might want to consider taking it."

Not a lot of job opportunities come up for ex-cons, I want to point out. But I keep my mouth shut. Cheryl doesn't deserve cutting comments. She's probably one of the main reasons I'm walking around a free man, no longer on parole, making a salary that I'm able to live off of.

For however long that lasts.

"I'll keep an eye out."

"I don't want you to think I'm pushing you out, Cole. I care about you. And no one is better with these furballs." She gestures to Sansa, who has decided to hook her claws into the already frayed fabric of my work shirt.

"I know." And I do. Logically, I understand that if Cheryl had unlimited funds, she'd probably employ me until I reach ripe old retirement age.

But even knowing this, I can't help having flashbacks to the other times in my life when I felt safe only moments before finding myself abandoned.

Chapter Seven

SUMMER

The fortress of books has been reconstructed.

He knows how to put them away. There's no reason to go over. None at all.

Only, there's a single volume, one that sits on the very corner of the table, that isn't part of the structure. The book seems completely separate from Cole's collection. Maybe it was left there by another patron.

I must shelve it.

"Are you okay to cover circulation?"

Karen raises her head from the magazine spread on the desk in front of her. "You're going to go talk to the tattoo guy?"

"What? No. Of course not. I'm going to check the tables for stray items."

Karen pushes her cat eyeglasses up her nose, glancing between the almost completely empty reading room and me. "I don't care if you go talk to him. It's slow. He's got good taste in books. I want to read this article without you interrupting me. He has a crush on you. Everyone wins."

Having worked with Karen for close to six months, I'm getting used to her blunt way of speaking. At least, I thought I was.

"He does not have a crush on me. I wasn't going to talk to him. And you shouldn't even be reading on the job. No one wins!"

Wait, no, that's not what I meant to say.

Karen flips the magazine's cover up to reveal it's the monthly publication put out by the American Library Association.

"Professional development. Go flirt."

"I'm not flirting. I'm doing my job!" I whisper with only an edge of frantic in my voice.

"Look. Summer. Can I call you Summer?"

"It's my name. So yes?"

"Summer. You're a good librarian. Great, actually. Top-notch. Sometimes it's intimidating to be around you. You're a catalyst for imposter syndrome."

"I don't mean to—"

Karen waves me quiet. "My issues. Not yours. My point is, you want to be a flustered human for the last ten minutes of your shift on a Sunday night? I can deal with that. In fact, I welcome it. So please, go 'shelve books.'" She uses finger quotes around the last two words, and I find myself smiling at her dry delivery of an extremely sweet sentiment. Briefly, Karen reminds me of Cole.

And once again, my focus is drawn toward the reading room.

"Okay. Alright. I will go *shelve books*." I put emphasis on the last words, trying to imply that is exactly what I plan to do.

But from Karen's snort, I can only imagine it sounded like some sort of dirty innuendo.

I can't win.

On quiet feet, I stroll around the reading room, eyeing every surface for some item I could put away.

There's nothing. Nothing other than that stray book not being used within the fortress. It's not even close enough to the piles to be considered a draw bridge.

I must put it away.

Cole's head is completely obscured. I could approach and retreat without alerting him to my presence. I will be sneaky. Use my quiet librarian superpowers to approach without disturbing him.

The old carpet helps in my task, muffling my footsteps. I hunch my shoulders, bending over slightly to make sure no bit of me pops above his towers. When I'm within reaching distance, I stretch my arm out as far as it will go. My fingers brush the plastic protective cover.

So close. Just another inch.

"Summer?"

I squeak. An actual squeak. I'll have to go around to the other patrons and assure them that the library isn't infested with mice, because the sound that just came out of my throat was not something a human should make.

In my single-minded approach to the table, all my attention had been focused on the stray book. Which means I didn't realize my crush decided to stand up, and has potentially been watching me creep around.

Luckily, I have a quick recovery time in awkward situations.

"Cole Allemand! Happy Sunday night!"

And by quick recovery time, I mean, I continue to exist in the awkward because it is my natural habitat.

His cool-colored gaze sweeps over me, then settles on where I'm fingering the stray book.

Oof. Better not use that phrasing out loud.

"Are you stealing my books?"

I straighten fists on my hips. "Excuse me, sir. These are the library's books. And even if you have a momentary claim on them, I resent the implication that I am a book thief. I was merely shelving this one title that I doubted was part of your Sunday-night collection.

"Why do you think that?"

"Because it has been left out of your fortress." I gesture at the towers that surround his work space.

"An oversight."

"So." I let my fingers slide away in defeat. "This is one of yours?"

Cole reaches over his wall, plucks the book off the table, and places it on the top of one of the piles.

"Yes."

Damn him. *Let me shelve for you!*

"Fine. I'll leave you alone."

"Wait." His command stops my retreat.

When I glance back, he traps me with his intense stare.

"Did you need help with something?"

He shakes his head, and the hope bubble that had formed in my chest pops.

"Then I should wait because...?"

From the twist of his mouth, he seems to chew on some words. I turn fully back to face him, suddenly wildly interested in what might emerge from his mouth next.

The suspense is brief.

"How was your date?"

"My what?"

"Your date. Saturday night," he clarifies.

An uncomfortable spike of fear scrapes against the inside of my ribcage. I take a step back. "How do you know about that?"

Cole watches the retreat with shrewd eyes.

What is he thinking? Is he upset at my caginess?

Is he angry?

My pulse beats a rapid rhythm under my skin.

Karen is here. Daniel is working security tonight.

"He asked you out on Thursday. I was there."

And like that, the fear evaporates.

"Of course."

I hate this. The bouts of panic that come from uncertainty. For so long, I'd lived with a different kind of fear in my life. Finally, I'd thought I'd found safety. Security.

But the little box tucked under my bathroom sink is a constant reminder that someone decided to take my safety away again.

"Summer? Are you okay?"

Cole moves around from behind the table, but he still keeps at a distance, as if he's worried I'll flee.

I was considering it. Now I feel silly.

"Yes. Fine. Just thinking. About my date." I hate lying.

"Was it bad?"

Not surprised he thinks so from the weird reaction I'm pairing with talk of it.

"Um. Well. It wasn't good." This I can at least be honest about.

Cole's brows dive at sharp angles, giving his face a fierce energy.

And, to my surprise, I'm not in the least afraid of it.

"Did he do something to you?"

"What? Oh. No. He was... Well, I'm sure he was being a genuine version of himself. The date should have been nice."

Cole's face softens, and he leans a hip against the table, settling in for a conversation.

I'm not supposed to be talking to him. I'm supposed to be shelving books.

"But it wasn't?"

I shrug and scan the room for any items that may have magically appeared and need to be returned to their rightful places. "We didn't have much to talk about."

"Really? But you want to know *everything*." Cole over-exaggerates my previous statement to him, but from the secret curve at the corner of his mouth, I can tell he's not mocking me. Only forming an inside joke.

His lighthearted response and sexy smile draw me back in.

"I do! And he had to know some stuff, right? But I just..." Realizing what was about to come out of my mouth, I cut myself off. "No never mind."

Cole leans toward me, smile inching wider. "What?"

"It's a horrible thing to say, and I make an effort not to say horrible things."

"Please, Summer." The sound of my name in his smoky drawl has my eyes fluttering.

"Please what?"

"Say something horrible to me."

"I can't," I whisper.

"Yes, you can. You can be bad if you want to."

Oh damn. Those words cause some delicious clenching down in my gut. It's almost too much. But what is definitely too much is the way he's staring at me.

"I didn't care."

"About what?"

"About anything he had to say. About *everything* he had to say." I cover my eyes, ashamed of how good it feels to admit my complete disinterest in a fellow human being. "He was like a walking, talking white noise machine."

There's a snort, and a warm grip on my wrist. My eyes fly open to realize Cole has tugged my hand down, and he's wearing a snarky smile.

"Are you smirking at me?" I try to sound annoyed, but all I want is to stare at where he's holding my wrist.

"Yes," he says.

Oh goodness. Pleasurable shivers skitter along my spine.

The five-minute bell splits through the quiet library, shocking me enough to wrench my wrist from his grip. Embarrassed at my erratic movement, I grab an armful of books off the top of one of the stacks.

"I can put these away!"

"No, Summer." He spreads a large palm over them, pressing the stack down until I have to release them. "I will."

"What about these?" I reach for another pile, but Cole steps in front of me, his body almost flush with mine, acting as a barrier between my seeking hands and the hoard of books.

"I'll take care of the ones I don't want to check out."

Of course. I know that, but my hands want something to grab onto.

So they won't reach for him.

I silently scold my hands and my nerve endings that all seem to have become addicted to him. I shouldn't be surprised. Bad boys are like drugs in that way. They make you feel good. So good that you get dependent. You think you need them to survive.

And that's when they disappear.

That's when you find out just how much destruction a life can handle. How painful it is to live with the wreckage of a broken heart.

I want a man to love, and I know the kind of man who will make me feel safe.

A nice guy. Not a bad boy.

Not a Cole Allemand.

I know he's not right for me. Knew it the second I saw him in a grocery store parking lot a few months back. Seeing him outside of the library threw me off, but I was just about to recover and offer a friendly wave when he shocked the hell out of me.

Cole walked up to a random tan SUV, and without any provocation, dragged his key along the entire length of the vehicle. Even a good twenty feet away I heard the metallic screech of metal on metal. Once he finished vandalizing the car, Cole tucked his keys in the back pocket of his black jeans, then strolled into the store, wearing a smile of smug satisfaction.

I don't know if he saw me or not, but the guy wasn't being sneaky. The act was brazen and unapologetic.

Leading up to that moment, I'd started to scold myself for automatically assuming Cole was a bad boy just because of the way he looked and his aloof attitude.

Now I know better.

So why can't I stay away from him?

"Sounds good. I'll leave you to it. Have a good night." This time my retreat is purposeful, rather than driven by fear.

"You're not going to check me out?" Cole's smile disappears, a confused twist to his mouth taking its place.

I've been checking you out all night, I'm tempted to retort.

Classic library humor. Still, it's true. And exactly why I need to have a locked door in between me and this tempting man.

"Karen can handle it. I have some stuff to finish in my office. Librarians do more than steal books from distracted patrons!" I add a forced chuckle, trying to help my bad joke land.

Cole doesn't laugh, or smirk, or even let the tiniest corner of his mouth twitch.

He just watches me stroll away.

I shouldn't know that he watches me, seeing as how my back is turned to him.

My guess is the same way that all that delicious metal pierced into him blocks my helpful telekinetic signals, they also act as amplifiers for his Icelandic eyes. There has to be some supernatural or scientific reason I can feel his stare on my skin because I refuse to believe Cole Allemand affects me this much simply by existing.

That wouldn't be fair.

But of course, I know more than most that life is rarely fair.

Chapter Eight

COLE

Any updates?

I stare down at the text I sent over an hour ago and again wonder if I should put in the investment to upgrade my phone.

It's not that I want a smartphone. The way people depend on them grates my nerves. Especially because I know I'd be just as bad if I let myself give in and purchase one, paying for not only the wildly expensive technology, but also the bank-account-draining monthly plan.

Those small devices are capable of so much, I'm uneasy about what I might be tempted to use them for.

I've done a lot to distance myself from my past, but old habits die hard and all that.

Only, I'm worried my texts might not be going through. Or maybe that she's missing mine. Not that I have any evidence that this is happening. Only a paranoia that I'll miss my chance.

I'm considering sending another follow up when my phone rings. Some of the tension seeps out of me at the sight of my literary agent's name on the screen.

Looks like my message did get through.

Camila Blake prefers talking to texting, which I'm reluctantly okay with. At least it means I get answers to my questions faster, rather than staring at a screen, wondering if her message got lost in the ether.

"Camila," I answer the call.

"Cole." She doesn't push me for pleasantries anymore, knowing by now that I'm not the chatty type. "I got your message."

"And?"

"And I wanted to assure you that we have your manuscript making the rounds. It's good. You know this. And I have high hopes. There are a few editors in particular that seem interested in adding more paranormal-fantasy crossover to their lists."

"And have you heard from them?"

"Only that they're reading the submission package I sent them. I'm sorry, Cole. I know you're wanting a more definitive answer than that. But the traditional publishing process is a slow-moving machine. These things take time. Years, possibly."

Years. The word isn't a revelation, but it still twists at my guts.

I need this now. But telling Camila that won't do any good. She's already busting her ass for my work. But these long stretches of silence have me feeling like I'll never publish my work.

That I'll never find that respectable second income stream.

That I'll never impress a certain librarian with my author status.

"I get it. Thanks for calling me."

"Of course, Cole. The best thing you can do is keep working. Write more. Finish another manuscript, and we can shop that one, too. Up your chances. Do you have anything you're working on?"

Camila's hopeful tone sparks a surprising prick of guilt in the back of my brain. The only project I've been able to concentrate on lately is not ever going to be a piece of work she can sell.

"I have ideas. I'll send you whatever I finish."

"Good. That's great. And you know I'll contact you the minute I have a bite on your manuscript."

"I know. I'm just... I know."

"Hang in there, Cole. You've got great talent. It'll happen for you."

"I've got to go."

After hanging up, I still feel shitty. Anxiety has the lines of my composition book blurring in front of me. Frustrated with my inability to concentrate, I chuck the blank pages across the room and collapse back on my bed, staring at the small water stains on the ceiling.

The conversation I had with Cheryl the other day plays through my head. My job is in jeopardy. My income on the line. Just when I thought things were falling into place, everything threatens to slip away.

Money doesn't have to be a problem, a small tantalizing voice whispers in the back of my mind. *You know how to make money. A lot of it. And fast.*

Yeah, I do. I learned early on that my ability to create something from nothing wasn't a talent everyone possessed. That I had skills plenty of people would pay for.

No matter if the transaction was morally suspect.

I could stick to the gray areas of the law. Return to my more innocent rule breaking.

With the plagiarism checkers professors use today, students can't simply go online and copy-paste their assignments anymore. Not if they don't want to get caught.

No, what they need is original work. Something I've never had a problem with producing at a high quality and in a timely manner. If anything, my time behind bars gave me more practice with writing and educating myself on a wide range of topics.

It wouldn't take much. Look around on social media for some jock bitching about a professor. Maybe swing by a kegger or two to pass my number around. I did it when I was sixteen. Could start up again with little effort.

My eye snags on a book on my bedside table. The spine has a white label with the book's call number printed in clear block letters. That font always makes me think of Summer and the way she mouths the letters and numbers to herself when she's shelving books.

What would Summer think of me writing college research papers for money?

A woman who is interested in everything would probably be baffled at the idea of someone not willing to do their own work.

Would she be impressed that I can write an academic paper on almost any subject presented to me?

Maybe. But not if it meant I was breaking some kind of rule in the process. Summer is too good to approve of rule breaking. I've seen her stand at a crosswalk with absolutely no cars in sight, waiting far longer than necessary to receive the pedestrians' crossing light.

It'll be hard enough to convince her to overlook my criminal past when she eventually finds out. No need to shovel more shit on the pile by revisiting my old ways.

I'll have to find some other option to keep my head above water. Something that won't lose me the librarian before I've even had a chance to get her to fall for me.

Chapter Nine

SUMMER

"Summer."

At the sound of my name in that familiar voice, I try not to cringe. I glance down from the ladder I've climbed to hang paper snowflakes from the ceiling tiles. And there he stands, staring up at me.

"Joshua. Hello." My knee-jerk reaction is to ask if there's something he needs help with. That is my job after all. But from our last interaction, I don't expect this conversation to be anything library-related.

"Can we talk?" He holds out a hand as if to help me down.

Some people might think the gesture chivalrous. No doubt I would have a few weeks ago. But now I can't help noticing how his extended hand has a layer of expectation to it. That I will abandon whatever task I'm doing and go talk to him. Not taking into account what I want, or what important duty I might be performing.

Seasonal decorations might not seem imperative, but I think they're important. I believe that lending an air of charm and good cheer to this public space helps to make the place more homey. Provide a sense of welcoming. Let the patrons know we care about this space, and we work to make sure everything looks nice for them.

But all Joshua sees is me performing a task less crucial than whatever he has to say to me.

"Aliyah is working the reference desk right now. She can help you find whatever you're looking for." I tilt my head toward said desk, where my coworker watches this exchanging with questioning eyes.

"I need to talk to *you*."

Damn it to the archives of hell. I was having such a good day.

"I'm working, Joshua. If it's not library-related—"

"Please." He stretches his hand even further, almost as if he's going to grab mine. That would be a disaster, seeing as how I'm carefully pinching delicately cut snowflakes I spent my entire shift on the circulation desk creating.

"Fine. Wait." Gone is my people-pleaser tone, and from the way Joshua frowns at me, I can tell he misses it. Yes, well, showing up in the middle of my work day to demand my attention about a personal issue is not the way to get Happy Summer.

Carefully, I step down from the ladder, keeping my balance on my own rather than accepting help from Joshua.

"I want—"

"Not here." Now it's my turn to cut him off. "This is my place of work." Without checking to see if he's following, I stroll across the reading room to the reference desk.

"I'm going to take my fifteen-minute break, Aliyah. Can I leave these with you?"

The middle aged woman stares up at me in surprise, pushing aside her curly hair as she nods.

"Sure."

"Thank you."

Her shock is understandable. Everyone who works an eight-hour day is due a sixty-minute lunch break and a fifteen-minute break in the first and second half of our shifts.

However, while I'm pretty good about claiming some time to eat and get a breath of fresh air, I have never bothered with the shorter breaks. What's the point? That amount of time is perfect for a smoker maybe, but what am I going to do for fifteen minutes?

Apparently, re-break up with a guy I barely started dating. I'm sure that's what HR had in mind for these fifteen minutes.

Walking outside, I discover the sun has sunk below the horizon, even though we're just past five p.m. The darkness of the evening causes a shiver of apprehension to trickle down my spine, and I make sure to choose a bench bathed in the light from the library's front windows.

Joshua sits beside me, closer than I would have preferred, but at least he's not touching me without my permission.

"Okay. You have my attention." I shift my body to face his while still keeping air between us.

"You ended things without letting me say my piece."

Deciding whether or not to go out with someone is not a debate, I want to point out.

"Fine. Say your piece."

"You're being very short with me."

"If that's your piece, then I have work to get back to." I go to rise but he places a hand on my shoulder.

"Wait. I'm sorry. You're right. Please, just let me ask you something."

I try not to sigh too loudly as I settle back on the bench.

"And that is?"

"Why did you end things?"

This question strikes me as willfully ignorant. It's not like I ghosted Joshua. When he texted me about going out again this weekend, I called him to thank him for the dates we had gone on, but also to say I didn't find myself interested in continuing things. True, I left this all on his voicemail, but does two dates require more than that?

Not in my book.

"Like I said in my message, you're a nice guy, but I think I should feel more if I want to be romantic with someone."

And by *more*, I mean *anything*.

"After only two dates? That's barely any time at all. You're not giving me a real chance."

Who says I have to?

The thought pushes at my lips, demanding to be spoken aloud. But since I try not to say harsh things, I opt for a softer approach.

"You may feel that way, but I am satisfied with the amount of time we devoted to finding out if there are romantic feelings between us. There aren't any on my end, and I'm sorry if that is not what you want to hear, but it's the only answer you'll get from me."

"I'm a good guy, Summer. But it takes me longer to open up. To show someone the real me. I want to do that with you. You're amazing and beautiful and sweet. Please, just one more date. We can do anything you want, and I swear I'll love it."

All the words he speaks sound like good words. They should be what I want to hear. But every plea he makes only notches up my discomfort. My hands fidget, tangling and fisting in my skirt. I wish I had a nice heavy pile of books to hold on to.

If I tell Joshua yes, then he will forever think that my no is worth nothing. He will push and pester, show up at my work, scratching away at my no, sure that if only he keeps at it long enough that the word will change to one he prefers.

"Thank you for the compliments, but my answer is the same." This time when I stand, I make sure to move out of the range of reaching hands. Still, Joshua also rises from his seat, and I realize for the first time how much larger than me he is. With his broad shoulders and close to six-foot height, I find a wall of man in between me and my escape route.

Where is security when you need them?

"Just give me a minute, Summer."

I don't have to give you anything! I want to scream, feeling panic prick at my skin as the dark parts of my mind taunt me with recent memories. The image of a box I keep tucked under my bathroom sink pastes itself across my mind's eye.

Is it him? Is he the one?

But he doesn't know where I live...or does he?

"Let's get a drink. My treat." Joshua reaches for me, just as I catch sight of a familiar figure over his shoulder. "We can—"

I don't stay to listen to the rest, dodging around his hulking form and jogging toward the tall figure who looks like safety.

"Cole Allemand!" His name springs from my throat, overly loud in the humid night. I don't care.

My potential savior freezes mid-step. Most people would have whipped around in shock at the ridiculous way I just yelled at them. Not Cole. He turns only his head, sharp eyes searching until they land on me.

That's when the most tempting smile I've ever seen melts over his mouth.

This may not have been my best idea, but I'm committed.

"Summer."

Damn him and the sexy way he says every word in existence. Especially my name.

"I'm so glad you've arrived on time for our appointment," I pant, breathless from my sprint. I should probably do more exercise than weightlifting stacks of books.

He raises a single brow, and of course, it's the one with the barbell piercing, which makes it so much harder to rip my attention away from.

"Our..." He trails off as I fall into step beside him. I realize then that his smile has fallen away as he stares back the way I came.

I don't look behind me, too worried Joshua will take that as an invitation to follow.

"Our appointment. Yes." Cole holds the door open and gives a half-bow for me to go in before him. He steps through directly after me, and I imagine I can feel the heat of him through the material of my dress.

But that's ridiculous.

Besides, my body is mainly flushed because of adrenaline. Before Cole showed up, my nerves had been in debate between fight or flight. Flight won out.

"My office," I announce to maybe no one. Maybe him. I don't know. For just a minute or two I want to be in a place Joshua is not allowed to follow, in case he decides to try.

For all I know, he's trailed my steps for longer than I've been aware of his existence.

Down a hall, through a locked door that only I and housekeeping have a key too, I enter my tiny office. It's filled with things I love and acts as a home away from home.

Once I've collapsed into my office chair, I realize Cole has indeed taken my words as an invitation.

Sort of.

He doesn't step into my space. His lean body lounges against the door frame, his icy gaze sweeping over my little satellite home.

My hands find a throw pillow, and I clutch it to my chest. The mass of it calms me as if it is an impenetrable armored breastplate that will keep me safe from the world.

Any moment now, he'll say something. Any second, he'll throw out a comment, and I'll have to focus and come up with an answer. Any moment I'll be expected to function.

Any moment...

Doesn't come.

Cole stays quiet at his post outside my door. He looks everywhere but at me, his lovely blue eyes tracing over my framed book covers before sliding down to the knickknacks covering my desk. He spends so long examining things that are mine, but not me, that my pulse is able to find a steady flow, and my heart can return to its nondescript beating.

Any moment becomes the moment I choose.

"I used you to escape an uncomfortable situation. I'm sorry."

He shrugs, eyes still not meeting mine. "Use me any time."

Don't say things like that, my reasonable brain whispers even as my lady parts conjure all the ways a man can be used.

"I'm keeping you from your meeting." The clock on the wall lets us know he has only a few minutes to join the other writers.

Coles nods but doesn't move to leave. Instead, his stare finally meets mine.

For some reason, his normally cold gaze found a way to radiate heat.

"I wanted to ask you something."

The statement scorches over my already sensitive nerves.

Please don't ask me for something I can't give you, I beg silently. *Can't I just be a librarian?*

His long fingers reach up to fiddle with a stud in his ear lobe, and he thankfully breaks eye contact with me.

"Can you help me with some research?"

I try to figure out if there's some secondary meaning to his question.

None that I can detect.

"Yes! That is my job."

A smirk tugs at his lips. "Exactly."

"What are you researching?" This I can handle. This is what I got my degree for.

"Genetic mutations. The structuring of DNA. Advances in prosthetic technology."

I chew on my lower lip, thinking. "That's some technical stuff. I could find the basics online. We'll probably have to order you some texts through interlibrary loan, but for the really good sources..." I trail off, considering the offer I'm about to make.

"Yes?" he prompts me, and I find myself staring at Cole's feet. They have yet to cross my threshold. Something about that restraint makes me feel safe. Well, safe enough to go slightly above my normal librarian duties.

"How would you feel about meeting up with me outside of the library?"

Chapter Ten

COLE

"Cole Allemand! Over here!" Summer calls out my entire name as if worried I won't recognize her.

I cross the university campus, heading toward a concrete picnic table Summer has taken over with her laptop and a pile of books and papers. As I approach, she stands, and I lose track of whatever thoughts were in my head.

She's in jeans.

Shouldn't I be more bowled over by Summer wearing skirts? Normally I am. But today, seeing her in pants, I can admire every beautiful curve.

Summer is shorter than me, but I wouldn't necessarily call her slim. She's compact. Like a gardening shovel. Sturdy and ready to work. Easy to maneuver.

And I want to maneuver her underneath me.

I shake my head to push the thought aside. That's for the future, when she's fallen for me.

"You found me, " she calls out as I draw closer, waving me forward and indicating I should settle in beside her at the table.

"Hello," I say because she deserves a proper greeting. She deserves everything.

"Hello," she offers back with a smile so bright my retinas begin to char. I enjoy each blinding second.

In addition to her stretchy jeans, Summer has on a long-sleeved shirt with the university's name printed across the chest.

"Camouflage?" I ask, tilting my head in the direction of her chest.

Summer smooths her hand over the front of the shirt. "Kind of. I did go here. So I guess I'm showing my alumni pride. And there are no rules against the public being on campus. Also," Summer leans closer to me, her voice dropping as if we're conspiring, "I know a little trick. Not breaking any rules, but they don't tend to advertise it. So I'm giving you an in."

She winks, and it's the most fucking adorable thing I've ever seen. Summer pretending to flout the rules even as she follows them, her delighted smile giving away that she could never do anything wrong.

She's too good for me. Which is why I need every advantage on my side before she finds out just how bad I've been.

"I'm a lucky guy." I lean in to her too, bringing myself close enough to smell her. Maybe that's weird, but I've been dying to know what her scent is. Because that's one step away from knowing how she tastes.

One year my grandmother lived in Southern California. She rented a small house with a roof covered in curved shingles and a backyard full of lilac bushes. Summer shares that purple flower's gentle floral scent that makes me think of sunny days and fresh blooms.

Before heading over here, I took a nice long shower, scrubbing vigorously, trying to make sure I don't smell like cat piss.

"Librarians are good friends to have." Summer grins, then reaches out to angle her laptop so I can see the screen. "Now, here's what I want to show you. See here?" She maneuvers the cursor and brings down the Wi-Fi menu. "We're on the university's Wi-Fi. Anyone can access this as long as they are on campus."

"I can get free Wi-Fi at your library," I point out, not understanding why we're going through this extra step, but still enjoying how close Summer is leaning to me.

"Yes, but this Wi-Fi gives you access to all the databases the school pays for. Do you know what that means?" For a second I thought I did, but when Summer grins up at me, unfiltered excitement spilling from her soft brown eyes, my brain briefly shorts out. All I can manage is a shake of my head.

"It means you can access hundreds of thousands, maybe even millions of academic articles that are normally behind a paywall. There is so much scholarly, peer-reviewed research, and all you have to do is come to the campus to access it."

Forcefully stifling my attraction for the librarian, I let her words sink in.

Shit. That is a fucking amazing workaround.

"You're a genius."

Her plump cheeks turn a tempting cherry color. "I'm not. I just know how library licensing works." She pushes her laptop toward me. "You wanna have a go?"

I'm about to when I notice one of the tabs she has open.

"Wikipedia page for *Feminist views on prostitution*?"

"Oh, yeah. That's normally why I come here." She waves a hand dismissively.

Briefly, I struggle to make words come out of my mouth. Eventually, I manage, "To research prostitution?"

Summer laughs, a deep booming noise that takes over her entire compact body. For some reason, I have the urge to gather her into my arms while she does it, so I can experience the joy shake through her gorgeous body.

"No. Oh my gosh. Well"—she shrugs, still chuckling—"technically yes. But not because I have any particular interest in the subject. I'm just researching it for the Wikipedia article. I'm a Wikipedia editor."

"You have a second job?"

"No. Although I should probably have one. Maybe clear out my student loans faster. But anyone with a computer and internet access can edit Wikipedia. Unfortunately, over ninety percent of the editors are men, which means the articles tend to focus on traditionally male-centered topics. I've made it my mission to help make Wikipedia a little more female friendly."

"This is your hobby?"

"One of them. I mean, I enjoy researching anyway. Why not make sure some good comes out of it?"

"You use the university's databases?"

"Yes! Exactly. I come here to access information the general public may not be able to afford. And it's not plagiarism or anything. I cite all my sources. Other editors will delete your entries if you don't. Plus, it's just the right thing to do."

I have to rest my chin in my hand. Give my head a break.

It's as if Summer has made it her mission to both tempt and shame me. If she knew my past, I'm almost certain she wouldn't be giving me that bright smile of hers.

She'd judge me and have every right to.

Reflexively, I glance down at my phone, hoping to see a missed call, or at least a text from my agent. Something indicating my ace has been dealt. That I've turned into the man this amazing woman could never resist.

But my screen is blank.

"Enough about me. We're here for you. Now I did some initial searching. You know, just to get a feel for your topics, and I think we should start with this database." Summer proceeds to guide me through a scholarly focused search, pointing to different buttons and suggesting more search terms than I considered.

When I first asked Summer for help, it wasn't truly about the research. I'm pretty confident in my ability to find information. The request came to me because I wanted to spend time with her. I'm not satisfied with the few moments before closing where she tries to help me put my books away. Those minutes are great, but I want more.

Still, with the uncomfortable dating situation she was running from, I was even less confident about receiving a yes if I put myself on the line and asked her out.

So I asked for research help.

And, as I marvel at the lists of academic articles appearing after each search, I realize I need help.

This is amazing.

Summer is amazing.

I want her to sit on my lap so I can put my arms around her as she explains how to expertly navigate databases. She can show me how to refine searches as I kiss her neck. She can wax poetic about the benefit of mining reference lists as I slide my hand up the inseam of her jeans.

Her librarian talk makes me hot.

I can't help it.

But I stumble out of my fantasies when I realize we're going to have someone join our research duo.

A woman approaches our table, walking across the grassy area with purpose. She looks official, with a name tag and a suit jacket. My shoulders tense in preparation for us to get dismissed from the campus. Maybe Summer could have passed as a student, but I doubt anyone thinks I belong here.

"I should go," I mutter.

"Go? Why? Research isn't a five-minute process, Cole. I mean, you know this. You spend hours in your book fortress. You can't expect a database to give you what you're looking for in seconds just because it's electronic. Here. Let's try another search."

I struggle against a glare. Not at Summer. Never at her. I want to scowl at the official-looking woman who's only ten feet away. I want to send her on retreat with the warning of my eyes, so she can't demand we leave and therefore break this delicious contact between my leg and Summer's. My arm twitches, aching to snake out, wrap around my little librarian's waist, and pull her closer.

Instead, I lean down to whisper in my companion's ear, earning a subtle scent of her floral perfume. "We've got company."

Summer glances up, eyes immediately settling on the woman. Instead of hurriedly moving to pack her things, Summer grins wide.

"Jasmine! I thought you didn't have a break today!"

The woman shifts her gaze between the two of us, eyes lingering just a touch longer on me even as a welcoming smile curves her lips. The stranger has on a dark purple lipstick that looks interesting against her mahogany skin. Summer only paints her lips brighter colors, and I wonder what she'd look like in a darker shade.

But I guess that's me, wanting to draw her over to the dark side.

"Professor canceled our meeting last minute, so I figured I'd check if you still made it out here. You brought a friend?"

The woman, Jasmine, stands over our table, the sun lighting up the edges of her riotous curls. She makes no move to sit.

"I did. This is Cole Allemand. He's one of my patrons at the public library. Cole..." Summer faces me with her sweet smile, but I'm barely able to appreciate the glow of it when I register that her hand has landed on my leg. "This is Jasmine Campbell. We were in the same master's program for Library Science."

Summer's gesture is innocent. I bet she barely even notices the fact that her fingers are resting on my thigh. But I can barely concentrate on anything else.

"Nice to meet you, Cole." Jasmine extends her hand for a shake. The polite thing to do would be to stand. But that means I lose Summer's touch. So I just reach my long arm out to return her grip.

"And you." My voice is rough, wanting only to whisper dirty things in the ear of my companion.

"So, you helping Summer with her mission to rid Wikipedia of misogyny?" Finally, the woman settles at our table, sitting on the bench across from us before steepling her fingers against her lips. She has purple nails, too.

"Nah," Summer says. "I'm still on a solo mission. Cole just wanted help with some research, and I told him about all your lovely databases." Her voice takes on a dreamy quality.

Jasmine chuckles. "You could have had regular access to them if you went the academic route."

"You mean, Summer working at the university?" I ask. The thought sends a hint of panic through me.

Is she leaving her job? How can I casually woo her with my author status if she's not around to hear about the achievement? What am I going to do if I can't see her, talk to her, for even the scant time I allow myself now?

"We do have an open position." Jasmine directs the comment at my librarian.

My hand acts on its own, covering Summer's, gently pressing her palm into my jeans, silently begging her to stay with me. Just a little longer. Once I've convinced her to fall in love with me, she can work wherever. Because we'll be connected already.

"Thanks, but no. You know I love public libraries." Summer waves the offer away with her free hand, the motion easing my anxiety.

"I guess." Jasmine appears skeptical, but she lets the matter drop. "So you two are researching together?"

The way the woman says *researching* makes the word sound dirty.

I like it.

"All the time. I can barely keep up." I use a deadpan tone to respond, earning me a grin from Jasmine and a squeeze on my leg from Summer.

"Careful, Cole. Jasmine loves causing trouble. We're not *together*." Summer shoots the last word at the other woman like a scolding.

I don't like that.

"Of course not." Jasmine leans across the table toward me, lowering her voice as if we're planning a conspiracy. "You look interesting. Summer only ever dates boring men."

"Jasmine!"

I force a small smile, playing as if I find her comment amusing.

But it has me worried.

I'm not car-chase exciting or anything, but people don't tend to categorize me as boring.

Tattoos, facial piercings, and a criminal record will do that.

I'm going to be a published author, I remind myself. Still not boring, but the right type of exciting to catch Summer's attention.

"Well, I only came out to say a quick hi. Good luck with your research. We still on for trivia tomorrow night?" Jasmine stands from the table, and Summer gives her a thumbs up.

"Definitely."

"Cool." I expect the woman to walk away with a wave, but she turns to fully face me.

"Cole?" Her voice has lost its teasing edge, and her eyes bore deep into mine.

"Yes?"

"She's too good for any man. You won't ever deserve her. But no one does, so just put in a solid effort and make sure she's happy."

"Jasmine!" Summer jumps up from her seat, glaring at her friend. I mourn the loss of her hand. "That's not funny. He's my patron. You're making this awkward."

"Oh, am I? Sorry." She doesn't sound sorry, wiggling her fingers in a mocking goodbye before strolling away.

Tense silence remains in her place. With stiff movements, Summer lowers herself back to her seat. Somehow, she ends up settling with a few inches of empty space between us.

Jasmine's proclamation rings in my head, twines through my chest. The words were half warning half...encouragement?

Did I just get a seal of approval?

Still, the seal means nothing if Summer doesn't want to be with me. And I don't like how much physical and mental space she's putting between us.

Which is what prompts my next question.

"Am I only your patron?"

"I...uh...I mean...what else would you be?" She fiddles with some papers in front of her, not meeting my eyes.

Shit. That stings.

But she's Summer, so it's not like she meant to stab me in the chest with her innocent question. And I can't help remembering the way she sprinted toward me for an escape from the walking, talking white noise machine. At least she prefers me to him.

So I give her a break, clarifying rather than getting defensive or shutting down like I tend to do.

"Your friend." I don't frame it as a question because in this moment I decide I *am* her friend. I will do my damnedest to tempt her into more than that. But if at the end of the day Summer tells me no, I may lessen the amount of time I'm around her.

But it's impossible she'd be my enemy.

And she can't be nothing to me.

So, for now, she's my friend.

"Yes." My librarian sighs as a brilliant smile spreads over her face. And she's just evil enough to direct it my way. "Yes, you're right. Cole Allemand, you are my friend, and that is the best offer I've had in a long while."

"Seriously?" I frown.

She laughs, poking me in the shoulder. "Stop scowling. Never sell yourself short!" Summer scoots an inch closer, and I feel like I've won a mile. "So. Research. Let's do it."

Yes. Let's do it.

Chapter Eleven

SUMMER

"You do not drive this."

"Hmm. That's odd. Because all my recollections lead me to believe the exact opposite. In fact, I *do* drive this." I give the roof of my junker a friendly pat, hoping that my hand doesn't come away with too much of the rusted paint that's been flaking off the car for years.

Cole stares, face in slack disbelief, as if I've told him a geriatric alligator is my mode of transportation.

I shouldn't have let him walk me to my car.

"Does it turn on?"

"Of course it does! How do you think I drive it? The Flintstone method? You think I have some holes in the floor and just foot-pedal it around town?"

"Honestly—"

"No. No more sass. It works. Most of the time. And it has remained mostly mobile for the last eight years. That's all I ask of it."

"What about safety?"

"There are seatbelts." One of them even buckles properly.

"Your bumper—"

"Is there!"

"Barely."

"Barely is enough for me. Look, Cole. I'm not sure what your idea of a librarian's salary is, but after rent and food and student loans, plus all the other expenses that pop up randomly, I'm lucky if I can tuck a little away in my savings. I don't have thousands to spend on fixing up this car or to buy myself something newer. Maybe one day. But not anytime soon. It's this or the bus, and this gives me more control over my schedule and my life."

Please don't die on me, I silently throw out to my mess of a vehicle, knowing I'm constantly tempting fate when I tell people it drives.

I glare at Cole, ready to mount another defense, only to realize he doesn't look amused or exasperated. That's how people normally look when they see my car.

There goes quirky Summer in her beat-up Volkswagen. Isn't she a hoot and a half? Bet she loves driving that wreck around town. She wants her car to have personality!

False. I would take the most boring car on earth if it ran smoothly and got decent gas millage.

But Cole isn't looking at my car like I made a choice to go the wacky route. He stares at the Frankenstein monster of auto parts and appears legitimately angry.

But angry about what?

"I have a friend. He manages an auto shop. He won't work for free, but he won't screw you over either." Cole's tongue fiddles with his lip piercing, and I'm distracted for a moment.

Shaking my head, I think over what he just said.

"There are so many things wrong, sometimes I think denial is the best move forward," I admit.

"Summer." Cole growls my name and shoots a scowl at me. "Driving this is dangerous. Let me set something up. I swear he won't push you to fix more than you have to."

Gah. I hate going to mechanics. They always discover more problems than I had when I arrived. Probably because I don't know all the ways a car can combust. Plus, I don't understand any of their magical auto mumbo jumbo, and I can't afford it either.

But Cole is offering me help, and I'd be a grinch to turn him down.

"Alright. Okay. But you need to warn him that I'm going to be an abrasive, distrustful customer who constantly questions his motives."

"That's hard to believe."

"Doubt all you want, but discussing the many shortcomings of my car is not the way to get on my good side."

His eyebrows spike up at this. "Am I on your bad side?"

All my consternation fades as fast as it rose with his question.

"No, Cole. Of course not. We're friends. Even if you are trying to make me a more responsible driver."

That earns me a lip twitch, almost a real smile. "I'm not normally the responsible one."

"Never hurts to try new things." I slide my key into the door and try not to let on how much muscle I have to put into turning it to unlock the car.

"If you give me your number, I can pass it on to my friend."

"You don't have my number?" *How have I not given it to him yet?*

Cole shakes his head. I hold out my hand for his phone. I'm a little surprised when he puts one of the older, pay-by-the-minute devices in my hand.

"Can you text on this or calls only."

"It gets texts, but you can call me whenever."

"About car stuff."

Cole shrugs. "Sure."

That *sure* holds more meaning than the tiny word normally does, but I let it pass, working on typing in my information. When I'm listed in his contacts, I call myself, waiting for the vibration in my back pocket.

Instead of hanging up, I pull out my smartphone and answer. "Hi Summer! It's me, Summer."

Cole rolls his eyes, but his lips curl at the corners. With a grin, I hang both up and return his. I expect Cole to return to the curb. Instead, he moves in close, reaching for the rusty handle of the door. With a decisive tug, he wrenches the thing open, the gesture very chivalrous as he bows me inside. Once I'm settled in the driver's seat, he pushes the door closed, gentle enough to make sure nothing of mine gets caught, but firm enough to get the ancient latch to catch.

The window lets out a god-awful screech as I use the manual crank to roll it down.

Resting his arms on the sill, Cole's face is level with mine.

"Go ahead," he murmurs, causing shivers to scatter over my skin.

"Go ahead and do what?" Because with his face this close to mine, there's one specific action that's taken up residence in my mind. That can't be what he's asking for, can it?

He doesn't expect me to...kiss him, does he?

"Start the engine. Prove to me this thing can run."

My breathlessness flees as I growl at him. "You want proof? Here it is, ass face."

To emphasize my not-at-all witty insult, I turn the key in the ignition, praying all the while.

Click. Click. Chug. Chug.

Nothing.

Cole rubs his hand over his mouth, hiding a smile that has no trouble creasing his eyes.

"Shut up," I mutter, even though he didn't say anything. The second time I turn the key, the same pathetic noises sound, but then there's that beautiful hop and catch.

"Ha! Told you." I smirk at Cole just as he grimaces toward the hood. My bet is he was hoping the car would give up so I wouldn't be driving around in it.

Too bad, buddy. I take what I can get, and this car is all I got.

"Fine. But I'm still calling my friend."

"Okay. See you tomorrow?" Sunday afternoon means Cole's book fortress needs to be constructed.

He nods as he moves to go. But then he pauses, hands shoved deep in his pockets, icy eyes capturing mine.

"And Summer?"

"Yes?" *I sound normal, right? That wasn't super high pitched and breathless. Not at all.*

"This *car*." He seems to have trouble saying the word and I scowl at him. But he doesn't let my evil eye stop him. "And the bus aren't your only options."

I push back. "It's too far to walk to work."

His lips tighten, then relax into an almost smile.

"When you need a ride, call me. I'll be there for you."

Then, finally, he strolls away.

And I'm left wondering who exactly Cole Allemand is.

Chapter Twelve

COLE

I don't hate Dr. Marlin, I remind myself.

It's hard to remember though, with Summer grinning up at the man and using her breathy voice whenever she responds to his questions.

Dr. Marlin heads the library's writers group, and he tends to be one of the few people I put the effort into having a cordial conversation with. The guy is an ingenious storyteller, with a Ph.D. in creative writing, and a tenured position at the local university, where he teaches semester-long courses I would kill to be able to afford. Still, I get the benefit of his wisdom every Thursday evening, and I should count myself lucky for that.

Normally I do. But Summer is staring up at the man like he cured cancer and wants to name the drug after her. I don't think she's doing it on purpose. The gold wedding ring shining bright as a warning from his finger would make the man off-limits to a standup woman like Summer.

The problem is that Dr. Marlin is an author. Two of his books have made it to the *New York Times* Best Sellers list in the last decade.

As I wander back to our meeting room, I can't help remembering another instance of Summer interacting with another man who had similar credentials.

The library was hosting an event, a visiting author reading passages from his latest book before participating in a Q&A with the audience. Since it was my day off of work, I showed up, taking a seat toward the back, interested to hear what someone who has a successful writing career would talk about.

Summer and her friend, who I know now is Jasmine, sat in front of me, not seeming to realize I was there.

"Oh my gosh, I might faint." Summer's frantic whisper grabbed my attention.

"Stop being weird," Jasmine said.

"I can't. We're in the same room as him. Holy crap. I just want to ravish him."

My whole body tensed, drowning in curiosity and jealousy.

"Are you serious?" Jasmine asked.

"Did you read his books? They're so good. The last one made me cry."

"Yeah, he's a great writer. That doesn't explain you wanting to sleep with him. He's like twenty years older than you and has a mustard stain on his shirt."

Summer shrugged, then leaned forward, her gaze adhered to the talented-yet-frumpy writer at the front of the room. "Authors are like rock stars to me. I can't promise not to throw my bra at him when he starts reading."

"Please don't."

"I'm not sure I'll be able to stop myself."

If I had thought I wanted to be an author before that day, it was nothing compared to after. Hearing how mad Summer was for some random old dude who wrote a good book, I couldn't help imagining what her reaction would be like if I casually slipped into conversation that I had a publishing deal.

She might crawl over the circulation desk to get at me.

And I'd be happy to help.

That overheard exchange let me know how I could guarantee a yes from Summer. Problem is, even though I signed with a literary agent over the summer, there's been no actual movement on my manuscript.

Which means I'm still coming to these writers meetings without any news, having to watch Summer get googly eyed around a guy who's actually accomplished something.

He's happily married, I remind myself. *And Summer isn't a homewrecker*, I beg the universe.

But what person wouldn't want the sexy librarian who stares up at them with hero worship?

Dr. Marlin enters the conference room without Summer on his trail, and I'm suddenly glad she didn't accept my invitation to attend the meetings. I'm not sure I'd be able to handle an hour of her gushing all over the professor.

He nods at me, and I force my chin into a dip, returning the gesture no matter how reluctantly. As the clock ticks toward six, more of our group show up. The chair next to me is filled by a teenager who appears perpetually uncomfortable with his gangly body. He reminds me of myself ten years ago. I've seen Summer talking to him with an aura of protectiveness hovering around her. I figure if she likes the kid, then I won't automatically ignore him.

Jamie. I think that's his name.

But small talk is not my skillset, so I just give him a silent nod, and he returns with a hopeful smile.

"You're Summer's friend, right?" The way he pairs me with the librarian immediately increases my view of him.

"Yes."

"She's great."

"Agreed."

That's it, but it feels like enough. Some of the kid's obvious discomfort eases, and he pulls out a well-used notebook that's not too different from mine. He's never shared in a meeting before, and I find myself wondering what he writes.

"All right, let's get started." Dr. Marlin stands at the front of the room, raising his hands to get everyone's attention. There are about fourteen people gathered. The group would probably be larger if it was widely advertised that Dr. Marlin is the leader, but he seems to like keeping the gathering smaller.

I prefer that, too.

"I hope you all found some time to write this week. Does anyone have an excerpt they'd like to share?"

Hands go up. Not mine, even though I did get a few thousand words on the page. I just don't feel like being the center of a discussion today. I'd rather sit back and listen. Maybe get inspired.

Then I notice the kid's hand in a hesitant half raise. His arms are so long, he could reach halfway to the ceiling if he committed. But that awkwardness still lingers. He's probably dealing with that voice in his head, the one that all writers have. The one that tells us our work is shit, and we shouldn't bother.

If Summer were here, she'd no doubt be vibrating in her seat, brain about to explode from the happiness of potentially getting to hear her young friend read.

Since she isn't here, I'm hit with a sudden urge to act in her best interest.

"We've never heard from Jamie." I throw a thumb to my right, bringing Dr. Marlin's attention to the kid, who can't seem to decide if he wants to put himself forward or sink into the floor. "I want to hear his stuff."

"Y-you do?" His adolescent voice cracks on the first word, and his face gets red as he meets my eyes then looks away, then glances back and away again.

"Perfect. I love to hear new voices. Especially young ones. Why don't you share, Jamie?"

"Okay. Yeah." The kid is still tomato red, but he's grinning as he flips open his notebook.

There's an interesting tingle in my chest. Something like pride and satisfaction.

I can't help thinking that Summer would approve of my actions.

Take that, Dr. Marlin.

Chapter Thirteen

SUMMER

My feet ache as I walk up the concrete steps to my apartment. It's only one flight, but the distance makes me think of mountain climbers on the last leg of Everest. The distance they have to traverse between the final camp and the peak isn't too far, but the weariness of spending a month on a mountain, breathing half the oxygen they're used to, limbs stiffening with the frigid temperatures, makes the ascent a battle.

I had a long day at work.

There are so many negative things that can happen when serving the public, and today, I hit the shit lottery. Sometime during the night, a vandal with a bottle of spray paint decided to draw a giant dick on the beautiful redbrick side of the library. It's going to take some intense scrubbing to get it off. Then a woman decided to scream at me about a twenty-cent late fee until we had to ask security to escort her out. As if the new wall art was inspiration, I had two porn watchers today on public computers. A kid threw up during story time and managed to splatter an entire bottom shelf of books. And, because the universe seemed to want to put a crappy period on my gross day, my car refused to start, so I had to ride the bus home.

Normally, Sundays are great days. And I'm too tired to pretend that one of the main reasons I look forward to them is because Cole

Allemand comes to the library on Sunday. He is a stoic, bright light at the end of the week as I let myself daydream about my crush.

But that was just another way this day let me down. Weeks ago, I agreed to work earlier hours today to cover a coworker's vacation. Which meant my eight hours were over long before Cole made his normal appearance. If today had been a fantastic workday, I may have found some excuses to stay later. But exhaustion ate away at me.

And what's more, I already know that tomorrow will be worse.

Finally, I summit my peak, reaching the landing, my apartment door in sight. Even though I wasn't caught in the puke splash zone, helping our children's librarian dispose of the contaminated books has me certain that I reek.

"Shower. Food. Bed," I chant to myself, a mantra driving me forward.

I just want to be clean and to curl up in a pile of pillows and spend the next few hours re-reading my favorite serialized fantasy saga in preparation for this week's new chapter.

But any spark of happiness that plan ignites is promptly extinguished when I unlock and open my door.

Sitting on the colorful rug in my entryway is an orange envelope. The familiar sight would be enough to twist my stomach with sickness, but what is lying next to it has me thinking I'm not done with puke for the day. Only this time, I'm the one on the verge of blowing chunks.

There's a little bird. Some gray creature with hints of green shimmering in its feathers.

I have time to examine it because it's dead.

The stiff body sickens me. I can't help thinking how beautiful the tiny animal would have been in life, flitting around and singing beautiful notes to the morning sun.

That's all been snuffed out.

Letting my bag slide to the floor, I step over the items, refusing to touch them. Not until I have gloves on. Once my hands are covered, I pick up the bird, blinking away tears as I hold it. For a moment, I waver over what to do, silently hoping my touch will somehow awaken it, allowing me to open my hands and let the bird fly away.

Instead, I just solidify the knowledge its life is gone. Outside, I stumble down the stairs, circling my building until I spot a flowering bush. I lay the bird underneath the branches in a semblance of a burial.

Back in my apartment, I lock my front door behind me, glaring at the mail slot that allowed the twisted gifts into my home. Tomorrow I'm buying a piece of wood, a hammer and some nails. Not that I expect closing off the opening will do much good.

With shanking fingers, I open the envelope.

Any hope I had that the poor animal somehow found its way in through my mail slot and died of natural causes is lost when I carefully unfold the newspaper article. The headline announces that a local family died from carbon monoxide poisoning.

The heavy black writing overtop of the printed words that has me choking on bile.

You're delicate like a bird.

Fear, thick as sludge, coats my insides. No shower will clean the dirtiness of this message from me.

With the note pinched in my gloved fingers, I shuffle across my small apartment, stepping into my bathroom. Under the sink, I extend my hand into a dark corner behind bottles of bleach and toilet cleaner until I feel the corner of a box I wish would disappear.

Instead, I pull the container into the light, lift the lid, and place the article on top of a pile of others just like it.

Chapter Fourteen

SUMMER

When I wake up, before my brain even starts functioning, the misery of the day settles on me like a sticky film. It's heavy, but not crushing. Not anymore. The feeling clings to me enough to make all my limbs sluggish, but not immobile.

This is not from the mess at work yesterday or even because of the creepy note. This day inspires a depression all its own.

Instead of sitting up in my bed and stretching like I normally greet the morning, I perform a slow log roll until I reach the edge of the mattress, then laboriously push my legs out from under the sheets. When I'm standing, I make a mental check.

One task finished among the hundred I need to perform to make it through this day.

This piece-of-shit day.

This day that makes me wish I smoked, just so I could walk up to every calendar in the world and burn away this day with a smoldering cigarette. This day isn't even worth acting as an ashtray.

And that's the mental state that persists throughout the morning and into my workday. Doesn't help that my shitty car is still sitting, useless, in the library's parking lot, and I had to sprint to catch the bus. The last thing I want is to be surrounded by strangers, but now my commute includes them.

Luckily, this Monday, things are relatively slow. Others might like to keep busy as a means of distraction from their misery, but the more I talk, the more likely I'll stray into unsafe territory and reveal my depressed state to some poor random library goer.

Best I keep my mouth shut and pray for the hands on the clock to pick up their pace.

I've set my mind to studying the strange shape of a coffee stain on the carpet behind the circulation desk when I hear the muffled approach of footsteps.

Deep breath. Try a smile. Nope, not going to work. Try a neutral expression. Hopefully that's good enough. Look up, scan the books, check off one more item on today's list of things needing to be done before you can sink into the oblivion of sleep.

But when I raise my head, all hope of staying detached from this interaction flutters away.

"Cole Allemand," I murmur, unable to infuse the words with my normal enthusiasm.

"Summer Pierce." A smile begins to flicker across his mouth but disappears just as quickly when he examines my attempt at a neutral expression.

"What's wrong?"

Attempt at normalcy? Failed.

"Nothing."

"You're lying."

"It's rude to point that out."

"It's rude to lie."

"I'm being nice to a library patron. I don't see how that's rude."

"Summer." Cole leans forward, holding my gaze with his fierce, frosty eyes. "You're unhappy."

"Yes! Satisfied? I've admitted it!" Cracks are forming in the brittle shell around my emotions. "But I'm not supposed to pile my shit on patrons. I'm supposed to smile, and help, and make sure you leave a little better off than you were before you arrived."

"And you don't want to do that?" he asks.

"Normally, yes. Every other day of the year I live for that. I eat it. I breathe it. I'm made of solar panels, and patrons' smiles of satisfaction are pure rays of sunshine."

His long fingers drum on the counter. "But I'm not your patron."

"Of course you are."

"Not *just* your patron"

I frown at him, stumbling over a reply, then realize what he's hinting at.

"You're my friend." The words come out on a defeated sigh. "Yes. Of course. But I don't like piling my shit on my friends either. Everyone's day is better if I find a way to keep smiling."

Silence stretches between us, but when I reach for the scanner again, he speaks.

"No."

"No?"

I'm surprised enough to glance up at him, meeting his intense gaze.

"Only give me real smiles. If you're sad, frown at me. If you're mad, scowl."

Frown? Scowl? Those would give only a hint at the deep pit of sadness that exists in my heart.

"What if I want to break down? Sob and cry and become an utter mess of a person. Maybe not even be a person anymore. What if I want to be a puddle? A sopping wet puddle of misery?"

Cole doesn't answer straight away. He runs his chilly eyes over me before glancing around the lobby area as if searching for something.

"I'll find another librarian," he says. "Tell them you need to take a break, and we can go back to your office. Then you can become a puddle." Cole takes a step toward the reading room, and I fully believe he's ready to pull Karen off the reference desk for me.

"Wait! Come back." My hand reaches out as if I might grab him. "That's sweet, but I'm serious about putting on a good face. This is temporary, I swear. Tomorrow, I'll be bubbly and positive, and it won't be work for me. Tomorrow my smiles will be truthful."

He watches me, his lips dipping into a frown.

"But not today." Cole doesn't add this bit as a question, only a clarity statement. He's starting to understand the gray cloud I'm temporarily living in.

"No. Not today. This day is..." For a moment I can't think of a word or even a metaphor thoroughly horrible enough to convey the fathomless sorrow that will forever stain this date in my mind.

"This day is...?" Cole prompts, leaning his hands on the circulation desk, regaining my attention with his icy eyes. The cool color is just soothing enough to coax words from my depressed brain.

"This day is the anniversary of the worst day of my life. If I had a choice, I would go to sleep on December fifteenth and then wake up on December seventeenth."

He stares down at me, probably searching for some indication of amusement or overdramatization as I'm so prone to. But this is not a day for kidding and light-hearted jokes. This day is too heavy. It weighs me down, threatening to forever hold my head under water until I drown in the misery of the past.

"What can I do?"

"Oh." The way he watches me makes me want to give him a solution to my sadness. Something that only he can achieve. But there's no tool in the world that can fix this broken piece of me. "Nothing."

His expression doesn't change, but I still get the sense he's disappointed.

Which is why I clarify, so he knows that no one can do anything.

"This is the day my dad died."

Cole grimaces, rocking back on his heels as he shoves his hands in his pockets.

"When did he pass away?"

"I was twelve." I offer this reluctantly. Almost defensively.

"I'm sorry. That sucks."

"It does suck. I know it's been fourteen years, and that people expect me to be over it. To have moved on. But I don't think that'll ever happen."

Cole nods. "He's your dad."

He says the words as if they're the most obvious thing in the world.

Like duh, of course, I wouldn't just get over the man who once was the most important person in my life.

Suddenly, I want to tell Cole about my dad. Funny, sweet stories cycle through my head, and I open my mouth to relay one.

Then it hits me. Just like it does almost every minute of this day.

He's dead. He's never coming back. I'll have no more stories with him.

"Get Karen," I choke out before sprinting away from the desk, down the back hall, into my office. The door latch barely clicks, and I'm on the floor trying to keep my sobbing quiet.

You're at work. This isn't professional. Stop crying!

No matter what I say to myself, I can't turn off the faucet. Every rational thought is overlaid with the image of my father. The picture in my mind almost foggy, blurred at the edges, as if time is eating away at my memory of him.

That makes me sob harder.

Only when I bury my face in a pillow and chant at myself to breathe through the pain, do I manage to calm down. But even when the tears slow and stop, my head pounds in a steady, painful rhythm. I feel like a mess, and I'm sure I look like one, too.

So, of course, there's a knock on my office door.

"Summer?"

Cole. Why? Why does the handsome bad boy I've allowed myself to secretly crush on have to know that I'm crying myself into a migraine at work?

Can't he just exist outside of a permanent five-foot radius of me?

Let me look at him. Fantasize about him. Maintain an image of a put-together woman around him.

"Can I come in?" His voice drifts through the door, but he manages to keep his volume low.

When I swipe at my cheeks the skin feels tender, as if I have a fever. "Did you lose your ability to see in the last five minutes?"

Silence, then, "No."

Damn. It's one thing to know I'm breaking down in here. It's another to see the wreckage.

"Can you swear you'll keep your eyes closed if I let you in?"

Another pause. "Are you naked?"

I gasp and push up from the floor, suddenly indignant. "Of course not!" I whip the door open to glare up at his sharply handsome face.

In comparison, mine must look like a red, swollen mess. I don't cry pretty. I'm not sure I've met anyone who does, so maybe I shouldn't be so self-conscious about it. But I just wish I wasn't crying at all.

Cole doesn't seem like the kind of guy who lets his emotions run rampant.

"Here! Feast your eyes upon the personification of misery." My hands fall to my sides in defeat. Maybe this is better. I should drive him away anyway.

He's quiet, and I find I like how Cole thinks about his responses before speaking. The words seem to matter more.

"Do you want a hug?"

A Cole Allemand hug? Does such a thing even exist? "Are *you* offering a hug? You don't seem like a hugger."

"I'm not."

"Well, I don't want a hug full of lies." I cross my arms, knowing that I'm being obstinate. But that's what this day does to me.

Cole's mouth twitches. "I'm not a hugger. But I'd like to hug you."

Well then.

He spreads his arms in an invitation.

And there's suddenly nothing more I want in the world than to accept.

Cautiously, I step forward, realizing my hands have a slight tremble as I reach for him. The second I'm close enough, Cole wraps his arms around me, holding my head to his chest with a large palm cupping the back of my skull.

I creep my arms around his trim waist, fisting my hands in the material of his sweater. My whole body shudders at the contact.

Cole Allemand is a masterful hugger.

He engulfs me, and I relax into his embrace.

"Karen is at the front desk." He speaks quietly, the words brushing against my hair.

"What did you tell her?"

"You felt sick."

Heartsick more like. But damn, I'm grateful to the man holding me. If the episode that just occurred in my office had played out in the front lobby, I may have been forced to change my name and shell out for plastic surgery to avoid the mortification of coming back to work and everyone knowing about my emotional breakdown.

I owe Cole.

And who knew bad boys were such good huggers?

"Thank you," I mutter against his chest.

Step away from him. Stop relying on him. This is creeping beyond the realm of friendship.

But my body doesn't want to listen to my mind today, so I remain in the circle of his arms.

"She said you should take the rest of the day off sick."

"But I'm not sick."

"So what? You don't want to be here."

"It seems dishonest."

Even though I'm arguing with him, I can't help pressing closer, soothed by the way his hand rubs circles on my back.

"You should go home."

Stubborn man.

"I still have things to do today. Even after work."

There's a pressure on the top of my head, and I realize Cole is resting his chin on me. Like he has no immediate plans to end this embrace.

For the first time today, I feel...not happy, exactly.

But slightly less despondent.

"Do you want to be alone?"

"Rarely." The word comes out before I truly think it through. But it's true. I'm an extrovert. People make me happy. Even when I don't want anyone to see how much of a mess I am, I can't honestly say that I want to be alone.

"Let's go. You and me. We'll do your things together."

"You're putting your name down for a shit job. I appreciate the offer, but you should get out now while you still have some kind of respect for me. That is, if you even do."

His arms loosen, and I stifle a whimper of regret.

But he doesn't make an escape. Instead, Cole clasps the top of my arms to stare down at me.

"I respect you."

My tender face burns hot. "Okay."

"I want the shit job."

A grimace forces its way out before I can stifle the expression. "I am not going to be fun today. What's more, I might even be mean," I say.

"Really?"

"Well, I'm sure as hell not going to be nice."

"That's okay. You can be mean to me."

A heavy sigh creeps out of me. "I don't want to be mean to you. I just need to be miserable and not have anyone expect me to be anything else."

"Sounds like a plan."

"I'm serious."

"I am too."

"After I get off work, I'm going to a cemetery," I warn him.

"Then looks like I'm dressed correctly."

Cole isn't wrong. He's wearing his normal uniform of black shirt and black jeans.

"Do you always dress for a funeral?" I pluck at the dark material, suddenly very unhappy with how loosely it hangs on him. He needs to eat more. Maybe I should add more apples to my fridge.

"Black is easy." He speaks the words in a low voice, and I realize he's pinched a lock of my dark brown hair between his fingers, fiddling with it.

As if he plans to distract me from my misery by making my heart beat faster.

"Black works for me today." I knock his hand away and step into my office, moving to grab my purse and pull on the over-sized cardigan I wear when the air gets chilly. Once my door is locked, I tilt my head toward the exit, an invitation to follow me.

Cole nods, iceberg eyes on me. Before taking another step toward the lobby, I find myself pausing, fingers reaching out to pluck at his sweater again.

"Black works for me today," I repeat. "But when I'm happy again—and I will be—I won't be able to stop myself."

"From doing what?" he murmurs, his stare seeming to catch on my mouth.

"From trying to paint you in colors."

Chapter Fifteen

COLE

"I think we need a safe word."

Good thing I already parked because that sentence has me choking on my tongue and coughing until my eyes water.

"You okay?" Summer watches me from the passenger seat of my truck, concern clear on her face. Apparently, her death trap of a car decided to break down, which means I have the perfect excuse to drive her around.

I nod, taking a swig from a water bottle in my cup holder. "Safe word?" My mind jumps to all sorts of sexy conclusions I didn't think were on Summer's agenda for the day.

"Yes. A safe word. You're being great friend. But I wasn't over exaggerating when I said I'm going to be a shit person to be around today. And I want you to have an out."

"An out?"

"That's what I said. A way to beg off if this all turns way too depressing for you to handle."

"Can't I just say that?"

"I don't know. Can you? Can you tell your friend who is grieving over her deceased father that you're done being the chauffeur of her misery limo? That you can't take witnessing any more of her sudden bouts of unexplained sobbing? Is that something you're up for?"

Summer stares at me from the passenger seat, holding my gaze with her unyielding one.

How is it that she's reliving the worst day of her life and still has some emotional capacity to worry about my feelings? I want to tell her to be selfish. To use me.

"I don't need an out."

She scoffs. "People rarely think they need one, until they do. So what does it hurt? We'll have a Summer's Day Of Depression Is Too Much For Me safe word, and if you don't need it, then you don't. But if you do need it, then you have it."

"Fine."

"Fine." She nods to emphasize agreement. "Choose a word you can casually say to me, and I'll know it's time for me to catch a bus home."

After considering for a second or two, I pick the first random word that comes to mind that I know I don't like.

"Pineapple."

"Pineapple?" Her dark brows do a confused dance on her forehead. "Where did that come from?"

I shrug. "I'm allergic. So I never ask for it."

"Allergic! Then that's a horrible safe word!" She throws her hands up, almost smacking them on the roof of my truck.

"Why?"

"Why? WHY? Just imagine I find you sprawled out on the ground, and you only say one word to me." She affects a feeble voice as she reaches a shaky hand toward me. "*Pineapple.*" The tone is that of an old man with maybe seconds until his death. She sits back, glaring at me. "What am I supposed to think?"

I know this isn't a laughing situation, so I keep my lips pinched tight together and shrug again.

"Exactly! I won't know if you're so worn out from my emotional neediness that you've decided to take a little lie-down while you send me on my way with the safe word, or if some rando came by and shoved a handful of pineapple down your throat, causing you to go into anaphylactic shock."

Somehow, I suppress the urge to laugh long enough to ask, "Are there a lot of pineapple wielding randos in this cemetery?"

Summer glares at me. "It's a bad safe word. Pick another."

I sigh, only to cover up how much I enjoy sparring with her. "Fine. Clementine."

"Clementine? What is it with you and fruits? No, never mind. Just tell me you're not allergic."

"I'm not."

"Good. Then clementine it is. If at any point today you've reached the end of your Summer tolerance, use clementine in a sentence, and we'll part ways with nothing more said on the topic."

"I won't abandon you."

"If you need to, then you should."

She won't relent on this, so I only shake my head and push open my door. Guess I'll have to show her that I'm here to stay, no matter how her grief manifests.

Side by side, we make our way from the parking lot into the graveyard. In classic New Orleans fashion, all of the bodies in this graveyard were laid to rest above ground.

The graves rise up on either side of the path, giving the sensation of walking through a village of tiny houses. An abandoned haunted village. Even with the autumn sun shining, there's an eerie feel. Yet at the same time, the place has a kind of beauty. Each structure holds a personality of its own, life only existing in the designs of the houses for the dead.

"Do you mind waiting here?" Summer draws me to a stop with a hand on my arm. Her skin is chilly, despite the warmth that still hangs on even into mid-December. "His grave is just ahead. I'm going to talk to him. Or myself. Either way, I'd like some privacy for this part."

"I'll wait here." I nod toward a stone bench that sits at the edge of the path. Vines have grown around the base, claiming the seat for the earth. Truthfully, I'm looking forward to sitting on it. I have my notebook with me, and I wonder what ideas may flow through my hands with this setting pushing into my creative consciousness.

"Take as long as you want." The stone is warm from the sun, making the seat almost comfortable as I settle onto it, stretching out my long legs.

Summer hesitates, staring down at me. Her eyes still look red and irritated from crying earlier, but the soft brown of her irises shines through. The sudden urge to capture her hand and tug her into my lap so I can hug her again is almost too strong to tamp down. I pull my notebook from my back pocket, clutching it with both hands to keep the reflex at bay.

Seeming to make up her mind about something, Summer nods, then strolls farther down the path. I'm glad she's still in sight when she comes to a stop. The idea of her wandering this place without me at her side causes a tightening in my chest.

Something like fear.

I want her safe. I want her happy.

I want her.

For now though, I'll take these bits she's willing to give.

Summer's mouth moves, but the words are lost over the distance. I avert my eyes, giving her the privacy she asked for.

How much hurt must she deal with, with thoughts of her dead father assaulting her all day?

Sometimes I wish my mom was dead. I'm glad I've never been one to blurt out my thoughts because I can only guess how hurtful that wish would be for Summer to hear. Her father is gone from existence, while my mother still lives and breathes. Where she does those activities, I have no idea.

But if she had died, if that was the reason I grew up without her, I doubt I'd have to deal with so much resentment chewing away at my gut whenever I think about her.

Uncomfortable with the familiar anger and depression gnawing at my insides, I shove away thoughts of the woman who never loved me. Instead, I gaze around the creepy, beautiful graveyard, and consider it as a setting in my story.

Lost in my writing, I'm not sure how much time has passed when a light tap hits my shoulder. Glancing up, I find Summer with new tracks of tears tracing paths across her cheeks. Moving purely on instinct, I drop my notebook on the bench and stand, my hands reaching to cup her face. My thumbs stroke across her soft skin, wiping away the dampness.

"You ready to go?" A friend shouldn't be cradling her like this, but she hasn't pushed me away. She seems to be in a dazed state of grief. My hands fall to my sides, not wanting to take advantage.

"Is something wrong with me? This shouldn't still hurt this much, should it?" Summer rubs a fist against her breastbone, as if the spot is sore and she's trying to soothe it.

I bend to retrieve my notebook, shoving it in my back pocket, then making the conscious decision to tuck Summer under my arm, guiding her back to the truck.

"Nothing is wrong with you, Summer. Absolutely nothing."

Chapter Sixteen

SUMMER

The day is still dismal, but talking to the memory of my father eased the sharp edges of my pain. My insides no longer feel cut up, shredded, and raw. Now there's only a soreness. An ache that throbs in time with the beat of my heart.

Today is a vocal heart day. The organ beats hard in my chest and demands attention. My heart commands that I fix it. Absentmindedly, I tap a finger on my breastbone as if knocking on a door.

I'm sorry I can't fix you. Tomorrow you won't hurt as much.

"Where to now?" Cole drives one-handed, and that grip is loose and assured. His other elbow rests on the sill of the open window. Wind ruffles his dirty blonde hair, emphasizing his slightly uneven cut. The sight of his messy locks would put my mother on edge.

Of course, not as much as his tattoos and piercings and fuck-the-world demeanor.

Mom would hate Cole before even talking to him.

And that thought annoys me. It pisses me off.

Then guilt assails me at the realization I'm thinking bad thoughts about my last surviving parent, a woman who loves me more than anyone else in the world.

And now I feel like a crappy daughter.

Maybe this is another reason to add to the pile of why the two of us don't grieve together. The first few years we set aside this day to spend with each other, thinking it might be like it is on TV, where everyone holds hands and shares happy memories about their lost loved one.

But we just cried, amplifying each other's misery by being walking, talking reminders of the man we both lost. Then we'd fight over stupid things and cry some more because we got mad at each other.

Once I moved out to live on my own, we came to an understanding. We'd grieve our own ways, and the day after we'd get together for dinner and wine. Lots of wine.

Even after all this time, though, I still haven't found a way to fill this black hole of a day.

"Where to now?" I murmur, mulling over the question.

Keep driving until you reach December 17th, please, I want to tell him.

But we're still hours away from a new day, the sun sinking too slow for my peace of mind. Staring out the windshield, I catch sight of a playground up ahead. Parents hold their children's hands, leading them to parked cars, likely heading home for happy family dinners now that the daylight is fading.

And I have a sudden urge to keep the place from being completely empty.

"Pull in up here."

Cole doesn't question me, he just puts on his blinker and turns into the parking lot. Once the truck is in park, I push open the door, hopping down from the slightly elevated seat. The air is cooler, and I hug my cardigan around me. There's still a kid dangling from the monkey bars, a man with salt-and-pepper hair hovering close by, arms outstretched, acting as a spotter. Ready to catch the little girl if she falls.

Maybe this was a mistake. I avert my eyes, blinking fast and sucking a bracing breath in through my nose.

"If you cry on my shirt, no one will know. Because it's black." Cole appears beside me, arms slightly open in the offering for another hug.

"But if I snot on it, there's no hiding that," I point out, using my long sleeves to soak up the few rogue tears that made their way out.

"I could walk around shirtless." He smirks down at me, and my eyes roll on their own.

"I'd rather not get splattered in girl guts. You know, from all the women spontaneously combusting from a sudden onslaught of lust." Me included.

"You're giving my bare chest more credit than it deserves."

"Unlikely." My ribs expand on a deep breath, and I realize the little bit of banter has chased away the potential sobs. For now. "I haven't been on a swing in forever," I announce, heading toward the swing set.

It's one of the older kind with a rubber hammock-like seat suspended from two industrial-looking chains. Settling into it takes me back to a childhood I've avoided thinking about all day. But at least this bit is a good memory.

And to my immense satisfaction, Cole folds himself onto the swing beside me.

Rocking my torso and swinging my ankles, I begin moving in the soothing motion that has me wondering why I ever stopped coming to playgrounds.

All the while, my friend stays still.

"Swing with me, Cole!" I demand.

"My legs are too long."

"Bend your knees." I fly by him on another freeing pass.

"I am."

"All I'm hearing"—a pause until I'm headed back his way—"are excuses."

"Fine." Cole resettles himself on the seat, then proceeds to kick off the ground, bending his knees at the most ridiculous angle to keep from dragging his feet in the dirt. It's not long before he gets a decent rhythm going, competing with me for who can achieve the highest point.

"That's it! I knew you could do it. You're never too tall or too old to swing. Swinging is a lifelong sport!" I crow.

"You're a competitive swinger? Did they give you a college scholarship for that?"

"If only. But I told them I'd only ever swing for the love of the game. Once you bring money into the equation, everything goes to hell."

"Very wise."

As we pass each other, I catch glimpses of Cole's smile. That's when I realize my face is creased in the same expression. I'm smiling. Despite this being the anniversary of the worst day of my life, Cole Allemand has found a way to make me just a little bit less miserable.

"How do we know who wins?" the magnificent man calls out to me. I let myself sink back into our banter.

"We jump! Farthest from the swings is the champion."

"I'm taller than you."

"I know. Hence your long-legged conundrum."

"I may go farther than you."

"If you're trying to discover if I am a sore loser or not, the answer is no. I am very graceful in defeat. Which is quite impressive, seeing as how I am so rarely defeated." On the next pass, I give Cole a wink and am rewarded with a delicious chuckle.

"Fine. Who should jump first?"

"Same time. Count down from three."

He does, and at the go mark, I release my grip on the chains, letting gravity and acceleration have their way with me.

Cole lands first, falling to his knees and pitching forward onto his hands, barely keeping himself from face planting.

I am not so lucky.

I should have had the perfect landing, feet under me, balance the envy of all gymnasts. But the ground in the park is soggier than I expected. A huge clod of mud and grass dislodges under one of my feet, sending me toppling to the side. My shoulder catches my fall in a bruising impact, and I slide a few inches, gathering dirt and grass stains as I go, finally coming to rest by collapsing onto my back.

"Summer? You okay?" Cole's face appears above mine, his mouth twisted in concern.

For some reason, I focus on how the setting sun glints off the barbell that bisects his brow. The piercing glows as if lit from within. Or maybe the decoration holds a little trace of magic.

"Did that hurt?" I reach up, the tip of my finger only just touching the surprisingly warm metal. Of course it's warm; it sits against his skin all day.

Cole's eyelids flutter when I come into contact. I let my hand fall, worried I'm paining him with my examination.

"Just a pinch when I first got it. Everything is healed now. What about you? Are you hurt?" His Icelandic eyes trace over my body, dragging a shiver with them on their journey.

"I'll have a few bruises. Did I win?"

After one more visual examination, Cole seems satisfied that I'm not bleeding out in the middle of a children's playground, and he smirks down at me.

"Yes."

An answering smile tugs at my lips. "You're not lying to make me feel better, are you?"

Cole snorts. "I landed the farthest, but you slid further. We'll have to leave it up to the judges." Then, instead of helping me up, my library patron turned surprisingly supportive friend flips over onto his back and settles onto the damp earth beside me.

The ground isn't the most comfortable, but with Cole next to me, our arms pressed close, a tease of calm snakes through my veins. My sadness still lurks just under the surface of my skin, but the urge to cry has faded.

Fourteen years. My father has been absent from my life for longer than he was part of it. I don't know what it's like to be an adult with that supportive presence.

"Do you have a good relationship with your father?" I ask my question without looking at Cole, wanting to give him a sense of privacy when he answers, in case he says *no*.

"It's good. In a way."

"You're making me curious, so if you don't want to talk about it, I ask that you use less elusive, tempting answers."

There's a huff from him that I think might be some sort of laughter. Then Cole clears his throat and says more words than I think I've ever heard him speak at one time.

"My mom left him when I was younger. She left us. He had to raise me on his own. That meant working more hours to make sure we had enough money. I see that now, that's why he was always gone. But when I was a teenager, I thought he just didn't want to be around me since I look like her. So, like most surly teens, I got into some bad shit."

Bad shit. Bad boy. But he's not being bad *right now*.

When Cole pauses, I turn my head enough to watch him swallow, his

Adam's apple bobbing with the movement. As I'm considering whether or not I should ask, he makes the decision for me by continuing his story without prompting.

"I thought I was too smart to get in trouble. That I kept everything under wraps. But people found out. He found out. Things were bad between us for a while. But I grew up, got my shit together. We're okay now, but there's still a strain. Like he's waiting for me to turn back into what I used to be."

"You were young," I murmur.

Cole shrugs, then tilts his head to meet my eyes. "Young when I started. Took me a while to straighten out. And it's hard to let the past go."

Don't I know it.

Fourteen years, and this day is as raw as ever for me.

"What do you like about your dad?"

Cole doesn't take his eyes from mine, claiming a moment to think over my question.

"He's reliable. Sometimes stubborn. But if he says he'll be there for you, he will be."

"That's a good dad quality. What else?"

A light breeze blows a strand of hair into my face, tickling my nose. But before I can push it aside, Cole reaches out with one of his long arms, gently twisting the lock around his finger then tucking it behind my ear.

I tell my silly heart to stop its intense beating.

"He only knows how to cook things on the grill. So he grills year round. If he even tries to boil water on the stove he ends up burning the pot and cursing like a sailor."

"Oh no!" I grin, and Cole joins me. The expression almost hurts, as if my facial muscles never expected to be used in this way. Not today at least.

"He loves fishing, but he knows I hate it, so whenever he took me when I was younger, we would stop by a bookstore, and he would buy me whatever book I wanted. Even if it was a twenty-dollar hardback. And then I'd sit in the boat and read while he would fish."

My heart thumps hard with conviction, and I'm so in love with Cole's stories that I think I might cry. But not from despair. Just from an overwhelming level of emotion.

"I want to meet your dad." The words are out before I even realize the thought is going through my mind. Quickly, I break eye contact with Cole, staring up at the indigo evening sky. I brace myself for the awkward answer he'll give me.

Oh, sure, someday.

Eh, he's not really social.

Or, *I'll get back to you. Clementine.*

"He'd like that. We'll set it up."

I turn wide eyes back to Cole, but now he's the one examining the quickly darkening sky.

"I'm being weird. You don't have to make your dad meet me."

But he just shrugs again, the corner of his mouth twitching. Then, before I realize his plan to move, Cole rolls up on his elbow, staring down at me.

"Want to get a drink? I'm your DD."

The abrupt topic change and his hovering proximity have my brain stuttering over an answer. After a deep bracing breath, I get my thoughts in order.

"That's true. I could try to drown my misery in alcohol."

"You could." He nods, his mouth in a serious line.

"Do you think that ever works?"

"Maybe."

"It probably doesn't." My fingers twitch, wanting to reach up and touch the warm metal he's decorated his face with.

"Hmm." The sound from deep in his throat has my body relaxing in a way it shouldn't. We need to not be lying on the ground so close to each other.

I pop up, so fast the blood doesn't have enough time to reach my head, and I waver as if already drunk. Only once I'm steady do I speak. "I don't like drawing conclusions without doing the proper research. So to the bar we go."

Chapter Seventeen

SUMMER

Cole chose the bar, seeing as how I'm still one step away from autopilot.

Plus, I'm not interested in going to a place where people know me. I'm not the normal, happy, helpful version of Summer. I'd feel the need to put in the effort to try and seem normal. I don't have the mental capacity for that today.

Like I told Cole, I need the space to be miserable.

We grab stools at a worn wooden bar. Classic rock pumps in the background, loud enough to hear, but not too loud that we can't have a conversation.

"IDs." The bartender holds out his hand, waiting for our license to prove that we're old enough to imbibe.

"I wonder which age I'll be when they stop asking to see mine." I pull the card from my purse, passing it over. After a brief scan, he nods and turns to pour my beer.

"You've got a while to go," Cole intones, slipping his wallet out of his back pocket.

"You think I look that young?"

Cole shrugs, even as a smile tugs his lips. "Not young exactly. More innocent than anything."

I snort. "Innocent? Maybe before I started my job. But spend any amount of time working in a public library and you'll see a whole range of eye-opening things."

"Like what?"

"For one, the staff has a running tally of how many people each of us has had to politely ask to please stop watching porn on the public computers."

Cole barks out a laugh just as the bartender slides my drink across the counter. The guy accepts Cole's ID, giving it a slightly longer search than mine before handing it back with a half-smile.

"Happy birthday."

My muscles lock in place, the beer halfway to my mouth.

The bartender has turned away, and Cole is focused on sliding his ID back into his wallet. I can almost pretend that what I just heard was a misunderstanding. Something my imagination fabricated.

Almost.

"What did he say?" My voice comes out hoarse, and Cole doesn't look at me.

"Nothing."

"That was *not* nothing."

"Nothing important."

"Cole." I set my beer down. Scratch that, I slam it down. "Cole Allemand. You look at me now, and you tell me the truth."

His icy blue eyes snap up to mine, a hint of surprise in them.

"Summer, don't."

"This first one is on the house." The bartender is back, sliding the stout Cole asked for across the smooth wood surface.

"Son of a biscuit! It *is* your birthday!" I stare at him, flabbergasted by this realization.

Then the guilt hits.

"If I had a choice, I would go to sleep on December fifteenth and then wake up on December seventeenth."

I told Cole I wanted to skip his birthday.

"I'm a horrible friend."

He frowns, leaning toward me. "Summer, no."

"Yes, I am. Look at how great you've been today, and I've just...ruined it."

"You haven't."

But I'm off the rails now.

"This is supposed to be your special day! Where everyone you know celebrates that you came into the world."

"Not sure a lot of people want to celebrate that."

"Well I do! Oh my god. I took you to a cemetery. On your *birthday*." My breath comes faster, as if I'm about to hyperventilate on the fact that I've been the most depressing birthday companion in the existence of the world.

But Cole just shrugs. "I like cemeteries."

"You are too calm about this!" I reach for my beer and chug half the glass, hoping the alcohol works fast. Both to help me calm down, but also to ensure that fun Summer comes out in full force and saves the day.

Cole watches me, his eyes getting wider with each massive swallow.

Taking a break, I swipe the foam from my lip with the back of my hand, then lean toward my friend, intensity burning from my pores.

There's still time. I can save this.

"If you could have chosen anything to do today, what would it be?"

Cole's head quirks to the side, and his teeth just fiddle with the piercing in his lip in a very distracting way. But I'm even more thrown off when he answers.

"I did choose. I wanted to spend the day with you."

After that mic drop of a statement, Cole leans his elbows on the bar and reaches for his own beer, sipping at a more sedate pace. Meanwhile, I have to clutch the edges of my stool to keep from falling over.

Spend the day with me?

That's when another very important fact I had overlooked makes itself known.

Today is Monday. Cole comes to the library Thursday evenings and Sunday afternoons. I've never seen him in the library on a Monday.

But he came today. Because it's his birthday.

And he wanted to spend time with me on his special day.

My heart kerthunks heavily in my chest, and I press my palm against my breastbone, hoping Cole can't see the intense beating.

"Not the whole day, I'm sure." My voice has gotten breathy with confusion.

He stares at the thick dark liquid in his glass.

"As much as you were willing."

Oh my. Oh my goodness.

Why is Cole alone on his birthday?

Where are his friends and family?

If I weren't trying to make this day better, I might ask. But what if his family is all gone and his friends forgot? I'm not about to make him admit that.

Instead, I slide off the stool and wrap my arms around his trim waist.

"Summer?"

"Birthday present number one. I'm hugging you."

"I'm aware." His voice is wry, but one of his arms circles around my back, pulling me in tighter to his side.

Cole doesn't smell like musk. At least, not what I normally associate with the word.

No, he smells like spicy soap and warm days.

How does warmth smell? Like Cole, I guess, because that's the only way I can think to describe it.

"How old are you?" I tilt my head back far enough to look into his face.

"Twenty-nine. You?"

"Twenty-six, but today isn't about me." Having my arms wrapped around Cole is heavenly, but it also reminds me how little body fat he has. Birthdays are the best days to over-consume calories.

I step back and snatch a menu off a nearby table.

"Birthday present number two, I'm feeding you."

"You don't—"

"Cole!" I cut him off, hop back up on my stool, and lean in close, capturing his eyes with mine. "It is rude to reject birthday presents. Plus, I'm hungry." I'm surprised to find I'm not lying. Normally this day leaves me with a swirling whirlpool of grief that makes me nauseous every time I try to put some kind of food in my mouth. But now, for the first time since I woke up, I think I might be able to take down a plate of loaded fries. "Order food. It's on me. And then as we gorge ourselves we're going to plan how to spend these last few amazing hours of your birthday. Deal?"

Cole appears conflicted, his eyes dark sapphires in this dim bar, tracing over me. But after a brief hesitation, the resistance leaves his tense shoulders, and he clinks the rim of his beer glass against mine.

"Deal."

Chapter Eighteen

SUMMER

I expected Cole to suggest going to a rave. Or maybe getting spontaneous tattoos. Possibly choosing nipple piercings.

Basically, an activity I'd find both terrifying and exciting.

I'm wrong.

He wants to watch a movie.

The idea lacks normal birthday pizzaz, but who am I to tell the man what he wants?

And he doesn't even want to go to a theater.

It's not until I'm walking up his front steps that I realize going to a strange man's house is a perfect way to get murdered. Despite Cole's bad-boy look, I don't pick up murdery vibes, but the strange notes I get randomly stuffed in my mail slot are a clear indication I need to be cautious. I send a text to Jasmine as a precaution.

Jasmine: *Got you girl. Get some.*

Summer: *Excuse me, I will be getting NONE. He's a friend.*

Jasmine: *Sorry...you're breaking up...couldn't hear...*

Summer: *We're texting weirdo. Goodnight.*

I pray I'm not blushing when I tuck my phone back in my pocket.

Cole rents one of those shotgun-style houses where the rooms lead into one another.

The first room is a sparse living area with some couches that have seen better days and a rickety card table. The next room is a bedroom and has more personality than the first, with full bookshelves, a small wooden desk, a closet door cracked open to reveal lots of black clothing hung up.

Of course, it is Cole after all.

Without my permission, my eyes are drawn to the big bed pushed up against the wall. The thing looks deliciously soft, with a puffy blue comforter spread over it. Could use a few more pillows, but that's pretty much how I feel about every surface I see.

I wonder if Cole would accept pillows from me. I could sew him a black one. I could sew him twenty black ones if he asked.

I will make him a pillow, I decide. Unaware that this was his birthday, I didn't get him a gift. A few days late is better than no gift at all.

The bed moves, and I yelp.

Cole stalks over to pull back the covers, revealing an insanely fluffy black cat who has sprawled out in the middle of the bed.

"This is Smaug," Cole offers, wiggling his fingers as the cat playfully bats at them.

"Like the dragon?"

That earns me one of Cole's sly smiles. "Exactly."

Smaug stands from his resting place, stretching dramatically before he blinks a gorgeous set of green eyes at me. And I suddenly see a distinct relationship between cats and dragons. The name fits perfectly.

"How is Smaug with strangers? Can I pet him?"

Cole sits on the bed, running his hand down the cat's fluffy back.

"Let him sniff your hand. He'll decide."

I crouch beside the bed, extending my arm so my knuckles hover about an inch from the cat's face. After a hesitation, the animal leans forward to sniff my skin. My held breath comes out in a rush when he butts his head against my hand, demanding pets.

"I'm approved!" I whisper-cheer.

Cole smirks down at me, but I think I pick out a true spark of excitement in his eyes. "Good. Now I don't have to kick you out."

"I would have completely understood." For a few quiet moments, the two of us pay tribute to Smaug.

"Now I know why you always wear black," I murmur.

Cole quirks an eyebrow up in response.

"You don't want people to realize you're covered in cat hair." My fingers scratch just behind Smaug's ear, disappearing into his gorgeous dark fur.

Another smirky smile. "Sure. You caught me."

"How long have you had him?"

"About six months now. When he came into the shelter, I decided I was ready to bring one home with me."

He says this like he spends a lot of time at a shelter where cats are. Does he volunteer at an animal rescue or something? That's when I realize there's a huge blank space in my mind when it comes to Cole's profession.

"I'm sorry, Cole. We're supposed to be friends, but I don't even know what your job is."

He reclines back on the bed, keeping his upper body propped up on his elbows. "I work with the cats at a local animal rescue."

"Oh."

No. No no no. This cannot be allowed. A sexy tattooed man cannot work with cute animals all day. And not just work with them.

If he's employed at an animal shelter, he's *saving* them.

Would it be strange if I asked Cole to use his shower to drench myself in icy cold water to suppress my inferno of lust?

Yeah, that would be weird.

"You don't happen to have a picture of yourself at work...with kittens?" It's as if I'm in a torture chamber handing out recommendations for the best ways to cause myself the most agony.

Cole shakes his head, sending a riot of relief and disappointment through me.

"My phone is shitty, so I don't take pictures with it. But I can let you know next time someone drops off a litter, and you can come by and meet them."

If this is Cole's birthday, why am I the one getting the best fucking gift in the world?

"That would be acceptable." I maintain an overly formal tone because I don't want to terrify Smaug with the excited squeal that's clawing around in my chest. But I still think it's unfair that Cole is distractingly gorgeous in addition to working with cute fur babies. When the shelter put out the job ad, it would've been good to add a line like...

Applicant must have a face and personality equivalent to a dumpster fire or else every straight woman and gay man in the vicinity of the shelter will die by panty combustion.

Before I experience said mortality, I refocus on the purpose of this evening: salvaging Cole's birthday. I gather the plastic bag of supplies I insisted Cole stop by the supermarket for me to grab.

"Thank you, mighty Smaug, for allowing me to enter your domain." I affect a curtsey, then step toward the door we haven't walked through yet. "Kitchen?"

"Here, I'll show you." Cole climbs off the bed and saunters ahead of me. Smaug lies back down and immediately falls asleep on the exposed sheets.

We walk down a short hallway where Cole points out the bathroom. Next, we enter another bedroom, but this one is a barren wasteland.

"Do you have a roommate?" If he does, the guy is a weirdo. There aren't even sheets on the bed.

"My friend Dash, the mechanic I told you about, moved out a couple of months ago. So not anymore."

"Think you'll get another?"

Cole just shrugs, so I leave it be and follow him through the next doorway into a small outdated kitchen. The space is a little shabby, but it's clean and more spacious than my studio apartment setup. Cheers to cooking where you sleep!

I set my load down on a tiny kitchen table and start unpacking things.

"You didn't need to get all this stuff, Summer." Cole picks up the packet of candles. I sprang for the twisty ones because I thought they looked fun.

"Birthdays are rarely about what you need to do. They're about fun times and weird traditions and"—I reach into the bag and pull out a plastic container with a small cake—"sugar."

The top is a blank canvas of white icing, but I have that covered. With a little blue bottle of decorating icing, I carefully write out...

Happy Birthday Cole!

I stare at the message. Short and accurate.

And boring. Cole deserves more.

Happy Birthday Cole! Silver medalist in the New Orleans Swinging Championship.*

The cake I got is small, so the message ends up spilling over the edge onto the side and wrapping around the entirety of the dessert.

But Cole's grin when he reads it is worth every awkwardly drawn letter.

"Do you have something to light these with?" I arrange the candles in evenly spaced disorder.

Cole rummages around in the cabinets until he comes up with a book of matches.

By the time I have them all lit, little droplets of wax are starting to drip onto the icing. But what's a birthday cake without a few wax sprinkles?

"Happy birthday, Cole. Make a wish!"

"No song?"

"Do you want me to sing?"

He doesn't answer, but I get the sense that he does and just doesn't want to ask for it.

So I bust out an operatic version of the Happy Birthday song that sends Smaug, who had peeked his head past the doorway, scurrying from the room.

As the last trailing notes titter away, I nudge the cake closer. "Now, make a wish."

He doesn't hesitate. With his eyes locked on mine, Cole huffs out a controlled breath, wiping out every little flame. All the heat from the cake seems to have transferred to his eyes.

I would pay good money to know his wish.

COLE

Somehow, I convinced Summer to not only spend the day with me but to come back to my house. I'm waiting for when I wake up and realize this is one of those shitty good dreams. The ones where life is perfect, and then you gain consciousness and find that none of it was real.

Summer sits cross-legged in the middle of my bedroom floor, stroking Smaug's ears as I scan through my thrift store DVD collection to figure out what the longest movie I own is. Summer scratches at her tights, and I wonder if it's an idle move or if the material is itchy against her legs.

She should take them off.

Of course, I want Summer to remove all her clothes, but I don't think she's anywhere near as invested in this as I am. And I'm determined to only ask her for things she'll say yes to.

Which is why I come up with a workaround.

It's a long shot, but things have been working out for me today.

"You want to know what I want for my birthday?"

Summer's delicious brown eyes home in on me. "Yes. More than anything."

I nod and take a chance. "I want to watch movies all night until we pass out."

She tilts her head, and I try not to hold my breath waiting for her answer.

"Birthday movie marathon?"

I nod again.

"I could be down for that. But are you also suggesting a slumber party?"

Probably wouldn't have used those words, but, "Yes."

Summer smooths her hands down the front of her dress. "Normally, I'm totally in for a slumber party, but I'm not prepared."

Holy shit. That's halfway to a yes.

"I'll lend you clothes. And a toothbrush. All that stuff."

The librarian moves to stand in the middle of my bedroom, silently deliberating. I wonder what each side of the argument is.

"Just movies?" she eventually asks.

For now. "And cake. And popcorn."

"You have popcorn?" Her hands clasp under her chin, and I can't help smiling in response to her eagerness.

"I do."

That seems to seal the deal.

"Okay, Cole Allemand. I will have a birthday movie marathon slumber party with you."

Fuck yes. I'm the luckiest man. Moving to my dresser, I dig around in my drawers, coming out with a pair of basketball shorts and a T-shirt.

"These okay?"

"Mmhmm." Summer accepts the clothes and retreats to the bathroom.

And I'm left with the knowledge that she's stripping just one room over.

Calm down. It's not stripping. She's just changing clothes.

Changing into my *clothes. Her bare skin touching every inch of that fabric.*

A groan threatens to give me away, but I bite down on my knuckle and fiddle with the remote to give myself something to do.

"Men's clothes do not take hips into account. But I love these pockets. I could fit my whole life in these things."

I turn at the sound of her voice, and take an involuntary step backwards.

If I thought dressing her in my baggy clothing was going to help with my lust, I was fucking kidding myself.

Summer is right. The shorts stretch tight over her shapely ass. Normally the tempting view would be covered by the T-shirt, but since she's so determined to enjoy the pockets, she has the thing hiked up enough to show every bit. Even a tantalizing sliver of her belly.

I want to kneel in front of her and press my mouth to that slim stretch of exposed skin.

"You're not wearing jeans to a slumber party, are you?" Summer lets the shirt fall, allowing my brain to focus on her words.

I wonder if she just wants me to be comfortable or if there's an underlying motivation to her suggesting I change. Instead of answering, I revisit my drawers, pulling out another pair of shorts as well as a tank top.

What would she do if I told her I normally sleep in briefs?

Would this slumber party devolve into an underwear pillow fight?

I wouldn't complain.

"Be right back."

After changing, I duck into the kitchen and microwave a bag of popcorn, trying to focus on the task at hand rather than the fact that the sexy librarian I've been lusting after for months is spending the night.

I've been with plenty of people. This isn't any different.

Except that it is. Summer is different somehow. Maybe it's because even if we were going to have sex tonight, I know I'd still show up to the library hoping she'd come over to my table to talk to me. I want her to say yes to more than one night.

I want her to say yes to long-term with me.

But for now, I'll bribe her with popcorn and cute cats.

Making my way back to my bedroom, I could swear I hear her humming "Jingle Bells."

"I smell buttery delicious—" Summer's sing-song cheer cuts off when her eyes land on me. She stands in the middle of the room, seeming slightly dazed.

I glance down at the bowl I'm holding, then look behind me, searching for what has her so shocked.

"Your tattoos are dragons," she whispers, taking a step toward me, and I realize what's set her off balance.

"Yeah. You've never seen them?"

She shrugs. "I know you have tattoos, but I've never had the chance to study them before. It's frowned upon to stare at library patrons." Summer's regained her teasing manner as she approaches me, her gaze trailing over my ink.

I imagine her fingers taking the same path.

"How many do you have?" She circles behind me, and I feel suddenly vulnerable with her focus trained on me but being unable to see her.

After a quick mental count, I answer. "Ten."

"Wow. And ouch. Are they all so different from each other?" Summer appears on my other side, examining a dragon that winds around my right bicep to my forearm, done in traditional style with thick lines and bold colors.

"Yeah. I got kind of addicted a few years back. Found the best artists in the city. Asked each one to design a dragon in whatever style they wanted."

"And they cover..." She trails off, and a charming blush creeps up her neck, infusing her cheeks.

A cocky smile pushes at my mouth. Summer is thinking about my body, and it's obviously affecting her.

"Rough estimate. Eighty-five percent of my skin is covered."

"Eighty-five?" Summer's eyes drop to my covered torso, then to my exposed calves, then creep up to right around my waistline before flying back up to my face.

"Yes," I say.

And as I watch, a little shiver quivers over her.

She likes my ink. I'd bet money on it.

Good. One more thing I can use to tempt her into saying yes to me.

"Movies!" She practically shouts the word, whirling away from me to stare at the screen. "What are we watching?"

"You sure you don't want a say?"

"Your birthday, your choice. So what's it going to be?"

I slide a disk into the DVD player, and a beautifully familiar instrumental blares from the speakers.

"We're taking a trip to Mordor! Perfect slumber party binge choice," Summer announces as she crawls onto my bed. I watch her gather the few pillows I have, plumping them and arranging an almost nest-like situation before settling herself among the mass.

"I would like to preemptively apologize for the amount of wistful sighing that's likely to occur whenever Legolas is on the screen," she announces.

"You're into pretty boys?" My voice comes out in a more surly grumble than I intended as I climb onto the mattress beside her, propping my back against the wall. But can I blame her? I had a huge crush on the guy, too.

"The heart wants what the heart wants. And mine wants an elf-man with badass archery skills." Her fingers pluck a few kernels of popcorn from the bowl in my lap, and she hums happily while chewing them.

Silently, I congratulate myself. Earlier today, Summer was so miserable she ended up sobbing in her office. Now she's made herself comfortable in my bed while bantering about crushes and making content eating noises. For most of the human population, I would be the worst possible person to bring their sorrows to. But for Summer Pierce, turns out I'm exactly what she needs.

Now it's my job to convince her of it.

Chapter Nineteen

SUMMER

There is little worse in the world than being completely comfortable while also having a full bladder.

Slowly, I rise into wakefulness, drawn there by the pressure that demands I use a toilet. When I blink my eyes open, I realize the delicious warmth that surrounds me isn't from a mound of pillows.

It's a man.

Specifically, it is Cole Allemand.

I know this because the arm draped across my chest has a colorful dragon twisting down it. We must have fallen asleep while watching the movie. At least, I did, because I have no recollection of seeing the ring get tossed into the fires of Mordor.

I wonder if we naturally ended up in this position, our bodies seeking each other out during the night, or if Cole gathered me close to him when he realized I was dead to the world. Either way, this is too decadently comfortable to be legal.

And yet, as I realized the second I woke up, I need to pee.

With a level of regret I decide not to ponder on, I slide out from underneath Cole's arm and tiptoe to the bathroom. After flushing and washing my hands, my eyes snag on the Mardi Gras cup with a toothbrush resting in it. My mouth is fuzzy from a night of sleep, and

I'm vain enough to not want to risk anyone catching a whiff. Two minutes later and I'm minty fresh.

Once my bathroom business is done, I'm left with a conundrum. It's seven a.m., which is technically late enough in the morning for me to reasonably get up, get dressed, and get out.

But I don't have work today, and I'm not meeting my mom until later, so I could easily argue for another hour or so in bed. A little bit longer in Cole's arms.

Friends don't usually sleep wrapped around each other. I didn't spoon with Jasmine the couple of times I crashed at her place after a bar crawl. She slept in her bed, and I bundled myself up in a blanket and passed out on the couch.

There was no mention of a couch last night.

But what if friends don't spoon because society tells us we can't? What if there can be a perfectly platonic spooning?

I decide to spurn society's rigid dictates. My returning to Cole's bed is tantamount to a protest. I'm standing up for my right to spoon a friend. Or, rather, I'm lying down for my rights.

With the excuses made, no matter how flimsy they are, I cross the bedroom and carefully crawl onto the bed, trying my hardest not to jostle the sleeping temptation of a man.

Now, I could easily stretch out in the empty space next to him. There's plenty of room.

But that's not a true protest, is it?

So, pretending my fingers exert no more pressure than a butterfly's wings, I grip Cole's wrist, lifting up his arm as I roll into his chest.

Success!

All that librarian ninja training has paid off. Not that my job has taught me how to sneak into men's beds. That's not a necessary skill for my profession.

"You came back."

All the loose relaxation I was trying to ease into evaporates.

Cole is awake.

My logical brain cells tell me I should climb out of the bed. I should leave. But those other brain cells, the ones that have a close relationship with my heart and my vagina, beg me to turn in his arms and face him.

The win goes to group number two.

When I shift enough to gaze into the cool blue of his morning eyes, I want to whimper at how delicious and sleep mussed he looks.

He watches me, lids heavy, but still seeming to see so much.

"I was comfortable," I whisper, wondering if I should've just left. But he was the one who wanted a birthday slumber party. Not that post-morning cuddling is a normal occurrence at those.

My hands seem to have their own worries of him backing away because next thing I know, I have a hold of his waist, pulling myself closer to him. There must be a medical reason my body is not responding to logic. If he asks, that's what I'll tell him. Just need to go to the doctor and set myself to rights. Nothing to worry about.

Cole dips his head, and to my shock, he traces his nose along my hairline, then down near my ear, until he reaches my mouth and breaths in deep.

"You brushed your teeth," he mutters.

"I used your toothbrush!" I blurt. Blood floods into my cheeks. "I'll buy you a new one."

The slight tug of fingers at the nape of my neck has me tilting my chin up and fighting a purr. If a perfectly platonic spooning exists, it's not going to happen between Cole and me. My hips shift restlessly, and I realize that there's another part of his body that's awake.

When my thigh brushes his hardness, Cole buries his head in the pillow, which only slightly muffles his low groan.

"Sorry!" I move to retreat, but Cole half rolls his body, pinning me with his hips, his cock pressing into my hip, his upper half held above me on bent elbows.

For a moment, we simply stare at each other, as if both trying to read the other.

I want him. And I want to stop pretending that I don't. I can only lie to myself about so many things before my brain explodes. So, trying to make things clearer for us both, I let my hands creep around his trim waist until my fingers span wide on his back. Muscles roll and tense under the thin fabric of his shirt.

"Can I kiss you?" he asks.

I'm already leaning toward him, but he stops me by gently cupping my chin, holding me at bay.

"What's wrong? Do you need to hear me say yes? Here it is, me saying yes."

Cole's lips twitch. But he also shakes his head.

"The first time I taste your mouth, I don't want you to be thinking about how I have morning breath."

"Oh." I gasp out a confused chuckle. "So you were asking for the future?"

Again, he shakes his head.

"Can I kiss you here?" His fingers release my chin, trailing lower, to the insistent pulse pounding in my neck.

"Yes." Maybe it's a good thing he doesn't want to kiss my mouth because, apparently, I swallowed a frog recently.

He teases my neck, tracing back and forth with his surprisingly soft lips. Ever so often, I feel a light touch of something with no give, and I know that his piercing has brushed against me. My teeth clench in an attempt to keep my moans at bay. For some reason, I don't want him to know how wild his gentle caress is making me.

But it's impossible to keep quiet when his tongue flicks against my collarbone.

Cole Allemand's mouth is on me, and I might die.

My fingers fist in the sheets so I don't tug his face up to mine. That doesn't stop the pleading words from tumbling out of me. "Just kiss me on the mouth! You are torturing me!"

"No," Cole growls before gently biting my collarbone and earning him a whimper from me. "Not yet."

Suddenly, all his delicious warmth is gone. He levers himself out of the bed, striding from the room.

"Am I supposed to stay here?" I call after him.

"Yes."

With a sexually frustrated sigh, I collapse back on the pillows. Then, only a second later, I hear the sound of scratching. When I roll to my side, I realize it's not scratching.

It's brushing.

Cole leans on the doorframe, meticulously working a toothbrush over his teeth, all the while his gaze rests on me. I never thought dental hygiene could be so hot. The thought that the same toothbrush was in my mouth is strangely erotic.

Counting down the seconds until he's done and will come back to the bed, I'm surprised when he pauses the repetitive movement, and gestures for me to follow him.

Under his sexy spell, I do as directed.

I come upon Cole in the bathroom rinsing his mouth. He grabs a hand towel to wipe away the remaining drops on his lips then turns to face me. Before I know what's happening, his grip is at my waist, and I'm boosted to sit up on the bathroom counter.

With the extra inches of height, I'm that much closer to Cole's mouth, and he takes advantage of the fact. Fingers clasp my chin, and a thumb brushes over my bottom lip. Then he leans down to press a kiss where his touch just left.

He's gentle, and I'm surprised to realize I want Cole to be rough. I want to feel ravished. Consumed. Like I'm the air his lungs need to breathe.

Well, if he's not going to give me what I want, maybe I should take it.

Reaching up, I cup the back of his head, tangling my fingers in his sleep-mussed hair, and press myself into him. A groan tears from his throat, driving me on. His hands fist in my borrowed T-shirt just as I lock my ankles behind his waist.

Is this too wanton for a first kiss?

Doesn't matter when it feels this good.

Cole is fresh mint on my tongue and hot touches on my skin. The way my mind grows hazy with his kiss has me doubting reality. Maybe I'll wake up and find myself in my own bed in my own apartment, the sheets tangled around me because I couldn't keep from thrashing with phantom pleasure.

If that is what this ends up being, I'm going to enjoy every second.

Cole's tongue explores my bottom lip, then licks along the seam, requesting entrance. I part for him, unable to stifle the eager noises with my mouth open to his. Every sigh and moan pulled from me drives him deeper.

With my legs around his waist, the center of me presses against the hardest part of him. An ache, a longing to be connected with him in that way overwhelms me. It has me grinding against him.

"Bed," I mumble, trying to convey my want without detaching myself from him.

Cole pulls back, and I anticipate an eager race back to the mattress we were christening earlier.

But the bastard doesn't make a move to leave. Instead, he traces the shell of my ear with his tongue, causing a convulsion of pleasure to wrack my body and muddy my brain.

"What am I to you?" His warm breath is in my ear while his talented hands dig into the tight muscles of my back.

He makes concentrating hard.

"What?"

"You and me. What is this?" Cole asks the question in between trailing kisses down my neck.

"I-I can't think w-when you do that!"

But Cole doesn't stop. He only adds his teeth, making me shiver and moan.

"We're dating," he provides in a husky voice. A lifeline for me to grab onto.

"We-we're dating? You want to date me?" I gasp out the questions.

His response is to drop a hand to my ass and pull me hard against his erection. "Mmhmm."

"You and me?" I whimper when he palms one of my breasts, easily finding my hard nipple through the cotton.

"I'll make you feel good. I'll make you happy."

Everything in me is shouting, but I can't make out the words. Wasn't there some reason I shouldn't date Cole? Something about him being bad?

But that can't be right. He said he'd make me feel good.

"Say yes, Summer." And he's back to worshipping my mouth

Say yes?

Is it that easy?

When he pauses again, I take advantage of the opening.

"Yes."

His entire body goes as rigid as his dick.

"Yes?" Cole cups my cheeks, tilting my head so he can meet my eyes. His burn with an intensity that only makes my blood hotter. There's something in the tone of his question that has me smiling

"Yes."

This earns me a Cole Allemand grin, and I consider if it's possible to self-combust just by looking into a gorgeous man's face. Iron arms envelop my waist, lifting me from the bathroom sink. I love the floating feeling, finding myself giggling in eagerness.

"Bed now?"

"No." He lets me slide down his body until my toes touch the tile of the bathroom floor. "Bagels now."

Chapter Twenty

COLE

Best. Birthday. Ever.

Chapter Twenty-One

SUMMER

A table in the corner sits filled with delicious finger foods, so it's no surprise I've gravitated there. Nothing messy, of course, but hearty enough offerings to make sure no one at this open house has an empty stomach.

"Empty stomachs don't feel like home." My mother's words echo from years ago.

As she stands by an ornate fireplace, chatting with a young couple, I can imagine her saying the same exact line today. That's how things are with her. Different, and yet the same.

When I was sixteen it was my responsibility to make sure the snack table for the potential buyers remained fully stocked and attractive to look at. Now Mom brings in caterers who craft delicate, yet still homey-feeling fare.

I didn't arrive at this spot because I miss my post as unofficial server. I'm just here because I'm hungry. Not that I would admit that to my mother. She would twist the conversation around to me not buying enough food because I spend so much of my earnings on my student loans.

The debt looms over me, creepy tentacles teasing, interest rates amassing. Sometimes I'm so knotted up by the numbers that I'm not even hungry. Which makes it easier to apply part of my food budget toward paying them off.

Couldn't have been happy with a bachelor's. No, I wanted that Master's in Library Science. I wanted a full-time, relatively secure position. Need to spend money to make money.

Not that many people would call the salary of a public librarian a lucrative investment.

But, one day, after my student loans are paid, I'll be able to start saving for a place to live with more than one room. I won't have to look so closely at my grocery receipts. Maybe I'll treat myself to a fancy cappuccino drink rather than a simple black coffee.

One day my salary will feel like enough, instead of just scraping by.

One day I'll feel secure. I'll feel safe.

Until then, I might as well supplement my income with some open house flatbread squares and fresh-baked cookies.

"Summer baby, glad you could make it. Just another half hour and things will slow down." My mother says all this in one breath as she presses a kiss against my cheek and whirls away again, eyes locked on a well-dressed woman running her manicured fingers along a window sill.

One of the waiters who passes by with a tray of waters and white wine gives me a pitying look. I let an easy smile spread across my face, hoping to convey I'm not upset in the slightest about my mother's abrupt greeting. This is her job. And she loves it. I'd never ask her to stop in the middle of what she's doing and pay attention to me. That would be like her showing up to the library and expecting me to ignore patrons so we could have a chat.

No way. Not going to happen.

For a long time, I watched my mother struggle to get to a point in her life where she found happiness and contentment. She has that here, at her successful real estate business. Finally.

After filling a tiny plate, I set to roaming and end up finding the comfiest place in the house, a window seat that is sadly lacking in throw pillows. Settling in, I pull out a tattered paperback I paid a quarter for at the library's used book fundraiser last week.

I'm deep into the story when a light tap on my shoulder pulls me back to the present.

"Are you with me?" My mother smiles down at me, waiting for me to replace between the pages the crumpled receipt I was using as a bookmark, and focus my eyes on her.

"Yep." The book fits easily in my purse. They're not the most durable, but I love the portability of mass market paperback books.

"You know, I didn't have to search anywhere else for you. I knew you would end up in this seat." Mom settles on the bench beside me and toes off her heels.

"Best seat in the house." I shift my legs so she has more room to sit. "Is everyone gone? Think you have some on the line?"

"At least three. One couple already called and left a message."

"Think they'll get it?"

She peers out the window, then meets my eyes. "Not if I buy this place for myself."

"What?" My eyes flit around, taking in the banister and high ceilings I can spy from my seat. Despite my lack of knowledge about property, I'd be naive not to realize this is a pricy piece of real estate. "You want this? You can afford it?"

Mom smiles wide, taking no offense at my baffled tone. It's just that, for so long, both of us would've been lucky to afford to rent a place as large as this house's garage.

"Business has been going well."

"That's fantastic." My heart squeezes with happiness for her. "You want a place this big though? You don't think it's a little much for one person?"

She reaches out to tug on a strand of hair that's come loose from my French braid.

"It wouldn't be too big if you moved in with me."

No. The word is sharp in my mind, and it's all I can do to keep from cringing at how harsh the thought was.

Still, the answer will always be no.

"That's a sweet offer, but I'm okay on my own." I have to be. I have to prove I can survive in the world on my own. Because you never know when all your safety nets will be torn away.

But then a dark questions scratches at the back of my mind: is my safety already gone? The strange, vaguely threatening notes are still showing up at my apartment. Not every day, or even every week. But just as I start hoping the sender has grown tired of me, another appears.

What would my mom say if I told her? If I moved in with her, would they stop?

Or would things escalate?

"I can give you a home now." Her warm palm cups my face, and I shy from my fears, forcing a smile free.

"You always gave me a home, Mom."

"Studio apartments and decaying rentals were not homes."

"Mom." I reach up and tangle my fingers with hers, admiring her pristine red nail polish I'd never be able to maintain. "*You* were my home. Everywhere we went, it was the two of us, so I had a home."

"Summer baby. You know how to say the most perfect things." She brings my hand to her mouth, pressing a kiss to my knuckles, then wiping away the lipstick. "But you're only agreeing with me. We can be an *us* again."

"We're always an us. But I need to build my own life. Rely on myself. You know why."

That gets her to sigh in defeat. "Of course I do. Of course. Strong women can do it on their own. I just want you to know you don't have to."

"I'm saying no, but only because you showed me that I could. But if you want to buy this house for you, then go for it."

She frowns around at the place. "No. You're right. It's too big for one person."

My mother's profile is beautifully illuminated by natural light from a picture window. She is a gorgeous woman, inside and out, and I suddenly feel bad that I'm one of the few people who gets to love her.

"Maybe if you decided to date someone and things get serious you'll have a reason to buy a big house." My fingers playfully poke at her side.

She bats my hand away, a scowl marring her normally friendly countenance.

"That won't happen."

I should drop it. We were having a good moment. But this issue, completely valid though it is, always hovers like a dark shadow in our future. The day that I'll want to bring someone special into my life.

"You never know. This city is full of handsome, *nice* men. One could sweep you off your feet."

She scoffs, and irritation scratches under my skin.

"I, for one, look forward to the day I find someone to love."

My mother turns a fierce gaze on me, reminding me of a mystical fairy giving a dire warning to a naive heroine in some ancient tale, knowing the girl won't heed her advice.

"You don't need a man. They are practically pointless."

Dad wasn't pointless, I want to growl. But I don't because then she'll excuse herself to the bathroom, and if I try to follow her I'll hear her sobbing on the toilet.

I do not bring up my father to my mother, especially not in an argument.

"Just because I don't need something doesn't mean I don't want it. Or him, more accurately."

"Him?"

"Yes. Him. I date men."

"But that sounded like there is one particular man that you want." She's got her shrewd eyes working on piercing my armor of indifference.

"Well, I went on a date." Panic has me continuing. "With a guy named Joshua."

Guilt seeps through me like black sludge.

It's not that I lied. I did go on a date with Joshua. But there won't be any more. And if I was referring to a specific *him*, Joshua was not that him.

Cole is that him.

But I shake my head at that thought. Cole is...dangerous. I think. He looks it anyway. Gives off that vibe with his tattoos, and piercings, and one shade of black clothing.

And making out with him the day after his birthday does not mean he's my someone to love.

He's my someone to kiss. Temporarily.

And temporary men are not the kind to get my mother riled up about.

"And what makes this Joshua so special?"

Nothing.

"I'm not saying he is. I just want you to know that I go on dates, and one of these days it might turn into something more. If it does, I would love it if you didn't lay into the guy simply because he identifies as male. Think you can do that for me?"

She grimaces. "I'll think about it."

That's probably the best I'll get from her, and I have to admit that it's progress. Before I can make any other pleas on behalf of the male populace, my mother shocks me with her change of subject.

"I have a box of—of your father's things. In the car. Things I'm not keeping. You should look through it. Take what you want. The rest I'll donate."

"Wow, Mom. Really?"

She stands and smooths her hands over her immaculate skirt. "It's not everything. Just some things. My therapist suggested it."

"You're seeing a therapist?"

"Don't sound so shocked."

"I'm not! I mean, I am. But I'm happy shocked. Therapy is good. I'm glad you're going." It's been fourteen years, and I'm almost certain my mother handles the day of my father's death just as poorly as I do. Maybe even worse.

I wonder if she spent yesterday going through his things. Maybe that was cathartic for her.

I probably would've been a sobbing mess.

Not that I wasn't anyway.

"I'll take a look."

Today, I feel better. Today, I think I can handle a task that involves my father's old things.

Today, I have the memory of Cole's kisses to bring a smile to my face whenever sadness threatens to creep in.

Chapter Twenty-Two

COLE

My worn sneakers slap against the pavement as I jog down another street. Beside me, Paige has no trouble keeping up. Some days I wonder if I'm holding her back. She's been running for longer than I have.

Paige Herbert is a gorgeous woman. Tall, soft curves, buttery blonde hair that makes mine look like an unwashed dirty mess. When we run, sometimes I keep track of the number of heads she turns, as a way to pass the time.

She's oblivious, which I'm glad about, seeing as how she's been dating my best friend for over a year. The two of them just moved in together, leaving me without a roommate.

Not that I'm mad about it. Dash deserves a partner like Paige.

"How would you feel about a brief affair of a sexual nature?"

Her words are worse than a crack in the sidewalk, tripping me, sending me sprawling. The concrete scrapes my hands as I try to catch myself, but I still hit the ground hard. Curses tumble out of my mouth as I roll over onto a patch of grass, taking the pressure off my abused palms.

"Damn, Cole. That was a hard fall. Are you okay?" She's kneeling over me, her face all concerned, looking so innocent, like she wasn't the one to send me crashing down.

"Okay? Are you fucking kidding me? I can't believe you'd ask that. That you'd do that to Dash!"

I've known Paige almost as long as Dash has, and I never thought that she would sleep around on my friend.

"He's the one who suggested you. I was thinking Charlie, but he's not coming home until New Year's."

Dash suggested this? Yeah right. "And you can't wait a few weeks to fuck another dude?"

Paige flinches back, eyes wide as if I hit her. I feel more like strangling her. Dash is a good guy, and he loves Paige more than anything. The idea that not only would she betray him, but that she wants to do it with me, has vomit rising in my throat.

And I realize how much I've come to love Paige myself. She's among a small number of people I've let into my life. The only woman other than my grandmother.

This is a betrayal, and I want to punch something.

"What are you talking about, Cole? I don't want to sleep with anyone other than Dash. Why would you say that?"

"Because you just propositioned me."

Paige sits back on her haunches, brow furrowed, her lips moving in silent words. Suddenly, she claps a hand to her mouth with a slight gasp, shaking her head before she lets it drop.

"No, Cole. No that's not what I meant. Oh hell. You know I say things wrong sometimes, but come on. You don't actually think I want to cheat on Dash, do you?"

"If someone else had told me, no I wouldn't have. But you said what you said."

She kneels next to me, hands gripping my shoulders as if she needs to force all of my attention on her. It's already there.

With a deep breath, Paige speaks slowly, and carefully. If I didn't know her, I'd think she was doing this because she considers me to be slow. However, I've learned that sometimes Paige needs to concentrate to make sure her words come out in normal human talk rather than confusing Paige rambling.

"I have a writer friend coming to town to visit for a few weeks. She is free-spirited and fun and would probably like a handsome guy to flirt with. Maybe also sleep with if there's attraction. I was trying to find out if that would be interesting to you. If you'd like me to set you up. With her." She lets go of my arms, sitting back again. "Not me. Dash fulfills all my needs on a daily basis. Sometimes multiple times a day."

"That's enough. I get it." Feeling like an ass, I duck my head as I move to stand, trying not to wince as my raw palms brush against my pants.

"You're not pissed at me, are you?" Paige rises beside me, helpfully brushing some dirt off my shirt.

"No. I should've known that's not what you meant."

Maybe I would have if my mind wasn't pulled in multiple other directions. My job. My book. Summer.

Thoughts of her make me want to smile, and drive away my annoyance with the misunderstanding. Also, they give me a good reason to turn Paige down.

"Sorry. Can't be a fuck buddy on loan."

"Oh god, Cole! Is that what I'm asking? That sounds horrible." My friend's face bleaches white in horror, which has me laughing. She softens at the sound, but still watches me with worry.

"No. I mean, yes, that's kind of what you're asking. But it's not horrible. Mainly because you're asking rather than just setting it up." I tilt my head, indicating we should start running again. Once we've re-established our steady pace, I explain myself. "I might've said yes at some point. But I'm seeing someone."

Not just someone. The best one. Every time I think of that kiss, my fingers curl, wanting to be gripping Summer's soft body again. And calling it "a kiss" isn't even accurate. There were a lot of kisses. One right after another. The two of us got drunk on kissing.

There's never been a better birthday.

"Who? Do I know her? Or him? Or they? I don't think I've ever asked your preference."

I shrug. "Any are good. But she's a she. Summer. She's a librarian." There's a certain amount of pride in my voice when I speak about her. She a fucking awesome librarian. Smart and clever and great with everyone she talks to.

And she spent an entire morning kissing *me*.

She could have anyone, like that fucker Joshua. But on her worst day, *I* comforted her. And then she showered affection on me, the likes of which I never remember receiving. Not even the first handful of years of my life when my mother was still around.

"Ooo. A librarian. Good choice. It's always good to have a librarian on your team."

"You just want more people to talk about books with." We jog in place at a crosswalk, waiting for the light to change.

Paige grins wide. "Obviously. Let's get dinner. We're taking my friend out anyway. It can be a whole group thing.

"I'll ask." And I can imagine it now. Us out to eat, laughing and having a good time, and me with my arm across the back of Summer's chair. Maybe even wrapped around her shoulders. As the night wears on, potentially moving her to my lap.

Where I could tilt her face toward me for a kiss any time I want.

Interesting. I might be into PDA.

SUMMER

"You don't have to help me clean up, Amy."

The stout woman waves me off with the hand that isn't holding a towering stack of used coffee cups. "The job will go quicker this way, and I have a slow afternoon."

I catch on her words, straightening fast.

"Would you mind staying then? It's only, there's someone I'd like you to talk to."

Amy glances at me then around the empty room as if to say *Where have they been for the last two hours?*

I get her point. The library's weekly Wednesday midday coffee talk just ended. AKA, the perfect time for someone to talk to her. It's the whole reason she's here.

When I was hired a year ago, the library was already providing free coffee for an hour each Wednesday. I glommed onto the idea, and grew it into something bigger:

Coffee Talk.

Sure, the title doesn't sound too exciting, but the information we learn from each session is valuable.

I realized early on that those taking advantage of the coffee most often were our homeless patrons, which had me thinking about what else they might like. As per my usual method, I began to research. But it didn't take me long to realize the easiest way to figure out what they wanted was to ask them.

They were already showing up for coffee, so I just turned the coffee time into a chat time. Before long the event extended an extra hour, and I invited employees from local nonprofits geared toward helping the homeless to attend as well.

Hence, Amy's presence.

She's here every Wednesday to answer questions and give guidance and advice on the many issues someone who lost their home might face. She lets them know about programs and jobs and tons of other services I know nothing about. She is an angel in jeans and a blazer.

And because of her, our attendance has doubled, making it easy for me to demonstrate the benefit of the program to our director.

Knowing that not everyone has the best intentions, or complete control over their mental faculties, one of the security guards is also normally nearby. But I've asked that they pour themselves a cup of coffee and take a seat when they're in the actual Coffee Talk space.

I love everything about this event, except for the timing. Of course, it works great for the patrons that don't have jobs or places to be during the day, a group in need I'm excited to help. However, it doesn't lend itself to helping people who are busy during the day.

People who have school.

People like Jamie.

"He's a teenager. He's in school. But I think something is wrong at home, and he may not be sleeping there anymore. But he won't tell me."

"So you want to see if he'll talk to me?" Amy grabs some paper towels to wipe up a spill.

"It's worth a shot."

"Of course I'll stay. I can work off of one of the library computers, and you can let me know when he arrives."

A plan. We have a plan, and maybe tonight I'll be able to go to sleep knowing Jamie is safe and cared for.

A few hours later, I see a familiar head of unruly dark hair stroll across the reading room. With a quick wave for Amy to join me, I follow him to his spot.

When he sees me approaching, I'm greeted with the sweetest grin.

"How are you doing, Jamie?"

"Just fine, Ms. Pierce. Just fine. Here, look." Jamie settles his backpack on the table and carefully unzips it. He pulls out a folder and from that produces a stapled bunch of papers.

When he hands it to me, I scan the title.

Beautiful Buildings: The History of Architecture in New Orleans

And under the title is scrawled a hand-written ninety-eight percent.

"Is this your history paper?"

Jamie nods, a huge smile on his face.

"This is amazing! Jamie! Holy goodness gracious. You kicked ass!"

There's an intentional throat-clearing next to me, and I glance over remembering who is there.

"Oh, sorry. I wanted to introduce you to my friend. Jamie, this is Amy. Amy, this is Jamie. Amy usually comes for our Wednesday Coffee Talks. Jamie comes to the library to write A-plus papers, apparently."

The teenager's eyes, which had taken on a wary quality when I introduced the woman, lighten at the praise.

"Nice to meet you, Jamie." Amy has one of those beautiful voices that could probably calm a charging grizzly bear. She holds out a hand, which Jamie shakes.

"I'll be right back, you two talk." Well, that wasn't the most subtle approach, but I still make my escape. I pause by the reference desk, considering if I should go to my office and wait for Amy to let me know they're done talking, or if I should hover here.

There's not much time to decide because a moment later Jaimie charges out from between a set of bookshelves, scowl carved deep onto his face. He's on his way out, and a spurt of panic has me following.

"Jamie! Jamie, wait!" I run after him, trying to keep up with his long-legged stride. Luckily, he pauses just outside the library front doors, brought up by the heavy rain coming down. I silently thank the weather for stopping him, even if I hate that this might be what he has to sleep in tonight.

But that's the problem. I don't know.

"Jamie. I'm sorry. Please, just give me a minute."

From his profile, I can see his jaw clench, but he doesn't plunge into the downpour. As I try to figure out exactly what went wrong, he growls, "I don't need charity."

Damn. There's that pride again.

And I can't help someone who refuses to be helped.

"What your life is outside of the library is none of my business. I made assumptions, and I'm sorry if they offended you. But I worry. And in case something was going on in your life that you didn't feel comfortable talking about, I just wanted you to know there are options. But we never have to talk about it again. Just, please come back inside. Please. I want to read your paper and help you with research, and I have something for you."

For a full minute, he's silent, staring into the cascading water. If he steps away, I'm not sure I'll be able to keep my hands from grabbing for him.

Luckily, I'm not tested. His gaze drifts to the side, just catching on mine.

"Coffee?"

A grin cracks across my face. "Would you believe they doubled my order again?"

"No," he mutters but turns to walk back inside. I almost sag against the brick wall, so relieved he didn't decide to disappear on me. When we pass Amy, who's leaning against the circulation desk, Jamie doesn't even acknowledge her. I give her an apologetic wave and receive a reassuring smile in return. I duck into my office to grab the coffee cup and the other thing I'd picked out for him, hoping it's not another spark to his fuse.

"Coffee." I place the cup down on the desk beside him. "And one more thing."

Jamie stares up at me, eyes wary, so I start on the guilting offensive.

"I'm not sure if I mentioned it, but my father passed away when I was younger."

The kid looks like I slapped him, and I hope I'm not triggering some bad memories for him.

"Recently, my mom had me look through a box of his stuff she planned to donate. This was in it." I hold up a worn bomber jacket. Maybe I don't know all the high school fashions, but I'm pretty sure leather jackets never go out of style. "It's way too big for me, but I don't like the idea of just giving it away. I wondered if you might be interested?"

"Ms. Pierce..." Jamie's eyes are wide in what seems to be a kind of wonder. He pushes up from his chair and reaches for the jacket.

The thing fits him perfectly. My dad was a tall guy.

"Don't feel obligated to take it. I just like the idea of knowing where it ended up."

Jamie runs his hands over the leather, then shoves his hands in the pockets.

"This is... Thank you." The kid looks at me with shining eyes, and I have no doubt he appreciates the gift.

"You're welcome. I'm at the reference desk at four. Come see me. And bring that paper. I wasn't kidding about wanting to read it."

Jamie swallows deeply and gives me a nod.

When I get to my office, I check my phone and see two texts waiting for me. The first is from Amy.

Amy: *Not the first time I've gotten that reaction. But he has my number and some information. Sometimes that's the best you can do. See you next Wednesday.*

That and the fact that I was able to convince Jamie not to run off makes me feel a little better. Then my attention focuses solely on the second text.

Cole: *Dinner w/ my friends tonight?*

My mind stumbles. Cole is asking me out. To eat food. With his friends.

Is this a 'meet the girl I made out with and maybe want to do dirty things with in a bed' kind of friend dinner?

Or is it a 'shit I kissed this girl but I only wanted to hang out with her in a platonic fashion so I'm going to incorporate her into my existing friend group dinner?

My phone buzzes again.

Cole: *I can drive. Dinner at 7. I can be at your place early if you want to make out before we go.*

Well, cross reason number two off my list. My heart starts up its heavy beating, seeming to double in size and claim much-needed space from my lungs in my chest cavity.

I'm having trouble breathing.

But that doesn't affect my thumbs' ability to type. A nervous giggle escapes as I read back my scandalous message.

Summer: *I took the bus and work till 6. Pick me up then and we can make out in your truck.*

Cole's response is immediate.

Cole: *Yes.*

Chapter Twenty-Three

SUMMER

"You look beautiful." Cole's words shock me.

It's as if he was rummaging around in my brain, hearing all the insecurities I was cycling through in regards to my outfit. I have on my preferred work attire: a T-shirt dress and an overlarge cardigan. Super comfortable, easy to move around in, but not exactly what one might wear to impress a guy's friends.

Do I need to impress his friends?

No.

Do I want to?

Hell yes. Life is easier when people like you. Plus, I want to get on their good sides so I can figure out more about Cole.

The bad boy who calls me beautiful.

"Thank you. You're beautiful, too." And I mean it. Cole's wearing a black dress shirt, the sleeves rolled up to show off his inked forearms. The illustrations on his skin paired with his lean build give him a fierce appearance, like one of his dragons.

And to me, that's beautiful.

Cole glances my way briefly before refocusing his eyes on the road. He doesn't ask if my compliment was a mistake or a slip of the tongue.

He doesn't correct me, saying I meant to say handsome. He just accepts that I think he's beautiful.

Or he thinks I'm joking and doesn't laugh.

It's hard to read Cole. Which only makes me want to more. He's a banned book I'm not supposed to take off the shelf. But every flip of the page feels too good against my fingers to put him back.

"Do you think your friends will mind I'm crashing dinner?"

"They asked me to invite you."

"Really?" *He talks about me with his friends?*

"Paige did." He reaches across the center consul to twine his fingers with my fidgeting hand. "You'll meet her, Dash, and maybe Paige's friend from New York."

"Paige and Dash. Okay, that's easy enough to remember."

Cole pulls into a parking lot, settling his truck in a spot farther from the bar than most people parked. When he pulls the key from the ignition, everything seems to go dark. I can only discern the outline of his face from the restaurant lights behind us.

"We can head straight in, or..." Cole lets his sentence trail off, giving me the option to fill in the blank. I get the sense that if I took option one, he'd be fine with that. The idea of Cole trying to guilt me for not kissing him seems ludicrous.

He's the one that took me out for bagels rather than taking me to bed.

And despite how delicious that excursion was, no amount of cream cheese could get me to stop craving Cole.

"I choose *or*." My seat belt unbuckling sounds loud in the truck cab. Shifting around until I'm on my knees on my seat, I brace myself to make a wanton move. "That okay with you?"

Cole watches me, his eyes sharp as ice. When I tilt his way, his hands shoot out to steady me, and then I find myself guided onto his lap. With my knees on either side of his hips, the cotton of my dress bunches up around my thighs. I pull my mind away from that part of my body. If I think on it too long, my fingers might reach for Cole's zipper.

Trying to make my hands behave, I tangle them together behind Cole's head, leaning into his chest to bring our mouths close.

"Do you still want to make out with me?" I doubt he would've helped me into his lap if the answer was no, but it's always good to have clarity.

"Fuck yes." The way he mutters the curse has me shivering in anticipation. Then his mouth captures mine, and I'm no longer starving. I'm feasting.

Cole cups the back of my head, tilting me at the angle he wants, teasing my lips with his tongue until I open for him. The taste of him isn't like any food. He's a man, and he tastes like it. With his flavor on my tongue, I can't help thinking about sex. And when I think about sex, my hips rock in agreement with the direction of my thoughts.

"Summer." Cole growls my name against my mouth, as if chastising me.

I pull back, panting and blushing.

"Sorry! It's just...been a while. And you're..."

"I'm what?"

My brain stumbles over comparisons. "You're like drinking an entire bottle of red wine. I'm drunk and horny around you."

Suddenly, I find myself crushed against Cole's chest. He buries his face in my neck, groaning as if in pain.

Did I knee him?

"Cole?"

"Want me to take care of you?" His question comes out low and rumbly, paired with his touch brushing along the edge of my underwear. His hand found its way up my skirt at some point.

Thoughts of what he's offering tumble through my head. We're in a public parking lot, minutes away from me meeting his friends. But all I can focus on is how delicious it would be to orgasm right here, in Cole's truck, on his lap, his fingers bringing me there.

I want to lose myself in him, just for a little while.

"Yes." The whisper thickens the air in the cab of the truck.

Cole's open mouth brushes over my pulse, the heat of his breath burning my skin. The sensation is almost enough to distract from the tug of elastic as he pushes under the cotton of my panties.

But the moment a fingertip traces over my folds, nothing short of an explosion could take my attention away from the space between my legs.

Cole caresses my entrance, his finger becoming slick with my arousal.

I'm on the verge of begging for him to push inside me, when he moves away. But he doesn't leave me. Instead, his touch claims that perfect, sensitive spot that men often forget.

Cole Allemand pays tribute to my clit.

Intelligent thought ceases. My brain reverts to its primordial roots, where all it cares about is indulgence. I want to rub myself against him, mindless and wild. Nothing matters but the skill with which he teases my nerve endings. The edges of my vision blur because who needs to see when all their body is meant for is pleasure?

"Yes!" I gasp, realizing I've been chanting the word as my nails dig into Cole's shoulders.

He leans his head back, lids heavy, watching me as his fingers pluck me apart piece by piece.

"Do you... Should I...?" Thoughts and words are half-formed as I detach one of my hands from its death grip and finger the top button of his jeans.

The hand that isn't playing me like an expert grabs my wrist. He draws my palm up to his mouth, holding my eyes as he shakes his head before running his tongue over the meaty part at the base of my thumb.

"This is for you. All for you."

Who can complain about that? When he releases my wrist, I lean forward, pressing my body into his, tucking myself into his hard chest. It's that pressure, the connection of us touching in so many places, that has my insides tightening in eagerness.

Cole grips me to him, his hold so engulfing that I find myself restrained. All I can do is pant and feel the steady circular movement of his touch on my clit.

"You gonna come for me? You like me stroking your pussy?"

Send me to the archives of Hell. His dirty talk starts an erotic tremble in my muscles.

"I want... I want..."

"Tell me. I'll give it to you."

"Inside," is all I can gasp out, but he picks up on my meaning.

His vise around my waist loosens, and his second hand sneaks between my legs. One, then two fingers push into me. A satisfied moan mixes with the wet noises of him entering me.

"Fuck, Summer. You're soaking. This all for me?"

My head nods on its own. I shouldn't like the possessiveness in his voice, but my brain is stewing in a hot tub of lust, and the idea of Cole owning a part of me turns the heat higher.

He tilts his head, then a lot of things happen at once.

His tongue traces the shell of my ear.

His thumb and forefinger gently pinch my clit.

His fingers curl inside me.

I come apart in a torrent of pleasure.

A yelp leaves my throat, and as all my muscles clench and pulsate with my orgasm, my whimpers fill the cab of his truck. Damn, I sound like I'm about to start sobbing.

When I come down from my high, we're both breathing heavy. Cole's fingers are still inside me, as if he's loath to leave.

And as the bliss of orgasm clears from my mind, a blush I can't fight off infuses my face.

That just happened. It wasn't some sexy daydream I had on my lunch break.

Cole Allemand just fingered me in his truck while whispering dirty words in my ear.

Dragging in a deep breath, I sit up and eye the passenger seat, trying to figure out the best way to maneuver back into it.

"Summer?"

"Hmm?" My eyes have trouble meeting Cole's.

Where did all my confidence go? Was it fueled solely by my sex drive?

"You okay?"

"Me? Of course! Super great. Full of endorphins. Could probably run a marathon!" While avoiding his gaze, I spot the tightening at the corners of his mouth.

This is getting awkward. I'm making it awkward. But what did I expect when I jumped on the idea of hooking up with a bad boy? That I'd somehow be chill about it? That I could act nonchalant?

I've been allowing myself forbidden fantasies about Cole for *months,* and now his fingers are *still inside me!*

"Look at me," he commands.

"I am." The piercing in his lip is part of him.

"In my eyes."

"So demanding," I mutter, using a good deal of will power to force my gaze up to his, wondering if he can see the sunburn color of my skin even in the dim car. In the darkness, I can't make out the blue in his irises, but the powerful chill of his gaze is still present.

"Did you like this?" Cole emphasizes his question by curling his fingers, which has me gasping.

"Yes! I did. Very much."

"Are we good?"

"Yes." Just because my mind is all over the place doesn't mean I'm upset with Cole.

"Do you still want to meet my friends?"

"Yes." I'm sure adding more people into this is going to make everything even more convoluted, but I still have this ridiculous urge to know who the important people in Cole's life are.

"Okay." Gently, he slides his touch away, readjusting my underwear so it's no longer shoved to the side. "Kiss me." The command throws me off after his questions, but my eyes snag on his piercing again, and it's almost like the shiny metal hypnotizes me, enticing me forward.

Still, I have enough sense to keep my mouth closed as I press it to his. If I were to get another taste, I don't think I'd be able to stop myself from begging to repeat what we just did.

Cole lets me retreat, using his palms on my ass to help get me back in my seat.

As my heartrate normalizes, I take stock.

I am thoroughly debauched. My thighs still tingle, and my center feels swollen and sensitive. The damp fabric of my panties rubs against my vulva, an uncomfortable sensation with how sensitive I am now.

No way can I interact with people like this. I reach under my skirt, hooking my thumbs in the elastic waistband.

"What are you doing?"

"Taking off my underwear." I lift my ass to slide them down my thighs.

"Because...?"

"Because you made them all wet."

Cole's jaw clenches, then he's leaning over the center consul to capture my mouth in a searing kiss that leaves me panting. He pulls back just enough to trace his tongue over my bottom lip.

"Sorry." He says the word but doesn't sound in the least bit contrite.

"Sure you are." I'm breathless as I speak, shifting away from him so I can try to bring order to my thoughts. "Anyway, I'd rather spend the rest of the night going commando than wearing damp panties."

He returns to his seat. "So you're just...not going to have underwear on." Cole says the sentence like he's speaking to himself, staring out the windshield as he does.

"It's not like anyone will know," I point out, finishing my shimmy until I have the blue polka dot boy shorts off. They hang from my pointer finger as I consider where to store them.

All of a sudden, a long-fingered hand reaches out, snatching the material from my grasp.

Cole palms the panties, then opens his glove compartment and shoves them inside, shutting the little door with a definitive click.

When I meet his eyes, they burn into mine.

"I'll know."

Chapter Twenty-Four

COLE

"Oh my god! Cole, wait!" Summer whisper-yells at me, tugging on our clasped hands.

We've only made it halfway across the parking lot, and I'm hoping this change of direction has to do with Summer wanting to go another round.

Instead, she stares up at me, eyes wide in almost delighted horror.

"What?"

"I can't—" She buries her face in my chest, and it takes me a second to realize her whole body is shaking from laughter.

"Summer?"

"Sorry!" She tilts her head back, still chuckling, actual tears gathering in the corner of her eyes. "It's just, next time remind me to make out with you *before* I put on my lipstick."

My attention drops to her mouth, and I realize the burgundy color on her lips is smeared at the edges.

"You're saying this is all over my face?" I brush a thumb over her bottom lip, eliciting a shiver.

What I wouldn't give for a mirror.

"Not *all* over. Just in the main make out spots. Here, I can fix it." She rummages around in the purse hanging from her shoulder. I keep my hand on her waist, holding her close, fiddling with the large knitted cardigan she's wearing over her dress.

A second later, Summer rips open a small package that looks a hell of a lot like a condom. Turns out it's a wipe.

"Keep still." She reaches up to pinch my chin, then proceeds to clean my face, making me feel like a kid who couldn't eat his ice cream cone without smearing chocolate all over his cheeks. That image lasts only for a second because her movements become less abrupt and more sensual. The cool cloth swipes over my mouth, massaging my lips, her gaze focused solely on the way she strokes me.

After what we just did in my truck, I had to tuck my hard dick into my waistband to keep from walking around with an obvious boner. Having her look at me like this, touch me in this intimate way, is not helping anything get soft.

"Okay. I think I got it all." She retracts her hand but then holds the wipe out for me to take. "Think you can fix me up, or should I just wipe it all off?"

Without answering, I pluck the cloth from her and cup her chin in my palm.

She wants to wear her lipstick on her perfectly shaped mouth? I can make that happen.

Using just a corner of the damp little wipe, I concentrate on tracing the edge of her lips, getting rid of all the smears I'm responsible for. The sight of her disheveled has my blood hot, but the image is only for me. The rest of the world gets adorable put-together Summer. I'm the one who gets sensual, wild, sex-mussed Summer.

When I'm done, there's no trace of the way I ravished her other than the flush on her neck and cheeks.

"Am I good?" she asks, as if there's a possibility I'd say no.

"You're perfect."

For that answer, she decides to torture me, sinking her teeth into her bottom lip.

Shit. I want to fuck up her makeup again.

Instead, I twine my fingers with hers and turn back toward the bar, glad that the rain stopped before we arrived. There's no way I'd keep my hands to myself if she were wet, too.

Well...wetter.

Through the crowded restaurant, I spot my friends, Dash and Paige. They've claimed a table in the back corner, and it looks like Paige's friend decided to join us.

"They're over there." I point the way to Summer, wrapping my arm around her waist and pulling her against my side to keep her away from the crush of bodies.

"Oh yeah! You have a picture of them at your place. But who's the brunette?"

"Paige's friend. In town visiting for a few days."

"She looks so..." Summer trails off in a distracted way.

We're almost halfway across the room when Summer gasps.

"Is something—"

"Shhh!" Summer shushes me, all the while shoving me in a different direction than the table.

"What—"

"In here! Now!" Summer is deceptively strong, pushing me into a room with little effort before slamming and locking the door behind her.

If not for her panicked look, I might think she wants to repeat what we just did in my truck. Hell knows I want to.

"Summer. Talk to me. What's going on?"

Instead of answering, she starts to pace, chewing on her thumbnail all the while.

Seeing her pass by a urinal, I feel the need to point out, "This is the men's bathroom."

She stops and spins toward me. "It's not my fault this restaurant decided to subscribe certain genders to certain toilets!"

This is an interesting version of my librarian. Kind of reminds me of her birthday freak-out. I'm just wondering what it is about my friends that set her off.

"Dash and Paige are nice," I offer, in case that has her worried.

"I'm sure they are." She's back to pacing.

"If you're not ready to meet them, we can reschedule."

Instead of calming down, Summer steps into my space, balling the collar of my shirt in her hands. "Do you know who they're sitting with?"

The brunette? "Paige mentioned her writer friend would be in town."

"Writer friend?" Summer's voice squeaks "That is *Marianna Tweep*."

The name sounds vaguely familiar, and I wonder if Paige has mentioned the woman before.

"Do you know her?"

"Of course I do! Well..." Summer steps back, her hands releasing my shirt only to flutter frantically as if they're domestic birds set loose from their cages. "I know of her. Whenever she puts pen to page it's an instant bestseller. And she writes memoirs, so it's like I know her intimately. But I've never met her. And you'll see why."

"I will?"

"Don't you get it? I'm going to gush!" Summer's confession is agonized, her palms pressed to her forehead as if she might have a fever. "I'm going to gush all over her, and your friends are going to tell you to shun me!" She starts pulling paper towels out of the dispenser one at a time, until she has two massive handfuls.

"Hey, babe." I keep my voice mildly curious. "What're those for?"

Summer stares at her hands, then back up at me, her expression completely baffled.

"I don't know!" she wails, pacing back and forth across the tiny room. "Help me, Cole!"

My librarian is adorable, but I keep that to myself.

"Do you think alcohol might help?" I ask.

"Maybe. I'll try anything."

"Okay. Stay here. I'll get you a beer. What do you drink?"

When I have her order, I slip out of the bathroom and weave my way toward the bar. My route has me catching eyes with Dash, who throws a curious look my way. I gesture that I need a minute, and he nods. That's one of the great things about Dash. He doesn't push when it's not necessary.

Back at the men's bathroom, cold beer in hand, I knock lightly.

"Occupied!"

"It's me."

Summer whips open the door and waves me inside, immediately taking the beer off my hands and sucking down a huge swallow. At first, her wacky reaction amused me, but now I'm legitimately worried she's going to give herself a panic attack.

"Let me know if you want to leave."

"I don't want to leave! I want to live in her brain!"

"Okay." My hands go up in surrender. "How about I head over and say hi, and you text me if you need another beer before you come to the table."

Summer only stares wide-eyed at me over the rim of her glass as she steadily chugs the contents.

All I can think is how perfectly my plan would have worked if I had gotten a book deal before asking her out. I mean, things seem to be progressing at a good pace on their own, but I wouldn't have had any worries about her interest if there was a publishing contract behind my name.

"It'll be fine." I lean down and press a kiss to her forehead before slipping out of the bathroom again.

Three sets of eyes stare up at me when I reach the table.

"Everything okay?" Dash asks as he stands up to give me a one-armed hug.

"Summer is in the bathroom." And the warmth of her presence diminishes slightly when I look over at Marianna, the woman who has my girl downing a beer just to function.

Marianna Tweep is *Playboy* magazine centerfold gorgeous. Even dressed in jeans, she looks ready to walk a runway with her ebony hair and red-lipped smile. Paige was probably paying me a compliment when she thought this woman would be interested in me. And at one point in my life, I would've been all about getting with her for a night.

But she's not Summer.

I look to Paige. "She's nice?" Maybe talking about the woman like she's not here isn't the most polite route, but if this famous author is an asshole, I'm not letting Summer anywhere near her.

Paige seems to understand, smiling up at me in a reassuring manner. "She's the best."

I nod, returning my attention to the bombshell. "My girlfriend loves you. She's going to be weird about it."

"Weird how?"

"Weird perfect." I glare.

"Oh good. That's the best kind." A purely joyful smile splits across the writer's ruby lips.

And I feel strangely at peace with the situation.

"Hello." The stiff greeting comes from just behind me, and I turn to see Summer hanging back a couple of steps, her hands wrapped tightly around her almost empty beer glass, her eyes flicking to the visiting author and then away from her just as fast.

Moving to Summer's side, I wrap an arm around her waist and guide her forward, eyeing each person at the table, daring them to say anything to make Summer feel bad.

"Hello! I'm Paige. This is Dash. We're Cole's friends. This is Marianna. She doesn't know Cole, so you're not the only newbie at the table. Come. Sit. Join us. Eat some fries." The blonde is all eager cheer, shoving her food toward us.

"Nice to meet you all. I'm Summer." Her voice is likely to crack, it's so stiff.

Everyone at the table pretends not to notice the way she moves robotically, sitting in her chair as if the function was programed into her coding rather than a decision she made as a human being.

I'm not a good conversation starter, but I dig in my brain for something to say that will put Summer at ease.

"Want another beer?"

Not gonna win any genius awards here. Her huge eyes flick to me full of panicked thanks. She knows I'm trying, even when I'm bad at it.

"Summer, did you know I once met a prince?" Marianna asks.

My girlfriend's head whips around so fast my hands twitch to reach out and check her neck for injuries.

"I— No. No, I didn't know that." My librarian is breathless as she leans toward the woman, enraptured before the story even begins.

Briefly, I wonder if this dinner is going to end up screwing me over in a way I hadn't expected. I know I'm gone on Summer, but she hasn't agreed to anything more than dating. I should've clarified I meant exclusively. Paige never said if Marianna is interested in women as well as men.

And that's not something I thought to ask Summer.

As the gorgeous writer starts speaking again, I reach under the table to clasp my date's hand. Her death-grip return squeeze is slightly reassuring.

"I did. But you see, it was not planned. I was dining out with a dear friend in London, and all of a sudden the waiter appears at my table with a note on a silver platter, as if it were part of the meal." While Marianna describes this, a group of men in Saints jerseys shout at a TV mounted above the bar, making it clear we're in a different type of establishment than the one in her story.

"What did the note say?" Summer is homed in, her eyes tracking as Marianna sips her beer.

"Well," she pats her lips with a napkin, "it was an invitation. Apparently the prince, who shall remain nameless and country-less for this story, was also eating there and recognized me when I walked in. You see, I was in London for some television appearances and other publicity for my new book. I am a writer if you did not know."

I fight against the urge to roll my eyes. Summer nods vigorously.

"So, what did you do?" This question comes from Paige, who seems just as enthralled with her friend's story.

"Of course, I politely declined. The offer was generous, but I was with a friend. If a prince were to walk in here and ask for my attention, I would do the same."

Grudgingly, I admit to myself that that was a badass kind of move.

"But if you turned him down, how did you two meet?" Summer asks this. I'm surprised to find she's no longer on the verge of crawling over the table anymore. Instead, she relaxes slightly, her grip on my hand becoming more pleasant than bone-breaking.

"You see, this prince did not take my refusal well. He decided if I would not join him at his table, he would join me at mine."

Damn. Rich people are pushy assholes. Not that this is news.

"The man strolled over, had the waitstaff push an additional table against our very cozy two-person arrangement, and then he sat beside me and proceeded to complain about the wine the sommelier had selected for him and comment on my outfit choice during one of my appearances."

"He insulted your outfit?"

"Oh no. He loved my outfit. Claimed it showed every one of my delicious curves to its best advantage. In fact, my outfit was so lovely, he had not been able to listen to a word I spoke and therefore wanted me to tell him about my book."

"What did you do?"

Marianna gives us a smile that promises a fantastic response, but she teases us by taking a long leisurely swallow of her beer and patting her lips dry before continuing.

"I kissed him."

Our table is almost as loud in our reactions as the football fans.

"What?"

"No!"

"He didn't deserve to lick your dirty dishes!" Summer pounds the table with her fist, finally sounding more like herself.

Paige is the only one smiling, too. She watches Marianna with knowing eyes. "What happened next?"

The woman taps a finger against her red lips. "He was quite surprised. And then pleased. The prince placed his hand on my knee and asked why I had kissed him. No doubt he was expecting me to say that I couldn't resist, or that I had always wanted to sleep with a prince."

She takes a moment to meet each of our eyes, and I'm hit with the level of her skill. Marianna is a masterful storyteller. No wonder her books sell by the millions. If she ever holds a class, I'll empty out my savings account to attend.

"But I told him the truth. That I had hoped I could live a fairy tale." Now she leans close, drawing the four of us in with her. We're puppets on her string. "Only, I wished for a fairy tale in reverse. I wanted to kiss a prince and have him turn into a frog."

Dash chokes on a laugh as Paige gives a happy whoop. Summer rests her head on my shoulder, giggles spilling out of her.

"Needless to say, he did not stay. And I left the exchange with all my illusions of princes shattered. I do not believe I have met a more insufferable person." Marianna grins at me across the table.

That's when the true purpose of her anecdote dawns on me.

This whole display was not to brag about her celebrity acquaintances or to dazzle us with her storytelling abilities.

Every word was for Summer's benefit. Not only is my librarian relaxed, leaning into my side. She also knows that there is a very low bar she needs to hurdle to keep from being the most annoying person Marianna has ever met.

I give the author a small nod, and she winks in return.

As long as Marianna doesn't have plans to tempt Summer away from me, she's cool in my book.

When things settle, Summer speaks up in a not-at-all robotic voice. "I'm sorry. I just have to say, I devoured your latest book. I never thought I'd find sex dungeons interesting."

"What?" Dash and I ask in unison.

"Wasn't it great? I edited it." Paige works remotely for an NYC publisher, and Marianna must not only be her friend but one of her writers. "I had to do some research myself to make sure my commenting was on point." she adds, like her words aren't just setting off a bomb in my ex-roommate's mind.

"Research? What kind? How is this the first I'm hearing of this?" Dash tugs the menu out of his girlfriend's hands so she has to look at him.

"Oh stop. It's not like I went to one. I meant reading. Watching videos. Making sure I knew the terminology and how things look."

"You've been watching sex dungeon porn? Without me?"

"It was for work."

"Does it have to be?"

Paige slaps her hand over Dash's mouth even as her eyes laugh.

Then Marianna launches into a description of the interview process for becoming a dominatrix.

Despite the fascinating conversation, it's not long before Paige's lips pinch, her eyes twitching toward the bar then back to me, a clear message in them.

After the message I texted her and Dash before this dinner, I expected something like this. But Summer's hand is twined with mine, and she's eagerly asking Marianna intelligent questions, and I have a delicious beer in my hand. I want to pretend like everything is right in the world.

I ignore the message.

So Paige shouts it at me.

"Let's go get the next round, Cole!"

A grimace threatens to curve my mouth, but I force out the semblance of a smile. "You want anything?" I ask close to Summer's ear.

She beams up at me. "Just a water, please."

I press my lips to the side of her head, breathing in her sweet scent and praying to the universe that Paige isn't about to tear my world down.

Chapter Twenty-Five

COLE

"Why are you asking us to lie to her?"

Paige and I stand at the bar, far enough away from our table to have a private conversation, but close enough to see our three companions chatting.

"Because it's not important," I mutter.

Before Summer and I arrived, I texted both Dash and Paige, telling them to keep info about my stint in prison to themselves. Not that it's a topic we normally discuss, but seeing as how it's the catalyst for Dash and my friendship, there's a chance it could come up.

"If it's not important, then just tell her. Dash told me almost immediately." Paige drums her fingers on the bar top as she stares up at me, confusion dipping her brows. She has a small scar that bisects one eyebrow from a car crash she was in in high school, and I find myself focusing on that rather than meeting her eyes.

"It's not important, but some people think it is."

"And you think Summer is one of these people?"

"I don't know." And I'm not willing to risk it. "She's a rule follower." And for a good chunk of my past, I was not. I want her too badly to risk her judgment. I'm being selfish, and I don't care.

"Do these lies have an expiration date?"

I firm my mouth and only answer when Paige's normally sweet features morph into a glare.

"When I'm sure she won't care."

"So maybe never?"

"Do you think I'll make a bad boyfriend?" I ask instead, avoiding her question. But I also want to know the answer because I can't help thinking how easily I could screw this all up.

Paige chews her lip and huffs, eyes tracing over me. Finally she responds, still not sounding particularly happy. "In every category other than honesty, I'm sure you'd be awarded an A. But honesty is a big category."

Paige would know. The relationship she was in before meeting Dash ended because the guy was cheating on her, and she found out only by walking in on them.

"I would never lie about something that would hurt her."

"Just the act of being lied to can hurt."

That gets to me, and I rub at my chest in an effort to ease the guilt.

"Could you stop saying smart things?" I growl. "Just...look at her, Paige."

We glance over together. Summer is telling some story that has her gesturing wildly with her hands and both Dash and Marianna laughing into their beers.

There's a flush in her cheeks, an eager glow in her eyes, and a wide smile that invites everyone around to join in on her happiness. Everything about her says *this woman is sweet and kind, and good.*

She's the opposite of me. I've never wanted anyone or anything so much as her.

"She's great." Paige rests her hand on my forearm as she speaks, the touch demanding my full attention. "Which is why I don't want you to mess things up."

Her voicing my worries ratchets up my anxiety. "I need time."

My friend turns back to stare at Summer as I order our drinks. Once I've signed my name on the check, she tilts her chin toward me.

"Summer is your succubus?"

A guy at the bar gives my friend a long, strange look. Well that'll teach him not to listen in on private conversations. I, on the other hand, understand exactly what she means.

Paige read over my manuscript before I sent it out to agents. She works as a professional book editor and was the only one outside the writers group I trusted to give me honest feedback. Just now, she's referencing the love between my warlord protagonist and the beautiful succubus from a warring nation. My book is essentially a romance, with the warlord pursuing his love despite the world telling him it's forbidden.

Summer feels just as off-limits to me, but I could give a shit.

"She is."

My friend grumbles to herself before sipping from her beer. After swallowing, she sighs.

"All right. Okay. To be honest, I didn't tell Dash everything right off the bat either. But"—she holds up a finger to insist on my attention —"things didn't start to feel real between us until I did. So keep that in mind."

I nod, holding my breath, knowing Paige isn't done.

"Friends don't lie to each other about big stuff, and it seems like you want Dash and me to be friends with Summer."

"I do."

"Then figure this out, Cole. Find a way to tell her that works for you." Her words have me preparing another nod, but she keeps going. "And if she doesn't take it well, then maybe she's not the person for you."

That has my muscles locking. Paige makes it sound so casual. Like things not working out for me and Summer is somehow acceptable.

And that's where we diverge.

"Let's take these to the table." I pick up my beer in one hand, grab Summer's water in the other, then clasp Marianna's beer with a skillful maneuver of my fingers.

Paige doesn't stop me, and I hope that means she's done with this topic.

Back with our group, Summer beams up at me and reaches to help with the glasses. I let her warm fingers brush against mine, remembering what it felt like to have them digging into my shoulders and tangling in my hair. I consider telling everyone I forgot something important in my truck and dragging her back outside to push my hand under her skirt again.

Which only reminds me that Summer doesn't have anything on under her dress.

I sit down fast to hide the reaction my body has to that thought. At this rate, I'm going to be hard the entire night.

Summer turns her attention back to Dash. "How did you and Cole meet?"

Fuck. Of course she'd ask that. Summer wants to know *everything*.

Dash glances at me and I try to convey to him how important it is that he lies. Or evade. Or pretend to pass out.

"We were neighbors." Not completely untrue. We did live right next to each other for a stretch of time. "Then we were roommates."

Tension eases from my chest knowing that Dash has my back. For now at least.

"Oh right! You're the mechanic! Cole gave me your number. He seems to think I need to get work done on my car."

"And you don't?" Dash asks.

"No. I do. I just think if I tell Cole he's right too many times he'll get a big head. I can't have bigheaded people walking around my library, knocking books off the shelves with their ears. It would be cataloging chaos."

"I love librarians."

I eye Marianna, trying to ascertain if her comment is innocent or suggestive.

The woman smiles at the both of us, so I can't tell.

Feeling possessive, I rest my hand on the bare skin of Summer's thigh, just below the edge of her skirt.

Her eyes flick to mine, a tinge of red decorating the tops of her cheeks.

Maybe it wouldn't matter if Ms. Tweep is interested. I seem to be able to hold the librarian's attention, even with a *New York Times* bestselling author at the table.

Which means if this relationship crashes and burns, I doubt I'll have anyone to blame but myself.

SUMMER

I have reached the chillest level I can possibly acquire while sitting at a table with Marianna Tweep. My gushing has been kept to a minimum, and the woman doesn't seem to be searching for a quick exit or a police officer to put in between the two of us.

Success.

"Bathroom," Cole mutters before pressing a kiss to the side of my head and unfolding himself from the bench we're settled on.

Paige and Dash's eyes track him as if he's a creature in the zoo that fascinates them. Marianna smiles around at the crowded restaurant, and I finally take a moment to examine Cole's friends.

They're a cute couple, Paige all curves and beautiful blonde hair, while Dash is sharp angles and dark edges. Also, they've been nice to me from the second I sat down, despite my babbling.

Which is why I feel slightly guilty I'm about to scold them.

Only slightly though.

"Cole's birthday was last week."

Marianna refocuses on me, her mouth widening to a grin. Paige and Dash stare across the table at me, both appearing confused.

"That's right," Dash nods, as if he thinks I am looking for clarification.

"I found out when we were sitting in a bar and the bartender wished him a happy birthday after looking at his ID. Now, mind you, this was a last-minute plan to get a drink." And admittedly had a very good conclusion, so I shouldn't be complaining. But I can't let this go. "So I'm wondering, what exactly would Cole have done if I hadn't been able to spend half the day with him. On his birthday."

I think they're picking up what I'm putting down when Dash grimaces and Paige bites her lip.

"Cole gets breakfast with his dad on his birthday, and then he likes to spend the rest of the day on his own. I've known him for a few years now. The first couple, I tried to get him to do something. He didn't want to. But that's Cole. If he doesn't want to do something, then he won't."

"But he didn't spend the day alone. I was there," I point out.

Instead of looking defensive or annoyed, Dash gives me an almost rakish grin. "You were. You know you're the first person he's introduced us to."

"Romantic person," Paige adds.

Oh, they're good. Master topic changers. I'm so tempted to follow the trail they're trying to lead me down, but I can't let things go just yet.

"Please just tell me he got something more than the horrible day I unknowingly doled out."

"Horrible day? Hmm, this sounds like a good story." Marianna leans her elbow on the table, chin in her hand, gorgeous eyes on me.

And all my words become as easy to grasp as bubbles, popping into nothingness when I attempt to catch one and give it to her.

"I'm sure it wasn't bad," Paige offers with a reassuring smile.

That refocuses me.

"We went to a *cemetery*."

"The cemetery tours are interesting. I was planning on taking Marianna on one before she leaves," the blonde offers.

"We didn't go as tourists. He escorted me to my dad's grave."

"Oh. Um. How did that go?" Paige cringes even as she asks the question.

"Well it went fine for me because I didn't have to cry alone. But it wasn't my birthday."

Paige reaches across the table, twining her fingers with mine in an almost intimate gesture that I find immensely comforting. "For Cole's birthday, Dash installed a new sound system in his truck, and I got him a subscription to the magazine *Writer's Digest*. The night before his birthday, we went to his place, made him dinner, and drank some beer around his fire pit."

Cole has a fire pit? I need to check that out.

"If he wanted to spend the day with us, we would've dropped everything in a second, and he knows that. But he didn't even text us. So, whatever Cole did on his birthday was his choice. It was what he wanted to do."

"Or who he wanted to do," Marianna murmurs with a wicked smirk.

Damn, my face feels hot.

But there're so many different causes, I can't figure out how to calm down. Paige's description of their birthday gifts has me embarrassed that I ever doubted them. But her insistence that Cole chose to spend the day with me has my pulse all fluttery. Then Marianna's comment brings the embarrassment back around.

Not that everyone thinks we slept together. But that everyone thinks we slept together when we haven't.

Why didn't we? I basically gift-wrapped myself for Cole, and he chose bagels. Over sex.

What's up with that?

Does he...not want me like that?

My mind traces back to his truck. That was glorious and sexy.

And I'm the only one who got off.

But he was turned on.

Right?

It's hard to think of him as a fuck buddy with no fucking.

"You want another drink?" The question pairs with a hand on my back, and I jump in my seat. Paige lets our fingers detangle, smiling over my shoulder at the man we were just discussing. "Everything okay?" Cole leans down to meet my eyes, probably thrown off by my reaction and my tomato complexion.

"Yes! Of course. Are you okay? How was the...bathroom?"

Cole's lips twitch. "Fine."

"That's good. Hate it when you have a bad trip to the bathroom. Ruins the whole night."

Dash snorts and Marianna raises her glass in a cheer.

"Drink?" he asks again.

"Yes. Please. Another beer would be great."

He nods and heads off toward the bar.

Dash and Paige watch him again. They clearly think Cole is acting out of the ordinary. But I don't know what normal is for him, so I have no means of measurement.

Questions rattle through my mind.

If I was someone else, I might let them fester.

But I'm a librarian. Finding answers to questions is my job.

Chapter Twenty-Six

COLE

"Why didn't you get me naked on Tuesday? I mean, I was practically *begging* for it."

My hands jerk, causing us to swerve in the lane. I'm quick to straighten us out again, but that doesn't do anything to get rid of her words.

Shit, now I have to drive with the fantasy of Summer lying in my bed, completely bare, crowding my mind. I glance to the side to make sure she's buckled in in case I rear-end someone.

"You didn't beg," I mutter.

"Do you want me to?"

Fucking hell. "Summer. Stop."

Her burgundy lips curve in an adorable scowl. "I don't get you, Cole. One minute you're all over me, the next you're saying 'Let's get bagels!' I mean, yeah, those bagels were delicious, but they weren't what I wanted in my mouth." She stares at me, and I think I'm sweating more than the evening calls for. "It was your dick, FYI. That's what I wanted in my mouth. Which I thought was pretty obvious."

I flex my fingers, wanting to fist them in frustration. Why do I always say the wrong thing around her? Hearing all this dirty imagery is not helping me focus.

"Can we talk about this when I'm not driving?"

A huge sigh gusts out of her, and she presses her palm against her chest. "Are you feeling guilty? Because of my dad and what that day was to me?"

"No."

"Then..." She trails off, shaking her head in confusion. "You know, this doesn't have to be more. We can still be just friends."

"No." I try not to growl at her. "We're dating." She agreed. Hell, she's the one bringing up the idea of us sleeping together.

Her hands fiddle with the seatbelt across her chest. "Does dating involve us sleeping together?"

"You want to fuck?" Curses tumble through my brain, all directed at myself.

That's what I say to her? The girl I want to think of me as long term gets *You want to fuck?*

I'm an ass.

Summer taps her nails against the old leather of the seat. "Well, not on the side of the road. I tend to be a fuck-in-a-bed kind of girl. Also, I'd rather not have a pity fuck. I mean, you're so handsome my eyes want to pop out of my head and follow you around, so I'm sure I'd get off. But I also don't sleep with someone unless they're having as much fun as I am. So I guess that's a long way of saying, I wanted to fuck when I thought you wanted to fuck, but now that I know you don't want to fuck, I do not either."

"I never said I didn't."

"Not with your words. But you've had opportunities and let them pass by. I mean, you're not abstinent are you?"

"No."

"Okay then, there we have it. Not-abstinent Cole Allemand has had multiple chances to do the deed and for some reason didn't. My guess is the answer is the most obvious. That you don't want to."

We're a mile from my house, the last few minutes of the drive passing at a tortuous pace because Summer thinks I don't want to sleep with her.

"You're wrong."

"So you do want to fuck me?"

"Since the first day I met you."

Her face reddens, and she presses her palms against her cheeks as if to wipe the color away. "I don't believe you."

I turn onto my street and speak to the windshield. "You were wearing a blue dress and a bunch of jingly bracelets. When I asked where the writers group was meeting you smiled at me like I said you won the lottery. So yeah, I wanted to find a private room, push your skirt up, and make your jewelry rattle." My final word is emphasized by me shifting the truck into park.

We're back at my place, and I'm done passing up my opportunities.

"It's not sanitary, but I want to lick all of your piercings." She whispers the words like a confession, and my hard-on from earlier makes a reappearance.

"Get inside. Now."

"We're going to fuck?" The way she asks the question, as if delighted with the idea, has me growling and ripping off my seatbelt.

Summer's smile is all excitement and teasing as she unbuckles her own, shoves open the car door, and sprints for the front porch. I'm right behind her, key in hand, arm wrapping around her waist. We're barely inside before our mouths find each other, hungry and searching.

We stumble through the front room, locked together. She's delicious, and soft, and all mine.

Falling onto my bed, our next mission is getting rid of every piece of clothing between us. Love her little dress, so easy to remove in one motion. My stupid clothes make things more difficult. There's the zipper, and shoes and socks that need to come off before my pants can. I wish I had claws to tear at them, but the experience becomes more fun when Summer lends a hand, kneeling on the bed in only a bra, pulling the legs of my jeans until they slide off.

The teasing triangle of dark curls at the apex of her thighs sets a fire in my mind, made hotter knowing I have the view because I confiscated her panties earlier.

How could she think this wouldn't get physical between us? I can barely keep my hands off her. My fingers want to rub her clit until she's whimpering, promising to be mine forever if I just give her the release she craves.

Curious fingers trace over the designs on my body. Now that I'm naked, she can see every mythical creature claiming an inch of my skin.

Despite the glory of her soft touch, I'm not satisfied. Parts of her are still covered. Mainly, her nipples. I need to see those peaks get tight with pleasure, silently begging for my tongue to tease them.

Grabbing Summer's hand, I tug her down so her front lands on the cushion of my mattress and I can reach the clasp on the back of her bra. But the second my fingers finish with the tiny hooks, a distinct darkness, low on Summer's body, catches my eye.

I move lower, fascinated.

"What is this?"

Summer shifts to look where I'm staring. "Oh, my tattoo?"

I have a brief mental glitch.

Once recovered, I sling my leg over both of hers and press my palm into her lower back, holding her still so I can examine the little lines of ink. The picture is simple, and I rub my thumb across it to make sure it's not just a pen drawing. But even as the pad of my finger puckers her plump ass cheek, dragging over the silky skin, the image remains, showing no signs of smearing.

A happy face. Summer has a happy face the size of a quarter on her right ass cheek.

"What are you doing?"

Glancing up, I catch her gazing at me over her shoulder. Those beautiful brown eyes so curious I want to give them something to be shocked about. Bending my neck slightly, I drag my tongue over her tattoo, keeping hold of her eyes the entire time.

Lips part, lashes flutter, and her back contracts on a gasped breath.

"You have a tattoo," I growl, even though I'm fucking overjoyed by the discovery.

"Should I have told you?" Her question is breathless.

"You should have shown me. Sooner. Months ago. Fuck me, Summer."

"I want to," she practically whines, wiggling under my steel grip that still has her pinned to the bed.

But I don't let her go. I don't think I'll ever be able to. My fingers sneak in between her thighs, finding damp curls. She gasps at my searching touch, raising her ass another inch off the bed as if she's hoping to give me better access.

And I need to be inside her.

But I want her just like this.

"Can you reach the nightstand?"

Summer glances back at me, then stretches an arm out, fingers tapping against my bedside table.

Good. "In the drawer. Get me a condom."

Her hands fumble around, searching blindly as I keep her body pinned to the bed. Finally, she passes a foil packet to me.

"I'm going to take you like this." I palm an ass cheek, and her hips grind into the bed. "That good?"

"Yes!" Her voice is all lusty exhale, the sound making my balls tighten.

Quickly, I have the rubber out and rolling onto my cock. Keeping my hand pressed into her lower back, I shift over her body, settling my aching head at her entrance.

"You ready for me?"

"Please, Cole." She arches her back, another invitation.

Slowly, I slide into her. A small corner of my brain worries I'll pass out from ecstasy before I make us both come. With my hips taking over the job of holding her down, I brace an arm by her shoulder and slide my other hand between her belly and the sheets until I plunge into her curls and search out the top of her slit.

Summer's nails dig into the blanket, and she rocks back into me, begging with her body.

My thrusts are measured. Despite all the talk of fucking, I want this to be more than that. Not jackhammering into her. This is about showing Summer all the pleasure I can bring her. Convince her to come back to me every day with hungry eyes and a wet pussy.

"Cole," she whimpers my name, writhing beneath me.

"You gonna come for me?"

Summer lets out a moan as I circle that sensitive little nub with the pad of my finger.

"I want..." Her half-finished thought has my curiosity raging.

"Tell me. Tell me what you want." This time I press deep into her, emphasizing my words.

"I-I need you to..." Again she hesitates, her neck turning red.

I lean over her, pressing my chest against her back.

"Say it," I command as I pull out and enter her again.

After a small gasp, she relents. "Pinch my clit."

That's right. In my car, that's what had her going over the edge. With an evil smile she can't see, I maneuver my thumb and forefinger to either side of her pleasure center. For a handful of seconds, I tease her, pressing only light enough that she knows I'm there.

"Cole." My name comes from her lips like a hiss.

I fucking love it.

So I reward her, giving Summer what she needs.

Her wet heat pulsates around my cock as my ears are caressed by her choked little gasps.

Curses flow from my mouth on their own, and I rise to my knees, pulling her hips up with me. My palms grasping her upper thighs, thumbs digging into her soft ass, I watch with torturous pleasure as I slip in and out of her pussy until the sight and the feel drag me into the most intense orgasm I've had to date.

As I come, my thoughts go haywire, blood rushing so loud that I can't hear myself shout her name.

But I still feel the sweet shape of it on my lips.

SUMMER

With Cole's hands on my ass, his leg between my thighs, his chest smashing my boobs in a surprisingly glorious way, I am pinned to the shower wall. After orgasming in the bed, we decided to christen the bathroom. The tile was a cool shock at first, but the warmth from my skin balanced the temperature out.

Everything around me is warm. The wall at my back, the spray of the water, the man I've wrapped my arms around, the breath we share.

This is what a dragon must feel like. Toasty warm all the time.

But warm is too mild a word for Cole.

He is scorching. Every spot we touch, which is a hell of a lot of spots, burns. He burns so good. My muscles are as liquid as the droplets trickling down my skin. Good thing Cole is holding me up. I'm a baked soufflé, on the verge of collapse.

His lips devour mine, stealing my breath every time I remember to gasp one out. When I inhale it's all him, filling my lungs with Cole.

I don't consider that it's probably better practice to fill my lungs with oxygen.

I'm too gone.

And then I am gone.

...

...

When my brain starts to function again, my first thought is...

What's that annoying tapping?

Then Cole's voice comes to my ears like someone slowly turning up the volume on a car radio.

"Summer! Come on, open your eyes. Please." There's a desperation to his words that helps draw me up from the dark fog. I blink and wonder why Cole is crouching over me.

Why am I not pressed up against the wall anymore? I liked it there.

"Fucking hell. You scared the shit out of me." Cole's hot hands cup my face, and I my brain tilts again. "Oh no. No you don't."

He moves, and suddenly the overwhelming warmth is cut with a surprisingly refreshing chill.

"What...?" I move my head around and realize I'm lying at the bottom of the tub.

"You passed out. Here." Cole clasps me under the armpits, supporting all my weight as he helps me stand.

On wobbly legs, I step out of the now-cold shower. Cole keeps me upright by sliding an arm around my waist and bracing me against his side. A moment later, a fluffy towel presses against my damp skin. Cole wraps me in the thing, securing it under my arms, before he settles me onto the toilet.

"Head between your legs. Deep breaths." His palm on my back

guides me down, and I finally can breathe normally. My head clears as blood winds its way back to my brain.

I also realize that Cole's erection is bobbing not too far from my face as he crouches beside me.

"You're still hard," I point out.

Cole huffs out a laugh that doesn't sound amused. "My dick is selfish. Ignore it."

"I don't want to hurt his feelings," I murmur.

Fingers briefly press into my back, then begin to rub soothing circles. "You're still loopy."

"Sounds like normal." I grin into my lap, this whole situation suddenly hilarious. A snicker sneaks out, then a chuckle.

A second later I'm full on snorting, with laughter spilling out of me in waves.

"Definitely still out of it," Cole mutters, pushing the wet strands of hair away from my face.

"I-I can't believe I-I p-passed out!" My snorts turn to hiccups, which is all the more comical to me.

Cole looks worried though, scooping me off my seat and carrying me out of the bathroom. It's even cooler away from the humid space, and goosebumps prickle over my arms. We settle on the bed, Cole with his back against the wall, and me in his lap, still dissolving into a giggling mess.

When the hilarity has calmed down into random spurts, Cole presses his lips against the side of my head.

"How do you feel?"

I take mental stock of myself. My one elbow smarts. I wonder if I hit it on my way down. Other than that, just a little weak.

"I'm good. What happened, exactly?"

Cole's arms tighten around me, pulling me flush against his chest.

"We were kissing."

"Yep, I remember that bit."

"Then you just went boneless. I backed off to see what was up and you slid down the wall. Scared the hell out of me."

"Oh no. I'm sorry." I rub my hand over his chest, only now realizing that his heart is racing.

Pushing myself up into a seated position, I take full stock of Cole. He's still naked, but instead of lounging on the bed in his normal relaxed style, his muscles all have a hard, tense look to them. Plus, when I meet his eyes, I find myself looking into overly wide pupils.

Maybe I'm not the one we should be worried about.

"How do *you* feel?" I ask, cupping his face in my hands.

His lids close as a deep breath fills his chest. "I'm not the one who passed out."

"But if you were, I would've been pretty shook up." And I realize just how much when the scenario flashes through my mind. "So, how do you feel?"

"Fine."

His answer is too quick to be genuine. "I don't think you are. You can tell me if something is wrong, Cole. I swear I won't judge you."

He watches me, and his tongue fiddles with his lip piercing before he gives me an answer. "A few years back my dad had a heart attack."

Guilt stabs past my ribcage. "And me passing out reminded you of that?"

Instead of saying anything, Cole sits up to wrap me in his arms and tug me back down to his chest. We lay in his bed, cuddling for a long time.

"If you ever feel lightheaded, tell me," he whispers eventually.

"I will. I promise."

His reaction to this whole situation has my world tilting out of balance. Bad boys aren't supposed to be sweet and cuddly. They get uncomfortable when having to deal with real issues, like a girl losing consciousness. They dump a bucket of cold water on her, ask if she's drunk, then call a cab to send her home.

Cole cradles me like I'm a family treasure made of glass.

My mind still swirls as my body reminds me we've been going at it for a few hours now. Maybe I just need to sleep, and then things will make sense.

"I should head home," I murmur a second before a yawn almost cracks my jaw in half.

"Stay the night," Cole whispers against my damp hair.

"Okay."

"That was easy." I hear the smile in his voice even as my eyes fight to stay open.

"Too tired to move." And Cole's chest suddenly feels like the softest mattress. Okay, maybe not the softest. The guy could probably do with some larger meals. Still, he's pretty comfy.

"You want a shirt to sleep in?"

I shrug. "Naked works fine." Maybe it's the lingering effects of losing consciousness, but the idea of sleeping without clothes doesn't spark even a hint of modesty.

Cole slides us down in the bed and pulls a sheet to cover us both. He mutters something that sounds an awful lot like "You're perfect," but I don't quite catch it.

My mind is in that murky half-sleep state when a thought occurs to me.

"You know what this means right?" I whisper against Cole's chest.

"What's that?"

"You're literally too hot for me to handle."

The sound of his snort is the last thing I remember before falling asleep.

Chapter Twenty-Seven

SUMMER

"You've been driving this for how long?" Dash's question drifts over from his place under my car's hood.

Defensiveness has me answering in a harsher tone than I normally use. "Since college. And I'll have you know, she only lets me down once, maybe twice a week!"

"There are cars out there that only let people down once, maybe twice a year."

"There are also grand mansions with swimming pools. Just because something exists doesn't mean it's within my price range."

The guy throws a smile over his shoulder at me. "I get that."

My brief spurt of affront drifts away, especially when I remind myself that Dash is giving me a deal.

After hanging out with Cole's friend and realizing Dash was the mechanic he's been pushing me to go see, I finally gave in. The decision became easier when I was stuck between two man-spreaders on the bus during my commute to work yesterday. I'd rather not have to deal with that nonsense if I don't have to. Paying to get my car towed to Dash's shop hurt, but I know when my Volkswagen is up and running again, I'll have slightly less stress in my life, and that might make the spending worth it.

Plus, I've decided to use this time to gain some insider knowledge on Cole. Since I'm allowed to hang out in the shop with Dash while he works, I assume he doesn't mind if I throw a few questions at him.

"Are you and Cole pretty close?"

"Sure." He doesn't tell me to be quiet because he needs to concentrate, so I push a little more.

"How close?"

"You asking if we fucked?"

"What?" I have to grab my stool to keep from falling off. "Why would —I don't..."

Shoot. Now I want to know.

"Did you?"

"Would it be a problem if we had?"

I think about it. Cole with Dash. In a bed. Doing naughty things.

Then my face explodes with a wild blush because that image doesn't necessarily bring up only jealous feelings.

"Maybe if you're still doing it. I don't like being involved with someone when they're sleeping with someone else."

Dash nods. "Paige is the only one for me. Cole and I never did anything. But he's been with guys. Not lately, though, I don't think. Should probably talk about that with him if it's a problem."

Guys aren't a problem. But that huge word hovering over this conversation is.

Exclusive.

Synonymous with monogamous. Which I equate to relationship.

Then we arrive at serious.

And I cannot be serious about Cole.

I skirt around this turn I didn't expect, bringing us back to my original question.

"What I meant to ask was are you close friends or just casual hang-out buddies? Like...do you trust Cole? Is he a decent guy?"

Maybe this is just hooking up, but I still don't want to share my bed with a total dick. I just want one part of him to be a dick.

I look at Cole, and I think bad boy.

Then he does some random nice thing, and I'm re-evaluating my assumptions.

But what do I expect from Dash? There's got to be some kind of bro code that mandates he sings Cole's praises. Soon this garage will be full of compliments, but will any ease my worries?

"Paige and I have a dog."

"Um, that's cool. Very cool. I'll probably make uncomfortably high-pitched baby talk noises if you show me a picture. However, I'm missing the connection to my question."

Dash uses his arm to wipe some sweat off his forehead, leaving behind a smear of grease. The petty part of my heart is glad he and Cole were never intimate. Dash is too sexy for his own good. How would I even be able to compare?

"She found the dog and called the shelter. That's how we met. When she came in to adopt it."

"That's sweet." Such an adorable meet cute. I wish dogs were allowed in the library.

Dash nods. "But Paige can't get over that fact that *she* found her. That if she hadn't been out running that day in that part of town that maybe no one would have. So now she jogs in shitty neighborhoods, keeping an eye out for abandoned animals to report."

"Wow. That's next level badass angel stuff."

Dash scowls at my car's engine, but I get the feeling the aged machinery isn't what put the expression on his face. "It's dangerous. She knows some self-defense. A decent amount. But she was still running on her own. It was killing me. I tried going with her, but I'm shit at running. After a mile I was dying. She was sweet about it, 'cause that's Paige, but I could tell it frustrated her."

He reaches his hand up like he's going to comb his fingers through his hair. Luckily he stops himself at the last minute, reaching for a rag in his back pocket to wipe away some of the grease instead.

"So what did you do? Train? You didn't tell her to stop, did you?" I wonder how that confrontation would go down. I get the feeling a woman who jogs through dangerous neighborhoods to search for abandoned animals wouldn't just roll over.

Dash seconds that thought with a snort. "Once, soon after we first met. She just dodged around me and continued running." He smiles while reliving the memory, then shakes his head as if to clear it. "I told

Cole about it. Just venting. Then the next time she showed up at my place in her running gear, Cole pulled on his sneakers and told me to sit that one out." Dash strolls over to his work bench, switching out his tools.

I wait impatiently on my stool for him to keep talking. "So he went running with her in your place?"

"He *goes* running with her. At least twice a week the two of them go for miles. We never talk about it. He never says why he goes. But I know." Some bolt-type thing clanks as it hits the cement ground. Dash crouches to pick it up, fiddling with it instead of returning immediately to whatever mechanic magic he was working. "He goes because I was worried about my girlfriend and he wanted to help. Cole just does stuff for the people he cares about." Dash smirks. "And if you mention it, he gives you this look." The mechanic meets my eyes then, his mouth curving even more. "This look that says *Of course I'm helping you, asshole. So shut the fuck up about it.*"

Laughter bubbles up in my throat, spilling out and echoing around the garage. I can picture that exact expression on Cole's face.

"He's not warm and fuzzy. But if you're one of the people he cares about, I'd say you're lucky." Dash shrugs, then leans back over the engine.

And I'm left to puzzle over one more confusing piece of Cole Allemand.

COLE

"Bite me."

"Are you telling me to fuck off, or are you literally telling me to bite you?" Summer asks.

When I invited my librarian to come over to my house, I wasn't planning on immediately falling into bed with her. But sometimes these things just happen.

Now I have her gorgeous naked body sprawled over my chest, and I'm wondering if she's up for fulfilling one of my fantasies.

"Literally."

"Is this because of the braces?" She taps a nail against her front tooth. "And my great teeth?"

My moan mixes with a laugh.

"Maybe. But I also want you to mark me."

"Ooo. Someone has vampire fantasies." The grin I'm treated to is wicked, somehow making me harder. "Do you want me to dress in all black leather and sneak into your window in the middle of the night?"

Can a man come just from listening to the woman of his dreams describe naughty scenarios? Because I think I just did.

"Would you?" The words are a garbled growl of hope.

Summer rises to her knees, staring down at me with a teasing smirk as she reaches out to fiddle with the stud in my ear. "Hmm. Maybe for a special occasion."

"Christmas?" It's the closest special day I can think of.

Summer bounces and claps. "Yes! That is the perfect holiday for sneaking into someone's house. You won't know if I'm Santa or a mistress of the night!"

Chunky jolly man with a beard vs my gorgeous librarian?

"I think I'll be able to tell."

"You never know." She traces a finger down my sternum. "I've always imagined Santa as a very sexy mythical being."

Guess I'm not her normal type.

"Do you have Santa fantasies?"

"I mean, he's basically a lumberjack who hands out gifts. Who wouldn't want to fuck that guy?"

Any guy Summer wants to fuck, is the guy I want to be.

"Okay."

"Okay?" She tilts a brow. "You want to fuck Santa?"

I suppress a snort and keep my face serious. No matter how weird her kink is, I never want Summer to feel bad about it. She's the most upbeat, supportive person I've ever met. Anyone who shits on her dreams deserves a fist to the face.

"No. But if you dress up as a vampire, I'll dress up as Santa."

Summer leans over me, her fingers digging into my bare chest, eyes sparking with lust. "You would do that for me?"

I would do anything for you.

But I keep that to myself.

"There are weirder kinks. I'm not exactly the right build though." I glance down at my slim, slightly underfed body.

"I'm not looking for the belly." Is she panting? "You find the outfit and call me a ho, and I will demolish you. You'll want to relocate to the North Pole and pretend it's Christmas year-round."

This is the weirdest conversation I think I've ever had, and I spent years in prison. I never thought I'd be hard as a rock and laughing. Gripping her soft body to me, I roll us both until Summer is pinned under me. This is my new favorite place: nestled between her spread thighs.

She stretches her arms up, then wraps them around my neck. There's a tease of her nails scratching the hair at the nape of my neck. My whole body tingles in response, and I stretch, loving the satisfying crack of a few of my joints.

"Guess we have a deal." To seal it, I press a hot kiss against her lips. Then I give in to the urge to tease her. "But only if you're good. Santa doesn't just slide into anyone's chimney." I pair the image with a slow thrust into her warm, tight pussy.

"But I don't want to be good." Summer pouts, shaking her head. Her heels dig into my ass, pulling me hard against her. Lips and hot breath brush against my ear just before her words. "Put me on your naughty list. I want some *Cole* in my stocking."

There's a deliciously sharp sting on my shoulder paired with her hips rocking.

She bit me.

Chapter Twenty-Eight

SUMMER

My arms ache from shelving all day. Normally there's more staff around to trade off the duty, but with Christmas Eve tomorrow, a lot of people asked off work.

I'm not resentful. Just sore.

Even clicking through my emails sets off little pangs of pain. I wish my apartment had a tub, so I could take a nice long soak after work, but I guess I'll just have to settle for a hot shower.

Maybe Cole could come over and massage my shoulders.

Is that what dating people do? That's not solely in the realm of boyfriend-ness is it?

A sigh drifts from me. Better not slip into the gray area. I'll find a way to massage my own shoulders.

As if he knew I was thinking about him, Cole's name appears on my phone screen above a text.

Cole: *U work tomorrow?*

My tired brain can't grasp why Cole might be asking this, and I figure the best way to find out is to answer.

Summer: *Nope. Library is closed for the next two days.*

Cole: *U have family plans?*

Summer: *Later in the evening. Nothing during the day tho*

Cole: *Early dinner at my Dad's house?*

My phone lets out a clank as I drop it on my desk. I get up, walk out of my office, scurry down the hall, push into the bathroom, turn on the faucet, and splash cold water in my face. When I look at myself in the mirror, I realize how bad of a decision this was when black streaks drip from my not-waterproof mascara-covered lashes.

"Damn it."

Using a stiff paper towel, I'm able to dry off and clean myself up. All of this does a decent job at pushing away the tiredness of my long pre-holiday shift. And in the time I take for myself, I'm able to reason that I misread his text.

Sexy, tattooed, bad boys do not invite their fuck buddies to Christmas Eve dinner with their families. Doesn't happen. Eight hours without a lunch break short-circuited my ability to comprehend the written word. Or the typed word.

I start back to my office, but I'm waylaid by no less than three mini-crises.

A patron racked up a thirty dollar fine on a book they claimed to have returned months ago.

A cluster of computers decided to stop connecting to the Wi-Fi.

All the stalls in the men's bathroom mysteriously ran out of toilet paper.

By the time I make it back to my office, an hour has passed, and I've completely forgotten about the text from Cole that I misread. That is until I notice I have another message from him.

Cole: *No big. Forget I mentioned it.*

I struggle to focus, opening up our exchange to decipher the meaning of his text.

My tired brain didn't misread his first question.

Cole invited me to spend Christmas Eve dinner with his family.

And I ghosted him!

Panicked, I dial Cole's number, silently praying he doesn't send me to voicemail.

"Summer?"

"All the toilet paper disappeared!"

"What?"

"And there was fine drama, and the Wi-Fi was possessed by demons!" I pace around my tiny office, punching some of my throw pillows as I pass. One has a reindeer stitched on the front and jingle bells on the edges that rattle when my fist hits its fat cushiony-ness.

"Is this some code I don't know?" Cole's dry voice has a calming effect, helping me center my thoughts.

"Library problems kept cropping up. That's why I didn't answer. Am I still invited to dinner?"

There's a pause that carves into my heart, making it and my head ache. "You want to come?"

"Yes! If I meet your father, then I'll know where you came from, and then you can't be brooding and mysterious anymore."

"I can still brood."

"True. Unless your dad is some super upbeat guy who works as a chocolatier for a living. Then you can't brood anymore. Anyone who grew up with an unlimited supply of chocolate has no right to brood."

"What if he's a pineapple farmer?"

"Oh my god. Is he? Did you break out in hives whenever he hugged you? I'm sorry. I take it back. You have unlimited permission to brood."

There's the sound of a reluctant chuckle weaving through our phone connection.

"He's not a pineapple farmer, is he? You dirty liar. For that, no more biting for the rest of the year."

"Summer," he growls.

I grin to myself, loving this little sense of power I have over his pleasure. And over mine.

"You brought it on yourself, Cole Allemand. I'm going to bite so many things in front of you. Apples. Chips. Gum. Strangers on the street."

"Okay. I'm sorry. Forgive me."

"Hmm. Maybe next year."

There's a stretch of silence, and I can hear the tension radiating over the line. When he finally breaks it, there's a delicious dark note in his voice.

"I'm going to bring you to the edge with my fingers and tongue so many times you'll be begging to come. You'll get so pissed at me you'll want to scratch me up. You'll want to bite me. And when you do, you'll have the best orgasm of your life."

Silence. Except for my heavy breathing. I'm panting, imagining what he just described. Dampness gathers between my legs, and I can feel my pulse beat in my clit.

"Damn you to the archives of hell, Cole."

He laughs like the bastard he is. "Come over tonight."

"Okay."

"And come to dinner tomorrow."

"Okay."

I think my quick agreements surprise him, but I'm honestly too horned up to deny him anything. After a hesitation, he responds with a smirk in his voice, "Get back to work, Summer."

"Don't tell me what to do," I huff. Even though I do need to get back to work. Plus, I just let him tell me a bunch of other things to do without argument.

To maintain a sense of power, I hang up.

Okay, honestly, I hang up because I don't feel capable of saying goodbye. I could spend the rest of my shift bantering with him. Plus, our conversation was quickly veering toward phone sex, which I just now decide is expressly forbidden while at work.

I must maintain some sense of professionalism.

It's not until I'm out at the research desk, helping a woman look up information about college night classes, that I remember I had qualms about going to Christmas Eve dinner at Cole's dad's house.

When he retracted the offer, my heart went into panic mode.

But why does my heart have a say in any of these decisions? All Cole decisions should strictly be held between my brain and my vagina. Logic and lust.

No other L-words need apply.

Chapter Twenty-Nine

SUMMER

He got me to bite him.

The second I arrived at Cole's house last night, he started in on his promise. Demanding hands stripped off my clothes and lay me across his bed. He tongued his way down my body, then licked me until I whimpered and begged. But my pleas didn't get him to stop his delicious torture, so I cursed him.

Then I shoved him off me, straddled him, and sank my teeth into his pec a second before sinking down onto his hard cock.

Currently, Cole drives with one hand on the wheel. The other rubs his chest in the exact spot I left a mark. Something like a smile hides at the corner of his mouth.

Any other day I'd be all smug satisfaction. But I can't concentrate when all I can do is stare.

He's wearing a sweater.

Only, sweater is too tame of a word.

Some people might call what he's wearing an ugly sweater.

But I think it's gorgeous.

Cole has forgone his normal black attire, opting for a knitted creation worn by only the biggest fans of Frosty the Snowman. The background is an icy blue, bringing beautiful emphasis to his eyes, but taking up the entire front of the sweater is a happy, top-hat-wearing, carrot-nose-sporting snowman.

My brain can't handle how adorable this sex-on-a-stick man looks in his seasonal wear.

"You're quiet," Cole murmurs. Flicking my eyes to the dashboard clock, I realize we've been driving for ten minutes without me saying anything.

"Your sweater." The first words I'm able to manage.

Cole's face stays blank, and he gives a little shrug. "Yeah?"

"How...when...where..." I can't settle on a single question, not sure what I want to know first.

"My grandma bought it for me. She'll be at dinner." Cole's mouth is tight at the corners, and I can't figure out why.

Does he think I'll make fun of him?

Does he love his sweater and worry I'll judge him for it?

I lay my hand on his thigh, giving a quick squeeze. "I. Love. It. *Love* it. You look amazing."

There's a hint of a smile twitching over his lips, which I count as a success. "*You* look amazing." His hand rests on top of mine, giving me a squeeze back.

The compliment warms my cheeks. I've never had a holiday dinner at a guy's house before, so I wasn't sure how to approach it. While I'm not as on-theme as Cole, I did opt for a dark green dress and a set of sparkly red flats I refer to as my Dorothy shoes. I'm my own little Christmas tree.

Five minutes later, we pull into the driveway of a small house. Cole puts his truck in park, then jogs around the hood to help me down. I don't need help, but I like the feel of his strong fingers tangling with mine.

Before I can take a step toward the front door, Cole pulls me into his chest, tilting my chin up so he can capture my mouth in a not-family-friendly kiss. He moves his lips over mine, hot touch searing my skin.

After momentarily giving into my knee-jerk reaction to melt against him, I shove at his chest. Cole stumbles back a step, his stare fixated on my mouth, eyes unfocused.

"Rude!" Working hard to calm my panting breath, I smooth my hands over my dress to make sure there are no wrinkles.

"Summer—"

"You can't get me all hot and bothered seconds before meeting your dad!" Planting my fists on my hips, I glare at Cole.

He blinks a couple of times before collecting himself. Cole shoves his hands in his pockets, then he has the audacity to smirk at me. "Why not?"

And there's that bad-boy mentality.

I wish it didn't send pleasurable shivers all along my nerve endings.

"Because I'll have a hard time holding conversation if I'm thinking about licking that delicious dip at the base of your throat."

Cole's eyes widen, and he smooths a palm over his collarbone, his Adam's apple bobbing as he swallows.

"And for the love of Wite-Out, I'm wearing lipstick again, you dope." Rummaging in my purse, I pull out a small mirror and an individually packaged makeup wipe. After fixing the smeared edges of my own lips, I quirk a finger at Cole, beckoning to me.

The cocky bastard is smiling as he steps forward. My fingers clasp his chin, and I wipe him clean of red smears.

Why do I get the feeling he likes messing up my makeup? If he keeps doing it, I'm going to make him pay for my next tube of lipstick.

"Okay. We're presentable. And definitely *not* horny."

Cole snorts and takes my hand, drawing me toward the cute little house. He doesn't bother knocking, instead opening the front door and yelling, "Dad! We're here!"

When there's not a response even after a few seconds pass, I raise an eyebrow at Cole.

He runs a thumb over my knuckles.

"He's probably out back, grilling. Let's go find him."

As we snake through the house, I note framed photos hanging on the walls of a tall thin man next to a surly blonde boy. I make a mental note to return and examine them later. Through a sliding glass door, I spot a lanky, grey-haired man bent over a decent-sized grill.

"Hey, Dad," Cole says as we step out into the backyard.

Mr. Allemand glances up at our arrival, his sternly set mouth hinting at a smile.

"Cole." A familiar pair of blue eyes flick to me in silent question.

"This is Summer Pierce. Summer, this is my dad."

"Nice to meet you, Mr. Allemand." I move forward, holding out a hand and hoping my lipstick cleanup was thorough enough.

The man gives a curt nod in greeting, returning my handshake.

"Summer is a librarian. At Downtown Public."

Is that a hint of pride I detect in Cole's voice?

Mr. Allemand nods, his gaze flitting between me and the grill. "That's a good job. You help a lot of people, do you?"

"Oh gosh. All day every day." Is my voice too bright? I can't help it. I want Cole's dad to like me, and when I want someone to like me, I slip into cheerfully informative mode. "That's why I chose to get my Master's in Library Science. I've always loved how libraries, especially public ones, help the community. And I wanted to be a part of that." Still, I don't want to talk about me. "But my job is small beans compared to both of yours."

Cole and his dad both raise the same eyebrow when they look at me, and the sight is a funny kind of adorable.

I explain myself. "Because, you know, Cole is saving and caring for animals. And you're keeping people safe when they travel. Cole told me you're an aviation meteorologist. I would be in constant panic mode if my forecast determined if a plane flew or not. I mean, what if there's a random tornado you didn't see on the radar? Or a freak hail storm?" Realizing what I just said, I press my knuckles to my forehead. "Damn it, listen to me. It's like I'm trying to stress you out. Please ignore all that. I'm sure you're amazing at your job. No need to worry about planes crashing." Mortification hits me hard, and I whirl toward Cole. "Make me shut up! I can't stop saying the wrong things!" I wail.

Then I see a glorious thing.

Cole grins.

The expression takes over his entire face, effectively rendering me speechless.

As I attempt to reboot my brain, he leans down to plant a quick kiss on my slack mouth. "You're doing fine. Right, Dad?"

My gaze somehow detaches from Cole's face, flitting over to his father. The stern man's eyes grow wider, but then he clears his throat and returns to his general expressionlessness.

"It's no bother."

The man seems unshakable. Of course, I've known him for less than five minutes, so it's not like I've discovered the true spectrum.

"How's the job?" Mr. Allemand asks his son.

Cole starts talking. Not the enthusiastic babbling I just displayed, but he's going into more detail than I've heard him use most times.

He's relaxed here.

When I told Cole that I wanted to discover the mystery that is him, I wasn't completely joking. There's normally a dark hesitance to him. Whenever I see that in another person, I'm drawn to it. I don't want to be, telling myself those are the types of people most likely to lash out or leave. These dark people are the ones who will hurt me. But I'm pulled in, curious to discover what the root of the darkness is. Where did the twisted tree grow from?

So I came here, wanting to meet Cole's dad. Would the man be arrogant and loud, overpowering his son with a booming voice? Pushing the creative man I know into the shadows? Or maybe disapproval would flow off him, eyes catching his son's piercings and tattoos, judgements dripping from his mouth.

But Mr. Allemand isn't those things. He's...quiet. Like Cole. Observant, like his son, too. I notice his sharp eyes take in every movement Cole makes. But not as if he's judging him. He's simply noticing it all.

And I also see the way Cole looks at his father. The way he leans toward the man, not exactly eager, but something close to that.

"And you're still writing?" Mr. Allemand asks when Cole finishes his work stories.

I'm just about to bristle at the question, thinking maybe this is where the man cuts his son down, when I notice Cole's solemn nod. "Every day."

"Good."

Good.

Forget all my previous prejudices. This man is an angel.

"And he goes to the writers groups at the library," I add, eager to let the man know about the great work his son is doing. "That's how we met. I kept bugging him."

Cole looks like I announced I juggle bananas with my feet for fun. "You didn't."

"Come on. Of course I did. You and your book fortress? I'm like an evil conqueress, always trying to tear it down at the end of the day."

"That's not bugging."

"Okay then, pestering."

"No."

I roll my eyes, knowing I'm right. He never wanted my help putting away his books. Guess I'm lucky my constant asking wasn't a total deal breaker.

My mind catches on how focused I am on whether or not Cole liked me. Like it's imperative information. But I shove that to the side and instead focus on the bribe I brought.

Well, bribe is being generous. I like to think of it as an enticement to consider me an optimal choice for his son to spend time with.

"Just forget it." I wave away Cole's scowl, turning my full attention his father. "Thank you for letting me join you all. I didn't want to come empty handed, so I brought a little something. Cole mentioned you like to go fishing." Reaching into my bag, I pull out a glass jar with red and green ribbon twined around the lid. Inside, the cookies I spent all morning baking in my toaster oven fill the container.

"You made fish cookies?" Cole asks, squinting his eyes at them.

"They're only shaped like fish. They taste like gingerbread," I say. When I spotted the cookie cutter in the supermarket, I got the idea.

Cole gently takes the jar from my hand, staring through the glass like my little desserts carry all the answers to the universe. The intensity of his gaze sets me on edge.

"What's wrong? Are you allergic to gingerbread? I guess I should've asked, but I thought it was only pineapple." Damn it. I'm terrified I just messed this dinner up.

"He's not allergic." This comes from Mr. Allemand, who steps away from the grill and pries the jar out of his son's hand. "Thank you, Summer. That was kind of you."

My cheeks heat with embarrassed pleasure at the compliment.

"Why don't you get the young lady a drink?" Mr. Allemand phrases this like a question, but it lands like a pointed command when he stares at his son.

"Yeah...a drink." Cole seems off balance, and I can't help worrying there is something wrong with my gift.

Did he have some mysterious problem in his past with cookies?

But then a strong set of arms snakes around my waist, pulling me into a hard warm chest. A second later, lips brush against my hair as Cole leans down to ask, "What sounds good? Beer? Wine?"

"Oh, if there's wine I'd love some. If not, beer is fine." Too late I realize I've yet again left myself open to being offered a glass of something sickly sweet. My problem is that whenever I hear the word wine, I automatically assume it's going to be a dry rich liquid.

"Your grandma told me to buy a bottle of red. Check on top of the fridge." Cole's dad waves us away, returning to whatever he's grilling for dinner.

With a hand on the small of my back, Cole turns me toward the house.

And only once we've stepped away from the older man do I fully acknowledge the tightness of my nerves. Normally, I'm great at one-on-ones. But hell, I wanted Cole's dad to like me. The reasoning behind that longing is something else I don't want to dwell on.

Still, for the last ten minutes, I was extremely nervous.

"Can I use the bathroom?"

Cole points me down a hall once we step through the sliding glass door.

Locking myself in the small room, I take stock of myself.

When I get nervous, I sweat. Luckily, I tucked an emergency stick of deodorant into my purse. I need a second to reapply. And maybe swipe a bit under my boobs for good measure.

Overall, not a disaster. Let's see if I can keep it that way.

COLE

"You have to have a wine opener somewhere," I mutter, searching through all the drawers in his kitchen. Different kitchen implements rattle around, but nothing that looks like it could remove a cork from a bottle.

"Stop that, Cole." My dad comes into the kitchen, a scowl on his face, just as I pull out the drawer under the microwave.

This one doesn't have any cooking utensils. What it is filled with are envelopes. A decent stack of them. All with thick red letters stamped on them.

Bill enclosed.

Final Notice.

Overdue.

"What the fuck are these?"

"Language."

I ignore his chastising, reaching for one of the pieces of mail. They don't even look as if they've been opened.

But Dad almost snaps one of my fingers off when he crosses the kitchen to slam the drawer shut.

"It's not your concern."

"Are those medical bills?"

"We're not talking about this."

"I told you to tell me about any money you owe. I'll pay it."

"You won't." He opens a smaller drawer, coming out with a meat thermometer. "Open the can of cranberry sauce, would you? Your grandmother will be here soon." My dad, always evading tough discussions rather than facing them head on. At least that's how it works if the issues are his.

I conveniently ignore any possible resemblance I might have to him in this area.

"I'm the reason you owe this money."

"You're not."

"Yes. I am. We both know how you ended up in the hospital."

"Cole—"

"That's some lovely smelling soap you have in the bathroom. Is it apple cider? Very seasonal." Summer strolls into the kitchen, her hands pressed to her nose. She's all positive sunshine, and I hate the fact that there's already a dark cloud over this visit, whether she realizes it or not.

Who am I kidding? The second Summer stops sniffing her fingers, she bounces her gaze between the two of us, picking up on the tension in the room.

She's too perceptive.

"Not sure," my father answers, voice gruff. "Just grabbed one off the shelf."

"Well, kudos to you and your ability to pick random amazing things. Is there anything I can do to help?"

"Distract my son," my father says, almost making a joke.

"Dad..." I hesitate, not sure what I'm willing to talk about with Summer here. Despite the fact that this shit needs to be figured out, I'm too ashamed to have her know the role I played in my Dad's no-longer-perfect health. That would no doubt lead to why he has no savings to pay what his health insurance didn't cover.

Lawyers are expensive.

My struggle for words comes to an end with the sound of the front door opening.

"I'm here!" My grandmother waltzes into the kitchen, a riot of color.

She has on a floor-length dress and feathered earrings, along with a tasseled shawl. People sometimes mistake her for one of the fortune tellers that set up tables in the French Quarter. Doesn't help that she's probably carrying a deck of tarot cards in her bag right now.

Summer's eyes go wide, flicking between me and the vibrant woman I somehow share blood with.

"Oh, look at you." She comes straight to me, setting affectionate hands on my shoulders. "That sweater is everything I hoped, and you make it more. You know, I found that when I lived in Alaska a few years back. Beautiful state, but the winters are rough. Dark all day and cold enough to kill a yeti."

With a bigger audience, I know I have to give up on the argument with my dad. For now.

Instead, I smirk at my grandmother. "Is this made of yeti fur then?"

She gives me a cheeky grin. "If only. That stuff is expensive. I love you, but not enough to purchase mythical creature clothing."

"You two," Dad grumbles, leaving the kitchen with his eyes on the backdoor.

Mama Al, as she insisted I call her since I was old enough to talk, watches the surly form of her son retreat. "Beer can chicken?"

"Can't change a classic," I offer back.

"His heart?"

"We'll make sure he sticks to white meat." It's the best I can do. My father doesn't like to be managed. Hence the drawer stuffed full of bills he refuses to talk to me about.

"Now, if you would please introduce me to this darling woman you have beside you. Or is she a stranger who wandered in off the streets that I need to help shoo from the house?"

"Oh please don't shoo me! I'll be good, I swear!" Summer blinks up at me, making her eyes all wide and innocent looking. It's like I'm staring down at a classic princess cartoon.

And I can't help remembering how my first crush was Belle from *Beauty and the Beast.* Apparently I have a thing for brunettes obsessed with books.

Because I can, and because I know my grandmother won't care, I pinch Summer's chin holding her face still as I dip down for a kiss. My librarian lets out a little gasp of surprise, but doesn't pull away.

At Mama Al's chuckle, I break off the kiss and tilt my head, trying hard to suppress a smile.

"Summer, this is my grandmother."

"Penelope Allemand. Call me Mama Al." My relative holds her hand out, and Summer steps away from me to accept the offering.

"Nice to meet you, Mama Al. I love Cole's sweater. I don't think he's ever looked more handsome." When Summer loops her arm around my waist, I vow to wear more colors, more often.

"Agreed. But then, I think he gets handsomer every day." Mama Al pats my cheek with a hand bedecked in heavy silver rings. "Now it's a beautiful sunny Christmas Eve. No reason to spend it inside."

"I was just looking for something to open the wine." My eyes skip to the forbidden drawer again. "But no luck."

Summer runs her hand over my lower back, and I love the way she uses her touch to reassure me. "I can drink beer. Or water. Or whatever. I'm easy."

My grandma smirks. "Aren't we all honey? But here, I should have us covered." And the sparkling woman reaches into her mammoth of a purse. Other grandmothers have hard candies and tissues in their bags. Not mine. Stick a hand into her bag and you're likely to come out with a map of North Dakota, or a taser, or a length of rope. She's a survivor, and her accessories reflect it.

Today though, she pulls out a small corkscrew.

"Never know when you might come across some poor abandoned wine that needs to be liberated."

Summer claps in delight and follows Mama Al to the counter where they uncork the bottle and pour a decent amount of red liquid into two glasses before sharing a cheers. I'm momentarily forgotten, but that's fine by me. Having Summer be at ease with my family is just one more step in my quest to get her to fall for me.

Later, when we're situated out on the concrete patio, Summer, Mama Al, and I drinking while Dad grills, conversation ebbs and flows.

"You in a hotel nearby?" my dad asks my grandmother.

"I'm staying," she declares before downing a hearty swallow of wine.

"That's what we want to know." The roll of his eyes is almost audible. "Where are you staying?"

"In a hotel for the next few days. Then the house I've signed on to rent will be available for me to move in."

Silence descends over the group. Summer was quiet anyway, letting the family discussions take place without her input. She has no idea how much of a bombshell statement my grandmother just made.

"You're renting? Here?" Was that desperation in my voice? It's only, my whole life Mama Al has always been transient. She'd come to New Orleans for a few days, maybe a week, then she'd be off on a new adventure.

The longest she stayed was a time I didn't get to enjoy her company. Because I was behind bars. Mama Al stuck around then because her son was in the hospital recovering from a heart attack.

When my dad found out about my arrest, only minutes went by

before a pain shot through his arm and he clutched at his chest. Again, I only know this second hand. Because I wasn't there. Because I had landed myself in police custody.

"I thought I'd stay for a little while."

"Oh you should!" Summer leans toward the older woman, an excited smile on her red lips. "You'll be here for Mardi Gras."

"My thoughts exactly." Mama Al squeezes Summer's knee, then raises an eyebrow at my dad. "Plus, I want to play matchmaker."

I hide a smile as Dad glares at the corn he just put on the grill.

"Don't."

"Who said I'm matchmaking for you? I have plenty of friends in town."

Dad snorts in disbelief, and I reach over to ease Summer into my lap. Mama Al better not get any ideas about me. I'm perfectly happy with how my love life is progressing.

The afternoon continues with my grandma sharing travel stories and giving my dad small verbal pokes. We opt to stay outside when the food is done, propping plates in our laps and setting our drinks on the ground. Summer takes over the conversation, relating hilarious library stories that have my grandma laughing and my dad cracking a smile or two.

Everything is easy. It all feels right.

If only my mind didn't continue to trip back to that drawer in the kitchen.

Later, after I'm done loading the dishwasher, I corner my father in the family room.

"Dad. We need to talk about those bills."

He settles into his recliner with a groan, not meeting my eyes.

"Dad—"

"She's good," he cuts me off. "Kind. Does she know what you did?"

I clench my teeth, not wanting to get distracted from the matter at hand. But when the topic is Summer, I have trouble concentrating on anything else.

"No. She doesn't. The bills—"

"Are you going to tell her?"

"Yes," I snap.

Of course, he picks up on what I don't say. "When?"

For a good minute, I don't answer. Instead, I stare out the front window where I can see my grandmother pulling knitted shawls from her trunk and draping them over my librarian's shoulders.

Mine. Right now she's mine.

I'll do most anything to keep it that way.

"When she won't leave."

A long sigh drags my attention back to the family room. My father grimaces at the wall, a spot where over a decade ago, there hung a family portrait. Now the spot has a fish my dad caught and mounted.

"You're like me."

"So?"

"So." He seems to chew on his words, then finally lets them free. "You'll drive her away."

He could've punched me in the gut, and I wouldn't have felt so sick.

"If she loves me, she won't leave."

My father keeps staring at the fish, it's open mouth gaping, gasping for breath. Forever caught in the struggle for its life.

"That's not how love works."

Chapter Thirty

SUMMER

I find Cole in the kitchen, his knuckles pressing into the counter, his eyes trained on a closed drawer. The intensity of his stance screams that something is wrong. This isn't the first time this evening.

Approaching him like I would a wild tiger, if I had any kind of valid reason to walk toward a jungle cat, I keep my steps light and my expression calm.

"Something I can help with?"

Tense shoulders only grow harder. "No."

No. I hate it when he tells me no.

Let me help you, I barely keep myself from begging.

"Okay," I say instead. "Are you ready to head out? Got my jacket and my purse, but I can dump them in the closet if you want to hang around longer."

"You have plans," he reminds me.

I do. And they aren't ones I'd feel comfortable canceling.

"I do. But I can also ride the bus if you need to stay here. It's not a big deal." Would me leaving help? Is that what he needs? The fact that I can't figure it out frustrates me.

"I'm driving you." He speaks low, as if to himself. Cole's mind is somewhere else. Somewhere not great.

Another person might have backed out of the kitchen and waited by the front door to be collected. But his rigid form draws me toward him rather than pushing me away.

"Cole." When my palm rests on his arm, the muscle twitches, and his frigid eyes flick to me. "What do you need? Right now." He can't tell me no if it isn't a yes/no question. Can he?

The line of his mouth tightens, far from any kind of smile. I want to kiss him into happiness, but that's not how feelings work.

Tell me how to help you. I try to force the thought into Cole's head, afraid if I speak it out loud he'll shut down. His gaze traces over me, coming to land on my purse. The thing is faux leather, almost the same cool blue of Cole's eyes, and has tiny snowflakes dangling from each zipper. New Orleans barely ever gets snow even in the middle of winter, so I decided to carry it around with me.

"I need your bag."

I slip it from my shoulder. "To wear? It does kind of go with your sweater."

He doesn't even give me a lip twitch. Instead, Cole accepts my purse, setting it in front of the microwave and unzipping the main compartment. As I try to remember if there's anything embarrassing contained within, Cole pulls open the drawer he's been glaring at. The space is filled with envelopes, and he doesn't waste any time shoving them into my bag.

I don't move. The sight is too strange. As he clears out the drawer, I try to puzzle out what exactly I'm seeing. When every last letter is tucked into my purse, I still haven't figured anything out. Cole zips it shut, closes the drawer, and slides the bag onto my shoulder.

"Let's go." He cups my elbow, turning me toward the front door.

"We're saying goodbye, right?"

Cole stumbles to a stop, staring at me with wide eyes. "What?"

"To your dad and your grandma. I don't want to leave without saying goodbye."

He shakes his head, but not in a denial, more like to clear out errant thoughts. "Yeah. Let's say goodbye."

We find them upstairs in a spare bedroom, pulling old suitcases out of a back closet.

"Mama Al stores some of her stuff here," Cole murmurs to me as explanation, then raises his voice a touch. "We're heading out."

The peacock of a woman wraps me in a tight hug. "Loved meeting you, Summer. I'll come by the library to get a card."

"You better!" When I let her go, Mr. Allemand offers me a hand to shake. I take it, smiling wide, trying to ignore the burn of my purse pressing into my leg.

I hope Cole has a good explanation.

Once we're in the car, a thick tension makes my skin feel sticky. Like dirty humidity.

"Which way?" he asks at a stop sign, voice casual, as if I wasn't just used as a mule to smuggle something out of his father's house.

"What's in my bag?" I can't simply continue with my night without addressing this.

"Don't worry about it."

My teeth clench, then I force my jaw to relax. "I have considered your request, and I reject it. The worrying is already happening. Can't stop it now. Might as well tell me."

"Summer." He growls my name in some kind of warning. The chastisement might have carried more weight if his sleeves weren't covered in reindeer wearing sparkly harnesses.

"I could easily find out. But I'd rather you tell me. Please."

As Cole stares out the windshield, I only get half his face. But that's plenty enough to see how irritated he is. In another circumstance, I might have tried jokes or flirting. But something about the way he holds himself tells me this is a heavier matter.

"Medical bills. My dad's."

My mind conjures up an image of the man I just met. Mr. Allemand is tall and lithe, like his son, but his blonde hair has gray throughout, and wrinkles dig deep into the corners of his eyes. Still, he looked to be in decent health. Not that these things always appear on the surface. I wonder what ailment has resulted in the heavy weight on my shoulder.

"Where is your mom's place?" Cole's driven us back into the city.

"Why did you take them?"

"Summer. Tell me where to go."

"In a minute. Answer my question."

"To pay them. Now, where do I go?"

To pay them? The amount of envelopes in my bag hints this won't be a small task. From what I've seen of Cole's life, he's not sitting on some massive amount of cash.

"Do you know how much he owes?"

"I'll figure it out. Right or left?"

"Left," I answer, only half my mind on the direction we're traveling. Cole has no idea how much his dad is in debt, but he's just going to pay it?

"When you say you're going to pay these bills, you mean..."

"I mean, I'll write the places checks and put those checks in the mail. Then my dad won't have to get harassed anymore."

Damn, my heart clenches hard. Both at the nobleness of the statement, but also because I'm worried. Handling massive debt isn't that easy.

"And if what he owes is more than you have? What will you do?"

Cole doesn't hesitate. "I'll pay it."

"And go into debt yourself?"

"If anyone should be, it's me." There's more than a hint of self-loathing in his voice. Clearly, Cole thinks his dad's money problems are somehow his fault. This seems like a bigger thing, and I'm not sure I'm equipped to deal with whatever emotional turmoil he's in.

But if there's one thing I do know, it's how to manage debt.

I learned the hard way.

"That doesn't have to happen." I chew my lip, then cross my fingers and beg the universe Cole will be reasonable. That he'll let me help. "Let me take a look at the bills. I promise to keep everything confidential."

"What? No," he says as if the thought baffles him. "They aren't yours to deal with."

The polite thing to do would be to keep my nose out of his business. But I *can't*. "Well they aren't yours either."

"They're my dad's."

"And I bet your dad would like to dig himself out of this hole." Wasn't hard to tell that Mr. Allemand is a proud man. I'm betting that's why Cole had me smuggle these documents out of the house rather than asking to take them.

"Leave it alone, Summer, and tell me how to get to your mom's place."

"Cole. Please. Just listen to me. I. Can. Help."

"Not. Your. Problem."

"I know that." The words beg to be shouted at him, but I keep my voice composed. This is my agitated patron voice. With this voice, I've calmed many people who intimidated me more than Cole. It is a rare person who can remain stubborn in the face of my serene librarian persona. "But I also know how to help. And not in a vague, I'll do some research into the matter and get back to you, way."

We've hit a stoplight, but Cole won't look at me. His knuckles are a vivid white as he fists the steering wheel at ten and two. I can imagine the second we arrive he'll try to grab my bag from me, taking my only claim to this issue.

"Directions."

"Pull in there." I point to the strip mall parking lot, and Cole throws me a confused glance. "I refuse to tell you any more directions until you listen to me."

He mutters a few curses but pulls off the road and parks. Just as I thought, he reaches for my bag, but I've already shoved it behind my back.

"Give them to me."

"No. I'm the one who stole them. And now I'm going to help."

"The only way to help is to pay the bills. Which I'm going to do."

"Okay. Fine. You're going to pay them. But there are different ways to approach debt."

"Summer." Cole has unclipped his seatbelt, and he tries to climb to my side of the car, long arms circling behind my back.

"I was almost homeless!" I shout, my librarian voice nowhere to be found as I'm desperate for him to understand.

Cole freezes, staring down at me as he looms. "What?"

Seeing I have his attention, I moderate my volume. "When I was a teenager. After my dad died. My mom and I ran into some hard times financially. We struggled, but we figured it out." That time of my life was a stressful mess of constant moving to smaller and smaller apartments, and ignoring the phone when it rang because of the creditors on the other end of the line. "She doesn't owe anything anymore, and I'm only dealing with my student loans. I have a clear financial plan with scheduled payments, and I know exactly when I'll be debt-free." So what if it's a decade from now? I still have an end date.

Reaching up a hand, I cup his jaw. His lids close briefly as if he's in pain, but I get the sense he wants my touch. That he needs someone to reassure him the papers in my bag aren't going to implode his life.

"You shouldn't have to deal with this." His whisper is rough. Still, his words give me hope.

"I want to. Please, Cole. I promise I can make this easier for you. I'm not asking to pay the bills. Just help organize it all. Let me help."

A moment passes, then another. Finally, a soul-weary sigh steels the tension from his body, and his forehead comes to rest on mine.

"Is this a yes?" Damn my mouth. I shouldn't push my luck.

But Cole nods, and my joy fills the truck cab. My fingers tangle in his hair, pulling his mouth toward mine. He lets me kiss him for only a second, then moves away and returns to his side of the cab.

He's not happy. Yet. But I'll show him.

Chapter Thirty-One

SUMMER

"This seems a shady kind of business."

"Well, you know librarians. We work in the shadows. We're the underbelly of society. Sunlight burns my skin."

"Dear, be serious."

I sigh, letting my teasing tone drift away as I settle into a seat beside my mother. She has Mr. Allemand's bills spread out over her gorgeous mahogany dining room table and is in the process of moving them into different piles.

What do the piles mean? I have no clue.

Because I may have told Cole a little white lie.

Money is not my strong suit.

My mother though, she's become a genius with numbers. Mainly out of necessity.

"Okay, Mom. This is me serious. Why do you think this is shady?"

"Well, because you're having me look at this man." She holds up a document so she can examine it through her adorable sparkly blue reading glasses. "Malcolm Allemand. You're having me look at his bills. And there is some very personal information here."

"I know that. But we've had permission from a family member." After I essentially wrestled it out of him. "They're a friend. And it's not like I'm asking you to do something bad with this info. We're trying to help."

"But help who? Why are you bringing this to me?"

"Because, Mom." I take her hand in mine, meeting her gaze over her eyewear. "We know firsthand the anxiety and fear, and honestly, the embarrassment, that comes with this level of debt."

The corners of her mouth pinch, and she stares off to the side. "We do."

"But more than that, you figured out a way out of it. You are amazing, and intelligent, and you had me to worry about, so you clawed your way out of that hole for both of us."

"You make me sound better than I am."

"No. If anything, I'm underselling you."

Suddenly, I'm overwhelmed with memories of the time in my life where our mailbox was full of final notices. The weeks my mother and I went to a food pantry so we could afford our electric bill and still have something to eat. And through it all, how she found ways to show me love and support when she was probably battling a descent into depression.

On instinct, I lean forward to wrap her in a tight hug.

"Please, Mom," I whisper into her shoulder. "I think he's drowning in this and doesn't know how to ask for help. My friend wants to, but they're not sure where to start." I sit back so I can look at her. "All I'm asking is you bring some order to the chaos. Tell us how much is owed. What should be paid first. What's the minimum they have to pay to keep this from getting any worse?"

She chews on the corner of her lip, then sucks in a bracing breath. "Fine. I can do that." Another piece of paper goes into another pile. "I hope you're not very close with this friend."

Close is a relative term. "Why's that?"

In her neat script, my mother makes a note on a legal pad beside her elbow. "I'm not sure I'd be able to face this Malcolm Allemand, knowing that I'd riffled through all of his private information."

"No. Don't worry. I don't see you meeting him." Not Mr. Allemand. Not even Cole.

When he dropped me off yesterday, I didn't invite him inside. Guilt pinches at my nerves, but I stifled the feeling, excusing my actions by reasoning there was no point for him and my mother to interact.

That would only happen if Cole and I were actually dating. Like, for the long term.

I know what's going on between us can't be called a fling anymore. Not after meeting his friends and family. But it's still not a relationship. Because that would mean putting faith in Cole. Trusting him not to hurt me.

And I still know what a charming bad boy looks like when I see one.

If my mom had had the same sense that I do, we wouldn't have had to learn about the fear of debt the hard way.

But even the most intelligent women can be fooled.

So Cole and I, we're together. For now.

And one day we won't be. And I'll be the one to choose that day.

Chapter Thirty-Two

COLE

I'm going to tell her.

As I make this demand of myself, I glare at my steering wheel, like it will somehow try to convince me to do otherwise.

I might let it.

But my dad's words continue to replay themselves in my mind.

"You'll drive her away."

I wanted to tell him that I was nothing like him. But that's not true. Plus, my dad isn't a shitty guy. He's a good dad, and I don't want him thinking otherwise.

What I wanted to say was that Summer isn't Mom.

She's not. Not like her at all.

But my dad never hid anything from my mom. He was just his standoffish, grumpy self, and that was enough for her to decide she didn't love him. To decide she didn't love us.

I have Dad's personality, plus my delinquent past.

Summer might not be bothered by the first right now, but paired with the second, any doubts she has could be amplified. Still, if I can find a way to explain what I did, get her to understand that I'm different than that person I used to be, maybe we can move past this.

My phone buzzes in my pocket, and I pull it out to read a text.

Summer: *Are you sitting in your truck outside of my apartment like a weirdo?*

Shit. She caught me. Not that she wasn't expecting me, but I should've texted the when I arrived. Instead, I've been idling here for five minutes, debating with myself, no closer to figuring out what to say.

Cole: *Yes. Got lost in thought. Want me to come up?*

Summer: *Nope! B right down.*

Even though she's coming to me, I still turn off the ignition and step out. Circling around the hood, I'm just opening the passenger door when I hear footsteps on the apartment stairs.

Summer appears.

Only, she doesn't look like the normal Summer.

Normal Summer likes floral patterns and cheery colors like yellow and sky blue. She wears little makeup other than her colorful bright lipsticks.

This is not that Summer.

This woman has on a long-sleeved black dress that hugs her torso before flaring out, ending just above her knees. Her nails are dark, maybe black too. She has smoky eye makeup and a sinful red color painted on her lips.

"Look!" She skips toward me, stopping just a few paces away. "I'm all dark and brooding like you!" And then, as if she is intent on killing me, Summer does her best to scowl.

Blood roars in my ears, saying a final goodbye as it all heads south. Without thought, I'm reaching for her, fingers splayed, ready to grab her. To pull her into me. Cage her in my arms.

Want me like I want you. Don't leave me.

The thoughts whisper desperately in my subconscious.

But Summer steps back, a teasing tilt to her lips as if she's oblivious to my need.

"Wait! Check it out." Her hands go to her mouth, and a second later, she's smiling at me with a set of fake fangs. "I know this isn't a full leather getup like I promised, but I kind of look like a mistress of the night. Right?"

My heart hurts. There are literal pangs in my chest with each beat as I take in this amalgamation of adorable and sexy.

She is perfection.

I don't deserve her.

Because I'm selfish, I'll never tell her that.

My feet move forward, and I feel my knees go loose. So I kneel in front of her, wrapping my hands around her waist and pulling her close so I can bury my face in her chest.

"Are you okay?" Summer giggles as she asks the question, combing her fingers into the hair at the nape of my neck.

All I can manage is a shake of my head.

"Ah, my vampire powers of seduction are already working, it seems." Then she puts on a horrible Transylvanian accent. "I vant to suck your blood! And your dick!"

I'm laughing, and groaning, and fighting off the fear that she'll walk away from me.

I can't tell her.

Not yet.

I just need more time.

When I'm sure Summer loves me, I'll find a way to crack myself open for her. Something I've never done with anyone before. For her though, I swear I will.

But I won't risk scaring her off when she's still far enough away to leave me.

"Cole. We're on a public sidewalk, and you have your face in my boobs. This is not the smooth seduction of vampire lovers. Paranormal romance authors across the globe are cringing." Even as she chastises me, I hear a smile in her voice and feel the scrape of her nails down the back of my neck.

Fuck the world, I want to say. If I could spend the rest of the day on my knees, worshiping her, I would.

But then she might think sex is all I want.

And I do want it. Especially when she's in this getup.

Still, I need more from Summer than just her body. I want every piece of her to be tied to me. Which is why I'm taking her out on a date. Drinks, food, walking around with her in public.

Then I'll bring her back to my place and smear her lipstick.

With that image bright in my head, I stand, eager to start our evening together. Meeting Summer's gaze, I pick up a slight amount of apprehension, and I realize I haven't said anything since she walked out of her apartment.

"You're perfect."

A blush spreads, along with a pleased smile, and I swoop down to steal a kiss before guiding her to my truck.

Once seated, I slip my key into the ignition.

"Wait." Summer places her hand over mine to stop me from starting the engine. "Before we start the fun part of the night, I thought we could get the finance stuff out of the way."

Finances? Does Summer want to talk about splitting the bill? Because it's not happening.

"Here." She pulls out a binder from her floppy purse and hands it over to me.

"What's this?"

Summer flips open the front cover, and I see a series of colorful tabs. "Your new financial plan. Or, a few plans, based on how much you're able to pay each month." She leans over my lap, turning to the first section. "This is the total owed when you combine everything, but it doesn't all need to be paid at once. The bills with higher interest and penalty fees are toward the front. You'll want to take care of those first. Also," her dark-painted nails pinch the mass of papers, taking me to the last page, "if the monthly payments still seem like too much, these are a few non-profit organizations that specifically help with managing medical debt. Give them a call and you might qualify for some assistance."

As Summer calmly lays out how to address a number figure that threatened to ruin my life, I imagine a hand plunging into raging waters, pulling out my drowning form as I cough and sputter. There's riot of emotions mixing in my chest. Fear of the amount my dad owes. Shame that I'm the cause of it and that Summer has to see my dad's struggle. Gratitude that she would step in to help untangle some of the mess. Awe that she's willing to do all this for my family.

With care, I close the binder and place it on the seat between us. Then I cup the back of her head, pulling Summer in for a searing kiss before whispering against her lips, "Thank you."

And a stray thought spikes through my mind.

The past should stay in the past. Maybe I'll never have to tell her.

Chapter Thirty-Three

SUMMER

Cole always uses one of the library's computers before building his book fortress. He settles in front of one of the screens, arranges his notebook beside the keyboard, then begins to type at a slow, but steady pace.

I've wondered more times than the number of books in this library—and we have thousands—exactly what he's writing. Some type of story, obviously.

Is he putting together a novel? A short story?

Are the words just for him, like a hobby, or is he seeking representation?

Has he published anything? Can I read his drafts?

But I know that writers can be very sensitive about their writing, and I'd never want to affect Cole's confidence.

Not that I think it's likely I would be able to. Still, just in case, I've kept myself from badgering him about it.

Maybe I could ask Jamie.

No. I quickly squash that idea. If I'm going to learn anything about Cole's writing, it's going to be from the man himself.

Instead of going up to greet him, I decide not to be a distraction and go do my job.

But when I get back to my office, I face a conundrum.

For once, my email inbox is shockingly empty. I don't have reference or circulation desk duty until later. There aren't any events today that I'm coordinating. Plenty of volunteers showed up to help shelve books.

I have a chunk of free time to work on projects. And I know exactly which one needs my attention most. Still, I fiddle around on a news site and check the library's social media pages. Avoiding the task.

But putting this off is like not going to the doctor when I have a gaping, bleeding wound. Things aren't just going to magically get better.

I need to practice.

A few months ago, I received word that my submission to present at the Louisiana Public Library Conference was accepted. When I opened that email, I'd had a few seconds of excitement, followed by weeks of panic.

This is a good thing. Fantastic for your career. One of the goals you set for yourself!

If only I could enjoy all those perks without the accompanying terror.

It's not that I don't believe in my presentation. The topic is our library's approach to serving our homeless patrons. I've mapped out exactly what I want to talk about, the experiences I'm excited to share. I even got Amy to agree to co-present with me so we have both the librarian and social worker viewpoints.

So it's not the content giving me panic sweats.

It's the actual act of presenting.

This anxiety always grips me when I think of talking to more than just a handful of people. The fear comes on, tearing at my insides, mocking my once-confident thoughts. My eyes dart around, looking for the closest large object I can duck behind.

Why? I have no idea.

It's not rational. It's not like I'm being asked to speak in front of a crowd on the verge of rioting. This is a presentation at a library conference. The room will be filled with the most chill people in the world.

And still the panic comes.

Which is why I need to stop avoiding this and instead spend my free chunks of time practicing. With a resigned sigh, I push away from my desk, pull open my filing cabinet, and grab the script I typed up for myself. Maybe if I have every single word memorized, I can use the rest of my brain capacity to keep myself from freaking out.

I just need to visualize the crowd. Work through it that way.

An idea sparks in my brain, and I swipe through my phone to the app store, wondering if...yep. Those Silicon Valley programmers think of everything.

After downloading my new find, I'm ready to practice.

My eyes scan the first paragraph before I close them, trying to instill the words in my brain.

"Hello. I am Summer Pierce, and I work at the Downtown Public Library in New Orleans. Today, I am here with Amy Winters to discuss the efforts my library has made toward helping one of our most important patron groups: the homeless." Pressing my thumb against my phone's screen, the low clatter of applause sounds from the speakers.

That's right. I downloaded an app to mimic a crowd clapping for me.

And with my eyes shut, it helps with envisioning myself in front of a large gathering of people. My nerves ratchet up, but I suck in a deep breath through my nose and let it out in a large gust before continuing.

"We thought our efforts were important to share because we know libraries across the country, probably across the world, continue to grapple with how to serve this group." I'm getting into it, gesturing with my hands for emphasis, and pressing the clapping button again. Not that I expect to get continuous applause, but it helps keep the imagined conference room in the forefront of my mind.

As I get into the groove of this practice, my muscles loosen, and I move a bit, hoping on the day of my presentation I'll be able to remember not to stand like a creepy robot.

"Before I even joined the Downtown Public team, there was a popular event where—ow!"

My shin throbs, having just collided with the corner of my desk. Maybe pacing around my tiny office with my eyes shut isn't the best practice method. As I reach down to rub the sore area, my thumb slides against my phone, setting off a round of celebration for injuring myself.

That's when I hear a throat clearing at my office door.

Damn it to the archives of hell.

Glancing over my shoulder, I spot the delicious, rumpled, grinning form of my current fuck buddy. Cole watches me, amusement clear on his handsome face.

"You okay?"

"I wanted to walk into my desk," I declare.

"Did you?"

"No. But the gentlemanly thing to do is pretend that I did."

"And you think I'm a gentleman?"

"A woman can dream."

He uncrosses his arms only to shove his hands into his pockets. My willpower is tested as my eyes long to trace the dragons circling his arms. Every time I look at them, I find a new detail.

"Do you want me to go?" he asks.

My gaze flicks up to his Icelandic stare as I consider his question.

The answer is no. I didn't want him to witness my embarrassment, but now that he's here, the idea of him walking away has me bumming out.

But I'm at work. I can't flirt with Cole while I'm on the clock.

Thinking back over our many flirtatious conversations, I amend...

I can't flirt with him for an extended period of time while I'm on the clock.

But maybe he can help me with work.

"Are you busy?" I ask.

"I don't have to be."

"Okay. Then I'd like your help with something. But only if you promise not to mock me."

At this, a scowl creases his brow. "I don't enjoy making you feel shitty, Summer."

Briefly, I rock back on my heels. His statement caught me that off guard.

Is that what he thought I meant?

Is *that what I meant?*

Guys with his demeanor always seem one step away from a snarky comment that can cut deep despite a joking tone. Still, I have to admit, Cole and I might trade jokes, but he's never said anything truly at my expense.

I feel comfortable around him. My vulnerable underbelly is safe in his hands. Which is strange, and I'm not sure I like myself slipping into that comfort.

That still doesn't mean I can make him out to be a douche when he hasn't been one.

"No. I know you don't. I'm just stressed."

His frown softens, and he leans forward into my office even as his feet stay just outside the jamb.

"About what?"

After a bracing breath, I admit, "In a few weeks, I'm going to be presenting at a library conference. But I'm terrified of public speaking."

There. It's out. The upbeat librarian falls to pieces when she is in front of a room that surpasses double-digit occupation.

Cole watches me, and I want to know what's going on behind his icy eyes.

Instead of asking, I pick up a stack of books on my desk, straighten them, then put them back down. My hands want to fidget. They reach for my script, rolling the papers, unfurling them, folding some corners, smoothing them out. Anyone who comes to my presentation is going to see a sweaty woman gone temporarily mute, who can't stop jerking around like a puppet detached from a couple of important strings.

"I'll help."

"You will?" I step up to him, fighting the urge to step into him. To wrap my arms around his trim waist.

"What do you need?" His voice has gone low.

I need you to close my office door and ravish me.

Wait, when did my vagina develop the ability to form thoughts?

"I need a practice audience. Come to a conference room with me?" The one with big glass windows and almost no privacy.

Cole steps back, gesturing that I should lead the way. Once settled in the conference room, me by the projector, Cole at the opposite end of the table with my phone in front of him, keyed up to play false applause, I start at the beginning.

Two run-throughs and close to an hour later, I'm steadier and speaking fine without my script. But I'm uncertain my problem has been truly solved.

"Feel better?" Cole asks.

"I guess." Damn it. That sounds ungrateful. And after Cole has sat with me for a good chunk of time when he could easily have muttered *clementine* and bowed out. "I'm sorry. Only, I'm still just talking to you. You're one person. And I'm pretty sure you like me."

Cole snorts, and I throw him a smirk, then sigh out my frustration.

"This just isn't stressful enough. It's not close enough to the real thing."

Cole watches me, his tongue fiddling with his lip piercing. And now I want to jump him. But I'm at work, trying to solve a real problem.

"Do you wanna come by the shelter tomorrow?" His question throws me, the topic change so abrupt.

"Um, well I work tomorrow."

"After work."

I consider it. Getting to immerse myself in cute dogs and cats might not solve all my problems, but it does seem like an awesome stress reliever. My lips tug into a grin, and thankful warmth spreads through my chest. Cole might not be able to give me all the solutions, but at least he's finding small ways to help.

"Sure. I'd like that."

He stands abruptly, circling around the conference table. From the way he stalks toward me, I'm half worried, half excited that he'll lift me onto the table and have his way with me. But when the tattooed temptation of a man reaches me, all I get is a quick kiss on the corner of my mouth.

"It's a date." He steps back, smirking down at me as I blink away the sudden onslaught of lust. "Get back to work, Ms. Pierce."

"Don't tell me what to do," I grumble, fighting off a smile and a blush.

Cole gifts me with a dry chuckle, sauntering toward the door and scooping up his notebook as he departs.

As I try not to ogle his backside, I'm hit with a sudden wave of panic.

Tomorrow, I'm going to Cole's workplace. I'll see him surrounded by adorable animals.

What if I see him holding a kitten?

Does he know what he's doing?

Does he know how easily I'm falling for him?

SUMMER

"You can't be serious."

"I am."

I stare at Cole, wondering if this is some sort of joke, trying to make me look ridiculous.

Will he take out his phone and video me while I do this?

And I immediately feel guilty for thinking the worst of him again.

"Okay, even if you are serious, I don't see how this helps."

Cole leans back against a door, looking sexy as hell in a worn pair of jeans and a bright blue T-shirt with the name of the animal rescue across the chest. His work uniform. When I agreed to come to the animal shelter, I thought I'd be volunteering. Walking dogs, cuddling cats, handing carrot sticks to rabbits, or whatever.

Cole has different plans.

"You said you needed more stress. Trust me. This is the most unruly crowd you could imagine."

Even through the thick walls, I can hear barking.

"I don't think animals are allowed into the conference unless they're service dogs," I point out.

He shrugs. "Yeah. It's not the same. But it's more intense than talking to me."

True. Damn, I'm going to look so silly. But I guess that's another part of my anxiety I need to learn to deal with.

"Okay. I'll do it. But afterwards there better be kittens." Cole just gives me his sneaky smile and holds the door open. The sound is deafening. Before we went into the room, there was only an occasional bark. But now that the dogs can see us, they get vocal. We're in a large room with lines of kennels. There are so many furry, excited bodies wriggling and jumping around howling that it's hard to concentrate enough to even try to count them all.

Which I guess is kind of the point of our visit.

"Start whenever you're ready!" Cole calls out to me over the racket.

He backs up, giving me the floor. Or at least the space near the door that's as close to a stage as this room provides.

As I clear my throat, I try not to get mesmerized by how Cole drops his hand behind him, letting a whining mutt sniff his knuckles through the metal links of the kennel. The pup's tail wags so fast I'm concerned it might fling right off.

Do I look equally as smitten when I'm near the man?

"Here goes nothing," I mutter to myself below the chorus of woofs. Then I do my best to project my voice over the racket. As I touch on all the important parts of my presentation, the barking batters against my brain and wears at my nerves. Still, I imagine that what I'm saying might somehow calm the animals. That maybe they'll find hearing my voice soothing and settle down to listen.

They don't. And by the time I've made it to the end of my talk, my skin feels sensitive, and I have the urge to sprint out the door and run off this anxious energy.

I guess I know how the dogs feel.

Still, I got through it all. This was harder than chatting in an empty conference room, and Cole's encouraging smile makes me feel more secure.

Then his eyes flick over my shoulder, and he bites his lower lip before calling out, "Hey, boss."

I whirl around, realizing that a woman came through the door at some point during my speech. She's a sturdy-looking lady, with strong arms and her hair pulled back in a no-nonsense ponytail.

And Cole just said she was his boss.

"Oh my gosh. I'm sorry. This was... I'm sorry," I end lamely.

The woman stares at me, her gaze heavy and curious. "Do you really do all those things?"

"What things?" I try not to fidget under her scrutiny. Even though it was his idea, I hope Cole doesn't get in trouble. He was just trying to help me.

"The things you just lectured the dogs about. Those programs."

"Oh!" Not what I was expecting her to ask. "Yes. We do. The library is a public space, so it's our responsibility to serve the public. Every member, whether they have a home or not." I snap my mouth shut before I go back into my conference spiel.

The woman gives a sharp nod that I hope is one of approval. Then she turns to Cole. "You gonna take some dogs out, or just talk at them all night?"

My urge is to step in and defend him, but then I notice his smirk. "I'm gettin' to it. Need to show Summer the way of it."

His boss grunts, then turns her scrutiny back to me for a moment before speaking. "You're smart. And you care. Ever think of a way your library can help these animals out, I'm interested in working together." She heads toward the exit, throwing a last instruction over her shoulder at Cole. "Give her one of my cards on the way out."

When I look to Cole, it's to find him stepping up to my side.

"You did great." His hands cup the back of my neck, massaging muscles I didn't even realize had gone tense. "Want to walk a dog?"

Leaving off the conversation about my surprise audience, I grin up at him. "I think they deserve it after listening to me yammer."

His smile is almost what I would call sweet.

Over the next half hour, I get an introduction to handling the animals. None of the ones Cole has me work with are aggressive, just wildly energetic. But I get that. If I had to spend the majority of the day in my studio apartment, I'd be ricocheting off the walls and begging for someone to open the door, too.

Once I'm comfortable walking a dog on my own, Cole chooses two animals that get along well, Bunny and Calamari, for us to take out together. We walk them around the grounds, then all four of us enter a smaller gated running area where we can take off the leashes.

The two dogs take a couple of laps, sniffing every corner on their way. Cole hands me tennis balls to chuck, and I find myself laughing at the silly puppies charging after the yellow balls.

"You're good with them. Ever think about adopting?" Cole hooks a finger in the belt loop of my jeans, fiddling with the material as we watch the dogs wrestle.

All the time. I want to say. Wouldn't it be glorious to give a home to one of these poor creatures? To love and care for them. To get back from work and be greeted with enthusiasm and devotion.

But then an image creeps into my brain.

A dead bird, lying neatly on my front mat.

"Maybe one day. I'm just too busy right now." My excuse is lame and flimsy, but Cole doesn't push, for which I'm thankful.

If I brought a pet into my life, I know I'd worry all the time that whoever my stalker is might take offense and harm the animal in some way. I could never live with myself if that happened.

A burning anger fills my chest. This specter is always out of sight, but still somehow present, affecting my life choices. Hindering my freedom. Demanding a say when they have no right.

All because I'm scared of them. What they'll do to me.

What they might do to something I care about.

My eyes skip over to Cole then as he steps away to throw another tennis ball far across the fenced area, a rare grin adorning his mouth as Bunny rockets after the toy. The sight of his relaxed joy has me rubbing my chest. And I wonder if he's more of a danger to me, or if I'm more of a danger to him.

As if my tormentor knew about my angry thoughts, later that night, when I arrive home, there's another envelope waiting for me on my front mat.

Good luck stretches in thick black letters across a newspaper announcement of the library conference.

Grabbing the closest throw pillow, I bury my face in the soft object and scream my frustration and fear. Tears stream down my face as I shove the taunting message in with the others.

Only after I've double-checked the locks and shoved a chair under the doorknob for good measure do I let myself curl up in my bed covers. As anxious adrenaline quivers through my limbs, I long to have one of those sweet, yet intimidating-looking pit bulls to cuddle with.

Also maybe the sweet, yet intimidating-looking man who rescues them.

Chapter Thirty-Four

SUMMER

"Summer?"

"On my break," I mumble around a mouthful of sandwich, my eyes adhered to the screen.

"You want me to come back later?" The question comes with a wry tone that is only perfectly achieved by one man.

Tearing my gaze away from my screen, I realize Cole is standing in my office doorway, lounging against the frame, wearing a smirk. I swallow my giant bite, and from the painful trip it takes down my esophagus, I know I didn't chew it enough. But I'd rather not just sit here, staring at Cole, munching in silence.

After a sip of water, I wave for him to come in.

"No! Sorry, I didn't mean to snap. Please, come in. Sit down." There are plenty of soft seats to choose from. Of course, Cole picks the wingback chair I have right next to my desk. He sinks into the garage-sale find, resting an ankle on his knee as he leans back in the seat. Claiming it as his own.

"Enjoying your break?"

"Yes. But"—my eyes flick to my computer screen then back to his face—"are you in a hurry right now? Could you wait a few minutes while I finish something?"

Cole shrugs. "No rush. What do you need to finish?"

"Well, it's not that I need to. I just want to. Badly."

His pierced brow curves up, and I try to figure out the best way to explain this without gushing or sounding obsessive.

"So, there's this website. It's called EpicTales dot com. Basically, it's this freely available publishing platform where people can post serialized stories. So anyone can write an epic tale and then release a chapter at a time."

Cole's fingers play with a worn hole in the armrest of the chair. I've been meaning to patch that.

"And you read these stories?" His casual question holds no understanding of how amazing and addictive these epic tales can be.

"Yes. Well, mainly one story in particular. I'll sample others, but honestly, this one has ruined me. But in the best way. I'm addicted."

"Which one is that?"

My eyes flick to my computer screen, drawn there by my rabid need to find out what happens next. But I tear myself away to answer.

"It's called *The Seven Siblings*. And it is glorious! There's adventure and romance and intrigue. Essentially, it's fairy tale retellings, but the traditionally female characters like Snow White and Rapunzel are gender-bent. So they're men. But their romantic interests are still men, so it's gay retellings of those fairy tales. And that might make it sound male-centric, but there are also these strong badass characters of other genders throughout, like this witch that is pretty much constantly saving all of their asses..." I trail off when I realize Cole is smiling but still not looking at me. "I'm gushing. Sorry. And I'm doing a sucky job of explaining this. Which is why I am the reader, not the writer. Just take my word for it. This story is amazing, and a new chapter just got posted, and I'm not sure I'll be able to focus on any conversation with you until I know what happens next."

"Go ahead and read," Cole murmurs.

I can't tell if he's put off by my fandom or not, but I decide I can figure that out in a few minutes when I get done reading the next scene.

Leaving Cole to his thoughts, I refocus on my computer screen and take another, more reasonable-sized bite of my sandwich. When I reach the last line, an involuntary moan works its way out of my chest before I remember I'm not alone.

"This chapter no good?"

I glance back at Cole to find him watching me intently.

"The exact opposite. Too good. And it ends on a cliff-hanger! Of course, they mainly do. That's how they keep everyone reading. That, and by weaving an amazing story." I sigh and remind myself that I only have to wait a week, and then I'll know what the prince whispered to his lover.

"You like it that much?" Luckily, Cole only sounds curious, rather than disbelieving. If he scorned my obsession for *The Seven Siblings*, I might have to end whatever this thing is that's developing between us. No one gets to shit on the things I love.

"Like it? That's the same as saying Willy Wonka only *liked* chocolate. Or that Smaug only *liked* treasure." My office chair squeaks as I swivel it to face Cole head-on, our stares locked. "*The Seven Siblings* brings me pure unadulterated joy. I adore this story. This author..." I gesture at my computer screen. "The Inked Dragon, they call themself. They're one of the most engaging, wickedly creative authors I've ever read. If I had any idea who they were, I'd write them horrible love poems."

"Horrible?" Cole is full-on grinning at me now, which only makes me more flustered and drives more gushing nonsense out of my mouth.

"Not intentionally horrible. But my ability to write anything creative is sorely lacking. I'd probably end up rhyming 'perfection' with 'infection.'"

"Really?" Cole presses his knuckles against his mouth, and I have a suspicion he's attempting to stifle some laughter. "How would that go?"

I fight my own smile. "Oh. You know. *Your stories are utter perfection. They've taken me over like an infection.*"

He barks out a short laugh, then cuts himself off. Resting his elbows on his knees, Cole leans toward me, a fascinating spark lighting up the cool blue of his eyes.

"I'm surprised."

"That I like this story? Just because I'm a straight woman doesn't mean I can't enjoy reading about two men falling in love."

"No." He shakes his head, a wicked smile still in place. "I'm surprised you haven't made the connection."

His words linger between us, and I try to piece them into some sense, like a puzzle.

"A connection in the story? Do you read it, too? Is there some plot point you think I'm missing?" But how would he even know? It's not like we've had a full discussion about *The Seven Siblings*, which I could spend days digging into.

"I do read it. But that's not what I mean."

The second part of his statement barely registers because I'm too overwhelmingly excited to find out that Cole and I read the same story.

"You've read it?" My hands clap together under my chin as I gaze at him. "Do you love it? Are you up to date? Probably not, since the newest chapter just came out. I swear I won't spoil it for you. But oh my gosh. It is so good. Do you want to read it now?" I wave at my computer.

Cole tilts his head, examining me. I smile wide to let him know I'm serious.

"Do you mind?" He gestures at my computer, and I want to cheer. I've always had to wait until Jasmine and I have a girls' night before I can talk to someone about the story. But now, there's Cole. He's going to read it, and I'm going to have the best break ever getting a chance to discuss it with him.

Standing from my chair, I allow Cole to slide into my seat. As I move toward the vacated chair, Cole's arm wraps around my waist, and he pulls me back toward him until I'm situated on his lap.

A much better seat than my secondhand furniture.

Long arms around me, Cole scrolls to the top of the EpicTales webpage.

Moving the cursor to the left corner, he clicks on the "Log In" button.

"Why do you have an account? The site is free for the public to access. Only creators have..." My words disappear as Cole's deft fingers tap over my keyboard, filling in the username box.

The Inked Dragon.

All rational thought leaves me. My mind is blank, shock having wiped all thoughts clean as if my brain were a whiteboard.

Cole continues to type, filling in the password box before pressing enter.

The screen shows a dashboard different than the public view. There's a box labeled "Tales." In Cole's Tales box, there's only one title.

The Seven Siblings.

He clicks on it, and we're brought to another page, one long list of all the chapters I've devoured more times than I could possibly count. And at the top of the screen is a beautiful blue button that reads "Add New Chapter."

My little office has never been so silent.

COLE

Sometimes I surprise myself at how aloof I can act. How casual I can be about things that mean the world to me.

The Seven Siblings means more than can be put into words. And I would know, seeing as how I'm a writer.

When I was behind bars, there were days I thought I might go insane. That the lack of control over my life would break my mind. Those were the days that writing saved me. Writing this story. I started with the Rapunzel fairy tale, turning the captive into a man so I could get all my rage at being locked up down on the page in an authentic way.

I had debated my Rapunzel being saved by a prince or a princess.

Then my new cellmate Dash showed up, and I opted for the prince.

I may have had a slight crush at the time. Soon, I realized he was straight, and we were better as friends. But the story had already taken shape. And I decided all the fairy tales I'd been fed as a child could benefit from a queer makeover. So I had a mission. A purpose.

And when I got out, I had hundreds of thousands of words of a raw, epic story.

Briefly, I considered trying to get an agent or a publisher interested.

But it was too personal. I couldn't have someone picking apart this story that saved me. Demanding I make changes so the words would be more palatable to the general public. I decided only I would have a say in its formation.

That's when I sought out some way to publish it myself.

And so The Inked Dragon was born on EpicTales.

A full minute has gone by without Summer having spoken. For a normally chatty woman, this silence is eerie.

Then, finally, she breaks.

"You." The word comes out harsh, like an accusation.

"Me?"

"You show me this when I have mere minutes left in my break? When I have four hours left at my job where I have to function like a rational human being? How could you?" Summer stares at me, aghast.

"Are you mad at me?"

"I am..." She shoves up from my lap, pacing the tiny office, only to come back to me and fist her hands in my shirt collar. "I am ravenous." My librarian's eyes are wild, and an answering neediness unfurls in my chest.

"Tell them you're sick. Come home with me," I say.

"Cole!" She moans my name, releasing my shirt to bury her face in her hands.

I stand, gently clasping her wrists, making my voice coaxing.

"You want to know what happens next, don't you? I can tell you. I have it all written already. Want me to read it to you?"

"You're the devil!" Summer sounds halfway between laughing and crying, but when I pull her hands away from her face she's glaring at me. "Don't you tempt me. Don't you dare."

Before I can answer, I'm shoved backward, my legs hitting her desk surprising me into sitting on the cluttered surface.

And her mouth is on mine. Hot, needy, worshiping.

"Don't you dare"—she bites my lower lip—"spoil the ending." Summer licks the spot she bit, then backs away, her hand pressed to my chest as if to keep me in place. Her pupils are dilated like I'm a drug she's high on. "I have to work. But then I'm coming to your place. And you're going to read me my favorite scenes you've published so far."

"Am I?" I can't help teasing her when she uses that commanding tone.

Summer leans in close, her lips brushing my ear. "Yes. You are. You're going to read them to me while you're naked, and I'm licking your tattoos. Because I'm the luckiest girl in the world, and I want a taste of The Inked Dragon." Then she bites my ear lobe, and I almost come on the spot.

"Now," I growl. "We go to my place *now*."

Summer leans back, shaking her head, teeth pinching her bottom lip. "You did this, Cole. You got me all horned up right before I have to go back to work. If I'm dealing with a lady boner for the next four hours, then you have to deal with some sexual frustration, too. Fair is fair."

I can't help the scowl that pulls at my mouth.

Hours. I have to wait hours for her to fulfill her dirty promises.

Before today, I thought I was a patient man.

Chapter Thirty-Five

SUMMER

"You are confident. You are a kickass librarian. You won't have any visible pit stains." Mirror Summer glares back at me in her black blazer.

This is an uncharacteristically dark outfit choice, but it's the only thing that will make my last pep talk statement true. My conference presentation starts in fifteen minutes. I need to get out of this bathroom and set up my laptop with the projector.

"Hey, you almost ready?" Amy knocks on the door, startling me.

One last time, I blot my face with a paper towel, then pull open the bathroom door to find my presentation partner waiting.

"You okay?" she asks.

"Yep!" That was overly bright, but I believe my best route is to pursue enthusiasm to keep me from getting lightheaded. I will be too perky to be scared!

Ten minutes later, I'm at the front of a room large enough to hold forty people, and from the steady stream filing in, I wouldn't be surprised if we meet that number.

It's okay. Just imagine you're hosting four Coffee Talks simultaneously. No big deal.

Lying is not my strong suit, especially when I'm trying to misdirect myself.

My hands fidget with the remote for the projector, wanting to press the buttons just for something to do. The organizers have left us each a bottle of water, and I home in on mine, untwisting the cap and chugging down half the contents before I realize I'm not even thirsty.

Damn. Am I going to have to pee halfway through this thing?

I can imagine it now, me standing up here in front of a group of people whose respect I'm trying to earn, all the while clenching my thighs together to keep from pissing myself. Has anyone ever excused themselves in the middle of their own presentation for a bathroom break? Would I be able to fight off the mortification of returning to the front of the room after a stunt like that?

"Okay, looks like we're about ready." A smiling woman with a badge that proclaims her as one of the moderators approaches us. "I'll introduce you both, and then you can take over. Sound good?"

"Sounds great," says Amy.

"Mmphgerd," says me.

The moderator gives me a vaguely concerned look before turning to face the mass of gathered librarians.

Wait. Holy shit. A mass?

My eyes race over the audience, and I try to do the math. Logically, I know there's maybe a couple dozen. But my panicked brain shouts over that fact.

There must be hundreds of people in here. Thousands!

Heavy heartbeats pump too much blood yet absolutely no oxygen to my brain.

Just pass out. If you lose consciousness, you don't have to worry about anything anymore.

The doors crack open again just as the moderator reads off my name and job title from her notes. I want to yell to the back of the room that no one else is allowed in, but then my eyes catch on a glint of silver.

The shine comes from an eyebrow piercing.

Cole Allemand is in the building.

In the conference room.

In my audience.

In my eyeline.

He smiles at me when he notices my staring, then proceeds to lean against the wall in the back of the room, his arms crossed over his chest. He's wearing a ridiculous sweater covered in a pattern that resembles books.

The bastard snuck into a library conference to hear my presentation.

I could kiss him all over his perfect face.

But that would probably be a weirder thing to do than asking for a bathroom break.

Instead, he gets my sunniest smile. My heart still hammers heavier than necessary, but I find I can at least hear over the pounding.

The moderator gestures toward me before stepping aside.

And I think I've got this.

"Hello!" *Too loud.* "I'm Summer Pierce." *That's better.* "And I'm here to talk to you all about helping one of a public library's most important patron groups. The homeless."

Just like when we practiced, I talk to Cole. I give him my presentation. I look for his smile and chuckle when I crack a joke. His subtle head nods let me know I'm at a good pace. Amy's interludes give me enough breaks to finish my water, and I don't even suck the thing down like a drowning fish.

The time does not fly by, but it also doesn't stick in place. The minutes progress, I sweat, my voice only quivers twice, and before long we've reached our last slide, a picture from Coffee Talk a few months ago where I sit among a group of our patrons, us all cheesing the camera with steaming paper cups.

With the happy memory displayed for all to see, I pull out my last line, not even needing my notecards.

"And remember, just because someone doesn't have a home, doesn't mean they don't have a voice."

The enthusiastic applause warms my already flushed skin, but I can't help grinning in triumph. For the last ten minutes, Amy and I take questions from the audience, which I find to be a much easier task than presenting. Conversations I'm good at. Performing gives me hives.

When the moderator flashes the red card letting us know our time is up, we both thank the audience, and I breathe the first full breath I've taken in an hour. Librarians from institutions across the state, and even some from Mississippi and Texas, wander up to me afterwards, exchanging business cards and asking for my slides.

"You did great, Summer. Thanks so much for submitting this proposal. I'm glad we got to spread the word." Amy slings her bag over her shoulder, here only for our presentation.

"Thank you." I find myself blinking rapidly. Maybe it's the sudden release of stress. Or maybe it's hitting one of my career goals. First presentation at a professional conference! Whatever it is, happy tears clog the back of my throat.

Finally free, I head toward the back of the room where Cole still waits for me.

"You came!" I clap, staring up at him, sure there's worship on my face.

"Had to see you kick ass," he explains with a shrug, as if it's obvious I should've expected him to come.

I want to hug him so bad, but I can't help thinking about how damp the pits of my blazer are. Instead, I pluck at his sweater.

"This is the most amazing one yet. Another Mama Al purchase?"

He nods with a rueful smile. "She got it for me when she found out you're a librarian."

The indirect approval warms my chest.

"Why haven't you hugged me yet?" Cole asks, a smirk on his face, but under it I can tell a hint of insecurity lurks. Not surprising. I'm constantly wrapping myself around him. I love the feel of Cole's body against mine. Apparently, he's noticed.

"I'm sweaty. And it's stress sweat, so I stink." I smooth my hands over my blazer as if I have magical detergent hands. "Don't want to subject you to all this. They should have complimentary showers for anxious presenters. No one is going to want to sit within five feet of me." Anxiety returns, not as fierce as what paired with my presentation, but still a subtle sting. No one wants to be the stinky person in the room.

Cole steps up to me, hands resting on my shoulders before sliding up to the back of my neck, massaging the tense muscles.

"How long till the next presentation?"

I glance at my program where I've highlighted the sessions I want to attend. "Ten minutes."

He nods, scooping up my hand and tugging me toward the front doors.

"What are you doing? I don't want to leave!" It's hard to dig in my heels when I'm wearing actual heels, so I just try to shorten my shuffling steps.

"We're not leaving. Just come to my truck for a second."

"Okay, but I want to see this next one. It's about promoting health literacy!"

Cole's half-smile is all indulgence.

When we find his truck, Cole opens the back seat and unzips a small duffle bag. From it, he pulls out a black T-shirt.

"Oh, that's sweet Cole. But I'm trying to keep a business casual appearance."

"This is for me. This"—he reaches for the bottom of his sweater, pulling it off in one move, revealing his naked, tattooed chest to the empty parking lot—"is for you." And then he holds the glorious book sweater out to me.

"I couldn't." The words come even as I grasp the knitted glory.

"You want to," he coaxes, pulling his T-shirt on.

"I really, really do." I finger the fabric, then glance around the parking lot. "Okay. Cover me."

Stepping between the car and Cole's body, I briefly wish he was wider around the middle. Better to act as a human dressing screen and keep me from flashing anyone walking by. Quickly, I shuck off my blazer and navy blouse, leaving me in a white bra. Luckily the day is mild, so I'm not fighting a chill as I bundle the clothes into Cole's back seat. Then, excitement sparking through me, I pull the sweater over my head. And immediately I'm grateful for Cole's slim form. The sweater is a decent fit, only a tad looser than my preference.

"Okay, how do I look?"

He steps away, pulling on his T-shirt before turning to examine me. I strike a Peter Pan pose, arms akimbo. I figure the sweater has to look decent with my black A-line skirt, dark tights, and Mary Jane heels. Maybe not an interview-level outfit, but better than a T-shirt or a sweaty blazer.

Cole's eyes trail over me before answering. "Adorable. Sexy."

"I was going for professional, but I guess those will do." Reaching up, I pull his head down so I can plant a noisy, smacking kiss on his lips. "You are an amazing man, Cole Allemand." When I lean away, I'm delighted to notice a light shade of red high on his cheekbones. "What are your plans for the rest of the day?"

He clears his throat and shrugs. "I guess learning about how to promote health literacy?"

"You...what?"

He reaches into his back pocket to tug out a lanyard. Attached to it is a small plastic sleeve holding a card with the conference's logo and a printed name.

Cole Allemand.

"Paid for the day. Might as well get my money's worth."

He didn't sneak in. He paid to attend a library conference. Just to see me present.

Some strange heavy feelings spark in my chest, and my fingers reach out to fiddle with the lanyard. "I want you to wear this in bed tonight."

Cole's gaze flicks from my hand, to my mouth, to my eyes.

"My conference name tag?"

"Yes."

The grin that curls the edges of his mouth is the exact right amount of naughty.

Chapter Thirty-Six

COLE

I gave Summer my spare key. My excuse was that Smaug gets lonely when I'm at work, so she should stop by and see him. In reality, I just wanted to up the chances she'd be at my place.

Also, I'm slowly acclimating her to the idea of us living together. Like, maybe one day all her stuff will appear in my house, and she won't question it.

Today, I'm pretty sure my plan is working.

When I walk in the front door, I'm in a zombie state.

This was a shitty day.

Someone returned a cat, claiming that it was aggressive. It was hard to argue with their reasoning, seeing as how the animal swiped at me the minute I opened the cage door. But I knew this cat. I'd held him and played with him when he originally ended up at the shelter. The cat had been affectionate. Now it was terrified of something.

And I have no idea what.

That's the problem with working at a rescue. You can only help the animals as long as they're in your care. Once you send them off with a person, you just have to hope the home is a good one. That the animal will be loved.

This cat went through something. And now he's in quarantine for clawing me.

All I can do is make a note on the adopter's file, and spend the next few months trying to teach the cat to trust humans again.

And seeing as how most humans are shit, I don't expect the job to be easy.

My bedroom door is ajar, a light on inside.

Is she here?

Quieting my steps, I push into the room.

On my bed is proof that some humans aren't terrible. At least one is as close to perfect as someone can get.

Summer lays on my bed in a nest of pillows, half of them ones she's sewn for me. At least, she says they are for me. She tends to get more use out of them than I do. In the nest with her is Smaug, curled against her chest, his tail covering his nose. Both woman and cat have their eyes closed, napping even with the reading light on.

When I slipped my spare key into her pocket, I had hopes. None of them prepared me for this. For the utter contentment that fills my chest at the sight. This is what I want every day for the rest of my life.

Because I love Summer Pierce.

I think I've loved her for months.

She's what I want forever.

But does she want me?

For now. I think she wants me for now. But that's not near good enough.

Contentment is replaced by the beginnings of panic. Even though I want to crawl into bed with them, wrap myself around them and claim my little family, I don't. I continue on to the bathroom and turn the shower on. The water stays freezing cold.

Good. I need that.

I scrub every inch of myself, trying to scratch the worry off my skin where it sticks like a layer of film.

You'll drive her away. The voice in my head isn't mine. It's my father's. Which makes it hurt all the worse because that man would never lie to me.

"Fuck that. She'll stay," I mutter to myself.

After I've passed the point of shivering, when my fingers are pruned and my lips are numb, I finally step out of the shower. The soft texture of the towel barely registers on my skin. It's as if I've tried to freeze out the panic by numbing every nerve ending in my body.

In my rush, I didn't bring any clothes with me. I head back to my room, adamant that I'll keep my eyes off Summer.

I fail in the first second.

Smaug has wandered off, leaving her alone in the bed.

Before she looked adorable. Now she's sexy as hell, sprawled across my bed with her skirt hiked up.

Abandoning my search for clothes, I carefully settle on the mattress beside her. My fingers ache to touch her, to trace the curve of her nose, to brush the satin of her lips. If only I could imprint myself on her skin, claim every pore of her for myself.

Instead, I sit quietly, enjoying the serenity of Summer completely relaxed.

That is, until she sits up suddenly.

"Gah!" Her sudden movement has me lurching back, which means I slide off the bed to land ass first on the hardwood. I moan, rubbing my tailbone and realizing the towel I'd had wrapped around my waist didn't come off the bed with me.

"Why are you sitting on the floor naked?"

I meet a set of wild, confused eyes. Summer blinks rapidly, as if still waking up.

"I was sitting on the bed with a towel until you scared the shit out of me." Standing, I reach for the terrycloth.

But she beats me to it, snatching the fabric and clutching it to her chest.

"I wasn't *complaining* that you're naked."

A smirk twitches across my mouth when Summer offers me a teasing smile. Still, there's a shadow in her gaze that has me thinking she woke up so suddenly for a reason.

"Were you dreaming?" Combing my fingers through my damp hair, I scrutinize her face for a reaction. She's not too subtle. A grimace sneaks out before she bites her lip and shrugs.

"What were you dreaming about?"

Hesitation, then, "Scary things."

My urge is to dig further. Find out exactly what is unsettling the woman I love. But just as I go to open my mouth, she reclines on the bed with a sigh, stretching her arms above her head in a delicious way that makes her chest bow up.

"But you make me feel safe."

Shit. That hits me hard. Right in the middle of my chest.

Summer feels safe with me. That's one step away from saying she loves me.

"What can I do?" I rasp. *To make you love me?*

"Come to bed." She reaches a hand out, and there's nothing in the world that could keep me from accepting it.

I cover Summer with my body, pressing my mouth to hers, wanting to breath her in. Her response is to twine her arms and legs around me, holding me close as if scared I'll pull away from her.

Never.

With our bodies desperately twisted together, there's not even enough space to slide her dress off. Instead, I hike up her skirt and rock my hardness against her core, massaging her clit through a thin cotton barrier.

"Just like that," she moans, her lips brushing mine as they move.

I keep up the steady rhythm until she's panting.

"Inside me." Her command comes ragged and delicious.

Blindly, I reach out toward my nightstand, somehow locating a condom without pausing my onslaught. But I have to take a moment, only long enough to slide the protection on, then I'm back to worshiping her, tugging her panties to the side. She's so wet, I slide in easy, sitting deep in Summer's heat.

The tingle at the base of my spine warns me I'm not going to last long. So I stay still, my forehead dropping to her shoulder as I suck in deep gusting breaths.

"Cole," she whimpers my name, the sound almost my undoing.

But I can't start up again just yet.

Because I need this. I need her in my arms the same time I'm in her grip. I need the subtle scent of lilac mixing with the tartness of her arousal. I need to hear her beg me for more, convincing myself that the longing in her voice applies to more than just sex.

I need her to need me.

"Please. I'm so close." Nails scrape along my scalp as her hips rock, seeking the pleasure she knows I can give her.

But is pleasure all that she wants from me?

Still, I can't deny Summer anything. Not for long anyway.

"Say my name when you come," I command as my hand shoves between us, fingers circling her clit, massaging, then squeezing in a gentle pinch. Just the way she likes.

"C-Cole!" She stutters over the word as her inner muscles quiver and tighten on my hard cock.

I love you, I repeat to myself as I thrust inside her.

I love you. My hips press into her soft thighs.

I love you. Her hands pull me in for a searing kiss.

As my orgasm blurs everything else in my mind, two words play on repeat. A silent, desperate plea.

Love me.

Chapter Thirty-Seven

COLE

When I end the call, my phone slips out of my fingers. My muscles just can't seem to grip it.

Did I say anything? I'm not sure I spoke. Maybe I had a stroke. Hopefully Camila understands. Now that I'm off the phone, alone in my house, I want to talk to someone. I need to tell someone.

No, not just someone.

I know exactly who I want to tell.

Scrambling for my phone again, I'm about to call her when I stop myself.

A call isn't good enough. I want to see her face. I need to be in the same room as her when she hears.

So I text her instead.

Cole: *Come 2 my place after work.*

She doesn't answer right away, and I pace around my apartment, all anxious energy. After a few minutes my phone dings.

Summer: *Okie dokie. I'll grab food. What cha want?*

Cole: *No food. Just you.*

Summer: *Sex makes me hungry. I'm going to need food after you bang me good.*

An exasperated laugh dives from my throat.

Cole: *I'll have pizza waiting. Just come.*

Summer: *That's what you'll be saying later ;)*

She drives me wild with her silly teasing, but at least I have a task to keep me busy instead of just pacing.

A short while later, when I'm pulling back into my driveway with a fresh pizza, I see Summer's car already here.

Thank god.

I circle around back, taking three stairs at a time. In the kitchen I barely pause to put down the food before jogging to my bedroom. Summer sits cross-legged on my bed, her skirt bunched high on her thighs as she fiddles with the remote. Any other day, I'd kneel in front of her, slide off her panties, and give her a post-work orgasm with my tongue.

But today I have news.

"Did you get pizza?" she asks.

"I got a book deal."

Quiet descends over the room as Summer's eyes flick to mine, going wide.

"You what?" The remote drops from her hand, bouncing from my mattress onto the floor.

"I got a book deal," I repeat. "My agent called earlier and told me."

Slowly, my librarian unfolds herself, standing from the bed. "You wrote a book? And it's going to be published?" She sounds mystified.

Fingers tapping rapidly on my jeans, I anxiously wait for something other than her complete confusion. Maybe I should've told her about my manuscript and signing with an agent. As far as Summer knows, I just write my serialized story.

"Next year. As long as I sign the contract. Which I will," I say.

As she continues to stare at me, my fingers drum faster.

I'm not sure what reaction I expected.

No, that's not true. In my daydreams, I came up with a hundred different Summer reactions to this possible news.

I expected screeching and dancing and grabbing random things.

Something like when she found out about The Inked Dragon.

I expected gushing.

But Summer just stares at me, her lips parted. She's doing none of my hoped-for reactions.

So I keep talking.

"My agent has been shopping it around for a while now, and I wasn't sure a publisher would want it. I mean, fantasy isn't always the biggest seller. But my agent thought it was good, and a lot of people like *The Seven Siblings*, so—"

My words are cut off when Summer steps up to me. Another emotion has bled into her gaze. She's no longer bewildered. Now there's a pure wave of joy that crashes from her into me.

Her hands frame my face. She has soft palms, soothing like silk on my cheeks.

"I know you did this all on your own, but I am *so* proud of you." The words come on a low, worshipful murmur. They dig into me and caress every inch of my self-doubt.

"Summer..."

She shakes her head, smiling all the while, as if she knows I want to duck away from her praise as much as I want to bask in it.

"I am. You are amazing." Pride shines from her eyes, and my entire body clenches, my muscles going so tight I begin to shake.

This is better.

This is so much better than gushing.

I didn't realize that I'd want more. That I'd need more from her than an overeager fan reaction. If we hadn't known each other, if she hadn't cared about me first, her adoration would've felt empty. Fleeting.

But she's looking up at me with something like love.

This is better.

Especially when the affection in her eyes goes darker, more wicked. Needy.

Those warm hands of hers drop from my face, landing on my belt buckle.

"Do you want to celebrate?" she asks. Her question would sound innocent if it wasn't paired with the clink and slide of my belt being undone.

"Yes," I groan as her knuckles graze the skin on my stomach.

A clear shiver has her shoulders quaking. "Do you know how much I love it when you say *yes* to me?"

Her breathy statement clenches my gut. "I do now."

"So are you going to agree with me more often?" Summer waits, watching me as her fingers tease my waistband.

"Yes," I choke out.

Heavy-lidded, she leans forward, only tall enough to press a kiss to my collar bone. "Do you know how proud I am of you?" she whispers against my throat.

I know the answer she wants. "Yes."

"Good." Her teeth give my shoulder a gentle bite through my shirt, dragging a moan from me. As I try to wrap my arms around her, crush her body against mine, Summer places her hands flat on my chest, maintain a torturous distance between us.

"Do you know how amazing you are?"

She stares up at me now, brown eyes fierce.

Self-doubt pinches at my gut, and I cover the feeling with a smirk. "You want me cocky?"

Summer drops her hands to my waistband, undoing my zipper, gaze on mine the entire time.

"Say it, Cole."

"Summer—" I choke on her name when she drags her nails along my hip bones, urging my pants to fall down my legs.

"Do you know how amazing you are?" Her grip is on my ass, her eyes burning into mine, demanding I give her what she wants.

She wouldn't think I was amazing if she knew the truth. She wouldn't look at me like this.

But I'll do anything to keep her eyes on me.

"Yes," I lie.

Again, she leans forward, and I brace myself for teeth or tongue. But

Summer presses another light kiss to my collarbone, and I'm worried the gesture will kill me. Any time she treats me to that gentle touch, no matter where on my body, I can feel the affection. The caring.

Does she love me?

Her sweet kisses make me think she does.

Then Summer suddenly drops to her knees, and thinking becomes impossible.

Chapter Thirty-Eight

COLE

I'm riding a high for an entire week. Then I get the details of the contract.

The buzz doesn't immediately go away. In fact, it spikes when I see the quoted advance.

Fifteen thousand dollars.

Fuck, that's a lot of money.

Thousands of dollars. I'm getting thousands of dollars.

But I'm not some teenager on his first payday. I need to be smart about this money.

So I grab a pencil and paper and start doing the math.

The contract states that half will be paid upon signing, and the other half upon submitting a final product.

Okay, so that's seventy-five hundred now, and seventy-five hundred later. Still a good deal.

But then there's Camila's fifteen percent for her work as my agent.

I scratch out the equation in my notebook.

New total equals $6,375.

But, of course, can't forget taxes. A book I read on the business of writing suggested assuming you'll need to give at least forty percent to the government.

More numbers written out, and I find the final total.

Upon signing my contract, I'll be making roughly three thousand eight hundred twenty-five dollars.

The number shouldn't depress me, but it does.

This is thousands of dollars I didn't have before.

But I guess, in the back of my mind, I'd hoped for more.

The amount isn't even enough to pay off my father's debt. And if that's what I choose to do with it, I'll have nothing, no safety cushion, if I lose my job.

In any other situation, getting close to four thousand dollars would rock my world. But in this one, frustration burns in my chest.

I was so fucking stupid. I'd had this idea that as long as I got a book deal, everything would be okay. That my life would be easier once someone was willing to pay for my writing. That I would be set.

But what I have now is an advance small enough to give me a taste, but in the end, only serve to crush my hopes.

Three thousand eight hundred twenty-five. Why the hell does that number seem so small? It's huge. It's multiple paychecks.

But it's finite. Nothing to depend on. To live on.

Maybe all the time I spend writing, I should instead be filling out job applications. Doing something that'll result in more than three thousand eight hundred twenty-five.

The money isn't even in my hands, and I've already spent it. The total is zero.

I'm worthless. Nothing to be proud of.

I'm still staring at the contract when my phone dings. There's a stray hope that it's my agent, texting to tell me someone left a zero off the contract.

But the name flashing on my phone isn't Camila's.

And for the first time, I'm not excited to see a message from my librarian.

That is until I open it and can't help smiling at her ridiculous text.

Summer: *Hello, Cole Allemand. Please put Smaug on the phone. We have an important matter to discuss.*

Tossing the contract to the side, I recline on my bed and text her back.

Cole: *He doesn't have thumbs. I'll act as go-between.*

Summer: *Fine. Kindly tell him that while I adore his fluffiness, I insist he no longer takes naps on my favorite cardigan. I am awash in cat hair.*

That has me grinning, and I reach over to where Smaug lounges in a sunbeam and scratch behind the animal's ears.

Cole: *He says it's a compliment.*

Summer: *It's an act of war. If he does it again, I'm stitching him up in a throw pillow.*

I chuckle and text her more dismissive messages from my unrepentant pet, all the while enjoying the happy glow in my chest.

When our banter trails off after a while, I pull the contract back into my lap and reach for a pen.

Three thousand eight hundred twenty-five.

It's what I have. I'll make it work.

Anything I can do to keep my librarian.

Chapter Thirty-Nine

SUMMER

"Do you have one for every holiday?" I can't stop staring at Cole. And not for the normal, distractingly handsome face reason. Today, I'm transfixed because, in addition to his normal black pants and plethora of facial piercings, Cole has a naked baby on his chest.

More accurately, a cupid.

A giant flying cupid, holding a bow and arrow, hovering on a romantically red background.

Cole's Valentine's Day sweater.

In response to my question, the man just shrugs, but I'm sure he almost smiled.

"President's Day? Easter? Fourth of July? You can't tell me you wear a sweater in the middle of the summer in New Orleans. That's madness." But a delightful kind of madness I hope exists.

"Wait and see." Cole turns our shopping cart down another aisle.

He's probably just teasing, but I can't help thinking about the underlying meaning of his words. For me to wait and see, that means I'd still be with Cole in the spring and then into the summer.

Was that what he meant?

This whole day is throwing me off. Making me ask questions I've been avoiding.

Cole hadn't asked me about doing anything special today, and I hadn't figured out what my response would be if he did. For the most part, I don't think too much on what exactly our label is. The only word that's been thrown around is dating.

No one has even said exclusive.

Of course, I'm not going out with anyone else. I don't want to. Another reason I try not to dwell on these thoughts. Because then I would have to admit why I don't want to. And then I'd have to talk to Cole about being exclusive.

Or about ending things.

But this weird undefined dating we have right now is working. We see each other when we want to. Sometimes we're wearing clothes, sometimes we aren't.

There're no complications or expectations. Just day by day.

And some days, Cole and I go food shopping together. A few weeks ago, someone rear-ended me at a stoplight. What would've been a fender bender for better-maintained cars, was the kiss of death for mine. When I complained about the hassle of hauling my groceries on the bus, a necessary evil until I get a new car, Cole offered the use of his truck.

Now it's a scheduled date. Every Saturday morning he picks me up and we drive to the store to bargain hunt. It's weird how much I look forward to it.

So while most people who are dating someone have likely planned a special day with their partner, Cole and I are spending our Valentine's Day meandering through the cookware section so I can buy a new set of bowls.

Once I find a set that's both cheap and covered in cute blue swirly patterns, we move on.

Where we run smack into a Valentine's Day display.

The pink-hearted mass is impossible to ignore. Like a burning car on the side of the road. The two of us exchange quick-eyed glances that convey a nervous *should we do something* air. Or, at least, mine does.

If I wanted to be completely honest, I'd admit my main goal of today is to stay far away from my apartment. The last few years I've gotten notes from the mysterious creep in my life. On this holiday, they always use a red marker instead of black. So fucking festive, am I right?

Still, I decided not to let the darkness of the harassment touch anyone else in my life.

After the fuss I made about Cole's birthday, and the description I gave him of my mother's and my Christmas, I doubt he believes I normally let this holiday pass by without acknowledgment. Especially when there is someone kind of romantic in my life.

He's wearing his flamboyant sweater, obviously acknowledging what today is. He's made the first move. I have to do something.

A wall of colorful cards sparks my attention and has me dodging around the heart and glitter display.

"Summer?"

"Come here! I need you to do something."

The wheels on the cart squeak as he follows me.

"What?"

Planting myself in front of the greeting card display, I lock my gaze with his before deliberately closing my eyes.

"Spin me."

"Did you get a head injury I don't know about?" Confused amusement colors his question.

"Don't make me threaten you, Cole. Spin me!"

"You're odd," he mutters at a much closer range just before his hands settle on my waist.

"You love it." I grin in the direction I think his face is, still guessing as my eyes remain closed.

"I do." His answer brushes over my lips a second before he steals a kiss. Then his mouth is gone, and I'm being spun, despite the fact the I'm already beyond dizzy from his sneaky affection.

When my feet stumble to a stop, I remember my purpose, stretching my arms out in front of me and shuffling forward.

"I'm moving toward cards, right? You'd warn me if I was about to bulldoze some old lady?"

"Would I?" His voice sounds just off to my left just as my fingertips brush against stiff paper. Grabbing the first card I touch, I hold it up in triumph, finally opening my eyes and turning back to Cole, who watches with bemusement.

"I found it!"

"And *it* is?"

"My Valentine's Day card to you. Are you ready?"

Cole fights a smile as he watches me, leaning his elbows on the handle of the cart. "Yes."

After dramatically clearing my voice, I hold the card in front of me, as if I'm giving a reading of some beautiful novel.

"Happy Valentine's Day from the dog." Cole snorts, but I keep a straight face as I open the card to dictate the inside. "I know I can sometimes make life rough—to clarify, rough is spelled R-U-F-F—but know that despite dirty paw prints I leave on the floor, and those shoes of yours I chewed"—Cole has a fist pressed against his mouth in a vain attempt to stifle his laughter—"and all the drool I left on your pillow, I love you more than anyone else in the world."

I keep a goofy smile on my face, trying not to think about how the last bit of that sentence wasn't hard to say.

Not very hard at all.

"You do drool on my pillow sometimes."

"See? It was perfect." And now I feel better. The day has been acknowledged, but not with over the top gestures that feel disingenuous or put a strain on our new not-really-relationship.

I return the card to the shelf and make my way down the aisle, turning my thoughts back to the mental list I made of items to buy.

"What about mine?"

My legs lock up at Cole's question, and I slowly rotate to see he hasn't moved to follow me.

"Yours?"

His chin dips. "My card to you."

Then, stealing my breath with the joy of the playful moment, Cole walks to the middle of the aisle and shuts his eyes.

I can't move, barely breathing, both happy and scared, and wanting to hold him close until we become a set of people unable to be parted no matter how much time passes or space is placed between us.

As I reel, Cole's one lid cracks open in the wink version of a smirk, arctic blue eye peering down the length of linoleum tile at me. "You're supposed to spin me now."

"Oh. Yes. Of course." I hurry up to him, too eager and I know it.

Then my hands are on his waist, directing his body to rotate. He doesn't resist but turns with my encouragement. Eventually, I realize I've been spinning him for too long because I didn't want to give up the sensation of his soft sweater covering his warm, hard body.

When I let my hands drop, Cole slows almost immediately, reaching out his long arm. The smooth bastard doesn't even look a little bit dizzy as his fingers settle on a gold and red creation.

Never expecting him to repeat my silly game, I have no time to wonder what type of card I'd want Cole to pull.

Just one line in, I know this is the wrong one.

I know because I want the words too much.

"To my friend, my lover, my partner, my forever." His voice comes low and sharp as he delivers the sentiment without hesitation.

I stumble forward snatching at the card. "You don't have to read that!"

But he's taller than me, and faster apparently, holding it out of my reach.

"I want to," Cole says.

His determined tone quiets my frantic movements. Watching me as if checking for more snatching attempts, Cole's eventually satisfied and tilts the card so he can continue reading.

"Our lives have taken twisted paths, some leading into darkness, and others leading into light. There were many forks, other routes you could have walked. Every day, but today most of all, I am thankful you chose the way that crossed with mine. Now I know I will never have to travel alone again. You are my forever, my partner, my lover, my friend."

Silence falls between us. As Cole carefully refolds the card and replaces it on the shelf, I struggle to maintain my composure.

Why did that hurt so much?

How can his smoky voice say those beautiful words as if they're the truth?

Why does my heart want them to be?

Light pressure on my lips has my eyes refocusing, but before I realize Cole is kissing me, his mouth is gone from mine, instead brushing against my ear.

"Happy Valentine's Day, Summer."

He's back at the cart. He's down the aisle. He's around the corner.

And I'm frozen.

And I'm on fire.

Chapter Forty

COLE

"What's this one's name? Is it some type of food? Because I am going to eat her up!" Summer holds a squirming kitten next to her face and mimes chomping down on the little furball.

"Haven't named them yet. You think of some. I'll be back."

"Seriously? I can name them?"

I shrug like I don't know how excited I just made her. "Sure." Then I leave Summer alone with the crate of two-month-old kittens, heading to my office.

"Cole?" My boss's voice comes just as I'm grabbing some paperwork. When I turn to face Cheryl, she doesn't look in the best mood.

"Yeah?"

"Can we sit? I need to talk to you for a minute."

Shit. This isn't good.

When I'm in my dilapidated desk chair and Cheryl is settled in an old vinyl number, she gets straight to the point.

"I can only keep you full time for another month."

Dread clenches my stomach. She warned me. I knew this was coming.

I just desperately held on to a hope that her prediction was wrong. The idea of leaving this job is like staring over the edge of a cliff and having someone tell me I need to jump. When I got out of prison, this was my safe place. So many ex-cons struggle to find any kind of job, much less a decent one. Cheryl was my fairy godmother.

Guess I've been banking on her magic powers of protection for too long.

"Our last two fundraisers haven't brought in the money I was hoping for, and donations are down overall," she explains, regret clear in her voice.

"I get it." I know this isn't personal. But I can't help the rise of defensive anger.

"I'm hoping a month will give you time to find another position. After that, I can pay for some part-time, but it's going to be a big cutback."

"What about the animals?" If there's a shortage in staffing, that's going to have an effect.

Cheryl grimaces. "I'm reaching out to other shelters and rescues. Trying to lighten our load."

Fuck. I wouldn't feel so shitty about having to leave if I at least knew the place was going to continue on strong. But it sounds like I'm not going to be the only one out on my ass.

"I'll stay on as long as I can."

She nods, and we both stand. As I leave my office, the world has a hazy quality. Disorienting.

Which is why I almost walk directly into Summer.

My librarian stares up at me, eyes wide in shock.

Shit. She heard.

"I put the kittens back in the crate. Do you want to stay or head out?" Summer wraps her fingers around my wrist.

My workday ended a half hour ago. I stayed later so Summer could visit the litter.

"Let's go," I mumble, no longer meeting her eyes. How long is she going to want to stay with me once I'm unemployed?

Three thousand eight hundred twenty-five.

How did the same number get smaller in a matter of minutes?

Summer took the bus to get here, so we both climb into my truck. The second I start the engine, her questions come.

"Did you know the shelter was struggling financially?"

"Cheryl mentioned it." I shrug, like I'm not concerned. Meanwhile, my meager sense of stability crumbles.

"Why haven't you said anything?"

"It's my problem. You shouldn't have to worry about it."

"Damn it, Cole!" Summer slaps her hands to her jean-clad thighs. "Did you ever think that maybe I could help?"

"Summer," I growl, gripping the steering wheel tight. "I don't want your money." I bet she'd be annoyed by my stance if she knew the shitty ways I used to earn cash. But I don't do that anymore. Not even if I'm desperate.

"Well good. Because I don't have anything extra to give you. But that's not what I mean."

"Then what?"

"I don't know yet. Give me a second." Summer pulls the lever on the side of her seat, reclining it back all the way.

At a stoplight, I glance over to see she has her eyes closed.

"Napping?"

"Hush. I'm thinking. Let my brain work."

Despite my annoyance at the situation—I never wanted Summer to know how close I am to being jobless and broke—I can't help the corner of my mouth tugging up into a half-smile. She's fascinating to watch, even when half the time I can't keep up.

A horn honks behind me, and I realize the light turned green while I was busy staring at my passenger.

Summer stays in her prone position the entire drive back to my place, not even sitting up when I pull onto the gravel of my drive. Instead of prodding her, I shut off the engine and settle in to wait. At least now I can watch her without some impatient asshole laying on his horn.

She looks sexy with her messy ponytail and tight T-shirt. The cat hair covering the material isn't a deterrent, seeing as how that's how I spend most of my days.

I might think she was asleep if it weren't for the occasional word her lips form, as if she's talking to herself. Maybe five minutes pass before her eyes fly open, and a grin blooms huge across her face.

"I think I've got it."

"Got what?"

"A solution. Actually, two solutions. I need to do some research, and you'll have to be up for some more writing if you think you can handle that?"

"What are the solutions?"

Summer rockets her seat into an upright position and unbuckles her seatbelt. "Inside! We need a computer!" She's out the door before I can point out the flaw in her plan. My girlfriend hovers by the front door, bouncing on the balls of her feet, desperate for entry.

"Summer." I hesitate with my key even as she waves me to unlock my door.

"Come on, Cole!"

"I don't have a computer."

"I just—you don't?" A considering look fills her eyes, and I'll bet she's mentally rifling through all my visits to the library, searching for a time when there was a laptop at my elbow. I already know she's going to come up empty. The light dawns, and I'm expecting a piteous look. Instead, she just huffs an impatient breath and waves me on again. "Fine. We don't need a computer right away. I can look up some stuff on my phone to start."

I slide the key home, but pause again, earning myself an adorable growl from Summer. I meet her eyes over my shoulder.

"First thing you need to do when you get inside is strip."

That sets her off balance. She gapes at me as her entire face flushes a deep red. "Horny much? I'm all about seeing you sans clothes, but I seriously want to tell you my ideas first. I'm not sure I'll be able to concentrate if we're nude."

I bite my bottom lip to keep a smile at bay. "You need to change because you handled all those cats at the shelter. It's better if Smaug isn't exposed. It's a health thing."

Summer smirks. "Of course. A health thing. I promise to immediately remove my clothes when we get inside for your cat's health. Now open the flipping door, slowpoke!"

She wasn't lying. I've barely shut the door behind us and her sneakers, T-shirt, and pants are tossed into a pile beside the threshold. Summer strolls across the room in her sports bra and flowery panties. The edge of her tattoo peeks out from the lacy edge.

Suddenly, my mind gives a shit about money. All I want is to get her under me, her hands stroking my skin, her voice moaning my name. But when I follow her into the bedroom, I find my spot in her arms already claimed by my goddamn cat. Smaug lets out a content purr.

Little fucker.

"Put him down and get in the bed," I command.

Summer shakes her head and sways her body as if she's rocking a baby instead of an abundantly fluffy feline.

"Give me one of your shirts. I want to tell you my ideas."

"Sex first. Then ideas."

Summer snorts, then starts humming a Christmas song to my cat, essentially ignoring me. Can't a guy get respect in his own home? Giving in, for now, I pull a T-shirt out of my drawer and toss it on the bed for her, specifically choosing one that shrank in the dryer. When she sets Smaug down and pulls it on, the bottom of her ass peaks out. My librarian glares at me, but I keep my face as blankly innocent as I can.

"Fine. Play dirty. And to think, I'm going to give you my genius ideas and solve all your problems."

"All my problems?" My eyes dip to my waistband. Since I handled a shit-ton more animals than Summer did, it was even more important I not contaminate my place, meaning I stripped a second after she did. Wearing nothing other than a set of briefs, it's pretty clear what the sight of her is doing to me. A problem quickly arising that needs her fixing.

"That's it! No more talking near a bed!" Summer saunters out of the room, and I follow like the tamed animal I am. I find her in my kitchen, washing her hands at the sink. Good idea. Want to get clean before we fool around.

She flicks water at me, the cool drops on my bare chest making me shiver. I lean down to kiss her shoulder before nudging her out of the way with my hip and grabbing the soap. As I build up a decent layer of suds, Summer starts talking.

"Are you ready? Ready to hear my genius?"

"Hope you're not overselling." I tease her, knowing that even if it's an impossibly lame idea, I'll still make as if she's detailed the cure for cancer.

"Never. Here it goes. Two-pronged plan. Save your job and increase your income so you can help your dad with his bills."

Yeah. That's the dream. A larger advance from selling my book would've helped with number two. But that dream is already spent. I stay quiet and let Summer keep talking as my hands find a dish towel.

"You work at a nonprofit. So why not apply for a grant? And not just one! I'm betting that I could find tons of grants related to animal shelters."

The world around me rocks at her words. The idea didn't even occur to me.

Probably because I'm shitty at asking for help, and that's basically what a grant is.

"You mean, fund my salary with a grant?"

"Maybe!" Summer's hands are flying every which way. She reaches for the cereal boxes I keep on the top of my fridge. But she doesn't move to pour herself a bowl, or even grab a dry handful like I prefer. She just clutches the boxes to her chest like the Honey Nut Cheerios are somehow going to contain her excitement. "But maybe it would be enough to find a few to offset other costs in the shelter. So your boss isn't dealing with such a tight budget."

"That...could work."

"Right? And I could help, and I bet Jasmine would, too. She's written a few grant proposals for her library that got accepted. I think we could do this, Cole!"

I don't want to get excited about something that might not work out, but just having something to do, not sitting by passively while my life crumbles, is enough to give me hope.

If I thought I wanted to be inside Summer before, it's nothing compared to now. I stalk across the kitchen toward her, knowing my need must burn from my eyes.

She smiles wide at me but holds the cereal like a shield between us.

"Wait a second! That was just one prong! My plan has two prongs."

"Then you better get to it because I'm ready to lick your pussy until you pass out."

Her mouth bobs open a couple of times, and I make another move. She recovers and bats me away a second before I grab her waist.

"Prong two is Patronize!"

"I don't know what that is." Nor do I particularly care as I watch my T-shirt bunch up around her hips.

"Patronize. It's a website where artists can create an account for their fans to fund them. You post bonus content, and people pay for access. But sometimes they just pay because they like your work and want you to keep making it. You can reveal yourself as The Inked Dragon. Make a Patronize account for *The Seven Siblings*. Give your fans a behind-the-scenes peek at your process, maybe write a bonus scene or two each month. They'll pay to get to know you."

Summer's words have me pausing in my pursuit of her.

"You think they'd pay for that?"

"I know they would. My god, Cole. Have you seen the comments on your chapters?"

The comments? "No."

"You've got to be kidding me!" Summer plops the cereal box on the table and hurries back toward my bedroom.

I follow right after, unable to keep from sliding a palm over one of her ass cheeks. Is it my fault? When they're just bobbing there?

Summer gives my stomach a gentle warning slap before scooping up her purse and pulling out her phone. After a few swipes across the screen, she offers me a triumphant grin.

"The chapter you put up yesterday? That already has over five thousand comments!"

"Really?" I lean over her shoulder to verify. She's right.

"Imagine, Cole. If just a fraction of those people were willing to pay you a couple of dollars a month for your work." She tosses her phone on my bed then wraps her arms around my waist, staring up at me with excitement sparking from her eyes. "I'm not saying you won't still need a day job. But you could make some decent cash on the side."

Cash on the side. The phrase has a spike of discomfort running through me. That was just how I thought of my money-earning techniques back before I got arrested.

But Summer would never suggest something unsavory.

"This is legit?"

Her ponytail bobs madly as she nods her head. "The website takes a small percentage for hosting your account, and you'll have to pay taxes on whatever money you earn. But it's all above board. What's more, your fans are going to *love* it."

My fans. I never thought about having fans.

I knew that my chapters got comments on them, but I never read any. Truthfully, I was worried they were all going to be shitty. *The Seven Siblings* came from a raw place in my soul, during the darkest time in my life. For the same reason I didn't want to shop it around to publishers, I also didn't want to read the feedback from strangers on the internet.

I guess I didn't think there would be too many people out there who liked it. Which is why Summer's initial reaction to the reveal was so surprising. And now it seems she wasn't the only one fan-girling.

"You'll love it?" I ask. She's the measurement I use now.

"Let's put it this way. If The Inked Dragon was some random person I didn't know, and they all of a sudden announced they were starting a Patronize account with bonus content, I would sign up immediately. And I would also dance around my apartment like I was tripping on five cups of coffee. People are going to freak out."

"Would you dance around naked?" Despite her having maybe just solved my money problems for me, my mind can't stray too far from the fact that she's pants-less and wrapped around me.

"Only for you." Summer raises on her toes to kiss me.

I hold her close and set us off balance so we land on my bed with a bounce. She's laughter and light in my arms.

There's no way I'll ever let her go.

Chapter Forty-One

SUMMER

There's someone sitting at Jamie's desk.

No, wait. Jamie is sitting at Jamie's desk.

I'm slightly miffed that he didn't greet me outside like usual, but I remember it's in the low forties today. I'd never want him sitting outside in that kind of chill. After jogging back to my office to grab his cup of coffee and an apple, I approach him on stealthy librarian tiptoes. When I'm just behind his shoulder, I whisper for dramatic effect.

"Boo!"

What I expected was a small jump of surprise.

Instead, Jamie flinches away from me, curling in on himself like he's expecting a blow to land.

What the hell?

Then, almost reluctantly, the teenager shifts in his chair to face me.

Despite having seen a lot of things while working at a public library, I'm not able to stifle my gasped shock when I get a clear view of Jamie's face. His normally smooth skin is swollen in places, darkened, and discolored with bruising. One of his eyes squints shut, the lid fat and heavier than the other.

Then I notice his arms, skinny where they stick out of his T-shirt sleeves. There are bruises there, too. Some big. Others small ovals. Like fingerprints.

My body aches at the sight, but certainly nowhere near as much as his battered form does. Jamie wraps his arms around his middle as if that's all that holding him together.

You can't touch him. Don't hug him. He's terrified. Be calm. Don't cry.

Don't cry.

For his sake, don't cry.

"Jamie." Good, there's no wobble in my voice. "You don't have to tell me what happened. But I would like to know."

"You want to know everything," he mutters.

"You're right." I nod. "I do. Especially when it comes to the people I care about."

He shudders as if my words have a physical effect on him. Maybe enough to break through this wall built from pain and some kind of betrayal.

"My dad kicked me out."

I don't tell him I guessed that. I don't say anything at all. I just let him talk.

"He found out I was dating someone. A guy. He freaked out and said I wasn't allowed back in the house unless I fixed whatever is wrong with me."

"Nothing is wrong with you." I can't stop the words. But he needs to know. And I need to stop thinking about murdering his father.

Jamie stares off to the side, picking at the cover of the book on his desk, breathing in deep breaths, one right after the other.

"I've been sleeping at my boyfriend's. Snuck into his room when his parents were asleep and left before they woke up. But yesterday, I accidentally slept in. His mom walked in and found us in bed together. They had a similar reaction to my dad, only they didn't kick Craig out. Just me."

So much hate in the world, and Jamie has had to shoulder more than most.

"Where did you go?"

He huffs out a breath. "School. Then here. And then, last night, I tried going to one of those shelters. Just for a place to sleep."

I try to suppress a grimace. From the little I know about homeless shelters, I've picked up they can get lawless when the lights go out.

"It was maybe midnight when they jumped me. Not sure how many. They took—" His voice breaks, and I have to press my fist against my lips to keep a sob at bay. "They took my backpack. And your dad's jacket. I'm sorry, Ms. Pierce."

A tear leaks out of the corner of his swollen eye.

"Don't worry about that." How I've kept myself from crying up to this point is a mystery to me. "There's nothing you need to apologize for."

He rests his forehead in his hands, staring at the desk in front of him. "One of them knocked me out. One of the volunteers woke me up. School had already started, and I didn't have any of my homework, and I just couldn't see C-Craig, l-like this."

My arms ache from the need to wrap the young man in an embrace. There's nothing I want more in the world than to make him feel safe and cared for. But I'm also terrified that any sudden move will have him running from me.

"So you came here? You've been here all day?"

Jamie nods, still not looking at me.

Before I make any decisions, there's a piece of the story I don't have. I'm afraid to ask for it.

"You said your dad kicked you out. What about your mom? Is she in the picture?"

"She does whatever Dad says. He's the law. She follows it."

Damn. Damn it all to the archives of hell.

"Okay," I say more to myself than to him. Plans, solutions, fixes as temporary as a damp Band-Aid present themselves in my mind. At last, I settle on the most sturdy, even if it doesn't take much of the future into account. Jamie needs help *now*, and I can give it to him.

"I want you to stay with me, Jamie. You don't have to go back to that shelter."

"I can't..."

"You can. I have a couch, and pillows, and blankets, and food. You can sleep safe." How long has it been since he's slept somewhere without worrying what would happen the next morning, or even during the night? Even one night of that is too long. "If not for yourself, then do this for me. I'll worry until I'm ill if I don't know where you are tonight. Just stay over tonight, and we can figure out how to move forward tomorrow morning. All right?"

Finally, I get a nod out of him. Briefly, I wonder if his agreement only came from exhaustion, but I'll take what I can get.

"Good. That's settled. You stay here until the end of my shift, and then we'll head to my place. I'm going to grab you some ice for your face. Be warned, if you sneak off, I will spend the entire night scouring the streets for you. Don't test me."

Somehow, Jamie manages a half-smile, even as pain lingers in his eyes and movements.

But he doesn't leave.

For the rest of my shift, I circle past Jamie's desk regularly, making sure he's still there. He is, although at one point I find him with his head down. Worried, I approach, only to realize he's asleep. I leave him, and when I spot Daniel the security guard approaching him I grab the man's arm.

"He's had a rough day. Can we just let him sleep?"

Daniel glances down at my grip then covers my hand with his, giving a friendly squeeze.

"Sure, Summer. I'll leave him be."

"Thank you."

My mind is so hyper-focused on Jamie that I don't realize until fifteen minutes before the end of the day that Cole is supposed to pick me up. I still need to figure out how to buy a new car without destroying my savings. The need hasn't felt urgent, when most days Cole declares he's going to pick me up from work, and then we spend the evening, sometimes the night together.

I may or may not have a toothbrush at his place.

But today, the situation poses a slight problem. I'm going to have to tell Cole my plan, and I'm going to have to hope that Jamie doesn't shy away from exposing his vulnerability to another person.

Damn. What a day.

After throwing my purse over my arm and locking my office door, I go to collect Jamie. The teenager moves carefully, and I wonder how many more bruises he's sporting.

"Maybe we should go to a doctor. Make sure nothing is broken."

But the boy only shakes his head with a grimace.

I try to stifle my sigh and be content with the fact that he's not disappearing into the night to sleep on the streets. Out in front of the building, I spot Cole's truck.

"Sorry, Jamie. I didn't drive today. Are you okay with us catching a ride with Cole?"

Again, he keeps quiet, giving only a shrug. He's not the type to chatter, but this silent version of him is making my heart ache.

Cole circles around the hood and raises an eyebrow at me as I approach with my companion. Trying to brush away any tension, I offer a wave and a smile.

"This is Jamie. You know each other from the writers group, right?" I wait for Cole's nod before dropping the hopefully completely reasonable-sized bomb. "If you don't think we can all fit in the cab of your truck, we'll just take the bus. But Jamie is going to come home and stay at my place tonight."

Cole's eyes trace over the teenager, who I can tell is trying to put on a front of nonchalance. But it's hard for the kid to look casual when his face is a black and purple mess of bruises.

Finally, Cole speaks. "No, he's not."

And I wish like hell the man had kept his mouth shut.

"Yes, he is." I speak carefully to keep from raising my voice. "Jamie is my friend. He needs a safe place to stay. And I will be giving him that safe place in my apartment."

Cole shakes his head, destroying my false calm. "No, Summer—"

"Don't you tell me no!" I move in front of Jamie, taking on the fierce spirit of a mama bear protecting her cub. Sure, Jamie is a good foot taller than me and not my kid. But he feels like mine. And he's finally letting me help him. Tonight is the first night in months I can go to sleep knowing that Jamie is safe. "This is my decision, and I am happy to have Jamie stay with me."

Cole keeps on his icy, no-emotion face. "You have a studio apartment."

"So what? It's a relatively spacious one." Relative to a walk-in closet. "We'll do just fine. Jamie can sleep on the couch."

"He'll stay with me."

"And it's an extremely comfortable couch!" I announce before Cole's words register. "What?"

The guy with a countenance of a bad boy moves his eyes over my shoulder. "I have more space. And a spare bed." He's talking to Jamie, taking the decision out of my hands. Which might be better, seeing as how I'm having trouble comprehending the turn of events.

"You..." Jamie's voice is hesitant. "You don't mind?"

Cole pulls open the passenger-side door of his truck. "No. Summer will stay over, too."

"Oh, I will, will I?" I mutter with feigned heat before turning to the boy I've taken responsibility for. "Cole does, technically, have a bigger place than I do. We might be more comfortable there. What do you wanna do?"

Jamie reaches up to scratch his neck, and I try not to wince at his scabbed knuckles.

"A bed would be nice," he murmurs.

Cole's it is.

The ride to his place is silent, with me sitting in the back seat because my short legs fit better. Once we're inside Cole's shotgun house, Jamie stands awkwardly in the front room, eyes on his sneakers.

Before I can figure out something to say to break through the uncomfortable fog, Cole toes off his shoes and waves for Jamie to follow him. I tag along behind, a caboose on their train.

"This is my room. And Summer's." Cole says this in a no-hesitation, blunt, announce-to-the-world-that-we-sleep-in-the-same-bed kind of way.

My face grows hot, and I wonder if any other librarian has had to deal with this odd of a situation before.

"Could've guessed," Jamie says, and I feel myself on the verge of sputter. Then he tilts his head toward the bed. "All the throw pillows."

Cole snorts in agreement before moving on. I waver between staying put and following, eventually letting my feet shuffle forward. Jamie agreed to stay here, but I'm still not sure how comfortable he is around Cole on his own.

"You can grab a towel from here." Cole has a small closet open across the way from the bathroom, and he's pulling out sheets and a pillow. He shows Jamie the spare bedroom next, dropping his armload on the bed, then heads to the kitchen. "Eat whatever you want."

Jamie stands with his arms crossed over his chest. Not defensively. More like he's trying to hold the edges of himself together.

I can't even imagine the emotional turmoil swirling through him right now.

"Thank you," he mutters. There's a thick quality to his voice. I can bet that one of the last things he wants to do is cry in front of Cole. I can also bet he won't have much choice in the matter if we hover here another minute.

"Pizza!" I announce, and both guys turn to look at me. Good. "I'm going to order pizza for us. Why don't you hop in the shower Jamie, and Cole can lend you some pajamas?" When I lend a pleading gaze to Cole, he doesn't even hesitate before nodding.

"Yeah. I've got plenty."

"You don't have to—" the teenager starts, but I've already grabbed Cole's hand to pull him toward the front of the house.

"It's no bother! Cole loves sharing." When we're in Cole's bedroom, I shut the door, then press my ear to it. A minute passes, then I hear footsteps, the bathroom door shutting, and a moment later, the water turns on.

Thank the universe.

That's when I turn to Cole, find him rooting through drawers while Smaug meows at him from the top of the dresser.

"Hope he likes black," the man mutters, pulling out a black T-shirt and a pair of black basketball shorts.

Words fail me. All I can do is cross the room and wrap my arms around his waist. I try to pour all my gratefulness into the embrace.

Cole turns in my arms, then holds me close.

That's when the tears come.

Maybe I was equally worried about Jamie seeing me sobbing.

A warm hand strokes my hair, calming me. When I have my unsteady breathing under control, I tilt my head up to meet his eyes.

"You're kind of amazing, you know?"

Cole grimaces before cupping the back of my head, holding me still as he leans in for a kiss.

"Just trying to impress you." He whispers the words against my mouth. I'm not sure how true they are, but I figure a guy who's willing to help out a stranded teen to impress a girl is still amazing.

But I also pick up on his discomfort with the praise, and moving us back to safe territory, I ask, "What toppings do you want on the pizza?"

Cole shrugs then gives me a teasing smirk.

"Hawaiian." His fingers lightly trace over a ticklish spot on my neck that has me shivering.

"Hah. Yeah right." I curl my hands in his shirt, staring up at him with a fierce gaze. "I will murder any pineapple that tries to come near you, Cole Allemand. Nothing is allowed to hurt you, you wonderful man."

Chapter Forty-Two

COLE

As I stand in front of my librarian's door, I try to angle the plant in my arms so Summer sees its best side first. Normally, guys bring flowers to a date. I could've done that. But they'd be dead in a week. Why would I want to give Summer something that's going to die?

The door flings open, revealing my beautiful, grinning girlfriend. She has on some high-waisted shorts and a top that looks frilly and white, reminding me of a cloud. Her maple hair sits on the top of her head in a tight bun, revealing a delicious amount of neck.

"Welcome to date night— Cole!" She squeals my name as I press a hot, open mouthed kiss against the skin right under her jaw.

But it's her fault for tempting me.

Summer steps back, laughing and pulling me with her, one of her hands fisting in my short-sleeved button-up shirt.

A new purchase for me. I got my first payment from Patronize and decided to use a small bit of it to look halfway decent for this date.

Summer was right. I have fans. So many that I'm on track to make more than I do working at the shelter, which is wild to me. So much so that I'm not sure I can trust it. I'll have to get more than one paycheck before I start making any major life changes based on it, but this could solve enough problems to relieve a portion of the crushing stress always bearing down on my shoulders.

Hopefully my meetup with Jasmine next week to work on grant proposals for the rescue will be just as successful.

Still, my mind can't focus on anything that far ahead.

Not with date-night happening.

This is a huge step. Summer invited me to her apartment.

I've picked Summer up plenty of times, and I've helped her carry in shopping bags from our Saturday morning grocery outings. But we've never spent more than five minutes together in her place.

"It's small," she'd said to me with a grimace the first time I walked her to her door.

As if I would care.

Still, she wasn't exaggerating. Summer lives in a studio apartment, big enough for a bed and a loveseat and a tiny TV. A small wooden table pushed in the back corner holds her sewing machine along with piles of fabric. Throw pillow material.

Just existing means I take up a lot of space here, and maybe that's why we spend more time at my rental. The shotgun house isn't five-star quality, but we don't have to worry about knocking things over every time we turn around.

Despite the destruction risk I pose, I'm still over the fucking moon to finally get invited here.

"Did Mama Al buy you this?" Summer asks, smoothing her hand over my shirt.

"No. I bought it."

"But there are flowers on it."

She's not wrong. I was going to go straight black, but then I saw this in the department store. Still black, but with little roses all over it. One thought popped into my head.

Summer would like that shirt.

"Yes." I watch her face, now that I know her reaction to the word.

Her lids flutter, and she traces her fingers over my already-straight collar.

"I'm going to have a fun time unbuttoning this later," she murmurs.

And the win goes to her. And me. Can't seem to stop winning when I'm around her.

"Got you this." I offer my gift, and Summer's grin softens into a happy smile.

"A succulent?"

I shrug. "Sure." All I know is the plant is tiny and cute and reminds me of her.

"I love it." Summer carefully takes the pot in both her hands and walks to her window sill, where she arranges it in a happy beam of sunlight.

Do you love me? I want to ask.

But I won't. Not until I know the answer is yes.

She's not the only one who wants to hear that word.

"Hope you're hungry!" My librarian turns back to me with an almost nervous smile. "I'm not the best cook, but I think my shrimp scampi is halfway decent. Hasn't given anyone food poisoning as far as I know."

"Can't wait." I'll eat whatever she puts in front of me.

A few minutes later, I'm situated on her couch with a steaming plate of pasta in my lap.

"And a beer for my man." Summer sets the sweating can on a coaster on the coffee table before bending to kiss my cheek.

Meanwhile, I'm basking in the glow of her using possessive language about me for the first time.

Muttering about utensils, Summer sets her plate and glass of wine on the table, then retrieves forks for both of us. When she settles on the cushion beside me, the couch is so small that our sides press into each other. This makes me want to get rid of my kitchen table, so we can spend every meal side by side.

Only, the second Summer tries to pick up her plate, disaster strikes. The edge knocks against her wine glass, sending red liquid spilling across the table, streams of it dripping onto her fluffy rug.

"Damn it!" Summer springs up from the couch, and I follow after, setting my food down on the counter and searching for a way to help.

"There's some carpet cleaner under the sink in the bathroom!" Summer frantically waves me to go grab it while dabbing up as much of the spill as she can with paper towels.

Following her orders, I jog the few steps it takes to get to the only other room in the apartment. Crouching down in front of the vanity, I pull open the cabinet door and rummage through the different spray bottles. There's a general cleaner, but I keep looking in case she has something particular for carpets. At my place, I make sure to have some on hand, seeing as how cats like to throw up in random places.

Just as I think I've found a promising bottle, my attention snags on a box pushed into the back corner of the cabinet. Seems like a strange place to store anything that's not cleaning supplies.

I'm about to dismiss it when I register words written on the top.

Open if something happens to me.

Unease creeps down the back of my neck, freezing my blood and locking my body still. Meanwhile, my mind descends into a panicked whirlpool.

Something happen to Summer? What would happen? What could happen to the woman I love that would require her to keep a mysterious box hidden under her sink?

My joints practically crack as I flex my fingers, creeping them like spiders into the shadowy corner and pulling the box out. I stand, holding a spray bottle in one hand, and the ominous container in the other.

"What's taking you so l—" Summer's question cuts off. She stands framed in the doorway, stare affixed to the box, eyes going wide.

She looks terrified.

"Summer—"

"Don't touch that!" Her voice whips out harsh, dripping with fear. She lunges forward, hands stretching to grab the container from me.

I don't try to keep it away, but my grip doesn't release fast enough. In the frantic fumbling exchange, the box falls to the floor, the top swinging open. The contents spill across the linoleum.

My brain, too worried over the reason for this box's existence, hadn't had time to guess at what was contained within. Still, I'm not sure the items tumbling out are what I would have guessed.

Newspaper articles. At least twenty of them, cut out of their original pages. Writing is scrawled, dark and thick over the stories. The urge to read the words, and my natural inclination to help clean up the mess I made, has me crouching down.

Summer yelps and dives to the ground, hunching over the papers and waving me away with frantic jerks.

"No! Don't touch them!"

"Are they...important?" I can't get a handle on this situation.

I've seen Summer unhappy. Hell, I kept her company on her worst day. But she's acting like a cornered animal, lashing out in fear.

Is she afraid of me?

"No...yes." She sucks in a shuddering breath. "Maybe." One by one, her fingers pinch the corner of each article, picking them up like used tissues, and quickly dropping them back into the box she righted.

Despite the speed at which she cleans them up, I'm still able to tilt my head and read one. The title of the article mentions a shooting at a local park. The handwriting scrawled under the title makes my gut clench.

I can protect you.

Without thought, my hand extends toward the strange message, but Summer catches sight of the movement and grabs my wrist.

"Fingerprints," is all she whispers.

But it's enough. Enough to let me know that this box is full of some kind of toxic shit that is tormenting the woman I love.

"Summer?"

She doesn't make eye contact with me, just continues cleaning up.

"Where did these come from?"

Silence descends on the bathroom. She pauses, staring at one of the slim pieces of paper. I'm able to read the title of this one, too. A woman got attacked and robbed on the way home from her night shift.

I'll keep you safe is written on it.

"Someone leaves them for me. Or mails them." Her tone is detached, as if she's merely commenting on the weather.

Only, when Summer talks about the weather, she's normally still animated.

This cold disinterest makes me feel sick.

"Who?"

"I don't know."

"You need to go to the police." I never thought I'd utter those words, but I'll ask anyone for help to keep Summer safe.

"I did."

"And?"

She closes the box, leaning over to tuck it back under the sink.

"And they don't know either. There weren't any fingerprints on the first few, so when I kept coming in with more they suggested I move."

"What the fuck?" The words burst out of me, and I collapse back against her shower, shoving my fists against the cold floor. It's either that or punch a hole in the wall. "Move? That's bullshit. You can't just up and move!"

"I did."

"You did what?"

"I moved. This is the third place I've lived in two years. But it doesn't matter. The articles and things keep showing up."

"Things?" My muscles tighten as if preparing for battle. But I have no one to fight. No clear enemy to defend Summer from.

She's being tormented by a ghost.

For years.

"It doesn't matter."

"Yes. It does." I speak slowly because that's the only way I can keep from raging.

But she doesn't need me in a temper. She needs to feel safe around me because someone has been stealing that from her.

Summer settles, her legs crossed, her back pressed against the cabinet door as if to keep me from seeking out the box again.

"I don't like to think about it."

Of course she doesn't.

"Why do you keep it all?"

She pulls her legs into her chest, hugging them close and dropping her forehead to her knees.

"In case I find out who it is and need evidence. In case something happens to me and the police need clues. Just...in case."

"Nothing will happen to you." I growl the words, pushing myself up and prowling across the room on my hands and knees until I reach her side. Not trying to dislodge her from her protective ball pose, I simply wrap my arms around her, pulling her into my chest. With my body, I attempt to convey a sense of security, but it's almost as if the box gives off poisonous vapors that make the air in the bathroom toxic.

She can't stay here.

"You can't stay here."

"Don't you get it, Cole?" Summer looks up at me now, and I can see tears have snuck out from the corners of her eyes. "I move, but the crap keeps showing up. It doesn't matter where I go. They find me."

Despite the firestorm of anger in my chest, my thumb is steady as I brush away the dampness on her cheeks.

"Stay with me."

"What?"

"Pack a bag. Come to my place. Sleep in my bed. Let me keep you safe."

"This—this isn't temporary. There's no quick fix."

"Then pack two bags."

SUMMER

"I bought groceries!" I announce, hopefully loud enough for Cole or Jamie to come help me carry them. The plastic is cutting off the circulation in my hands. The front door hangs open behind me, and I hobble around, trying to close it with my foot, making sure Smaug can't make a break for freedom.

That's when I hear the voices.

There seems to be some kind of argument going on in Cole's bedroom.

And the voice shouting the loudest is distinctly female.

"You're an asshat!"

My hackles go up. No one gets to call Cole an asshat. Even if he's being one.

I drop the bags on the rickety card table in the front room before storming through the half-opened door. The scene throws me.

Paige sits cross-legged on the floor, shaking a feathered toy for Smaug's amusement. Cole sits on his bed, hands curled into fists on his knees as he glares up at a stranger. He doesn't have to glare too far. The woman is around my height, but despite her average stature, she gives off an aura of hidden power.

Like a grenade whose pin just needs to be pulled for all hell to break loose.

The stranger swings her focus to me, and I find myself swallowing a couple of times to clear my throat.

She's striking. I don't know if she's beautiful or just the embodiment of some goddess who could smite the entire city of New Orleans with a snap of her fingers. Strength is clear in the muscles that flex under her golden skin. Her features hint at Asian descent, and her onyx hair frames her face to perfection. She has one of those badass short cuts where the ends angle down to sharp points just below her chin. Coal-colored eyes trace over me, taking in every inch.

"You're Summer?"

"Yes." Damn it. I squeaked. But she's *so* intimidating.

"Hi Summer!" Paige's enthusiastic greeting has just enough pep in it to draw my eyes away from the stranger. The blonde grins up at me from the floor. "This is Luna. Dash's sister. We're here to teach you self-defense. How was work?"

"I—um—work was fine." My wild eyes bounce between the three of them. "Self-defense?" Finally, I settle on Cole.

He nods in a resolute kind of way. Like he thinks I'll disagree with him about the idea.

Maybe I should. Maybe this is an overbearing move.

But it doesn't feel that way.

This feels like an offer I'd be stupid to refuse.

My attention skirting back to Paige, I can't help thinking about her kind, upbeat nature.

"You know self-defense?" The question pops out before I can make sure no disbelief shows up in my voice. Then I recall the conversation I had with Dash about her running habits.

Paige nods. "My dad was a lawyer, and now he's a judge. We got a decent amount of death threats when I was growing up. My parents thought it was a good idea for me to learn how to defend myself. I'm decent, but I figured since we have a master in our midst that I'd bring her."

Paige gives an almost theatrical gesture toward Dash's sister.

A master? What does that even mean?

Seeing the question on my face, Cole explains. "Luna's visiting for a few days, and she does this for a living."

"Really?" Great, that sounded way too doubtful.

"Yes." The woman, Luna, answers in an efficient, but not necessarily offended manner. "I work with VIPs in Nashville. Mainly female country artists. Their crowds get rowdy, and you never know when some drunk hick might storm the stage. Good for them to know how to drop a guy fast. But I also cover fitness and nutrition in general."

"That's...wow." That's some resume. Unfortunately, that puts her way out of my price range. "I'm sorry, but I don't have VIP money to pay you. I barely even have P money."

Luna smiles, and it makes her face even more mesmerizing.

"This is pro bono."

"But...why? Why help me, that is. Not that I'm not grateful."

Her smile disappears as fast as it rose. "I owe Cole."

For some reason, that sounded heavy. Does she owe him for saving her life or something? I wouldn't put it past him. He's surly, but I still think he'd stick his neck out for people.

He has a strange teenager living in his house for Pete's sake. Which has me remembering to ask, "Where's Jamie?"

"At his boyfriend's football game," Cole says.

That's sweet, and has my chest feeling tight with hope. The kid won't have a normal high school experience, but at least he doesn't have to give everything up. I make a mental note to have a dinner and invite Craig over for it.

Now that I know where my unofficial charge is, I'm able to refocus on the oddness happening around me.

"What do you owe Cole for?" My curiosity hasn't gotten me killed yet, but it might one day.

Luna grinds her teeth, then sighs out a huff. "For watching out for Dash."

"Dash needed watching out for?" I think back on Paige's boyfriend, who seemed pretty capable of taking care of himself.

Luna's eyes darken, and she glares at Cole. He responds to the fierce expression with a clenched jaw and hard stare.

"You seem mad at Cole," I can't help pointing out.

She doesn't bother with a denial. "I am."

I find her honest, straightforward manner refreshing.

"But you won't tell me why?"

"No."

"And you're still willing to help?"

"Of course. Just because he's stupid doesn't mean I don't owe him. Now get changed and meet us in the backyard. Expect to get dirty."

"O-okay. Um, can I talk to Cole for a minute?"

"Sure thing," Paige says, uncurling from the floor and hooking her arm through Luna's, dragging the electric woman from the room.

When we're alone, I move to stand in front of Cole.

"Are you going to tell me why Luna is pissed at you?"

He responds with a tight-lipped frown that sets off warning bells in my chest.

"Were you two together?"

Cole's eyebrows shoot up, causing my eyes to fixate on his barbell. Why do his facial expressions have the power to so easily distract me?

"Me and Luna? Dating?" He shakes his head in one definitive motion. "No. Never."

"It wouldn't surprise me. I mean, she's..." I wave my hands at the place she'd been standing, struggling to find words to describe the enigmatic woman.

"Sure. But she's also scary as hell."

"True. Never took you for a wimp, though," I tease.

Cole growls a second before he leans forward, wrapping his arms around my waist and tugging me to stand in between his knees. Before I can say another word, he has my head in his hands, tilting my face to make it easy to steal a hot kiss. He's ruthless, plundering my mouth with his tongue, dropping his hold only to cup and knead my ass as he presses me to him. All I'm able to manage is a desperate clutching of his shirt as he ravishes me.

When we finally break apart, I'm panting, and there's a triumphant gleam in his eyes.

"I don't want someone to fight with. I want someone to play with." His murmur is liquid gold, scorching through my veins, promising beautiful things when the two of us are truly alone.

"Think you can send those two home?" My voice is all husky temptation that makes me fiercely proud of my seductress skills.

Cole's eyes spark with lust. But then the intensity leaves him on a sigh.

"Later. Right now, you need this." He stands from the bed, staring down at me as he cups my shoulders. "I want you safe when I'm not around."

"I'm not very good with violence." The admission forces its way from my throat. What if I can't learn self-defense because I'm too chicken to fight back?

Long, strong fingers massage the tense muscles in my neck.

"Just learn the stuff, okay?" His lips brush my forehead in a gentle caress that's a stark contrast to the hardness of his next words. "You never know how violent you can get until someone forces you into a corner."

The amount of truth twined in his statement tugs at my curiosity.

I get the sense that Cole's experienced his own corner or two.

Chapter Forty-Three

COLE

The dinner Summer suggested was supposed to be small. But somehow we end up with a whole crowd of people at my place.

Jamie and his boyfriend, Craig.

Paige, Dash, and Luna.

Summer, of course.

And my grandmother as the latest addition.

We've grown to a number that requires eating in the backyard. The setup isn't too bad. Despite the slight chill in the air, our group is comfortable around an old rusty fire pit. Plus, Summer keeps carrying out trays of steaming food from the kitchen. This seems to be her happy place. Making people smile.

I'm glad to also see a grin on Jamie's face as he talks to Mama Al about her year in New York City. Paige also adds in her take on Manhattan, the three of them leaning their heads toward each other. Meanwhile, Luna dispenses nutrition advice to Craig, and the high school athlete dutifully types out notes on his phone.

Dash looks my way, giving me a smile and a nod.

Wasn't too long ago the two of us lived in this house alone, back when our only concerns were making it through the day and paying rent on time.

I didn't realize then how starved we both were for something more.

Something like this.

"Brownies!" Summer announces, appearing at the top of the steps again with a baking dish. "The mix is from a box, so if you don't like them, blame Betty Crocker."

No one complains. Especially not me. How could I when I've got chocolate on my tongue and the view of my librarian sauntering in front of me, acting the hostess.

As she passes within reaching distance, I snake an arm around her waist. Summer squeaks, then chuckles as I pull her into my side

"Don't wash the dishes," I whisper before pressing a kiss to her shoulder. "That's on me."

Summer smiles down at me. "Teamwork. I like it." Then she bends at the waist to plant a firm kiss on my lips. When she steps away a second later, I grumble in protest, which only has her laughing again.

"I promise I won't clean! I just need to cover the food and put it in the fridge."

As she walks away, I could swear she sways her hips more than usual. Tease.

I love it.

"You're happy, then?" Mama Al appears beside me, settling into the folding lawn chair to my left.

"What?" I heard her. It's just, that question is kind of deep. For me anyway.

I was unhappy for so long, it's just what I know. A state of being I'm most comfortable in because it's familiar.

Am I happy?

How will the world shift if I admit that I am?

And is it something I can count on lasting?

Admitting that I'm happy might tempt fate. So instead, I shrug.

My grandmother smiles anyhow.

"You know, you're a good man. Not many people are willing to open their doors to those in need."

Another shrug. "He's a good kid."

"Don't sell yourself short."

I grind my teeth, not knowing what she's looking for from me. "If

Dad had kicked me out for having a boyfriend, I don't know what I would've done." At Jamie's age, I dated a lot of different people. Girls, guys. Then there was Tess, who didn't subscribe to any gender. Dad never said anything bad about any of them except for Rhett, who left cigarette butts in our backyard. Dad said that guy wasn't allowed at our house again until he learned how to properly dispose of his litter. I grumbled about it but broke up with him the next day. Truthfully, I didn't enjoy making out with a guy whose breath smelled like stale smoke.

"You would've survived. At least until I came for you." Mama Al sips her wine before adding, "Even if I hadn't—which I would have—you would've figured it out."

She's so confident. And yeah, I probably would have. Only, I'm betting my methods would've landed me in prison a few years earlier.

"A kid shouldn't have to worry about surviving." Across the fire pit, far enough away that Mama Al and my conversation is slightly private, Luna deals cards from a deck I'm guessing came from my grandmother's purse. Mama Al spent a year working in a Las Vegas casino.

"I want to take Jamie off your hands." Mama Al leans toward me, keeping her voice low despite our distance from the rest of the group.

"You what?" Again, I heard her, but I'm having trouble believing the statement.

"I want to offer him a home." She pushes, staring straight at me, her tone completely serious.

"Why?" My initial reaction is defensive. "Do you think I'm a bad influence?"

That gets a chuckle from her. "Bad influence? The exact opposite. You've shown him how generous a man can be." She leans forward to squeeze my knee. "But you're young. And busy. And you may not talk about it, but I know you're juggling a lot of things. I, on the other hand, have all the time in the world for some surrogate mothering."

Mama Al has always been supportive and loving. But she's also transient. Hard to pin down. And ever since the first night Jamie crashed on Dash's old bed, I've started to grow protective toward him.

"He's still in high school. You can't move him across the country because you get the urge to...feel the Seattle rain or whatever." Shit, that sounded harsh. Almost like resentment.

But that can't be right. I love my grandmother. I don't get mad at her.

Still, she's relocated for less.

"I bought a place."

"A house?"

She nods.

"Where?"

"Here. In New Orleans."

Mama Al has never owned property. Anywhere.

"I don't understand." The grandmother that flitted in and out of my childhood memories was not the type of woman to put down roots. As far as I know, she's never owned a house in her life. Not even when she was raising my dad.

The colorful woman sips her drink, reclining back in her chair to tilt her chin and gaze up at the night sky. "I was a free spirit."

"You still are."

"Yes, but I've decided on a different way of living. I had it in my mind I needed to be roaming in order to be free. But I don't. Not every day. Or even every week or every month. I can stand still and be free. And Cole..." She clears her throat, and I realize my grandma, a brick house of a woman, is fighting tears. "My sweet grandbaby. I should have stood still for you."

"It's okay."

"It's not. We both know it's not. You know I love you—"

"I know. I've always known."

"But you should have seen. I should have shown you."

Shit, now I'm the one fighting a thickness in my throat.

"I'm going to show you now, and hope it's not too late," Mama Al continues, reaching out to cup my cheek in her hand. "And I'm going to help this young man if he'll let me. I still have some mothering left in me, and I think he could use a warm home to come back to every day."

"That's a lot to do for a stranger."

"He doesn't seem so much like a stranger to me. For one, that magnificent woman you've fallen in love with cares for the boy. But more importantly, I see a lot of you in him."

Is Jamie like me? In some ways, it seems he is. Only, when I was his age, I at least had a house and one parent who loved me no matter what.

"Whatever he wants. I don't mind him here," I say. That's not completely true. I can tell Summer feels uncomfortable having sex with Jamie just one room over. When she stops my hands, I don't push her. But hell, I miss sinking into her as she sighs happily in my ear.

"Let's talk to him. I have plenty of space at my new house. Got one with a second bedroom. Figured I'd have visitors." Mama Al makes friends wherever she goes. One reason she'd probably turn out to be a better homemaker for a teenaged boy than I would.

Still, I want to make sure the kid knows I'm not trying to get rid of him. I don't like the idea of Jamie thinking he's getting passed around.

"I want to talk to Summer about it." For some reason, I feel like I should be consulting her about this. Like she's the teen's mom or something.

My grandmother offers me a soft smile. "You found a good one in her."

"Dad thinks so, too." Of course, he also thinks I'm going to mess it up.

Don't tell her about your past. She doesn't need to know.

The selfish words whisper through my brain, and I cling to them like they're some kind of wisdom. My eyes sneak toward the back door, wanting Summer to walk back through it and settle herself on my lap.

"She loves you. I can tell."

The words rock through me, and I don't know if my grandmother realizes how much pain they cause. It doesn't matter what everyone else in the world thinks. I need to know from Summer. Hear those words from her lips.

Without them, I'm just waiting for the ground to crumble from underneath my feet.

Until she loves me, there's always the chance she'll leave.

Chapter Forty-Four

SUMMER

This is a quick visit. Just picking up a few things. No reason to bother Cole about it. No reason for him to even worry. It's broad daylight for heaven's sake.

I keep up the silent rationalizing as I get off at the bus stop a block from my apartment.

When I packed the first time, I was flustered, with no organized list of essentials, which means I missed some things. Like face wash. And tampons.

Sure, I could buy more, but why would I when I've already spent the money?

The cost seems especially extravagant when I consider how I'm paying rent on a place I'm not exactly living in anymore.

Not that I want to officially move in with Cole. Last week, I was able to imagine myself as a temporary occupant of his house. Someone in need passing through, like Jamie. But then Mama Al made her generous offer, and Jamie accepted with a blush and a pleased grin.

And now it's just Cole and me, alone in his place. It seems important to have this apartment to come back to when things inevitably end between us.

"Ow," I whisper out loud, rubbing at my chest. The thought of Cole and me being over hurts so much that I experience the stab of it as physical pain.

And I have to admit that maybe I've let myself get too caught up in this. Too comfortable. I'm relying on Cole. Trusting him. I find myself thinking about him at all times of the day.

There was the way he looked at me when he read that silly Valentine's Day card.

And he keeps doing more things to make it hard to protect my heart.

Showing up at my conference.

Taking in Jamie.

Cuddling goddamn kittens!

And the way he writes...

Every week, I'm still eagerly reading the new chapter of *The Seven Siblings*. Even if the whole addition is a description of a gory battle scene, all I want to do afterwards is jump Cole's bones.

The hazards of dating a writer.

Now that I'm living in his house, seeing him every day, everything is worse. And by worse, I mean torturously better. I thought cohabitation was supposed to strain a relationship.

Maybe that'll come with time.

But I won't be staying for long.

I can't.

Even if I admit that I was wrong for assigning Cole the bad boy label, that he's even better than the button-up, cookie cutter, acceptable guy I'd imagined would fulfill all my long-term requirements, dating for a few months is too short for me to move in.

This is just temporary, I remind myself as I reach the stairs.

I'll start looking for a new apartment today. Maybe moving this time will be easier. I can ask Cole if he'd be willing to lend me his truck. Maybe this time my shadow won't find me. Or they'll get bored.

Rushing out of my apartment last week with a hastily packed bag was a bit dramatic. Seeing all of the notes for the first time was no doubt shocking for Cole. Still, it was an overreaction.

The thought comes just before I step onto the landing. And there, resting on my front mat, is a familiar orange envelope.

Fear claws over skin that's suddenly too sensitive.

He wasn't overreacting.

The notes have come so many times, I think I've been trying to desensitize myself to them. No one's ever approached me, so I can pretend that no one ever will.

But that's naive thinking.

I waver, feeling like the envelope is an extra deadbolt on my door, and that I have to give up my safety to unlock it.

Maybe I should wait for Cole to get off work and come back here with him.

That cowardly thought has me thinking of my mother's words. *"You don't need a man."*

Would she agree in this situation? I haven't told her about the notes. She'd only panic and probably push even harder for me to move in with her. Both of those outcomes make me anxious.

There's no reason for her to know.

There's also no reason to bother Cole. Leaving something outside my door does not mean they have access to my apartment. I'm alone here on my landing, in the middle of the day, bright sunlight almost blinding, practically shoving me toward my apartment with its cheeriness.

I continue forward, reaching out to rattle the knob just in case. Still locked.

Briefly, I leave the envelope where it sits, carefully opening my front door and scanning the studio space.

Everything looks to be the way I left it.

The first thing I do when I enter is pull the curtains back. I don't want to be entombed in this place if someone is hiding in my shower waiting to hurt me. Next, I pull out a box of plastic gloves I bought for this exact purpose. The latex snaps as I tug two on. No longer at risk of contaminating the materials with my fingerprints, I lift the envelope off the ground.

The smart thing to do would be to not open it and hand it over to the police. That's what I did with the first ten or so. But despite the fact that I've received these notes for years, the cops haven't turned up anything. Probably because a public librarian's non-violent stalker doesn't rate high on their priority list.

Clearly, we have different lists.

And even though seeing the news articles covered in creepy writing leaves me with a nauseous fear, I'm driven to pull out the contents. I'm worried that one day it won't be an article, but instead a picture of someone I love tied up in a basement with a ransom note attached. *What would a stalker even ask me for in a ransom*? I ponder as I pinch the metal clasp to open the envelope.

A pair of my panties? A nude picture? My undying love?

Anything goes when dealing with someone who is fine with silently tormenting me.

But no threatening pictures fall free.

However, the contents *are* different from the normal news article.

It takes me a few paragraphs to realize what exactly I am reading, but when I do, a darkness presses in on the edges of my vision. My knees decide they no longer want to support me. With no chair at the ready, my butt lands hard on the linoleum floor.

Not that I have the brain capacity to care.

In my gloved hands is an arrest record, printed out from some website but looking official nonetheless. The name at the top of the page hits my nerves, making my fingers quake and the paper quiver along with them.

Immediately, denials surge to the forefront of my brain. Then I flip to the second page, and staring up at me, face younger and more surly than I've ever seen, is Cole.

Apparently, I'm holding the arrest records for Cole Allemand.

Chapter Forty-Five

COLE

When I walk into my house, Summer is sitting on the couch we never use, her duffle bag on the floor beside her. My confusion turns to unease when she keeps her head bowed over a handful of papers rather than jumping up to give me the enthusiastic greeting I've become accustomed to.

Something is wrong.

"Summer?"

Even at the sound of my voice, she doesn't look at me.

"I went to my place today," she says, her voice lifeless.

I move to crouch in front of her, my hands hovering, hesitant to land. "Was someone there? Are you hurt?"

She shakes her head, but when I settle my palms on her shoulders she tenses as if in pain.

"This was left for me." Summer pushes the papers she's holding into my chest, and I have to let her go to catch them.

It doesn't take me long to realize what the documents are.

Dread leaches all the warmth from my body.

"You believed them?" The question comes out on some strange hope. As if another reality exists where I didn't spend years in prison, so there's nothing to confess to her, and we can continue happy like we were this morning.

"Excuse me." Now I get her eyes, full of self-righteous fire. "Of course I did more research. You don't think the first thing I did was find the nearest computer and look you up, hoping that this was some kind of elaborate joke?" My librarian stands, pacing away from me. "I found everything, Cole! The arrest record, the newspaper articles, the pictures of you in court! Are you trying to deny this?"

"No." I can't keep the growl from the word, wanting to strangle the person who has not only been making Summer's home feel unsafe but is now airing my dirty laundry in the worst possible way. "But I bet this is exactly what your stalker wants. You getting mad. Us fighting."

From the bewildered expression on her face, I can tell I said the wrong thing.

"This is not about them!" she shouts. "This is about you!"

"It's my past. It doesn't matter." *Fucking hell.* I wanted time to prepare what I'd say. Ways to keep her calm. To get her to move on from this as if it were nothing more than a speed bump.

Or, better yet, I just wanted her to never find out.

"My god." Her hands tangle in her hair. "I feel like I don't even know you. We're basically living together. I can't believe you never said anything."

"When could I have told you?" The question makes its way through clenched teeth. "When could I have told you about this shit and not have you walk out?"

"You've had months! Choose a day! Any one of them would have been better than finding out like this! From *them*." A shiver that conveys her disgust visibly travels over her body.

Without thought, I reach for her.

But she flinches away.

And everything in the world shatters around me.

"Were you going to tell me? Ever?" Summer whispers.

My hesitation is answer enough, and she turns her back on me with a wretched groan, putting more distance between us.

"I can't believe this. You were just going to keep me in the dark forever? How could you think this is any kind of real relationship with that hanging between us?"

"This is real. We're together. This is serious." I can hear the panic in my voice.

"Obviously not!" Her hands wave in the space between us. "Not when you're withholding huge things like this."

That has a spark of unfairness flaring in my chest.

"I'm not the only one."

She whirls to stare at me.

"Are you kidding? You think I have a secret arrest record I'm not telling you about?"

I grind my teeth, not sure if I'm helping or hurting my case with this next question. "Why haven't I met your mom?"

Summer looks like I slapped her. "What?"

"Your mom. She lives in town. You see her regularly. So why haven't I met her?" The insecurity, the hurt I've felt these past few months scratches into my voice.

"That's not what we're talking about."

"It's exactly what we're talking about. You've met my family because I'm all in. I haven't met yours because you keep expecting this to end."

"That's not why!"

"Does she even know about me?"

From the way Summer avoids my eyes, I have my answer. She paces away, agitation shaking through every inch of her body. When she returns to the space in front of me, I find myself staring into determined eyes.

"Okay, Cole. I'm demanding honesty from you, so I'll return the favor. Here's the truth. A few years after my dad died, my mom started dating someone new."

I lean back against the front door, my arms crossed, feeling defensive as I finally get the answer to a question that's been eating at me for months.

"She fell for him hard. And you know what? I liked him, too. He was charming and wild, and my mom was in love with him. She was laughing easier, smiling more, and for a while, I had the happy version of her back."

"And he broke her heart?" My hands clench and unclench in frustration. "Just because one guy didn't stick around doesn't mean I won't."

Summer gives me a look that lets me know just how ridiculous my assumption was.

"Yes, Cole. He broke her heart. They got married, just a small ceremony. And once they set up a joint bank account, he emptied it out and disappeared. All the money from her savings and my dad's life insurance, gone. Along with the first man she let into her heart since my dad passed." Summer straightens a stack of books on the card table, then picks them up as if the weight in her arms is comforting. "We had close to nothing. For years we struggled to get by, all because she trusted the wrong person. She loved the wrong person. Needless to say, she's got a lot more walls up now when it comes to men."

Summer stares down at the books in her arms, as if surprised to find them there. Dropping the stack with a frustrated huff, she turns back to me.

"So, you're right. I'm hesitant about introducing her to someone I'm dating. I never have, and I don't plan to unless I think it's something serious."

Silence fills the room, a heavy guilty presence.

Her reasoning makes sense, and I want to commit violence against the man who took away Summer's happiness. Took away her safety. No wonder she's so financially savvy. She and her mother had to be when that asshole bankrupted them.

"Did they catch the guy?"

She shakes her head, her fingers reaching back toward the books without her seeming to realize.

"He used a fake name. Fake ID." Her glare comes back to me then. "Sound familiar?"

Fucking shit. Yeah, it sounds familiar. Seeing as how making fake IDs, forging false documents, is exactly what landed me behind bars. And I started up with that shit when I was eighteen, so for all I know, I helped the guy who first tore away Summer's sense of safety.

How many lives have I had a hand in ruining?

"I'm sorry, Summer. I was a selfish piece of shit, and that's the only excuse I have. But I served my time, and I don't do that anymore." Stepping away from the door, I approach her, desperate to hold the woman I love. To comfort her.

My librarian backs away, pulling the stack of novels into her arms again, as if they're a shield.

"I don't think I can be what you're looking for."

Did a knife just get slipped under my ribs? Because that's what this pain feels like.

"Because your mom might not like me?"

"Well, I have a hard time wrapping my head around the introduction now." Her mouth twists in a sick imitation of a smile. "Hey Mom! This is Cole, the guy I love who I just found out was lying to me about his criminal past!"

The world tilts and tips. Then it settles, and I take another step toward her, more steady than I've felt since walking through the door.

"You love me?"

Summer's eyes widen in panic. "It was a hypothetical scenario!"

"You love me." The words are out. I won't let her walk them back.

"I never expressly said that."

"You didn't have to."

"Yes I do!" She chucks the books on the couch, then shoves me with a fierce glare. "I get to choose who I love. I get to say who is allowed in my life and who isn't! And if you don't respect that, if you don't stop trying to manipulate me into staying with you, then you're no better than the creep who sends me all those news articles."

The knife is back, slicing deeper this time.

"You don't mean that."

She shakes her head, but she doesn't retract her words. "I knew this would happen."

Feeling my eyebrows pop up, I ask in disbelief, "You knew *this* would happen?"

"Something like this. You have bad news written all over you. And don't tell me I'm imagining things because I saw you that day at the grocery store. When you keyed that car for no reason. Just that should've been enough of a hint!"

The day she's talking about springs to my mind, and if I weren't so rattled, I'd laugh.

"Seriously? You think that matters?"

"Of course it matters! Your actions show who you are as a person." Her mahogany hair brushes her shoulders as her head shakes. "I should've listened to the reasonable part of my brain. We should never have gotten involved."

I hate this. My fingers clench and unclench, wanting to grab hold of her, drag her into me.

But I manage one word.

"Disagree."

Her huff feels like a punch. "Disagree all you want. It's the truth."

"No." My panic manifests itself in anger, and I find myself arguing fiercely. "That's not the truth. You're looking for an excuse. An easy way out of something real. I'm not leaving you, Summer. And I don't mean I plan to follow you around or any of that shit. I'm saying that if someone is walking away from this, it's not me." Every part of my body strains toward her, but I keep my feet planted. "You think because I look like a bad guy that somehow makes me one. Well, now you know why I kept my past from you. I thought you had plenty of fodder already. So, if this ends, it's you. You're making that choice. Not me. If it were up to me, you'd move in permanently."

Wide eyes stare up at me, her mouth bobbing a couple of times before she finds words. "I can't talk to you. I can't do this."

Fuck. She's leaving me.

"I love you."

This was not how I wanted to tell her, as some last-ditch effort to keep her from walking out. She pushes past me to the front door, grabbing her duffle bag and clutching the strap with white-knuckled hands.

"Did you hear me?"

"You know what I heard?" The woman I love more than anything pauses, her hand on the doorknob. "Duct tape on a cracked window."

"What?"

"A quick fix." Her voice is low, pained. "I heard 'Shut up, Summer.' I heard 'Stop asking questions, Summer.' I heard 'Smile and pretend like this is all you need from me, Summer.'"

"That's not—"

"I like a lot of people." She cuts me off. "But I only love a few. And I need to trust the people I love." Her body shifts slightly, turning a few inches toward me. But her hand is still on the doorknob. "I'm not a thing to be kept. You took away my choice by hiding parts of yourself from me. I'm done being manipulated."

"Don't do this, Summer."

"Leave me alone, Cole."

Then she's out the door.

And I'm alone. All she's left behind is the tease of her lilac shampoo scent and the decimated pieces of my heart.

Chapter Forty-Six

SUMMER

"That may be the most gorgeous sweater I've ever seen."

Jamie grins at me, running his hands over the riot of green, yellow, and purple, while Mama Al preens under the praise.

"Thank you, dear. Picked it out myself. Doesn't it make him look so festive?" She plucks the shoulder of the somehow both gorgeous and eye-melting garment.

The sight is adorable and has my heart squeezing. The two of them are an odd pair, but I'm not sure I've ever seen Jamie happier. And I know, when he leaves the library, he'll be going to a warm, dry, safe place, staying with someone who cares about him.

There's no getting past that Jamie won't be with his parents, but I hope that he at least feels loved by a few people in this world.

"You have some writing you think you'll share today?" I ask, trying to re-focus my brain on positive things.

The teenager nods as a tinge of red paints the tops of his cheeks. "Yeah. Just something small."

"Bet it'll be great. Head on in, so I can talk to our favorite librarian. I'll be back later to pick you up." Mama Al shoos the boy away.

Jamie waves to us with his notebook in hand, then disappears into the meeting room.

Fully aware of the few overlapping topics Ms. Allemand and I share, I make sure to speak before she can.

"So, how are things going with Jamie?"

The woman smiles indulgently at me, not fooled by my push away from a certain conversation.

"As good as they can be. He's a sweet boy. Always doing his homework or writing. We had his boyfriend over last night for dinner."

"And what do you think of Craig?" After the bonfire at Cole's house, I like him.

Ms. Allemand leans on the circulation desk counter, and I'm glad there's no one forming a line, demanding I end my conversation.

"Seems like good people. Obviously adores our boy. He's a big star on their high school football team, you know? Seems his parents are the kind that don't believe sports and gay mix. Like their son will lose his abilities and college scholarship if he admits to fancying men." The woman scowls into space. "Ridiculous."

I agree. But I'm happy to hear the guy hasn't broken things off with Jamie just because they were outed. Craig gets a lot of points on my good list.

"Speaking of ridiculous," Ms. Allemand straightens and glares down at me, "what did my grandson do to mess things up between you two?"

"I—" Words catch in my throat, and I reverse my previous wish, suddenly longing for an endless line of patrons demanding my attention. "Wh-what makes you think he did anything? Maybe I did."

And I did. But I also didn't.

Cole's grandmother sighs and adjusts her bag on her shoulder. "I love my grandson. He's intelligent and passionate and has a secret heart of gold." I can see her grind her teeth before she continues. "But he's not afraid to twist the truth to get what he wants. And he most certainly wants you."

The accuracy of her words hurts as they hit the bullseye.

"He did do that," I murmur. And maybe someone else, someone better and more trusting than me would be able to help him learn from that mistake.

"I'm sorry. That must have hurt."

"It did."

She grimaces, then her face takes on a soft smile, and she reaches across the desk to lay her palm on the back of my hand.

"He's smart. And determined. If he finds a way to fix what he broke, I hope you'll give him another chance. I am the definition of biased, but I still think he deserves happiness. And damn do you make him happy." Cole's grandmother gives me a little, reassuring squeeze before backing away, feet pointing toward the exit.

"If you wait another minute or two, you'll be able to say hi to him," I offer, hoping my voice doesn't sound begrudging. And I realize the disgruntled emotion is caused more by the knowledge that Ms. Allemand is able to have a lovingly affectionate conversation with Cole, while I still have to be pissed at him.

She just waves to me and walks out of the library.

Leaving me waiting on my own. Glancing at the clock, I realize the writers' meeting is one minute away from starting.

Cole doesn't normally cut it this close, but no way would he have arrived without me noticing. Impatiently, I wait as another sixty seconds pass.

Still no Cole.

The meeting is starting, and he's not here.

I try not to let my impatience show as I smile at patrons and scan their books and secretly wonder why Cole Allemand has not shown up for the meeting for the first time in months. This is madness, and I can barely contain my confused annoyance.

When there's a lull, a full ten minutes after six, I dial Karen's office.

"What's up?"

"Can you cover circulation for a minute? I need to make a quick call."

"Sure. Be right out." A minute later she's at my side, affixing her name tag. "Everything okay?"

"Not sure. Just need to check on something. I'll be right back."

In my office, I fish my cell phone out of my purse, where I normally leave it unless I'm on lunch break. When I pull up Cole's number, I try not to let my heart break at the adorable image of a haughty Smaug.

I miss that little dragon fur ball.

After two rings, a smoky voice caresses my frantic brain.

"Summer?"

The sound is an electric shock to my nipples. Painful and arousing.

Strangely, I'm surprised to hear him. I had this idea, a wild notion, that in calling Cole I would somehow immediately find out what is wrong with him without ever having to interact with him. Like, I'd end up listening to a message along the lines of...

"You've reached Cole Allemand's voicemail. If you're wondering why I'm not at the weekly Thursday night writers group, it's because I ate a bad batch of shrimp and now I'm posted in the bathroom, spewing from both ends. Nothing life-threatening, just extremely embarrassing and uncomfortable. Leave your name and number after the beep."

Instead, I hear his actual voice, in real time, saying my name.

Luckily, he's not in the room to see my hands shake and the way I dramatically drop into my desk chair.

"Are you sick?"

A brief pause. "No."

"Did your work schedule change?"

"No."

"Then why aren't you at writers group?"

There's silence on the other end of the line, but I know the call hasn't dropped.

"You're not here because of me." I can't contain a groan born of pure guilt. "That's ridiculous, Cole! This is a public library. Just because we're not..." I can't finish the statement. Partly because I don't want to, but also because I'm not sure what we ever were. "You can still come here even if I'm here."

Another hesitation, then, "I can't."

"You can."

"No, I can't. In the beginning, I thought if you told me no, that I could take it. That I could still be around you." His sigh is so heavy, I can almost imagine it brushing my ear through the phone. "If that was true, it's not anymore. If I can't have all of you, then I can't be around you."

"But...your group."

"I'll find another."

There's an easy fix to this. I could just tell him that I want to be together. That him hiding his past from me doesn't matter. That I'm willing to forget everything and trust him.

No words come out.

"Get back to work, Summer." Cole murmurs the command. He doesn't growl like he's angry at me.

Not that he has any right to be angry. *I'm* the one who was deceived. But it's so much easier to be pissy with someone who is being a jerk. Aren't ex-cons supposed to be assholes?

"Don't tell me what to do," I mutter without heat.

He has the audacity to chuckle. "I love you."

"Goodbye!" Pressing the End Call button doesn't seem final enough, so I stuff my phone under a throw pillow and leave my office, locking the door behind me.

"Everything good?" Karen asks when I get back to the desk.

"Just fine. Nothing to worry about."

Who's the liar now?

Chapter Forty-Seven

COLE

"How's Summer?"

When did my dad get so chatty?

Normally, when Malcolm Allemand fishes, he doesn't want to say a single word. Just float and do nothing to alert the fish to the danger hidden within the intricate lure the man crafted.

But now he's asking questions I don't want to answer.

"Fine," I mutter, assuming it's the truth. I haven't seen her since the day she found out about the parts of me I was hiding. Last I heard her voice was when she completely ignored my declaration of love. Maybe she's not doing great, but my hope is she's at least doing fine.

As long as her creepy stalker hasn't tried to make contact.

Whenever I think of that shadowy figure, I can't help the combination of rage and anxiety that gnaw at my chest. Especially because now I'm not around to protect her. Not there at night to make sure she's safe even when she sleeps.

My librarian is out in the world, alone. And she wants it that way. Because she doesn't trust me.

"She broke it off with you, huh?" My dad's words have my fists clenching so hard, I snap in half the pencil I'm holding. The section with the eraser clatters against the metal bottom of the boat and rolls away from me.

"What'd you do?"

Nothing, I want to growl. But that's not true. Or at least the nothing I did means a hell of a lot.

"She found out about prison," I eventually admit.

"She found out, or you told her?"

"Found out."

"Shit, Cole."

"I don't need to hear it."

Dad readjusts his battered baseball hat. "I won't lay into you. Bet you're hurting enough as it is."

My mouth twists in a grimace, and I opt not to answer. A good fifteen minutes go by, where my dad pulls up a bull redfish as long as his torso. Once he's got the thing tucked away in a cooler and his line back in the water, I get another question.

"Why didn't you tell her?"

I pick up the errant pencil half off the boat bottom and erase my last sentence before answering.

"You met her. She's too...good. I just fuck shit up."

"Language." The chastisement is laughable, seeing as how he's apt to call someone an asshole for not accelerating fast enough at a green light.

"The boy you used to be messed up. People change. You changed."

"I still lie."

"You lie about something else?"

"No."

"So just one thing?"

"That's what I said."

"You tell her why?"

That has me pausing. "What do you mean?"

Dad shifts in his seat, his face pinching as if uncomfortable. "What did you say to her? When she found out?"

Shit. I hate reliving this. But I also know this is some rare, possibly insightful version of my father I'm getting. Maybe he can help me fix things. So I play it back for him as best as I can remember, cringing when I think on my exact words.

When I'm done, the boat gets silent, the only noise the small waves lapping against the hull.

"You said you didn't tell her because you thought she wouldn't give you a chance. That she'd leave," he summarizes.

"Basically."

Dad chews on his lower lip, staring out over the water.

I fiddle with the lead half of my pencil, drawing shitty stick figures in the margins of my notebook.

"She did leave you."

"Yes."

He nods, still thinking.

"You should lay it all out. Tell her everything."

"I—what do you mean? She already knows everything."

Dad shakes his head, scratching the back of his neck. "Naw. She knows you went to prison. She knows how you thought she'd react to that. But she doesn't know why you thought she'd react that way."

I'm still having trouble following. "What are you saying?"

"Actions. She's got all the actions. You've gotta lay out your feelings."

"I did. I told her I love her." Multiple times. And it didn't do anything but piss her off more.

"But you didn't trust her."

Dad's words are like a punch to the gut. Me not trust Summer? Try the other way around. "Of course I do!"

He doesn't respond right away, just lets me seethe while he reels in another fish. Once his line is back in the water, he breaks his silence. "What are you afraid of?"

"Nothing," is my immediate response.

"Liar."

I grind my teeth, even as I consider his question. "Losing her forever."

He snaps his fingers. "There's a start. What does it feel like when you think about the time you served?"

"That's in the past." Again, the response feels automatic.

But Dad is shaking his head. "I don't think it is. You don't have to tell me. You don't have to tell anyone. You also don't have to earn the love of that sweet girl. Build all the walls you want, but don't expect her to hang around on the other side of them."

The bench seat is suddenly extremely uncomfortable, and I find myself fidgeting.

"So what, you think I need to spill my guts? Tell my sob story? Earn her pity?"

"Earn her trust. Figure out what scares you most, and give it to her."

We're quiet for some time, each in our own head.

"Where is this coming from?" I ask. "Is this some kind of *if I'd done this with your mother she wouldn't have left* thing?" I'm immediately guilty for throwing her in his face.

But dad just gives the water a sad smile.

"No. Your girl is better than your mother. She liked playing house. Until she didn't. She knew I loved her, but that didn't matter so much to her. She didn't have walls or fears because she didn't have any cares."

"Summer cares about everything," I mutter. My dad nods.

"You should let her care about you. All of you. Not just the bits you think are good enough."

From the firming of my dad's jaw, I get the sense that he's done relaying wisdom. I'm still reeling from how intimate the conversation was. We never go deeper than me getting on his case about bills.

But I'm changing. Summer's changing me. The walls are coming down, and I want her to be around to see what's behind them.

Even if it's dark and grotesque.

Flipping to a new page, I start to write.

Chapter Forty-Eight

SUMMER

Don't read it.

The command has been playing over and over in my head for hours.

You don't need to read it. You'll only hurt worse after you do.

But even as I help patrons and set up tables for a new display, and call a vendor about issues with a database, my mind is on one thing that won't leave me alone.

The Seven Siblings.

Today is the day. A new chapter should be going up.

Any. Minute. Now.

The next step in the story. That beautiful fantasy epic that just happens to be written by the man I refuse to hand my heart to.

Unless he already took my heart when I wasn't looking.

Wouldn't be out of character.

Shame immediately reddens my cheeks, and I shove my head in the staff room's refrigerator as if I'm fascinated by Aliyah's bagged lunch, rather than trying to chill away my embarrassment.

That was a low blow, even to think to myself.

Cole may have done a crime, but he served his time. It's not truly the issues with the law that concern me, although they don't help with his case. I'm pissed about the lying. The manipulation. The withholding of information because he decided how I would react to it.

He doesn't know. And now I don't know either.

It's completely possible that if he sat me down, showed some true vulnerability when describing his sordid past, that I would've gotten over it. But the fact that he kept it from me only leads me to believe he might not think what he did was so wrong.

That he might do it again.

But then my memories of Cole crowd in, trying to push away the doubtful thoughts. He's the guy who cradles cats and offers his free bed to a homeless teen and writes such beautiful goddamn words. The conflicting ideas of the man threaten to drive me mad. As does the teasing chapter of his work.

The torment won't end. The chapter will never disappear. Just the opposite, there will be a new one next week. And the week after that, and the week after that.

Maybe reading more of the story will somehow desensitize me to him.

There's no real logic in that reasoning, but since I'm weak, I'm already folding.

"Just going to take my lunch break." I wave at Aliyah as I try to casually stroll past the circulation desk. As if I'm not headed back to my office to do something I shouldn't.

She nods at me over a patron's shoulder, not noticing, or at least not reacting to my anxious sweating. Feeling like I'm about to bring up porn on my work computer, I lock my office door with feverish fingers and sit at my desk, hunching over the keyboard.

When I navigate to the website, my heart thuds heavy in my chest when I see the thick words accompanying an unclicked link.

There's a new chapter.

As I stare at the bold words, a sudden rush of jealousy overwhelms me. For Cole to have uploaded this, he would have needed a computer. Since he's not using one at our library, then that means he went somewhere else.

Bet it was Westside Public, with their gorgeous view and spacious seating area.

Bastards.

Okay, they're not really bastards. I like Westside Public. It's just...I don't want him using any library but mine.

He'd come back here if you forgave him, a sneaky goblin voice whispers from the back of my brain.

I want to smother it with my rage as tears prick at my eyes.

It would be so easy. To show up at Cole's house, tell him I forgive him for lying, and then fall into his arms. The actions would come so naturally, I doubt I'd have to think much to do them.

The issue is the emotions lurking underneath the surface.

It wouldn't take much effort to say I forgive him. The words constantly push at my lips. But speaking something doesn't make it true.

So, in the end, I wouldn't. I can see myself emerging from the delicious haze of our reunion, the happiness of our being together again wearing away as I spent days, weeks, months with him, waiting for the next lie. He wasn't even remorseful when it came to the deception. Which assures me that he'd do it again just to get his way.

Cole can be kind and caring, but he's closed off. Unwilling to reveal the darker parts of himself to me.

And maybe that's partly my fault. I was judgmental. But that doesn't mean what he did was okay.

Debating with myself once again, I spend a good five minutes shoving a new box of pencils into my electric sharpener. The loud grinding and resulting sharp points is soothing in a way. But when the box runs out, so do my excuses. I twirl one of the pencils in my fingers as I stare at the screen. Only when I tuck the writing implement behind my ear do I reach for my mouse.

I circle the link a couple of times, trying to talk myself out of this. But the temptation is too great. The chapter is public now, and it will taunt me until I read it.

With a soft click, I open the next installment of *The Seven Siblings*.

The different layout catches my eye. Normally there's the chapter title, then we go straight into the prose. But this week, there's a message at the top of the page. And before I even read it, I lock onto a specific word.

Summer.

Blood thunders in my ears, my fingers grab a book off the corner of my desk, clutching it to my chest. Then, like I have something shameful to hide, I stare behind myself with wild eyes. It's as if seeing my name on this site has revealed to Cole that I'm reading his work.

He doesn't know, I reassure myself. My continued obsession hasn't been outed.

After a few calming breaths, I loosen my death grip on the random book, letting it slide from my fingers into my lap. Then I scoot back up to my desk, leaning toward my computer, and brace myself to read all the words that surround my name.

> *Most people think that spring is a good time for forgiveness. Everything in the world is new and growing, and the pain of winter can be forgotten. Can be forgiven.*
>
> *But spring has always felt too fragile to me for taking such an important step. In spring, heavy rains can come and wash away hopeful growth. One day is warm, the next is cold, the fluctuation confusing and disheartening. The nights, still long, can leave frost come morning.*
>
> *I've never truly trusted spring.*
>
> *Forgiveness requires steadiness. Reliability. It needs to burn through you until there's no doubt the past sin, the chill of winter, is gone for good.*
>
> *That's why I ask for forgiveness in the Summer.*

Shaking fingers press to my lips.

Probably every other reader of this story will think the author just decided to share a small piece of poetry. But I know what this is.

It's for me.

Whatever is in this chapter, it's for me.

For the past few months, Cole's characters in *The Seven Siblings* have been living out a fascinating interpretation of the *Beauty and the Beast* fairytale. Last week, we were left on a cliffhanger, as the handsome peasant discovered the truth of his beastly lover's curse.

A discovery of a dark secret. Of a lie. The parallel does not escape me.

I begin reading. The scene has no real action. Just two characters talking, arguing. The peasant is desperate to understand the motives of the beast. The words they throw back and forth aren't the ones Cole and I spoke to each other, but the feel of the scene is reminiscent of that night. Anxiety stings at my nerve endings.

Then I reach a line, the full thing italicized as if for emphasis.

> *"Why did I lie, you ask? I lied because I am a monster and you are perfection. I lied because I am selfish, and I want you. I lied because the truth of me is a dark twisted mass. I lied because I am terrified. Terrified of life without you in it. I am desperate for you, and I believed lies were the only way to keep you from leaving. If I had known that truth was the key to you, I would have shared every detail of my pathetic existence."*

The rest of the words are hard to comprehend, and it takes me a moment to realize that tears are obscuring the screen. Wiping them away, I consume the rest of the chapter. As the character's speech morphs into words from Cole's mouth, they read like a desperate confession.

I should've known that once he put everything down on paper it would flow smoothly. That it would make sense.

That he could use his pen to break my heart.

Chapter Forty-Nine

SUMMER

We were both wrong, I decide.

Cole kept things from me, but I was waiting for him to make a mistake. I never even gave a permanent version of us a fighting chance.

No wonder the man didn't want to be vulnerable with me.

But if I'm interpreting his story correctly, he just waved the white flag. The man offered to crack open his hard outer shell and give me a peek at the darkness inside him.

As long as I give him a chance

My lunch break is almost over, so I make a quick decision, pulling my phone from my purse and navigating to my contacts list.

The call rings once before getting picked up.

"Summer?" Cole's voice is guarded, but I know him well enough by now to detect a hint of hope.

"Cole Allemand." Even after all this time, I still love saying his full name. I breathe in deep, giving myself precious seconds to figure out how to ask what I want to ask. Something I probably should've had ready before I got on the phone.

"Are you okay?"

"What? Oh. Yes. I'm fine." I wish my cellphone was like the landlines from my childhood. That way I could have one of those twisty cords to fiddle with. Instead, I stack and re-stack items on my desk. "Could you give me a ride home after work?"

"You're still riding the bus." It's not a question, and Cole sounds unhappy. I'm not sure if it's because I'm asking for a ride when we're not together anymore, or if he's pissed I haven't gotten a car to replace my old one yet.

"The bus isn't bad. If picking me up is inconvenient—"

"I want to drive you." His words send happy little flutters through me.

Glad to know he doesn't detest the idea of being in a car with me. Maybe my olive branch will work.

"Well, good. Because I want you to drive me. I'm staying with my mom."

"Good. You shouldn't be alone."

I try not to roll my eyes. His concern is warranted. My safety is something I should take more seriously.

"So, if you don't mind, I would like you to pick me up from work, drive me to my mom's house, and then I would like you to walk inside said house with me and meet my mother."

Silence on the other end.

I guess that's better than hearing another woman's voice in the background asking Cole to hurry up and get back in bed.

"I know that whatever relationship we were building kind of imploded. But I want to rebuild. You're..." Damn, I think I might cry. Thank the universe I have my own office for these uncomfortable emotional breakdowns. "You're important to me, Cole. I don't want to lose you because I'm scared I'll lose you."

A beat of silence, then—

"You're off at nine, right?"

"Yeah."

"Does your mom like flowers?"

"Cole, you don't—"

"Can I kiss you when I see you?"

My face explodes with heat. Oh hell, my entire body does. I've missed this man.

Which is why I can't help teasing him.

"Only if you've brushed your teeth first."

His chuckle drifting from the phone is a cool compress on my aching heart.

I'm about to say goodbye when he stops me with a question. "Did you read the chapter?"

"Yes. I did. It was lovely and heartbreaking. Was any of it..." I don't know how to finish my question without risking him shutting me down again. I know how Cole shows his affection now, but I still want to know more of him.

"You inspired it. How I feel when I think about telling you about my past." He sighs, heavy. It breaks my heart but also fills it with love. "The first sixty or so chapters I wrote when I was incarcerated."

"The Rapunzel story?"

"Yeah. I felt trapped. Like I was going to go mad. A lot of that came out in the story."

Instantly, I decide to go back to chapter one and re-read *The Seven Siblings* from the beginning. Now with Cole in mind as I devour his words.

"All of your writing is gorgeous. But this week..." I choke on my words, clearing my throat and blinking away tears. "It meant a lot. And I think I understand now. And I'm sorry."

"You don't need to apologize."

"Too late. I already did."

His chuckle is a soothing balm, and the sore parts of me start to heal. Then he sighs.

"About the car that I keyed."

"You don't—"

"I do. You need to know. Because I don't regret it."

That has my teeth snapping shut.

Cole keeps talking. "I know the owner of that car. A guy named Martin. He's Paige's ex. They were engaged, but he cheated on her. Then when she was with Dash, the bastard tried seducing her."

"Oh." Memories of Cole's friend come to me then, of the sweet woman who quickly enfolded me into their group and later showed me how to fall without injuring myself during our self-defense lesson. Anger on her behalf heats in my chest.

"Yeah. So. I hate his guts. And I get it. Keying his car was immature. Should probably be the bigger man or whatever. But...when I love someone, I can't stand seeing them hurt. You know?" There's a vulnerable note in his voice, and I wish he was in my office so I could wrap my arms around his waist.

"Next time—" I clear a sudden blockage from my throat. "Next time we see his car, I'll stand watch while you slash his tire."

There's a smothered laugh from his end, then Cole speaks in his deliciously smoky way. "That'll earn you a spot on the naughty list, Summer Pierce."

Damn it to hell. Dirty thoughts are going to plague me for the rest of my shift.

"I need to get back to work."

"I'll be there at nine," he says. "I love you."

As I open my mouth, wondering if the same words will come out in return, I hear the beep of a call ended. He didn't give me a chance to respond, which only makes my heart hurt again. He didn't think I'd say it back.

And in that moment, I realize I want to.

I love Cole Allemand.

Fear kept me from admitting how deep my devotion goes. But not admitting it doesn't make it any less true. Cole never deserved my initial judgment. I put him in an "unacceptable" box before ever truly understanding the man. But all Cole has ever done is show me what a caring and compassionate friend and lover he is.

Yes, he's had a troubled past. And yes, he kept that from me. But not because he's still that person. Only because that's the person he feared I would think he is now.

I proved his fears right.

And I'm a fool. Because he's a good man.

The man I love.

My hands clutch at my phone, wanting to call him back and tell him. But my break is over, and he deserves to hear the words in person. So I attempt to exhale all my anxious excitement and return to work.

Somehow, I make it through the rest of the day without bursting through my skin. I'm so distracted that it takes me a second to realize whose books I'm checking out just a few minutes before the library closes.

"Joshua!" Wow. I said his name way too loud. At least I didn't call him Josh.

He gives me a tight smile. "Summer. How have you been?"

"I've been good." Better now that I know I'll see Cole tonight. The thought has me grinning wide. "You?"

The stiff quality of Joshua's smile disappears, and he leans closer to me. "I've been good, too. We should get coffee sometime. Catch up."

Damn it to the archives of hell. Not this again. Not now.

How many times do I have to say no for it to register?

To avoid a repeat of last time, I choose not to respond. Instead, I print his receipt and slide the books toward him.

"These'll be due back in three weeks. Enjoy!"

Joshua raps his knuckles on the top one then winks at me before picking them up and leaving. And I'm left feeling jittery and gross.

Luckily, the library is ready for closing, and my mind refocuses on the end-of-day tasks. It's not long before I'm grabbing my purse from my office and checking my phone.

Cole: *Stuck behind a car accident. Be there soon.*

I type a quick thumbs up then lock up my office.

"Hey, Daniel!" I wave down the security guard as I approach the front door.

He approaches with a friendly smile, and I at once feel safer. "Hey, Summer. Heading out?"

"Yeah, only, I was wondering if you mind waiting with me? It's kind of dark outside, and I'd rather not stand on the curb alone."

Daniel moves closer, cupping my elbow with his hand. "Of course. I'm here for you."

Once we step outside, he locks the door behind us. We're the last two to leave tonight, and I was in charge of turning everything off while he took care of the final walk-through.

There's no sign of Cole's truck, even when I peer down to both corners.

"I can give you a ride home," Daniel offers.

"Thank you. That's kind of you, but I have a friend picking me up." Friend. The word isn't exactly right, but I don't think I can call Cole my boyfriend until we talk a few things through.

"I don't mind."

"They're already on their way."

"Alright." Daniel shifts on his feet, and the sleeve of his jacket brushes my cardigan. "How are things going? We haven't talked much lately. You've had all your attention taken up."

There has been an influx of projects I've been working on. After a year at my job and speaking at the conference, my director seems to trust me to pursue more of my ideas without oversight. And I've been looking for any and every distraction from my disastrous love life.

"I guess I have been running around a lot lately."

"Hmm. Maybe you'll have some more time now that Allemand guy is out of your life."

I stiffen at his judgmental tone. Is he making a comment on me, Cole, or both of us?

"What do you mean?" My voice stays casual even as my mind sifts through ways to change the subject.

"Just that he was always coming up to you. Expecting all your attention. You're better off without him. The guy is bad news."

"Did he do something at the library?" I can't believe Cole would've gotten into trouble at my work and I not have known about it. Plus, this place has always seemed like a haven for him.

"Not here, no. But the arrest, and him going to jail. You're a good girl. Don't want to get mixed up in that."

Warning spiders creep over my skin, biting at my nerves. "How do you know he was arrested?" I ask.

Daniel shrugs, then goes to place his hand on my lower back as we approach the curb. "It was in the news."

Yeah, six years ago.

When we stop walking, I expect his touch to drop away. But it doesn't.

Instead, Daniel's fingers curl, pressing into the cotton of my dress.

"Daniel—"

"Why'd you even bother with him?"

His question has me teetering to the side, which the security guard seems to take as leave to grip my arm and keep his hold there. Adrenaline spikes in response to the unwelcome touches.

"What?" The word is useless when I want to yell *Stop touching me!* But something holds me back.

Daniel is my coworker.

Daniel is in charge of library security.

Daniel is alone with me on this dark sidewalk.

"I mean. The guy *looked* like a bum. You had to know you could do better. That you deserved better than him."

"I don't—"

"You need someone who can keep you safe."

I can keep you safe.

My stare catches on Daniel's, and the answer is clear in the smiling crinkle at the corner of his eyes. The world briefly stops, then it moves too fast, time flashing by in sync with the rapid pounding of my heart.

"Y-you leave me the notes?" I choke on a question that sounds innocent, but reveals a vile truth.

His thumb brushes back and forth across my sleeve as if he's comforting me. Every inch of my flesh tightens, trying to distance myself from this man.

"I wanted you to feel safe. To know I was watching over you. Not just at work, but in your home. Even if you moved. That's how much I care about you."

Care about me?

"I never wanted any of that." My voice is barely a whisper.

Daniel frowns, then his face breaks out into a smile. "You didn't need to ask for it. I did it anyway. And you feel safe around me now. That's why you wanted me to stand with you tonight."

Just as I'm wading through the toxic mess of this discovery, a heavy pressure rests against my lower back.

His arm.

Daniel wraps his arm around my waist, pulling me into him. Against him, in a sick imitation of a comforting embrace.

"I've been patient. Waiting so long for you to trust me. Seeing those other men that don't deserve you. Not like I do. I love you, Summer."

Acid rises in my throat. Those words aren't his to say.

"Let me go." As panic rushes through me, it forces my command out in a harsh whisper.

"It's okay." Daniel smiles down at me, his eyes on my lips. "We're off the clock, and it's just you and me here."

Just him and me. Where the hell is Cole?

But I don't have time to wait for him when my tormenter bends his neck, angling his head as if he plans to kiss me. There's no as if about it. Daniel's end goal is his mouth on mine.

Finally, my muscles regain strength. Palms flat on his chest, I shove the security guard as hard as I can. My main bit of luck comes from the fact that Daniel obviously didn't expect the move.

He stumbles back a step, then his face transforms into a scowl. Dark and scary.

I try to run, but he grabs the back of my dress. The neckline tightens around my throat as he jerks me back into his arms.

"Don't run away from me," he hisses into my ear.

"Let me go!" I try to scream the words, but it's as if I'm in one of those horrible nightmares where I'm aching to call for help but my voice doesn't work.

As I feel his hand low on my stomach, something of Luna's training flickers to life in my mind. I throw an elbow, then wing my head back. The soft give tells me I got his stomach, and the sharp pain on the back of my skull paired with a satisfying crunch has me praying his nose is broken.

Briefly, Daniel's grip slackens, and I stumble forward. In my haste, my legs tangle and I pitch to the ground, knees and palms scraping on the concrete. As I ignore the pounding pain radiating from my head, my eyes catch on something rolling across the ground.

One perfectly sharpened pencil. The one I stuck behind my ear and forgot about.

As I move to stand, my fingers wrap around the pointy number two.

But I don't make it to my feet. With a tight grip on my hair, Daniel wrenches me backwards. I land hard, pain shooting up my tailbone.

"Listen to me damn it!" He shakes me with the words, all of them garbled as blood from his nose drips over his lips. "I waited for you! You're mine!"

As if to lay claim, he uses his free hand to collar my throat, squeezing.

There's no thought to my next move, only animal instinct.

Swinging my arm up, I aim for the part of him not covered in clothing.

The pencil sticks in the pale fleshy column of his neck.

My hand falls away, already coated in the sticky, warm blood seeping from the wound.

Daniel stumbles back a step, his grip releasing my neck and hair. Both of his hands touch my makeshift weapon at the same time. Then his eyes roll back into his head, and he crumples on the ground.

Chapter Fifty

COLE

As I pull up to the curb in front of the library, I realize the writhing mass I caught sight of is a security guard. And he has his hand around Summer's throat.

I'm not sure the truck is fully in park when I shove my door open and sprint. By the time I reach the pair, Summer isn't being strangled anymore. Instead, she has her hands on the man's throat as blood seeps through her fingers.

"Oh my god," she sobs. "Oh my god. Oh my god. Oh my god—"

"Summer!" I grab her shoulders, trying to pull her away from her attacker.

But she just shakes me off, sobbing harder. "Don't die, don't die don't diedon'tdiedontdie—"

"Summer, let him go. I'll take care of it. Summer?"

It's like she can't hear me. Shock and panic overwhelm all reason.

I'm not too far from that point myself, desperate to find out if any of this blood is hers. But she won't listen to me.

"Summer? Please look at me. Tell me if you're hurt."

She doesn't respond, just gasps in breaths and mutters pleas to no one in particular.

A wild idea pops into my head.

"Clementine!" I roar the word. Finally, she jerks her frantic gaze up, meeting mine.

"What?"

Desperate to comfort her, I stroke a hand over her wild hair. "I just wanted your attention. Now I need you to listen to me. I'm going to apply pressure to his neck, and you're going to call 9-1-1."

She glances from me to the bleeding man, as if just comprehending the two of us exist in the same space. Then Summer gives a jerky shake of her head.

"No. No, you need to leave." She sobs. "You have a criminal record! You can't be around this!"

Fucking damn it. I love this woman.

"Summer." I keep my voice calm and steady, hoping that'll help her see reason. "You need to call an ambulance."

"Clementine! I will! Just get out of here first."

"You're using that wrong." Frustration has me growling. "And if you don't call the cops, I will. But I have bigger hands, and I can apply more pressure to the wound. So stop arguing and just let me help."

My words must break through the adrenaline soaking her mind. She lets her palms slide away from the bloody wound, fumbling in the pocket of her dress for her phone as I take over.

Those stains will never come out, I can't help thinking as my eyes trace over the bloody fingerprints on blue cotton. Great thing to be focusing on when there's a man bleeding out under my grip.

"Nine-one-one, what's your emergency?" I hear the operator say as Summer puts the phone on speaker. She's frantic in her explanation, but she hits the important parts.

She was attacked.

She took the man down with a pencil.

An ambulance needs to show up soon.

Her hands are shaking so badly that the phone slips from them. No longer concerned with the device, she crouches across the man's body from me.

"Are you hurt?" I ask. She didn't mention anything to the operator, but that could've been from shock.

Summer shakes her head. "Not hospital worthy. Just bruised."

Bruised. This guy laid his hands in on her, and now my hands are all that's keeping him alive.

"I thought you would hate him," she whispers, clutching her knees to her chest.

"There is no one on this world I hate more than this fucker. But his death won't be on your hands. You'd never get over it."

As we wait, Summer continues to shiver. I want to hold her in my arms, comfort her with my body. But I have to keep pressure on the wound, or else cause her constant mental turmoil knowing she killed a man.

"What happened?"

Summer doesn't just go around stabbing people, and she's not the type to bring on someone's temper.

"He's the stalker." Then she retraces the conversation leading up to the asshole putting his hands on her like she was an item he won.

It's all I can do not to tighten my hold until I cut off his air supply.

Red and blue lights flash as sirens sound.

Thank fuck.

Summer stares at me with wide frantic eyes. "Please. I don't want anything to happen to you."

Hope from earlier rises swiftly in my chest. I haven't destroyed things with her. She still cares about me.

"I don't care if the police put handcuffs on me the second they arrive. I'm not leaving you to deal with this on your own, Summer. I love you."

Chapter Fifty-One

COLE

"I have never met a woman so insistent that she stabbed a man." The police officer stares at Summer as if finding my librarian fascinating.

My urge is to step in closer, wrap my arm around her protectively. But if Summer has proved anything tonight, it's that she can protect herself.

Plus my hands are still covered in blood.

"Yes, well. I did. It was me. Not Cole. I know he looks more capable of stabbing a man than I do, but trust me, I'm the one who did it."

"Summer." My voice comes out low and urgent. Maybe she doesn't need physical protection, but this confessional babbling could put her in a different kind of danger. For fuck's sake, the police officer didn't even ask a question when they approached her hospital bed. She just started proclaiming things.

"What?" When she turns to meet my eyes, her pupils are too wide. She is still dealing with shock. "It's the truth. I'm not going to let you get in trouble for something I did."

"And are you ready to give your statement of what happened?" The police officer pulls out a notebook.

Summer goes to open her mouth, but I talk over her. "She's ready for a lawyer."

The cop focuses his eyes on me, and I keep myself from flinching away. Police and me do not mix.

"Cole—"

I cut her off for her own sake. "Are we under arrest?"

"No," the officer admits.

"Good. Then we'll wait here until our lawyers arrive and give our statements then."

I'm talking out my ass, but if I learned one thing during serving my time, it's to keep my mouth shut around the cops. Innocent or not.

"Alright. I'll be just down the hall whenever you're ready."

Once the officer is gone, Summer blinks up at me.

"Why do I need a lawyer?"

"Because you stabbed a man."

"In self-defense!"

"And they know that based off your word and mine. This isn't cut and dry, Summer. He attacked you when there wasn't anyone around to testify to what he did."

"That's ridiculous. I have bruises on my neck and arms in the shape of his fingers!" She holds up said arms, and I have to stifle the fury that burns through me at the sight.

"I know. It's not fair. But people have been screwed over by the law before. Everything will turn out better if you have legal counsel."

When we got here, the nurses asked each of us about emergency contacts. So Summer's mom and my dad received some kind of call, but I need to get this blood off my hands so I can do something useful, like find us legal representation.

"Summer!" The gasp comes from a curvy woman in a well-tailored suit who is jogging toward us, her heels clicking on the tiles. The brunette, who shares the same brown eyes as her daughter, rakes her gaze up and down the woman beside me, likely looking for any fatal injury. "Your hands," she whimpers, spotting the rusty, crusted blood on Summer's palms.

"It's not mine," she clarifies. "I'm alright Mom. Just a little shook up.

"What happened?"

"Don't freak out, but, for a little while now, I've had a...stalker." My librarian hesitates on the last word.

"A stalker?" Ms. Pierce's eyes widen then flick to me. Summer scoffs.

"No, Mom. Not him. I'm not currently sitting next to the guy who's been tormenting me for years." Her voice loses the biting edge as she goes on. "Sorry. I'm stressed. What I mean to say is, I found out it was Daniel. The security guard at the library. And he attacked me tonight."

The next few minutes involve a detailed replay of the events leading up to the assault, then the assault itself.

The whole time Summer speaks, her hands wring and flick and gesture wildly. If there was a stack of books around, I'm sure she'd be grabbing for it. Or maybe not, worried about leaving bloody fingerprints on the pages.

"And he was just lying there. Bleeding. And I was panicking. But then Cole showed up." Her soft gaze locks on me, and I don't feel deserving of the worship directed my way. "He kept a calm head. Took over putting pressure on the wound. Told me to call 9-1-1. I'm not sure I would've calmed down in time."

"I just wish I'd gotten there sooner." Fucking shitty drivers. A fender bender at a stoplight is the reason Summer's arms are covered in bruises and she has a man's blood literally on her hands.

"You were there when I needed you." She pokes the back of my hand, the dried gore on our fingers lending a weird cast to the gesture. But I appreciate it all the same. Summer tilts her head toward her mother, a confident smile curling her lips.

"Mom. This is Cole. We've been dating, and I love him."

Ms. Pierce's sharp gaze connects with mine.

The polite thing to do would be to formally greet the woman. But I can't move past what Summer just announced to the room.

She loves me.

"I love you, too." I rasp the words out, being a rude bastard by ignoring her mother and focusing solely on Summer.

"Oh good. That would've been awkward if you didn't."

A chuckle bursts from my chest, and I want to draw Summer into my arms. Affectionate gestures will have to wait until we're not covered in Daniel. Still, I lean down to kiss her cheek, then rest my forehead against hers.

"You scared the shit out of me," I whisper.

"She does that." Ms. Pierce's voice brings me back to the present, and

I turn to meet the woman's scrutinizing gaze. She gives a twist of her lips that is maybe a grimace, maybe a reluctant smile. "I would have preferred to meet you in other circumstances, but I'm glad you were there for my daughter when she needed you."

I nod just as a woman in a black pantsuit enters the room. "Hello, Pierce. What have I missed?"

The new arrival turns out to be a lawyer, who Ms. Pierce called when she realized Summer's situation involves the police. Yet again, Summer runs through the events of the night, and I can tell from the dip in her shoulders that she's tired of repeating the uncomfortable situation.

Unfortunately, she has to do it again for the police officer.

The lawyer leaves us, off to talk with law enforcement. Soon after she's gone, we're given permission to clean the blood from our hands. Finally.

Summer is nodding off against her mother's shoulder when the lawyer breezes back into the room, a triumphant smile on her face.

"They have security footage from the jewelry shop across the street," she announces.

"What?" Ms. Pierce rises from her perch on the hospital bed.

"Maybe the guard, Daniel, thought he was clear to assault you because the library doesn't have any outer cameras. But he didn't count on other storefronts. They have clear footage of him grabbing you repeatedly, you trying to fend him off, then the stabbing, then Cole showing up after he's already on the ground bleeding."

"If they have that footage, why didn't they tell us?" I can't keep the annoyed growl out of my voice.

The woman grimaces. "Probably just waiting to see if you admit to something else incriminating. Still, we have proof of self-defense. And I wouldn't be surprised if the police are able to get a search warrant to find proof of him sending you those stalking messages."

Summer shudders, and all I want to do is hold her. But her mother is in my way so I keep back.

"I'll be in touch tomorrow to discuss anything that needs to be done moving forward. Contact me with any questions you have." The lawyer holds out a card, which Summer accepts. I'm glad to see her hands are steady. The shaking has worn off.

"Cole? Cole, are you alright?" The familiar voice has me turning toward the door just as my dad bursts in, his face white as he steps up to me, cupping my face.

"I'm fine, Dad. All the action happened before I got there. Calm down. Breathe." He may be worried about me, but I'm just as anxious for him. Last time he got a shocking phone call about me, he had a heart attack.

Taking my advice, he sucks in a deep breath through his nose, but he keeps scanning me, looking for injuries.

"I'm serious, Dad. Summer is the one who got hurt."

My father's eyes flick to the side and land on my girlfriend, his gaze going soft as he looks at her. His hands fall from my face, and he steps toward her.

"Hi, Mr. Allemand." Summer gives a weak wave, and I notice now that her voice is hoarse. Probably from the bruising. The thought makes me want to storm through the halls of the hospital, find wherever they're keeping that piece of human waste, and finish the job Summer started.

Only, that would land me in jail, the stress of which would probably then kill my dad. With effort, I suppress my murderous impulses.

Instead, I steady my voice and make introductions.

"Dad, this is Summer's mom, Ms. Pierce. And their lawyer, Bethany Rothchild."

"And I was just leaving." The lawyer gives the room a nod as she departs.

"Ms. Pierce, this is my dad, Malcolm Allemand."

SUMMER

My mom, thank the universe, has an expert-level poker face. The only indication I get that she recognizes Cole's father's name is the slight twitch at the corner of her eye. I guess you run into a lot of odd situations while selling houses. Need to be able to roll with the awkwardness.

So much for my promise that she'd never meet the owner of the medical bills I asked her to organize. If I'd been thinking straight, I should have blacked out Mr. Allemand's name on all the documents before giving them to her. But I'd been desperate to help Cole and didn't bother to think things through. If I had, I might have realized I was already in love with him.

Which meant our families mingling was inevitable.

"Nice to meet you, Malcolm. It seems our children have gotten themselves into some trouble," Mom says, her voice calm, her eyes still holding an edge of concern.

"*I* got us into trouble," I correct before Mr. Allemand gets the wrong idea.

"That fucker Daniel got us into trouble," Cole corrects.

"Language," Cole's father scolds him, even as I watch him take in every inch of his son's body. Again. I'm glad we were able to wash the blood off our hands. The man doesn't need a reason for another heart attack.

"Sorry," Cole murmurs, his eyes flicking to my mother as his cheeks stain red.

"No need to apologize." My mom glares at the bruises on my arms. "He *is* a fucker. He's also a god damned piece of—"

I barely have time to hop off the hospital bed and clap my hands over Mr. Allemand's ears before he hears my mom's tirade. She spends a good minute describing in detail not only how horrible of a person she thinks Daniel is, but also the creative methods of torture she'd use on him if she could convince the police to leave her alone in a room with the security guard.

When she finally peters off, I glance up at Cole's dad to find him smiling down at me in the understated way he shares with his son. I let my hands drop.

"Sorry," I mutter.

There's a snort to my right, and I glance over at a smirking Cole. "Did Summer save your delicate ears, Dad? Keep you from swooning?"

"I appreciate the effort," is all the older man admits.

My mom waves a dismissive hand as if she didn't go off on a rant rated R for graphic violence. "I'm going to go see about getting you both discharged. You're all patched up. No reason for us to linger."

Then she's gone, her clacking heels demanding attention as she marches down the hallway.

"Yeah, so. That's my mom," I say by way of explanation.

"She's..." Mr. Allemand starts.

"Intense? Scary? Overprotective?" So many words to fill in the blank.

"Strong," he finishes himself. That's when I realize the man is still staring after my mother, even though she's disappeared from view.

Cole and I meet eyes, both of ours having gone wide.

Weird, he mouths.

Cute, I push back.

But he just rolls his eyes and guides me into a gentle hug.

"How are you feeling?" His question ruffles my hair.

"Exhausted." I sigh the word out with my entire body. "What time is it even?"

"Midnight," Mr. Allemand answers. "I'll start back to the parking garage. You text me when I should pull around front." Then the man shocks me by planting a chaste kiss on my forehead. "I'm glad you're okay." He cups his son's cheek with a hand but doesn't say anything more. Just offers a short, firm nod. Then he walks away.

"Yeah, so, that's my dad," Cole mutters into my hair. There's a thickness to his voice, but I decide not to push.

"I like your dad."

"I like your mom."

"That's good. That we all like each other."

Cole's deliciously comforting warmth disappears as he steps back. I'm about to protest when I spot the heat in his eyes.

"I don't just like you, Summer."

"Oh, yeah, duh." I rise up on my toes and plant a sloppily loud kiss on his lips before stepping back. "You love me."

"That's fucking right," he growls, wrapping me in another comforting hug.

"Language," I mutter.

When my mom returns to the room, she finds the two of us twined around each other, fighting a losing battle against our laughter.

Epilogue

SUMMER

One year later

With more reverence than I've ever shown another book, I gently place this one in its plastic stand under the *New Releases* sign.

The glossy cover of the hardback shines under the fluorescents, and I read the words on the cover again, as if they'll have changed.

War, Sex, & Magic

Cole Allemand

Finally, after months of edits and formatting, and marketing, Cole's book is out in the world.

I'm not sure I could be more proud. Not even if I wrote the book myself.

My boyfriend, acting the self-conscious artist, didn't let me read the story until it was in its final stages. He made the mistake of giving me a copy after dinner one evening. I stayed up until four a.m., reading. Then I woke him up and showed him how much I loved the book. Let's just say, he didn't mind the early wake-up call in the least, once I started kissing my way down his stomach.

Probably helped that he didn't have work in the morning, now that he's only part time at the shelter. Most days he's hard at work on his next novel and building a solid bank of future chapters for *The Seven Siblings*.

Not that he couldn't work full time at the shelter. Two of the grants he and Jasmine worked on were accepted. The rescue had enough money to build an entirely new space for the felines, as well as hire an intern. Jamie just happened to nail his interview and is now learning the ropes of running a non-profit.

Realizing I've surpassed my allotted staring time, I return to the cart that has the other, equally as good I'm sure, new releases. One by one, I arrange each title neatly on the three-sixty, multi-tiered display stand.

As I'm setting out the last few titles, a young woman meanders up to the display. Doing my best to act casual, I fiddle with one of the books as I watch her out of the corner of my eye.

After a moment of scanning the selections, she reaches out and plucks Cole's book off the stand I just set it on. She takes her time reading the inner cover, all the while I'm clenching my teeth together, trying not to shout, "*It's the best book ever! If you don't check it out then you're a fool!*"

That's probably not how a librarian should talk to a patron.

Another few agonizing seconds pass before the woman closes the cover and tucks the book under her arm.

When she turns toward the circulation desk, I abandon my task and power walk back to my office. Once the door is shut, I dial Cole's number. He's at work today, probably rolling around in a pile of kittens, so I get his answering machine.

"Someone checked out your book! And I didn't even make them do it!" I announce, not bothering to say who's calling. He'll know. "Anyway, I love you. Have a good day at work!"

It's dorky, but I'm not the only one who does it. I often return to my office on a break to find a phone message from Cole telling me about a funny animal story. And he always ends with the same command.

"Get back to work, Summer."

Those messages are often the best part of my day. At least, until I get off work and climb into Cole's truck.

I have a working vehicle now, but most days we carpool, twining our hands together across the center consul on our way back to the shotgun house we share. After letting myself love the man and accepting his love in return, moving in didn't feel so scary anymore.

And even with Daniel behind bars, I feel safer knowing that someone is waiting for me.

That Cole is waiting for me.

At the end of my shift, I find him inside, walking down my hallway, carrying a stack of books to check out.

"You sure you didn't make them?" Cole asks with a teasing smile before leaning down to kiss me.

"I swear! She just walked up and grabbed it herself. I'll record a video next time," I declare while switching the lights off in my office.

"Maybe don't," he chuckles.

After waiting for my boyfriend to check out, we walk hand in hand to his truck. I'm settling in the passenger seat when I realize my water bottle is leaking.

"Do you have any napkins?" I ask, popping his glove compartment open.

"Yeah. Should be some in there."

There's a hefty amount from a take-out place, and I grab a handful, holding them to the bottom of the bottle. Then my eye catches on something pink. Careful to make sure my hands are dry, I pinch the corner of the item and tug it free of the compartment.

"Happy Valentine's Day From the Dog," I read aloud. Then I choke up, realizing what this is.

When my gaze flicks over to Cole's, he watches me with a half-smirk. "You remember that?"

"Of course I do. But I didn't know you went back and bought it!" My grin is so wide it hurts my cheeks.

He shrugs, his smile showing teeth now. "It was our first Valentine's Day. The first day I was honest about how I felt. I wanted to remember it."

With numb fingers, I reach into my purse. One thing I always have on me is a book, and I pull out the cozy mystery I checked out the other day. Cole watches my hands as I flip open to the last page I stopped on. My place is marked with a well-worn Valentine's Day card.

"I wanted to remember it, too," I say.

Cole leans to my side of the truck, capturing my mouth in a hot kiss. When he breaks away, there's barely space between us for breath.

"You know, February fourteenth is next week," he points out.

Another holiday spent together. But can it possibly live up to this past Christmas, when I found Cole in his very own Santa suit, waiting for me beside a decorated tree?

My thighs tighten at the memory.

Maybe he would be willing to sport the outfit as a special gift to round out the night. But during the day, I already know what I want to do.

My lips stretch in an eager grin. "You trust me to spin you again?"

Rough fingers cup my jaw, tilting my chin up until I gaze into a set of Icelandic blue eyes. I shiver, but not from the cold. The eager quakes in my body are all anticipation.

"There's no one I trust more."

***

Thank you for reading! Did you enjoy? Please add your review because nothing helps an author more and encourages readers to take a chance on a book than a review.

And don't miss more romance novels like, **PAINTING THE LINES** by Ashley R King. Turn the page for a sneak peek!

And visit www.laurenconnollyromance.com to keep up with the latest news where you can subscribe to the newsletter for contests, giveaways, new releases, and more.

Sneak Peek of Painting the Lines

BY ASHLEY R. KING

Amalie scanned the bar, looking for Romina's raven hair beneath the dim lights. For a Tuesday night, quite the crowd had gathered inside Oakley's, a trendy hangout in midtown Atlanta.

"Can I get you something else?" Bryan, the cute bartender, asked with a boyish smile.

Amalie looked at her watch again. Romina was already fifteen minutes late. Tonight of all nights, when Amalie needed her best friend most.

Amalie's father, mega-billionaire Andrew Warner, had just dropped the hammer with his latest ultimatum, and Amalie needed Romina's sage advice, help, magic—*anything* that might help her figure out what to do. Her father had been pushing her to work for the family business, something she had no interest in doing. If she didn't, she'd be disowned and disinherited from the great Warner Hotel fortune. To some that might not be a huge deal, but to Amalie, who had no back-up plan, it was everything.

She sighed and took one last sip of her daiquiri. "No, that'll be all. Thank you."

With a quick nod, Bryan moved to the other end of the bar, where a seat had been claimed by a man who, even sitting down, was still taller than most. Amalie couldn't help but give him a once-over. He had a powerful frame, even if soft around the edges, like the forgotten build of an athlete lived under his skin. But something else snagged her attention.

Amalie watched with interest as the bartender seemed to contemplate cutting the guy off for the night even though it was only eight o'clock. The man bristled, spine stiffening, fingers tightening around the empty tumbler before him. But in a half-second, his eyes flicked up to one of the flat screens suspended behind the bar and he leaned forward, completely enraptured, his face oddly serene.

As a writer, or well, washed-up writer on the hunt for her next idea, Amalie was captivated by this guy's body language. One minute it looked like he might shatter his whiskey tumbler with his bare hands, and the next his eyes were glued to the television.

Amalie glanced at the screen, surprised to find a replay of the US Open tennis finals from several years ago. She knew enough about tennis to know the names of the Grand Slam tournaments and some of the cute players (hello, Rafael Nadal), but other than that, she was clueless. Her father, who loved tennis and watched it religiously, had tried to inspire a love of the sport in her, but...it just wasn't there.

Her eyes slid back to the enigma at the end of the bar. There was a catlike tension in the way he studied the battle between Rafael Nadal and Novak Djokovic, his entire focus narrowed to the game, his muscles twitching with restrained energy. Her writer instincts screamed that there was far more going on here than a bar patron watching the rerun of an old match. Cheering and clapping erupted on the screen.

"I could've done that! *Easily*!" The man pounded his fist on the bar and exploded from his seat with such force that his barstool tumbled backward. He was just as tall as she imagined, well over six feet.

Amalie gasped and took a step back. The man downed his drink, slamming the empty glass onto the bar with a thud, wiping his mouth with the back of his hand.

"Another," he growled at the bartender.

He shifted slightly and when he turned, she caught sight of his lovely eyes in the dim light, but they were marred with heavy bags beneath them.

"Hey, man. Julian, come on. You've got to chill," Bryan pleaded.

Julian. Amalie rolled that name around in her mind, tasted it on her tongue. She supposed he looked like a Julian, though to be fair she hadn't met a single Julian in her twenty-eight years. She studied him, his calves and thighs muscular beneath his khaki shorts. Yes, shorts, despite the cold. Even his arms looked like they had once been powerful, but judging by the slight beer gut he was rocking, Julian had missed a workout or two. He was ridiculously attractive, though, even if Amalie struggled to reconcile that fact with his brutish behavior.

She studied him further, imagining his story and committing his features to memory, a memory she would later take out, dissect, and piece together into one of her fictional heroes. Romina always teased that Amalie was more voyeur than participant in life. Perhaps that's why writing was so important to her.

Julian's burnt umber hair fell in unruly waves across his tanned forehead, his nose almost too flawless. But no, when he turned, she noted a slight bump, perhaps hinting at a fight at one point in his life? Or maybe, if he was like Amalie, a pretty nasty run-in with a suspiciously transparent sliding-glass door.

Julian's profile, with his sulky lower lip, was a thing of beauty, and she found herself wondering why such loveliness had been wasted on a staggering mess of a man.

As if feeling the levity of her gaze, or rather her judgment, Julian met her stare. Now *that* was completely unfair. His eyes stood out against his dark skin, a stunning green that reminded her of lush trees in the spring, and there were tiny lightning strikes of sparkling gold darting from the pupils.

Wait...

Holy crap, she was standing directly in front of him, having gravitated toward him without even realizing it. It didn't matter how hot he was, how *big* he was, she didn't want any part of this.

As if he heard her thoughts, he raised a perfect, dark eyebrow, a quirk she was sure was meant to be sexy and had probably worked on dozens of other women, but at that moment it only came off as sloppy and awkward.

"Like what you see?" he challenged. His sultry voice would've made her panties melt if not for the slur accenting it.

Amalie recoiled, cheeks hot as she leveled the behemoth with a sneer. "Excuse me?"

Julian tilted his head, studying her with a drunken intensity that made her squirm. "I said, do you like what you see? My place isn't that far...if you think you can keep your hands off me that long."

Bryan snickered as he shook his head, pretending to be mesmerized by the cleanliness of the beer mug in his hand.

"Can you believe the balls on this guy?" Amalie hooked a thumb toward Julian as she looked to Bryan. For what, she had no idea.

"A filthy mouth, too." Julian shot her a wink and sat back down at the bar. "My *favorite*."

"You are out of control." Amalie huffed. "I can't help it that I naturally gravitated toward *this*"—she waved her arms around, motioning and flailing at Julian—"train wreck. I thought I might've had my next book idea. But yet you disappoint, something I'm sure is very common."

There. She hated to be a mean girl, but he'd totally asked for it.

Julian reared back as if she'd slapped him but quickly recovered. "Enough of the spoiled little rich girl act. It reeks."

She faltered, the sting hitting home. "You don't even know me."

"Right, and you don't know me either, princess."

Princess? Anger burned inside her as she poked her finger into his surprisingly hard chest. "You have no idea who you're messing with, mister."

He puffed up, straightened his broad shoulders, and gave her a scalding once-over. "Yeah, I'm shaking in my boots. Listen, I'll have you know that you're looking at a US Open contender." He leveled her with a hard glare, daring her to argue.

Interest piqued, Amalie remained in place, her finger falling away. "*You're* a tennis player?" she asked through gritted teeth while mentally berating herself for continuing this conversation.

Julian paused a beat too long before answering with a shrug. "You could say that."

"Okay..." Amalie stretched the two-syllable word into three and cocked her brow as if to silently say, *I call bullshit*.

Julian blinked, but his gaze was still hazy as he responded with a surprising amount of vindication in his voice. "Actually, I'm going to qualify for the US Open." His eyes widened, as if his words were a revelation to him as well.

Interesting. Amalie's nails tapped the bar in an easy rhythm as she assessed him. "So I gather you used to play?" She almost mentioned his fading physique, but he was being oddly civil now, and she feared an observation like that would bring out the pig in him, *again*.

Julian averted his gaze, studying his hands, which now gripped the edge of the bar. He gave her a tight nod, then he seemed to slowly deflate. "I used to be the best. Before it all went to shit. Now I'm just a has-been, stuck selling pharmaceuticals day after day. I had everything I ever wanted right here"—Julian lifted a hand, palm open, his stare searing into his own flesh—"then I let it all slip away."

It was a surprisingly coherent statement, one that echoed and mirrored things Amalie felt about her own life. But before she could dwell on it, electricity hummed in her veins, the wheels in her head spinning wildly.

A tiny spark of sunlight filtered through the cracks of the prison that had slowly become her life as an idea quickly formed. Ever since New Year's Eve, she'd been mulling over goals, and writing a book was at the top of her list—this was perfect. The threat of having to work for her father receded as she pulled in a deep breath and let the realization settle over her bones. *This* could be her next hit, a novel that chronicled the rise to the top of a former tennis great. Hadn't her agent, Stella, recently hinted that sports romances were making a comeback? Besides, everyone loves a good underdog story. She could see the headlines now: *Washed-Up Tennis Player Makes Run for US Open*.

What were the odds that he played the only sport she knew even a little bit about?

Right now, it didn't matter that she hated tennis. It didn't matter that her father always rubbed it in her face that her older sister, Simone, was such a great player. It didn't matter that he'd tried to force Amalie to take lessons even though her instructor was the meanest person on the planet and cut her down every time she made a mistake

Her past with tennis was exactly that: *the past*. An opportunity had presented itself, and she was hellbent on taking it. Stella had been adamant that Amalie write something "real and honest," something more along the lines of her debut, *Breaking the Fall,* the story that shot her into the next-big-thing stratosphere at the ripe age of nineteen. Of course, Amalie didn't want to let her down. Stella Frenette of Frenette Literary had been a hard win after Amalie lost her first agent for being a little twit high on fame and her own wealth. She'd bailed on so many commitments and haggled over stuff so stupid it made film and book people walk away. Yeah, film—that's how close she'd been to the big time.

Somewhere along the way, Amalie also lost the gift of natural storytelling. Every time she set pen to paper or fingers to keys, it felt forced. Her words read like *See Jane run. See Jane jump. See Jane suck at writing.*

Her last two novels fell flat because the characters weren't realistic. To fix the problem, Stella suggested Amalie study real people. Her bestseller had centered around a heroine based on none other than her sister, Simone. The intimate knowledge shared by sisters had given Amalie the means to create a three-dimensional character readers adored, which was really no surprise. Who didn't love Simone?

Amalie's follow-up books hadn't had that benefit and suffered because of it. She struggled to craft characters who leapt off the page, and she had no doubt the reason was because, other than Ro, she hadn't let anyone get close. Not even her ex-fiancé, Maxwell. Not really. Amalie failed at human connection because people broke hearts, and her heart already had enough cracks. It couldn't survive another quake.

She cringed as she thought of her early writing days, trying to reconcile that person with who she was now. Sadly, though she was ready to write again, the human connection thing was still a problem. But maybe Fate had given her a workaround. Readers—and Stella as well—would love that this novel was based on a real tennis player—one who was gorgeous and, with some training, would have muscles popping by the time the tournament rolled around. It would be so easy to capitalize on his looks and to even use the momentum of his rise to the top for promotion of the book.

She couldn't let fear get in the way of her dream this time. She just needed to get this Julian fellow to the US Open.

Just as Amalie was about to open her mouth, Julian slumped over the bar, passed out cold. The bartender dipped his head and smiled. "From what I hear, he does this all the time. He's pretty popular with the ladies, so usually he's already secured one or two to go home with. Looks like he didn't get that far with you." He had the audacity to smirk.

"Hard to imagine that he's popular with the ladies when he acts like a Neanderthal."

Bryan leaned forward on the bar conspiratorially, his voice hushed. "He was different tonight. Besides, I think you got under his skin because you called his bullshit. But hey, that's just my opinion."

Amalie sized up the situation *and* Julian, her mind calculating a million possibilities at once. "Was he really a great tennis player?" she asked Bryan, needing to know for sure before she made her next decision.

Bryan nodded. "Hell yeah. You never heard of Julian Smoke? They called him 'The Smoke' in college because he was a beast. He was even pegged as the next tennis great of his generation."

Amalie studied Julian's face, willing herself to remember him from one of her father's endless tennis ramblings. "What happened?" she asked, bringing her gaze back to the bartender.

"That's his story to tell. You'll have to ask him."

Amalie drummed her fingers on the smooth surface of the bar one last time before releasing a deep breath and making a decision she was sure she'd regret. "Help me get him to my car, will ya?"

Don't miss more of the *Forget the Past* series coming soon, and find more from Lauren Connolly at www.laurenconnollyromance.com

Until then, find more romance with PAINTING THE LINES by Ashley R. King!

"King debuts with a delightful, character-driven rom-com! Fans of slow-burn romance will be swept away." – Publisher's Weekly

Amalie Warner wants another shot to prove that she can be a successful writer. After hitting the bestseller's list nine years ago, she's lost her spark.

Feeling pressure from her father to leave her writing behind and to work for her family's lucrative hotel business, she's desperate to find inspiration for her next big idea, something that challenges and excites her, something real.

Enter Julian Smoke, a failed tennis player making a dream run for the US Open. After a chance meeting at a bar, Amalie hates him instantly. He's cocky and arrogant, but Amalie knows his story could be her big break.

Could he be more? Everyone knows that in tennis, love means zero, but these two are about to change that.

Please sign up for the City Owl Press newsletter for chances to win special subscriber-only contests and giveaways as well as receiving information on upcoming releases and special excerpts.

All reviews are **welcome** and **appreciated**. Please consider leaving one on your favorite social media and book buying sites.

For books in the world of romance and speculative fiction that embody Innovation, Creativity, and Affordability, check out City Owl Press at www.cityowlpress.com.

Acknowledgments

Once again, I wrote a book set in New Orleans about someone working in an animal rescue, which means I have to thank Katie. You shared your knowledge and offered your spare room so I could explore the city. That picture of cake is for you.

Thank you to everyone who helped turn this rough draft into a finished product. Katy, you were a wonderful beta reader. The team at City Owl Press, you all keep making my dreams come true by putting my books out in the world. I am eternally grateful.

And a huge thank you to every single reader who picked up this book. You gave my story your precious time, and I appreciate every moment you spent with my words.

About the Author

LAUREN CONNOLLY is an author of romance stories set in the contemporary world. Some are grounded in reality, while others play with the mystical and magical. She has a day job as an academic librarian in southern Colorado, where she lives outnumbered by animals. Her furry family consists of a cocker spaniel who thinks he's a cave dwelling troll and two cats with a mission to raise hell and destroy all curtains. It should come as no surprise that each one is a rescue.

www.laurenconnollyromance.com

facebook.com/LaurenConnollyRomance
twitter.com/laurenaliciaCon
instagram.com/laurenconnollyromance

About the Publisher

City Owl Press is a cutting edge indie publishing company, bringing the world of romance and speculative fiction to discerning readers.

www.cityowlpress.com